DIVISIBLE MAN™
THE SECOND GHOST

by

Howard Seaborne

ALSO BY HOWARD SEABORNE

DIVISIBLE MAN
A Novel – September 2017
DIVISIBLE MAN: THE SIXTH PAWN
A Novel – June 2018
DIVISIBLE MAN: THE SECOND GHOST
A Novel – September 2018
ANGEL FLIGHT
A Story – September 2018
DIVISIBLE MAN: THE SEVENTH STAR
A Novel – June 2019
ENGINE OUT
A Story – September 2019
WHEN IT MATTERS
A Story – October 2019
A SNOWBALL'S CHANCE
A Story – November 2019
DIVISIBLE MAN: TEN MAN CREW
A Novel – November 2019
DIVISIBLE MAN: THE THIRD LIE
A Novel – May 2020
DIVISIBLE MAN: THREE NINES FINE
A Novel – November 2020
DIVISIBLE MAN: EIGHT BALL
A Novel – September 2021
SHORT FLIGHTS
A Story Collection – June 2022
DIVISIBLE MAN: NINE LIVES LOST
A Novel – Nine 2022

PRAISE FOR HOWARD SEABORNE

"This book is a strong start to a series…Well-written and engaging, with memorable characters and an intriguing hero."
  —*Kirkus Reviews*
  DIVISIBLE MAN [DM1]

"Seaborne's crisp prose, playful dialogue, and mastery of technical details of flight distinguish the story…this is a striking and original start to a series, buoyed by fresh and vivid depictions of extra-human powers and a clutch of memorably drawn characters…"
  —*BookLife*
  DIVISIBLE MAN [DM1]

"Even more than flight, (Will's relationship with Andy)—and that crack prose—powers this thriller to a satisfying climax that sets up more to come."
  —*BookLife*
  DIVISIBLE MAN [DM1]

"Seaborne, a former flight instructor and charter pilot, once again gives readers a crisply written thriller. Self-powered flight is a potent fantasy, and Seaborne explores its joys and difficulties engagingly. Will's narrative voice is amusing, intelligent and humane; he draws readers in with his wit, appreciation for his wife, and his flight-drunk joy…Even more entertaining than its predecessor—a great read."
  —*Kirkus Reviews*
  DIVISIBLE MAN: THE SIXTH PAWN [DM2]

"Seaborne, a former flight instructor and pilot, delivers a solid, well-written tale that taps into the near-universal dream of personal flight. Will's narrative voice is engaging and crisp, clearly explaining technical matters while never losing sight of humane, emotional concerns. The environments he describes…feel absolutely real. Another intelligent and exciting superpowered thriller."

—*Kirkus Reviews*
DIVISIBLE MAN: THE SECOND GHOST [DM3]

"As in this series' three previous books, Seaborne…proves he's a natural born storyteller, serving up an exciting, well-written thriller. He makes even minor moments in the story memorable with his sharp, evocative prose…Will's smart, humane and humorous narrative voice is appealing, as is his sincere appreciation for Andy—not just for her considerable beauty, but also for her dedication and intelligence…Seaborne does a fine job making side characters and locales believable. It's deeply gratifying to see Will deliver righteous justice to some very bad people. An intensely satisfying thriller—another winner from Seaborne."

—*Kirkus Reviews*
DIVISIBLE MAN: THE SECOND GHOST [DM4]

"Seaborne…continues his winning streak in this series, offering another page-turner. By having Will's knowledge of and control over his powers continue to expand while the questions over how he should best deploy his abilities grow, Seaborne keeps the concept fresh and readers guessing…Will's enemies are becoming aware of him and perhaps developing techniques to detect him, which makes the question of how he can protect himself while doing the most good a thorny one. The conspiracy is highly dramatic yet not implausible given today's political events, and the action sequences are excitingly cinematic…Another compelling and hugely fun adventure that delivers a thrill ride."

—*Kirkus Reviews*
DIVISIBLE MAN: TEN MAN CREW [DM5]

"Seaborne shows himself to be a reliably splendid storyteller in this latest outing. The plot is intricate and could have been confusing in lesser hands, but the author manages it well, keeping readers oriented amid unexpected developments…His crisp writing about complex scenes and concepts is another strong suit…The fantasy of self-powered flight remains absolutely compelling…As a former charter pilot, Seaborne conveys Will's delight not only in 'the other thing,' but also in airplanes

and the world of flight—an engaging subculture that he ably brings to life for the reader. Will is heroic and daring, as one would expect, but he's also funny, compassionate, and affectionate... A gripping, timely, and twisty thriller."
—*Kirkus Reviews*
DIVISIBLE MAN: THE THIRD LIE [DM6]

"Seaborne is never less than a spellbinding storyteller, keeping his complicated but clearly explicated plot moving smoothly from one nail-biting scenario to another. As the tale goes along, seemingly disparate plot lines begin to satisfyingly connect in ways that will keep readers guessing until the explosive (in more ways than one) action-movie denouement. The author's grasp of global politics gives depth to the book's thriller elements, which are nicely balanced by thoughtful characterizations. Even minor characters come across in three dimensions, and Will himself is an endearing narrator. He's lovestruck by his gorgeous, intelligent, and strong-willed wife; has his heart and social conscience in the right place; and is boyishly thrilled by the other thing. A solid series entry that is, as usual, exciting, intricately plotted, and thoroughly entertaining."
—*Kirkus Reviews*
DIVISIBLE MAN: THREE NINES FINE [DM7]

Any reader of this series knows that they're in good hands with Seaborne, who's a natural storyteller. His descriptions and dialogue are crisp, and his characters deftly sketched...The book keeps readers tied into its complex and exciting thriller plot with lucid and graceful exposition, laying out clues with cleverness and subtlety...Also, although Will's abilities are powerful, they have reasonable limitations, and the protagonist is always a relatable character with plenty of humanity and humor...Another riveting, taut, and timely adventure with engaging characters and a great premise."
— *Kirkus Reviews*
DIVISIBLE MAN: EIGHT BALL [DM8]

THE SERIES

While each DIVISIBLE MAN ™ novel tells its own tale, many elements carry forward and the novels are best enjoyed in sequence. The short story "Angel Flight" is a bridge between the third and fourth novels and is included with the third novel, DIVISIBLE MAN - THE SECOND GHOST.

DIVISIBLE MAN ™ is available in print, digital and audio.

For a Cast of Characters, visit **HowardSeaborne.com**

For advance notice of new releases and exclusive material available only to Email Members, join the DIVISIBLE MAN ™ Email List at

HowardSeaborne.com.

Sign up today and get a FREE DOWNLOAD.

ACKNOWLEDGMENTS

This is the Divisible Man's third mission. The flight crew remains unchanged. Once again, I gratefully acknowledge their roles. Stephen Parolini continues to guide the mission through his editing expertise. The brave test pilots who took this thing into the air on faith, my beta readers and life-long co-pilots, Rich "Maddog" Sorensen and Robin "Polly Pureheart" Schlei, deserve special thanks for the initial airworthiness inspection. I couldn't have done any of it without the ground crew at Trans World Data—David, Carol, Claire, April and Rebecca who keep the machine running and Kristie and Steve who continue the reconnaissance, so I can concentrate on flying. I can't say enough about my sharp-eyed radar operator, Roberta Schlei, whose thorough copyediting spots the bandits lurking in every paragraph.

And thank you, Robin, for always knowing I need to fly.

For Stanley Rankin.
You showed me the magic between paperback covers.

PART I

1

T he four worst words in any relationship.
    "We need to talk."

Andy lowered the martini glass to the checkered tablecloth and issued a serious look shaded by her long lashes. She's not a heavy makeup user, but for our date night she had applied something extra, to breath-taking effect.

"God, no," I said, "you're finally dumping me. Was it the toilet seat? Because I can work on that, I promise."

She flashed one of her smiles; the small, private one. The one that creases the corners of her lips and forces dimples to peek from her skin like shy spirits.

Her hand slipped across the table between the two long-stemmed glasses. She closed her fingers around the third finger on my left hand and slowly rotated my wedding ring.

"Pilot, if that day ever comes, it will be because you throw your socks in the laundry inside-out. My lawyer tells me that's a slam dunk in divorce court."

"Dammit! Tripped up by my own feet!"

We took a moment and like two dumb kids swallowed by first love, we stared across the table, across the martinis, across the flickering candle meant to bring romance to a cozy venue already awash in it.

I love this woman beyond any ability to measure.

Andy sat with me in the candlelight of Los Lobos, a small Mexican restaurant attached to the other bowling alley in Essex, a goddess in a blue velvet holiday dress. She'd done her hair up for our date night, wrapping her wavy auburn locks in a sculpted work of art that offered the added benefit of showing off her slender neck. Like a beacon drawing me into rising seas, a single tiny diamond mounted on a slim chain hung from her neck, dipping to a place I wanted to go. Her dress had a blessedly low-cut line on top and high hemline below.

We chose Los Lobos because we had a coupon and because the drinks are two-for-one during Happy Hour. Andy and I are on a tight budget. Los Lobos won't make anybody's list of Most Romantic Getaways, but tonight New York or Paris had nothing on it. A light snow descended outside the window. Holiday pepper lights hung from rafters. Mexican music warmed the ambiance.

"I'm serious," she insisted. "We've been putting this off since California."

She did not exaggerate. It had been a month. I can't say I'd intentionally avoided the subject, but I had readily accepted the way her busy schedule delayed confronting it. Andy had been promoted to Detective, however staffing in the City of Essex Police Department required her to carry on many of her patrol sergeant duties. November pulled a disappearing act on us. We found ourselves atop the first weekend in December, a scant twenty-four days from Christmas.

"Maybe we could save this discussion for a night when you're not seducing me with that dress," I suggested. A bald attempt at procrastination.

"Maybe I should put on my coat," she countered.

My hands went up in surrender.

"Fine, but after we talk, I get equal time to stare at you." I tried to pout. I'm not good at that.

"Love, at some point I'll give you this dress and you can stare all you want." It was a bribe because she went right to the matter at hand. "I want you to see Dr. Stephenson."

This again.

"I really don't see the point."

"How about to confirm that it's *not* a brain tumor! You insist it isn't. Why not make sure?"

I sat back and considered the question.

November marked five calendar months since I fell out of a disintegrating airplane on a landing approach to Essex County Airport. Five months later I'm no closer to understanding the cause of the accident, or the origin of the gift I took from it.

The investigator from the National Transportation Safety Board believes I hit something. Whatever I hit left no evidence. No paint scrapings on my airplane. No debris. The federal government doesn't like a void, and while the investigators at the NTSB don't judge, one individual from the Federal Aviation Administration decided that—absent a better conclusion—the blank space under Cause of Accident should be filled in with "Pilot Incapacitation." My pilot's license and medical certificate were suspended, pending a full medical evaluation. Pure bullshit, but bullshit with a Grade A government stamp on it. Which meant I had to leap through hoops, bend over and cough, and get re-certified. I went through all of it, including examination by a neurologist.

That's when things went south.

A few weeks ago, I sat in Dr. Doug Stephenson's office while he showed me images of my brain. He pointed at something that didn't belong. He ventured to say it didn't look like any brain tumor he had ever seen. It looked to me like wiring for a car stereo, but since I can't blast tunes out my ears, I leaped to the explanation that made the most sense to me.

I think the car stereo wiring in my head is what makes me vanish.

"I'm telling you, it's *the other thing,*"

My stance frustrated Andy. She prefers conclusions supported by evidence.

"All I'm asking is that we make sure," she said. "And confirm that it's not growing."

"That's not all you're asking. You're asking me to explain *the other thing* to Stephenson."

"You know, we really do need a better name for it."

"I'll get to work on that." I sensed an opening to change the subject.

"That can wait. And—yes."

"Yes, what?"

"Yes, we should tell Stephenson."

That took me aback.

"Seriously?"

Andy let the underbite to her otherwise perfect teeth jut slightly. The effect was both alluring and a warning. She leaned closer.

"I'm not the only one worried. Earl is concerned. He doesn't know about the scans and the—you know."

"It's not a tumor." I filled in the word she could not bring herself to use twice in a conversation.

"He wants you back, Will."

Nice try, I thought.

Earl Jackson owns Essex County Air Services. It was his airplane I wrecked. Since the crash, during my recovery and while the government demanded proof of competency, Earl kept me on the payroll as a ramp rat, parking and gassing airplanes, and a grease-monkey in the shop. A menagerie of useful. Earl's loyalty to me had the dual benefit of a steady paycheck and keeping me around airplanes. After talking with Stephenson about the new wiring in my head, everything changed.

The FAA will never remove a suspension once they get wind of a brain tumor.

Shortly after Stephenson did his show-and-tell, I walked into Earl's office and handed him my resignation. He tore it up, threw the pieces at me and told me to get the fuck out of his office. Since then, I've tried to make the point by not showing up for work. My paycheck direct-deposits as usual.

"Earl wants to talk to Stephenson," Andy told me.

"Stephenson won't tell him the problem. I don't care how close they are."

Earl Jackson knew Stephenson during the Vietnam War. No matter what their back story, Stephenson would never betray my patient confidentiality to Earl. I was about to point that out when I realized patient confidentiality worked in favor of Andy's argument.

"Earl's no dummy, Will. He knows something is wrong."

"You shouldn't involve him."

"I didn't involve him. He called me. He's been calling me."

Her eyes, subtle green flecked with gold, fixed on me and held a mildly angry stare as Julio, our server, deposited a fresh basket of chips and new bowl of salsa between us. Julio must have felt some heat on his hands because he slipped away quickly.

"Dee, flying is risk management. Being a cop is risk management. We both know how that works. We don't know the risks of someone—someone outside of our little circle of trust—finding out about *the other thing*. For starters, there are all the clichés. Winding up in a secret government lab. Having to wear tights and a cape. Becoming the boy toy of a female super villain."

She stabbed a chip into the salsa, suppressing a smile.

"The point is, *not* telling Stephenson why there are little wire-looking things on my brain scan is a means of managing risk."

"Knowing that the *thing* in your head isn't growing, isn't a tumor, isn't going to hurt you—that's also risk management." She pointed the salsa-painted chip at me. "You're the one who insists it isn't a—a *problem*. Prove it."

As so often happens in a debate with my wife, I felt the earth slipping away under my feet.

"I'll think about it."

"Well, think about it all you want, but Earl set up an appointment with Stephenson for Tuesday morning."

"We can't go Tuesday. We've got that thing with Sandy." Sandy Stone, a close friend who teaches kindergarten in Essex, also suddenly found herself the administrator of a one-hundred-million-dollar education trust fund—because I recently extorted one hundred million dollars from a corrupt old bastard and set it up in a trust. No good deed goes unpunished. Both Andy and I got roped into serving on a board to help Sandy manage and disperse the fund, even though I protested vigorously, citing the fact that I know nothing about such things.

"That's Thursday. Evening. Tuesday is all set. Earl wants you to fly down to Madison. Says you're going to get rusty sitting around on your ass." She smiled triumphantly at me.

To administer the *coup de grace*, she tugged the low neckline of her dress down slightly and said, "You may now stare."

"IT'S LANE."

We had just ordered dinner and the free Happy Hour second round when the phone in Andy's purse chirped. I gave her a reproachful look for picking it up.

"Wishing us a pleasant and un-interrupted date night?"

Andy read the incoming text. Her face said not.

"She needs us. Both of us. It sounds serious. See if you can get the check. I'm going to the Ladies and then to get my coat."

With no small regret, I watched Andy's short dress and long legs weave their way out of the room toward the hall with the restrooms. So much for our romantic dinner. I clung to hope for the remainder of our evening plans.

At the same time, I felt a low-wattage alarm at Andy's rapid assessment. Lane Franklin, the fourteen-year-old daughter of the office manager at Essex County Air Services, possesses an exceptional intellect and advanced maturity. She wouldn't send up a flare unless it was serious.

I found the waiter, explained we had an emergency, and asked for the check. He offered to ask the kitchen staff if the entrees had already been made. The news wasn't good when he returned. I handed him the coupon and enough cash to cover the bill plus a decent tip. Andy reappeared, slipping her arms into her winter coat. She hurried out the door.

"Hey!" I caught the waiter's attention. "Give our entrees to these folks." I pointed at a couple stepping into the restaurant and shaking flakes of snow off their shoulders. To the startled pair, I said, "Don't know if you want 'em or not, but we have a couple meals ordered and paid for, and we have to run. Babysitter problem. Merry Christmas!"

I hustled out, leaving surprise and hasty gratitude in our wake.

"WHAT, EXACTLY, DID SHE SAY?" I asked as Andy wheeled out of the parking lot. Andy's car has a better heater, and one of her cop habits is to insist on driving. She has a heavy foot, but tonight she gave ample respect to the snow that had been falling all afternoon, our first of the year. The temperature hovered just above twenty, which made the snow stick. Roads not treated posed a slick hazard. I wondered if Bob Thanning, who plows our driveway, might have the job done by the time we got home. Probably not. He tends to show up at four in the morning and wake us with his rattling diesel pickup.

Andy handed me the phone. I read the text.

"*Emergency. Need help. Serious. Bring Will.*" The address that followed wasn't Lane's home.

Andy's reply read, "*Coming.*"

"She might be at a party," Andy offered. "I had a talk with her. A couple months ago. You know, if you're ever in a circumstance you don't like, or you do something stupid and need an out, call me. No questions asked. It could be a situation like that."

"Lane's fourteen. Her wildest activity is Philosophy Club."

"Lane's a living, breathing, growing adolescent girl. An attractive one, to boot. With a mature mind and body. Don't think for a minute that boys aren't interested in her."

"Sounds like you two have talked about more than designated drivers."

"We have." Andy let it go at that. Lane, an only child, had found a big sister in Andy. According to Andy, Lane nurtured a bit of a crush on me.

The address took us to an unfinished subdivision on the west side of Essex. Andy followed a winding street to one of only four homes that had been completed before the housing market collapsed in '08, and the builder went bankrupt. The saltbox-style house stood beside an attached two-car garage on a landscaped lot. The property wore the appearance of stability and success. Fresh snow covered the driveway, which displayed no recent tire tracks. Christmas lights lined the eaves. Lane's bicycle lay on the lawn, becoming a snow sculpture as flakes gathered on the frame and tires.

"She rode her bike? At night, in the snow?"

"Dangerous," Andy said, scanning the house, the yard, and the street. She parked in the driveway and killed the lights. We stepped out of the car, closing the doors without attempting stealth.

A yard light came on as we stepped to the front door. The door opened before we could knock. Lane Franklin appeared. Her long black hair hung damp on her shoulders. She wore sweats, and the knees and thighs of her pants were wet. Despite her milk chocolate complexion, she looked flushed, like someone warming up after a serious chill.

"Andy, Will, thank you *so much* for coming!" Lane spoke at barely a whisper. She hurried us in the door. As soon as we were inside, she closed the door and turned to me. "Will, you need to disappear!"

"What's going—"

"Quick! You have to be here, but you can't be here!" Lane gestured with her hands, making an urgent winding motion. I glanced at Andy, who gave a play-along nod.

Fwooomp! I vanished. I relished the comfortable cool sensation enveloping my body. It chased away the winter chill. I immediately began to float, weightless. I clamped a hand around the belt on Andy's coat.

"Do I have snow melt on me?"

Lane did a quick survey. "Can't see any."

I had not yet experimented with disappearing in a snowfall. I wondered if I would show up as an outline of accumulating snow on my head and shoulders.

"Lane, what's going on?" Andy asked, her tone laced with concern.

"It's my friend Sarah. Hurry! And whatever you do, Will, don't show yourself!"

We moved into the house. Weightless and without my battery-powered propulsion units, I can only move by gripping objects and structure or by hanging on to my wife's coat. Andy towed me forward.

A dozen different scenarios involving kids, drugs, partying, drinking, sex, and other teen mischief ran through my head. I had no idea what to expect as we passed through a comfortable, tidy kitchen into an open-concept family room.

A girl, fair-skinned and blonde, the same age and size as Lane, sat cross-legged on the floor in front of an unlit fireplace. Like Lane, she wore comfortable sweats. A phone lay on the carpet at her knee. In her lap she held a large-caliber revolver. She sat with her small hand wrapped around the grip and index finger inside the trigger guard.

Andy stopped cold when she saw the weapon. I released my grip on Andy's coat and pushed against the floor with my toes. I immediately rose to the ceiling. I touched the ceiling with my fingertips, stopped, stretched my legs horizontally, then used the kitchen door frame to propel myself into the family room above the girl.

"Sarah?" Lane started forward, but Andy threw an arm out and stopped her. "Sarah, this is my friend Andy."

The girl had been looking down at her lap. At the sound of Lane's voice, she raised her head, showing us a petite and pretty face with long black lines of melted mascara on her cheeks. Wet smears ran to her chin. Her nose and eyes were red from crying. Her blue eyes were alert but fixed on a distance. I looked around the room for drug paraphernalia, empty bottles, anything that might complicate matters. Nothing revealed itself.

"Hi, Sarah," Andy said softly. "May we come in?"

Sarah didn't answer. She shook her head minutely, a gesture that said it didn't matter one way or the other.

Keeping Lane behind her, Andy moved into the room, slowly. She slipped her coat off and draped it over a chair. From the same chair, Andy pulled an ottoman toward Sarah, careful not draw too close. Andy sat on the ottoman with her hands folded on her knees.

My mission appeared clear.

Andy spoke gently. "Sarah, no one is going to do anything. We just want to make sure you're safe. Okay?"

Again, Sarah's head shook, side to side. Like it didn't matter.

I didn't have much to work with. The smooth ceiling lacked light fixtures or beams to grip. I fixed a course toward the space on the floor beside the girl and pushed off carefully. In mid-flight, I curled my legs up into a cannonball position. I arrived a few feet from the girl, adjacent to the fireplace hearth. The hearth had a slate stone surface with just enough overhang to grab. It anchored me within reach of the gun.

"Sarah is anyone else home?" Andy asked.

"My parents are at the movies," she replied in a small but clear voice.

"So, it's just you and Lane?"

"Just me and Lane. I told her to go home because she shouldn't be here when I kill myself."

Andy glanced at Lane, who nodded.

"But you know Lane. She's—she's—" Sarah began to cry. "She's a *really good person.*"

"She is. Lane is a really good person," Andy said. "She's my best friend. I tell her everything."

"Me, too," Sarah said, high, thin, weeping.

"Did you tell Lane about this? About what's going on?"

"Uh-huh."

"That's good. Maybe, since Lane is your friend, and Lane is my friend, maybe we could all be friends. Together. Just us girls."

"That would be nice. But I need to be dead soon. I'm sorry."

"The thing is, Sarah, I don't get to see Lane very much, and I miss her.

And it would really be nice to have another friend to talk to sometimes. Is Lane your best friend?"

"Lane is *the* best friend. OMG, she rode her bike all the way out here tonight, in like this snowstorm. That's like two miles."

"She cares about you."

"I really, really do, Sarah!"

"Sarah let's talk about it. Okay? Just us girls. Let's talk about why you think you need to be dead. Because that's kinda forever, and it would be so hard on Lane."

Sarah squeezed out the words, high and thin. "I need to be dead because I don't want to be a whore."

"Nobody can make you be a whore," Andy said. "Nobody."

Sarah huffed out a breath. She leaned forward and pushed her phone toward Andy.

"That's not true! See what he sends me? If I won't be his whore, he's going to put it everywhere. My parents will see it. My boyfriend will see it. Everybody will see it!"

Andy picked up the phone and opened the screen to a photo. Lane leaned over, but from her expression I knew she'd seen the photo. Andy's face remained neutral, despite the image she confronted.

"Everybody is going to see me naked," Sarah declared with helpless resignation.

"Who's doing this? Is it your boyfriend?"

"No! I don't know! Some guy. He just texted it to me. Then he started texting me and telling me what I had to do to keep him from sharing it with the whole world. He told me *exactly* what I had to do. Like, in really gross detail. And if I didn't…"

"Do you have any idea how this picture was taken?"

"No."

"Okay." Andy backed off the subject. "Your boyfriend—is he a good guy?"

"Yes."

"Would he have taken this picture? And maybe shared it with someone?"

"Ohmigod, no. He never…we never…did it. We don't do it. God. I only let him touch my boobs once!" Sarah suddenly burst into loud sobs.

Through the sobs, she cried out, "I'm going to kill myself and I never even got to *do it* once!"

She pulled the revolver out of her lap and swung it toward her head.

I leaned forward and clamped my hand down on the cylinder and hammer. My grip prevented her from bringing the pistol to bear on her head. Sarah startled. Her finger convulsed on the trigger, pulling it all the way through. The hammer snapped back, then forward, pinching the flesh of my palm. I tightened my hold, preventing the action from dropping the hammer and firing. I jerked the pistol upward, breaking Sarah's grip. To Andy and Lane, the weapon shot up a foot or two on its own, then floated away from Sarah's reach.

Sarah didn't pay any attention. She bent double and wailed. Andy flashed Lane a signal and Lane dove to the floor, pulling her friend into a tight embrace.

I eased the hammer down into a safe position and handed the revolver to Andy. With practiced fingers, she removed the ammunition and carried the weapon into the kitchen. She laid the revolver on top of the refrigerator and dropped the cartridges into a drawer. She spent a moment there, thumbing the phone. I pushed off the hearth in her direction. Lane and Sarah held each other, both crying.

"What the hell?" I floated to a position beside Andy and spoke softly.

"I don't know, how does someone get a picture like this?"

She showed me. It was Sarah, nude, standing full frontal to the camera. The picture had been retouched so that everything around Sarah was blurred. Her body glittered, wet. Water glistened at her feet.

"She must have let someone take it."

"Maybe," Andy didn't commit. "Keep out of sight. Look around, okay?"

"Got it."

Andy found a glass and filled it with water. She took a box of tissues from the kitchen counter and walked back to the girls on the floor. She dropped down beside Sarah and drew both her and Lane into a comforting hug. It renewed Sarah's capacity for crying.

2

———————

I cruised through the house. Had Sarah managed to kill herself, the newspaper article would have commented on what a happy, healthy home she came from. Appearances can certainly deceive, but the house had all the trappings of being comfortable, full of life and belonging to a close family. Photos told a story of mother, father and daughter loving and enjoying each other. Not just posed portraits, but candid shots that showed impromptu smiles, warm embraces, and caught-off-guard looks of love and admiration. A china cabinet displayed soccer trophies. Perfect-grade report cards hung on the refrigerator door. A piano sat in the living room, not as a dusty decoration, but with sheet music tipped against the front panel, including paper lined with stanzas full of hand-scribbled musical notes. Sarah composed, old school.

I cruised upstairs. Her bedroom looked practical. School books from Essex High School lay on a desk beside a laptop. Clothes lay on the floor. The bed was made but bore the impression of someone lying on it, along with more books and a bag of Cheetos. She had her own television and cable box. Clothing nicer than Lane's mostly second-hand collection filled a closet and overflowed onto a dresser. An electronic keyboard sat in one corner. MIDI cables ran from mysterious boxes into her laptop.

If there were signs of something amiss in the house, I didn't see them. In the photos, her father appeared young and well-groomed. Nothing I saw suggested his occupation. Her mother took pretty pictures that captured warm, friendly eyes. The house was tidy, but not obsessive-neat-freak clean, if the master bedroom and her mother's cluttered closet were any indication.

Conversation in the family room continued at a low murmur as I glided back through the kitchen. I floated into a hover over the kitchen island.

Andy, Lane, and Sarah had moved to a U-shaped sofa, with Sarah in the middle. The two girls sat like sisters, hugging. Andy sat with her legs folded under her, facing Sarah. Andy spoke softly, steadily, looking like a big sister telling bedtime stories to the siblings.

"Well, he's tall, handsome, smart," Andy said, ticking each item off on her fingers. "I met him when I arrested him—well, not really arrested him. I stopped him—like a traffic stop—but really, and don't tell anyone I told you this, I did it to ask him out."

"That's so cool. What else?" Sarah asked. Her voice carried weakness and strain, the traces of crying, but her question had the energy of genuine interest. I got the impression that this girl talk was about love, and about caring for and connecting with someone.

"He makes me laugh."

"My parents are like that, too." Sarah told a halting story of a couple that met over a steaming sink in a campus kitchen; two college freshmen serving time in a work study program.

"You're lucky to have them." Andy put a hand on Sarah's leg. "When are they supposed to be home?"

"They went to a four o'clock show. Mom always makes dad take us to the matinee-priced shows. They like to go to Los Lobos after."

Andy didn't mention the coincidence. She took a serious tack.

"Honey, you know I have to stay here and tell them."

"*No!*" Sarah's composure collapsed. "*No, please don't tell them!*"

"Sweetie, can you even for a second imagine that they love you less or care for you less than Lane and I do? Even for a second?"

"You can't show them that picture! You can't show my dad!"

Andy gave it a moment of serious thought.

"I don't think I will have to. Do you trust me?"

Sarah's head bobbed.

"I need to keep your phone. For police business. Okay?"

Another head-bob.

"Good. And I promise you, while I have your phone, no one will see this picture except me. No one."

I thought it a tough promise to make, but Andy seemed determined.

"Andy's a kick-ass cop," Lane said. "She shot a guy." Lane didn't elaborate on her role in that tale. I wondered if she ever told the story of her abduction.

"He was a very bad man who attacked me," Andy said. "As a rule, I don't go around shooting people."

"You can shoot this guy," Sarah said.

3

We heard them enter through the garage door. Sarah's parents came in on full alert. Andy stood ready for them, badge in hand.

"Sarah! What's going on? Is everything okay?" Sarah's mother, a blonde reflection of her daughter, asked urgently. Andy stepped forward.

"Mrs. Lewis, I'm Detective Andrea Stewart and a very close friend of Lane's."

"Hi, Mrs. Lewis! Hi, Mr. Lewis!" Lane waved. They waved back hesitantly.

"Robert Lewis, my wife Donna." The man shook hands with Andy.

I recognized him from the restaurant. He must not have looked too closely at Andy when we left, because he didn't recognize her as having been with the stranger who gave him and his wife two free dinners.

"Honey, what's going on?" Donna Lewis rushed to put an arm around her daughter. Sarah folded into her mother.

"What's this about?" Lewis wanted to know.

"Lane called me," Andy said. "Can we chat in the other room? I'm sure the girls will be fine here for a while."

Andy didn't wait for an answer but gestured for the parents to follow her through the kitchen, through a dining room, into the living room on the opposite corner of the first floor. The move inconvenienced me. I crabbed my way across the kitchen ceiling, pulled myself into the dining room using the doorway, and fixed a hover where I could see and hear them. Andy directed the couple to sit. The three adults formed a triangle on formal-looking furniture that probably saw little use.

"What's going on?" Sarah's father pressed.

Andy held up Sarah's phone with the screen facing away from the parents.

"Someone has taken a compromising photograph of your daughter and is using it to threaten her, and as an attempt to extort her."

"What photograph?" Mr. Lewis reached for the phone. Andy pulled it back.

"Your daughter would rather you not see it. It's up to you, but I'd like to endorse her position for the moment. It will be hard on her if she knows you've seen it."

"Has it been posted? Is it all over the internet?" Lewis demanded. "Oh, God!"

Andy shook her head. "I don't think so. Not yet. A threat's been made, but the person making the threat appears to be using it to pressure Sarah into providing sexual favors."

Donna Lewis pressed a hand to her mouth. "How could this happen? Did she—?"

"She says she hasn't had any contact with him. Sarah's been very forthcoming about all this. She said she has had no sexual contact with anyone. I'm inclined to believe her."

"Is it Michael? Her boyfriend?" Lewis asked, anger rising. "Is he taking pictures of her?"

"No."

"But she knows this person, right? Can you find him? Arrest him? Stop him?" Donna Lewis begged.

"She doesn't know who it is. The picture was taken without her consent," Andy said. "But it's possible we will be able to lure the person who took the picture into a position where we can make an arrest and prevent the distribution of the image. Possible."

"How could this happen? How did some stranger get this photo?"

"Sarah says she doesn't know how it was taken."

"That doesn't make sense," Lewis shook his head.

"I need to have the image examined," Andy said. "With Sarah's help, we might be able to determine its origin."

"Is it even her? I mean, did Sarah say it was even a picture of her? Not something doctored up?" Lewis asked. "One of those deep fakes?"

"Sarah seems to feel the image is genuine."

"That's ridiculous! Let me see it!" Lewis put his hand out.

Andy held the phone back again.

"Sir, I understand. Would you wait here a moment? Just a moment?"

He nodded. She stood and went to the kitchen. When she returned, she held up the revolver, but did not hand it over.

"Is this yours?"

Both parents looked at it, wide-eyed.

"Yes," Mr. Lewis said. "I keep it upstairs, in a gun safe."

"Does Sarah have access?"

"I taught both Sarah and Donna how to access it and use it. I think they're both safer if they have had instruction."

Andy sat down. She held up the phone again.

"Sarah called Lane, and Lane called me to come here tonight because Sarah said—because of this—" Andy gestured with the phone, "she had decided on suicide." Both parents gasped. "Your daughter had this weapon when Lane got here. When we got here."

I noticed the slip-up, the *we*. Neither of the Lewis parents, awhirl in their worst nightmare, caught it.

"*Oh God...*" Donna Lewis's eyes spilled tears.

"Now I want you to listen to me. You're asking to see this photo, Mr. Lewis. But consider the lengths to which your daughter was willing to go to defend her honor, to defend your good impression of her. For a moment tonight, she thought death would be preferable to having you look at her with the same eyes that have seen this." Andy let the point settle, then said, "So you can ask me again, and I will hand this over. Or you can let me take it with me. Your job is to care for your daughter. My job is to conduct an investigation. I can't promise anything, but if you let me take this, there's a chance we can find this person before he can threaten your daughter again or make this image public. There's a chance no one else will ever see this. It's up to you."

"Take it," Lewis said.

"Good choice. Now, your daughter needs you." Andy stood up. "And I would like to start moving on this."

4

G etting me out of the house became a bit of a trick.

After Lane embraced Sarah in a lengthy good-bye, Andy handed Lane her keys and told her to put her bike in the trunk of the car. Andy stayed behind to have a final word with the Lewis family. Part of that may have been a bit of theater designed to get me out the front door with Lane.

"I'm grabbing the back of your sweatshirt, kiddo," I whispered to Lane after she pulled on a hoodie in the front hall. "Lead the way."

Lane pulled me through the front door, careful not to let the storm door slam into me. She led me down the sidewalk.

"This feels funny. You have no inertia."

"Science!" I performed my best Thomas Dolby imitation.

When we reached her bike, I reappeared.

Fwooomp! Dropping to the pavement, my feet almost slid out from under me on the snow-covered driveway. The TV-weather prediction had been for up to half an inch, but accumulation already measured double that. I opened the trunk and helped Lane load her bike after shaking off the snow.

"Take the front seat," I told Lane. I slid into the back seat and—

Fwooomp! I disappeared again after strapping in. I couldn't be sure one or both of the Lewis parents wouldn't walk Andy to the car. The last thing anyone needed was for Sarah's parents to see some strange man appearing and disappearing.

"You're a good friend to Sarah," I told Lane. "You saved her life tonight."

Lane didn't answer. We watched Andy working her way out of the house, answering last-minute questions, giving last-minute instructions. Before saying a final goodnight, we saw Sarah push past her parents and close a powerful hug around Andy. They held on for a moment.

5

"May I have the phone?" Lane asked Andy as we backed out of the Lewis driveway. Andy handed it over. Lane bowed her head over the lighted screen while Andy drove. Seated in the backseat, I couldn't see what she was doing.

"Don't delete anything," Andy warned.

"I won't. I'm sending the picture to my e-mail."

"Why?" Andy asked, going on alert, ready to explain the obvious about letting this picture get out.

"I need to look at it on my Mac."

Andy drove us to Lane Franklin's tiny house in Essex.

"WHERE'S YOUR MOM TONIGHT?" Andy asked as Lane powered up her computer.

We stood in Lane Franklin's living room. Lane sat at a secondhand desk tucked in one corner. Lane has a skilled touch with Photoshop. Not long ago, she performed a key bit of photo retouching to help Andy identify a suspect in the killing of a state senator.

"Mama's out with the ladies from church. God, it was like pulling teeth to get her to leave me home alone! She's still so clingy!"

Since Lane's abduction last summer, Rosemary II struggled with allowing her daughter to go beyond arm's length. I understood. Looking at Lane, remembering things I didn't want to remember, I saw vulnerability, too.

Lane busied herself with her mouse. Photoshop woke up on her screen.

Andy and I leaned closer. In an instant, Lane had Sarah's photo fully framed on her iMac screen. Moving too quickly to follow, she created a rectangle of opaque color over Sarah's naked torso. With a few more clicks of the mouse, Lane magnified the image to a point where the pixilation made it nearly impossible to discern detail.

"There!" Lane pointed at the screen.

"What are we looking at?" I asked.

"Right here," Lane said. "Under her feet."

"Back it out a little," Andy directed. Lane complied.

We could see Sarah's bare feet. The blackmailer had blurred the image all around Sarah, possibly using Photoshop as well. But he had been careful not to let the blur effect wash onto Sarah. He left a tiny border all the way around her naked body. The portion between her feet escaped the effect.

"She's wet. You can see the water on her skin. And here," Lane pointed again, "that's water on the floor. But look at this pattern, right here along the edge of her foot. That's tile."

Andy and I studied the image cues as Lane pointed them out.

"It is," I agreed.

Lane looked up at us, her face bright with certainty.

"I know where that photo was taken!"

6

M ike Mackiejewski parked his patrol car behind Andy's car. We had been sitting curbside for less than ten minutes, but snow already covered the car. Mike stepped out and pulled on a coat. In his mid-twenties, a little shorter than Andy, Mike served under Andy's command for the two years he'd been on patrol with the Essex PD.

"'Sup, Sarge?" He looked at me. "Hey, Will."

"Hey."

He looked at Lane.

"Hey, Lane," he said, casting a questioning look at Andy. Everybody on the Essex PD knew Lane Franklin. Her abduction case went in the Win column.

Lane had not only convinced us of what she saw in the photo but insisted on showing us in person. Andy resisted, but Lane made the case that she had a stake in this, in her friend, Sarah. Andy agreed to let Lane tag along only on the condition that she call her mother and let Andy speak to Rosemary II. Lane saw no problem in that. She knew her mother would say Yes to anything Andy and I asked. After a brief conversation, Andy promised Rosemary II we would have Lane home by eleven.

"I need the security fob to get into the pool," Andy told Mike, gesturing at the glass doors at the end of the sidewalk. The high school pool has a public entrance for conference swim meets and for providing public swim access that had been a condition of the original referendum to build the pool.

Mike hiked up the sidewalk, pulling a heavy ring of keys from his jacket pocket. At the brick wall adjacent to the farthest glass door, he removed a metal cover from a small box. He found the fob he needed and swiped it across the small box. Something buzzed and snapped loudly. Mike reached over and pulled the door open.

"Want me to come in with you?"

Andy shook her head. "We got it from here. Thanks, Mike!"

We filed into the pool lobby, past the glass trophy cases, past the closed snack bar counters, toward the entrance to the pool itself. Andy's high heels clicked on the tile floor. Chlorine odor and humidity contrasted with the winter atmosphere outside. Of the two, I preferred the scent of fresh snow.

The pool annex, larger than the original high school gymnasium and smaller than the recently added athletic field house, offered eight Olympic-scale lanes, plus individual diving wells that included a ten-meter platform. I like swimming, and even enjoy diving off a good flexible board. No way in hell I'd take a plunge off a thirty-foot high diving platform.

We skirted the big pool and then the diving wells, both looking like vast sheets of glass. At the far end of the building, a pair of doorways opened to a hallway that led to the locker rooms.

"Hold up," Lane touched my sleeve.

Andy and I stopped and looked at her. We stood in semidarkness, illuminated only by small walk lights and the exit signs above each doorway. The halogen overhead lights hung dormant above us.

"Ever see those stupid movies where someone searches a room for a bug, then tears apart a light fixture and holds it up for everyone to see?" she asked. She pantomimed. "Hey, look, A bug."

Andy got it right away. "Completely overlooking the fact that the people listening can hear the whole thing."

"Right," Lane said. "That photo was taken without Sarah knowing it."

"Probably from a fixed position. Which means there's a good chance the camera wasn't some schmuck holding his iPhone up and pretending to scroll his play list," I offered, trying to keep up.

"Exactly," Andy said, looking past us at the dark entrance. "But a camera planted in a locker room—that would be quite a trick. If it's a fixed mount, how does the pervert collect his photos?"

"Transmitted," Lane said. "Maybe a Bluetooth connection or the school's Wi-Fi." She bounced up and down. "I bet it uses motion detection! The camera only wakes up and shoots when there's a subject. And it could be set to send the images as a compressed burst!"

"Hold on here," I said. "Isn't this getting a little sophisticated for some perv shooting locker room pictures?"

Lane gave me a join-the-century-old-man look. "Do you have any idea the technology that's in the phone sitting in your pocket? Oh—my—God! You can get all kinds of spy tech from Amazon. What we're talking about is totally doable."

"The point is," Andy put us back on track, "we could walk in there, wake up the camera, and have the camera taking and transmitting pictures of us fumbling around looking for a camera."

"Which would tip off our guy," I said. "And might point a finger at Sarah for going to the police, prompting the pervert to broadcast the photo."

Woman and girl both turned and landed expectant gazes on me.

"Do your thing, Divisible Man," Andy said.

"Wait! What did you call him?" Lane, startled, asked.

I looked around. "Any security cameras in here?"

Andy shook her head. "They monitor the halls and entrances."

Fwooomp! I vanished. I grasped Andy's arm to stay anchored.

"Oh! That is so effing cool!" Lane exclaimed. "Seriously, what did you call him?"

"Andy, I'll need to turn on some lights. Do you think that's a problem?"

"Shouldn't be. Janitors must go in there at night to clean and must turn on the lights in the process. If any of the high tech we suspect is at play, more than likely the camera pays no attention to lights turning on and off. The perv probably gets all kinds of photos of middle-aged janitors."

"Wait!" Lane dug into her back pocket and pulled out her phone. "If you find a spot you think is right, see if you can get some photos."

"Why?" Andy asked.

"I want to apply a blur effect on my computer," she said. She read Andy's confused expression. "We can't reverse his blur effect like they do in the movies. You know, 'Computer, enhance!' That doesn't really work. But we can shoot a picture that matches Sarah's photo, apply the same effect, and see if it matches up."

"Good thinking," I said.

Lane held out her phone. I put my hand around it and pulled it out of her hand. She broke into a bright smile, seeing the phone float before her eyes.

"The camera is on. Just push the button, here," she pointed.

"Got it."

I opened my jacket and pushed the phone in, causing it to vanish. When I pulled it back out and held it openly in my hand, it remained unseen, but I could still feel the shutter button. I pushed away from Andy's arm.

"Okay, I'm off. Hang loose."

7

I didn't get far.

The entrance from the pool s-turned into the women's locker room, shrouded in black with no light switches in sight. Not wanting to float blindly through a locker room darker than a coal mine, I abandoned the approach and went back to Lane and Andy. I reappeared. We repositioned in the lobby near the locker room entrance and I started again.

I found a bank of light switches and flicked them on. The entire locker room lit up.

Except for an absence of urinals and the use of more feminine colors, I didn't see much difference between the women's locker room and any men's locker room I'd ever seen. Regiments of square, powder pink lockers stood divided by low plastic benches. Mirrors above sinks lined one wall. Tile in rose and pink shades covered the floor, with white tile covering the walls.

I went high as usual, floating just below the ceiling and gripping the rows of lockers for propulsion. Maintenance needed to do a better job of dusting the tops of the lockers. I passed over several socks and a pair of panties, careful not to touch. At one point, I passed over a pair of swim goggles. They reminded me of ski goggles I had purchased and planned on using tonight as part of Date Night. If Andy and I ever got home, that is. Faith in that outcome faded fast.

Opposite the entrance, the shower rooms lay between the locker room and the pool. As I passed over the last row of lockers, I pulled myself downward and unfurled my feet under me. I let them touch the tiles in a weird, weightless trot that took me to the first pillar of shower nozzles in the expansive room.

Tile floor. Drains placed at evenly measured intervals. Chrome shower nozzles and water controls lining the walls. An orderly forest of stainless-steel pillars at attention in rows filled the center of the space. Here, the chlorine pool smell mingled with cleanser scent. A basic institutional shower room large enough to handle an entire gym class of girls.

I began to wonder if the camera streamed video. And I began to see a problem with a much broader scope than Sarah Lewis.

I studied the floor and the tiles Lane pointed out.

Lane hit the mark dead on. The tile matched the photo.

The image of Sarah showed a girl, naked, full-frontal to the camera, with her weight on her right foot, her hips cocked slightly, her left arm hanging limp, and her right arm raised with her right hand at the back of her head. She stood with her face upturned and her eyes closed, looking serene, or seductive—if taken out of the mundane context of an athlete trying to wash chlorine out of her hair.

After Lane saw the tiles and told us where to find them, she pointed out that Sarah had joined the freshman swim team.

I considered the image and the moment it had been shot.

She had been showering when the photo was shot, with her back to the stream of water. Where would she have been standing?

The question was not so much which nozzle was she standing at, but which one put her in a position where a mounted camera could snap her image?

I eliminated the outer wall. A trough at the base of the wall dropped half an inch below the rest of the floor. No such line could be seen at Sarah's feet. Also, the outer wall had white tile, with a band of rose-colored tiles running through it around waist height. Sarah's photo showed the same color band, but distant, blurred and higher in the frame.

That put Sarah at one of the central pillars. Three ranks of pillars, with four pillars in each, filled the center of the room. Each pillar sported four nozzles, set at cardinal points around the pillar.

I needed a matched pair. One nozzle to spray and a companion pillar for the camera.

Again, I considered the background of Sarah's photo. The color band gave a strong hint. It meant the photo had been taken in one of three directions, eliminating the shower room entrance as a backdrop, where no color band could be seen.

I did the math. There were nine options facing the back wall. Eight options facing the right-side wall, and eight options facing the left side wall.

Only twenty-five possibilities.

Again, thinking of the image of Sarah, I recalled that the blurred color band appeared high behind her, running even with her shoulders. Since the image had a slight down angle, it had been taken by a camera mounted roughly at the height of her face. The down angle on the camera and the location of the color band in relation to Sarah's body put the color band farther, rather than nearer to Sarah.

That stopped me.

How the hell do you mount a camera in a shower room at face height? *Holy shit!*

Floating beside the first of the pillars, I realized I was staring right at the most likely answer.

The shower nozzle.

Each pillar had four shower nozzles, mounted even with my eyes, which put them close to six feet above the floor. Each station had a pull-type knob that turned on the water, and a soap dish. Both the knob and the soap dish were mounted much lower, around bellybutton level.

The shower nozzle.

I studied the one directly in front of me. Slightly phallic (or perhaps strongly phallic, if you see things that way), the design formed a simple chrome cylinder with a half-sphere tip and a single outlet hole.

Or eye if the thing were a camera instead of a nozzle.

I reached for the control knob ninety degrees to my right, fixed a grip on the pillar with one hand and prepared to pull the knob with the other. Then I stopped.

If I create a stream of water, will the motion activate the camera? Then what?

I moved around the pillar and peered into the nozzle. It had a diffuser and tiny hints of mineral buildup. Normal. I moved to the next nozzle.

I found the camera on the fifth try. Center row, first pillar, the nozzle facing the back wall.

The exterior of the nozzle looked no different than any of the other thirty-one nozzles in the room. But when I maneuvered around to look into the single outlet hole, I saw a glint where there should be none. A lens.

Got you, you son of a bitch!

8

"Here," I handed Lane her phone. "I shot a bunch of photos from right in front of the camera. Should be the same point of view. There has to be at least one good one you can use for your blur experiment."

"That actually worked?" Lane seemed surprised. "With the camera *gone*?"

"Seems like."

"You're sure it's the camera?" Andy asked.

"As sure as I can be. But the question now is, how do we remove it without tipping off the pervert?"

"I know the answer to that," Lane said.

That came as no surprise to me.

"Going on the assumption that the camera is using the school Wi-Fi to transmit images, we simply shut down the Wi-Fi and remove the camera while it's out of touch," Lane explained.

"Exactly what I was thinking" I lied. Andy gave me a no-you-weren't look.

"Of course," Lane went on, "the catch is that the camera may perform a routine signal check—like a regular check-in. That's how I would do it. So that the perv will get an alert when it goes offline, or when it fails to check in."

"So, this could also tip him off that Sarah reported him. And make him release the photo preemptively."

"Maybe," Lane said. "But going offline could mean anything. Power failure. Software glitch. It doesn't have to mean that Sarah ratted him out."

"Except we don't get the chance to debate it with the guy," Andy said. She stood still for a moment, looking through the walls at the nozzle-camera with her mind's eye. "I really need to have that hardware looked at by an expert. That's going to take time."

"Target fixation," I said.

Andy and Lane looked at me.

"Target fixation," I repeated. "That might not be the right term for it, but we induce target fixation on the perv. We set him up to make an assumption about why the camera has gone offline. An assumption that steers him away from thinking Sarah turned him in. He gets his mind fixed on the answer he thinks *he* came up with and doesn't explore other possibilities."

I explained what I had in mind.

When I finished, Andy gave it a moment's thought, then said, "Okay. Let's try it. First, we need to take Lane home. Then we pay a visit to Chet Allison, the high school principal."

9

"We have another problem," Andy said after we dropped Lane at her door and made her promise to say nothing to anyone about what happened to Sarah, or what we found—not even to Sarah. Lane, both dutiful and smart, agreed, but she made Andy promise to keep her up to date on the case.

"Here." Andy handed me Sarah's phone.

"We have more than one problem," I said, taking it, and thinking further about the camera mount and location. "What's yours?"

"Scroll through the text messages on this thread."

She backed out of the driveway and started driving while I read. When I finished, I handed the phone back.

"That last one came in while you were in the locker room." Andy thumbed the phone to close the screen. She put it in her coat pocket while she drove.

The string of messages went from a coy, teasing hello to a tone of smug superiority, to showing Sarah the photo, then into a string of explicit messages telling the girl what, precisely, she would have to do to ensure the photo never went public. Sexually explicit messages.

The last note in the string said, *Candy Store. Midnight or the pix goes viral.*

"What the hell is the 'Candy Store?'"

"I don't know, but that only gives us two and a half hours." Andy fastened her eyes on the snowy road ahead. Falling snowflakes raced toward the windshield, then dodged our passage at the last second.

"Sarah must know, or he wouldn't have used it as a reference. This should make it easy. We find out where this Candy Store is and set a trap for the asshole. Grab him and this all ends."

Andy didn't speak.

"What?"

"Say we find out. Say we text him back and agree to the meet. Say we get lucky and grab him, which is only likely if he's a complete idiot, and I have my doubts about that. Then say he claims he was just driving by...saw a kid who looked like she needed help...doesn't know a thing about any photo, or camera, or computers. And say he's smart enough not to have any evidence where we can find it. Locks his phone. Hides his computer. Suddenly, we have nothing. We can't hold him. And we can't stop him from publishing the photo—which can happen with a click of a mouse or touch of a screen. Will, I know next to nothing about the web, how these perverts can lurk there, how they hide behind east-European IP addresses and trade their disease with other perverts on the 'Dark Web'—whatever the heck *that* is!"

"Got any friends at the FBI who handle this sort of thing?"

Andy laughed. "At nine-thirty on a Saturday night? With a two-and-a-half-hour window? And that's assuming they don't brush it all off as kids sexting each other."

I admit, it seemed unlikely to me that this situation would attract federal interest.

"We need to buy some time."

"So, buy time,"

Andy turned off Main Street onto a county road that would eventually slip out of Essex into farm country. She checked her mirrors, then eased the car to the side of the road and stopped. The snow fell heavier than it had all day.

"Do you think it will work?" she asked, pulling the phone out again.

"Yes, If you word it right."

She activated the screen and brought up the text messaging app. She located the thread that Sarah, thankfully, had saved. "I need to get to the station to run this number," Andy muttered to herself. "Although I'm sure it's a burner phone."

She busied her thumbs for a minute. Regarded her work. Made a change. Then showed me the screen.

"*Parents have me locked down. They're out of town tomorrow night. PLS don't post the photo!*" I read.

"It lets him dictate the schedule change."

"It's good. Send it. But then send another right behind it. Add *PLS. I'll do anything you want.*"

Andy looked at me, frowning.

"It's what he wants to hear. Sorry."

She tapped Send. Worked the phone. Tapped send again. After heaving a resigned sigh, she laid the phone on the console and pulled back onto the road.

Less than a hundred yards down the road, Sarah's phone gave an iron-ically angelic bell chime. I picked it up. I read aloud.

"*Bitch. You'll do what I tell you.*"

Andy continued driving.

"Let me," I said. I worked my thumbs on the screen.

"*PLS! Anything for you. Everything. Tomorrow night!*" I read it to Andy.

"Send."

The message flew from Sarah's phone, joining the snowflakes in the cold, black air around us. I felt something equally cold and equally black deep inside. A frigid simmering anger surrounded with contrasting heat. I had felt it before when Lane had been abducted. I felt it again, not long ago, when I found two children, two small girls, dead in a forest.

Murder.

I thought about Sarah, another helpless victim, and I touched that cold black thing in my heart.

Sarah's phone dinged. I picked it up and read the response to Andy.

"*Say it. Say you'll be my sex bitch.*"

Andy held grimly onto the wheel, perhaps suppressing the same feel-ings that were rising in me. There are times when I don't know how she does her job.

I worked the screen. When I finished, I sat still for a minute, holding the phone, with the message ready, but unsent.

I waited. Let him think this cost her, hurt her, made her cry. Let him think this pushed her to the edge.

The tires spoke to us in a steady wet whisper as we drove on.

I will be your sex bitch. Whatever you want.

I didn't read it to Andy.

I hit Send.

Looking out the windshield, I thought of the snowflakes charging our headlights, our windshield, as messages flying through digital skies. Some benign. Some silly. Some urgent.

Some malevolent. Sick.

I wanted to vanish, float free of this car, and chase the message I just sent—chase it down the path of this sick exchange. I wanted to find this worm and yank him out of his black fantasies into a cold, harsh light.

Andy turned off the county road into a subdivision marked with a pair of landscaped brick half walls. One side bore the name Covent Creek Estates in sweeping metal script. Oversized homes spaced out on five-acre lots spread into the night distance. Each one glowed in the snowfall, tastefully lighted for Christmas, a scene of winter postcard perfection.

We found the Allison home on a cul-de-sac. A jolly inflatable Santa Claus waved at us from the front lawn. Icicle lights dripped from the eaves. When Andy stopped the car, we sat for a moment regarding the phone in my hand.

Ding!

Midnight. Tomorrow. One minute late and the whole world gets to see your...

I didn't read the rest.

10

Nobody likes a knock on the door by the police.

Andy may have looked like a model on her way to a society soiree, but she held up her badge which caught Chet Allison's eye immediately. I saw his expression flick from *who's this lovely woman?*—to *it's the cops*—to *wait, I know her* in a split second.

"Sergeant Stewart?"

"Hi, Principal Allison," Andy greeted him. I noticed she didn't correct him on her new rank. Andy knew the high school principal through the police liaison program. The city maintained an office for an on-duty officer at the school. I remembered Andy telling me that one of the privileges of her sergeant's rank was avoiding high school duty. Too many rampant hormones running around in the halls, she said. I easily imagined Andy being a distraction for teenaged boys. "I'm so sorry to bother you at this hour, but we have a situation. This is my husband, Will. May we come in?"

Mildly bewildered, the principal of Essex High School swung his front door wide and ushered us into his home. We did our best to limit the snow on our shoes to a rug in his front hall. The house smelled like fresh baked cookies.

Allison looked young to me. Andy told me he'd only been at the helm of the high school for two years. Under short-cropped sandy-brown hair, he had a round face with a slightly pug nose. Shorter than my six feet, his physique carried muscle that might have once served a football team's defensive backfield. The man either had a gym membership or used the one at the school to stay fit. I didn't picture him as anybody's pushover at the high school.

His wife appeared, curious, stroking long blonde hair back behind her ears. Both wore comfortable sweaters and slippers. We had interrupted a cozy evening of television watching while the snow flew outside the window. Judging their age and the size of the house, I suspected children slept upstairs.

Allison shook hands with Andy, then me. "Please, call me Chet. I've heard your name, Will. Quite a story."

"Fifteen minutes of fame."

"Is there somewhere we can talk?" Andy asked, letting them know this conference wasn't going to take place at the front door.

"Please come in," the wife offered, "I'm Lisa."

We performed a second round of introductions and followed them to their kitchen, where they offered us seats and water. I had been hoping for coffee, and maybe a cookie.

"THAT'S DISGUSTING," Lisa Allison said after we explained the path that led us to their door.

"And very troubling," Chet Allison added. "Do you have any idea how long the camera has been there?"

Andy shook her head. "Not at present. I'm not sure we will be able to determine that. Unless we catch whoever put it there."

"My God," Allison said. "We've had dozens of girls use that facility. Not just from our school, but schools all around us. We've had conference swim meets." Allison ran his hand over his scalp, a man looking both ways down a road, and seeing trouble ahead and trouble behind. "Are there any other girls? Girls who have been contacted?"

"None that we know of," Andy said. "I'm afraid you're going to have to start compiling a list. I don't know if it will come to this, but we may have to reach out to anyone who has used the facility."

"There's a lot to consider here," Allison said. "Issues of liability.

Issues of privacy. Issues of trust. Not to mention the number of these girls whose parents are lawyers."

"Or who know lawyers," his wife added.

"All things to be addressed," Andy said, "but we have more immediate concerns. We have a small window of opportunity to connect the camera to the person behind it. I can't emphasize enough that it must be handled delicately. One misstep, and we tip off the perpetrator. We could lose him for good, plus be unable to stop him from broadcasting whatever images he's collected."

"A cat that can't be pushed back into a bag," I added.

"Are there any events scheduled for the pool tomorrow?" Andy asked.

"Sunday? No," Allison said. "I'd have to check for Monday. Regular gym classes may be using it Monday. And the swim team practices after school during the week. Plus, the next conference meet is Thursday. Boys and girls."

"No question, then. We're on a clock. But we have tomorrow."

"Detective, I appreciate what you're trying to do, I mean, in terms of catching this pervert. But I have a responsibility beyond that. Knowing what I now know, I cannot allow anyone to use that facility until it's been swept clean. Not that I have a clue how to do that."

"I understand completely. I think I may be able to offer help with the technology. But I need a little time before we go in and shut everything down. We can't go public prematurely. Going public will drive the perpetrator underground."

"God," Allison said. He looked at his wife, whose face wore furrows of deep concern. "We'll have to bring the Board up to speed on this. I need to call Al." I knew he meant Al Glower, the superintendent—not one of my favorite people. "Who knows what kind of legal issues we're looking at?"

"Legal issues that might be less daunting if you can show that you took immediate steps not just to remedy the situation, but also to catch those responsible," Andy pointed out.

Lisa Allison reached out and took her husband's hand. They traded looks laced with awareness not only of the threat to the girls he held himself responsible for, but to his job and career. I'm not an educator, but I've seen the way the public grabs pitchforks and torches to go after teachers at the drop of a hat, or with the flash of an internet posting. Chet

Allison had the police in his home, at his table, informing him of a situation, and in the same breath asking him to withhold information from the public. Any perception that he hesitated to act, even with the best of intentions, could be devastating.

Whatever messages were transmitted silently between husband and wife, the decision came rapidly and unanimously.

"Tell me what you want to do," Allison said.

"Thank you," Andy said. "This may take a while."

"Whatever you need."

"Good." Andy slipped her coat off her shoulders. "For starters, on behalf of my husband who is too polite to ask, would you mind making some coffee? It could be a long night."

"God! Thank you!" I exhaled and slapped my hands on the table. Lisa Allison laughed, and it broke the tension. She stood up and began rattling off gourmet flavors that meant nothing to me, so I let her choose. She went to work at expensive-looking coffee-making machinery on her kitchen counter, determined to show off some barista skill.

Andy pulled out her phone.

"I need to start making calls." She ticked off names. "Tom. Chief Don Schultz at MPD. Pidge. Earl, too."

I blinked at the names. Andy's mind ran well ahead of mine.

Andy raised an intimate look in my direction, and with her eyes, told me she was sorry for what was about to happen to Date Night.

11

"Do you remember Greg LeMore? Detective with MPD?" Andy asked me when I returned to the table after Lisa Allison finished showing off her selection of coffees and brewing equipment.

"Hairy guy? Great barista?"

"I just got off the phone with Chief Schultz."

Chief Don Schultz had taken charge of the effort to find and rescue Lane, an effort that unfolded in Milwaukee. Schultz had offered Andy a job, which she turned down. Andy's excuse had been that her rank as Detective had only been temporary, and that she hadn't yet earned the full promotion.

"And?"

"And he's agreed to lend us LeMore."

"Excellent. Why?"

"LeMore is a tech geek. Nerd. Whatever. Remember he was always on his laptop? That's his thing. I talked to him a little when we were wrapping up Lane's case. He builds all kinds of stuff for MPD. Surveillance equipment, tracking devices, cameras—all custom made. I told Schultz what we're dealing with and he jumped all over the idea of lending us LeMore."

I suspected Schultz's generosity doubled as leverage to get Andy to say yes to his job offer. My reluctance to see her accept the big city job kicked in on autopilot. But then it struck me that without my job at Essex County Air Services standing in the way we were free to move wherever Andy's career took her.

Until this moment, I hadn't fully considered how things had changed. The notion of uprooting took on new meaning. Why not? We were no longer a two-career couple. Maybe moving halfway down the state would get Earl to stop sending me paychecks and stop pushing me to see his neurologist friend. Maybe—

"Hello," Andy waved a hand in front of my eyes.

"Oh, sorry." I focused on her again.

"Where were you?"

"Having nightmare flashbacks of riding in a car with Chief Schultz."

"Well, he's giving us LeMore. But we have to go get him. He says he needs to see the installation firsthand."

The light blinked on.

"I was thinking, maybe you and Pidge could, you know…"

"Steal another airplane in the middle of the night from Earl? Wow. This is *déjà vu* all over again for a second time again. You do know we're sitting in a snowstorm."

"It's supposed to let up after midnight. Clear and sunny by morning. That's what the forecast said before we left home. And we don't have to steal the airplane. I can put in for the city to pay for the fuel."

I laughed. I don't think Andy has a clue what the fuel consumption of a piston-engine twin can be or how the price of aviation fuel hangs between four and five dollars a gallon. As it is, the city comptroller craps his pants when Andy turns in a mileage request for using her personal vehicle.

"Earl might bitch about us stealing his airplanes, but he's a warrior without a war. You tell him why we're doing this, and he'd beat us to the hangar and salute us when we take off. I'm more worried about finding Pidge on a Saturday night. That's what you had in mind, isn't it?"

Andy nodded. "I would have said Dave, but he's in Montana giving depositions until Tuesday. Do you think you can find Pidge?"

"I don't know why we bother. Nobody's going to ramp check me tonight. I can fly down to Milwaukee and back without Pidge." I allowed a little sulking into my tone. The feds may have suspended my license to fly, but that didn't mean I'd forgotten how.

"I don't doubt it for a moment, love. But you're forgetting the cocktails were had at dinner. Plus, this is a police investigation, and I can't have any element of it bending the law. Sending a pilot with a suspended license to bring in an expert whose testimony may be needed down the road...you can see where a defense attorney might try to twist that around. Go find Pidge. See if you can take her along. We're going to need her tomorrow night, anyway."

I wondered what that meant.

"Lemme have your phone," I said. "She won't answer mine."

"ANDY—(*HUFF*)—!" Pidge answered on the fourth ring.

"It's Will," I said.

"Fuck!—(*huff*)—Will! I thought it was—(*huff*)—Andy!"

"Are you in the middle of something?" I asked.

"Fuck—(*huff*)—yes! What's up?"

"Wait, are you...?"

"What the fuck do you think? Hold on a second!" Something rustled against the phone. I heard Pidge say, "Get off me, doofus!" More rustling.

Pidge returned to the line, breathless.

"What's up?"

"Were you seriously in the middle of having sex?"

"Aren't you? I saw—(*huff*)—you and your babe wife headed into Los Lobos a couple hours ago. So, by my—(*huff*)—watch, you should be at home now screwing each other senseless."

"Jesus, Pidge!"

"Can I take it this isn't a fucking social call?"

"Nope. The cavalry rides again."

"No shit?! For real?!" Every time I see Pidge, she reminds me that our trip to Montana was the best effing time she ever had and wants to know when we can do it again. My vote was never, but her enthusiasm came through the line clearly. "Fuckin' A!"

"Don't get your hopes up. I just need to run down to MKE and pick up a cop and bring him back up here. I need you, so we have a genuine government-licensed pilot on board. I'd ask you to do it without me, but you've been drinking, haven't you?"

"As much as possible," she confirmed. I didn't mention that several hours ago, so had I. The rule is eight hours, and that rule was about to be bent. On the other hand, I don't have a license, so by a twisted kind of logic, I guess the rule didn't apply. Besides, I wouldn't be listed as pilot in command on the flight plan.

The phone rustled again. I heard her say to someone "Put it back in your pants, pal. I gotta go!" Then to me, "When and where?"

"Make it an hour. Let's pull out Six One Nine," I said, referring to one of a pair of Beechcraft Baron light twin-engine airplanes in the fleet.

"Oh, no! Wait 'till you fucking see what Earl bought. I'll see you there in an hour."

She broke the connection.

12

I took Andy's car. Andy stayed at the Allison home. Her boss, Chief Tom Ceeves, told her he would join her there to work over the details of what Andy had in mind. At some point, they planned to move to the district office, which adjoined the high school. Andy told Chet Allison she wanted to start compiling a list of contractors, maintenance people, and anyone else with access to the pool. It promised to be a long night.

At the airport, I worked the keypad on the security gate, waited for the gate to rumble open, and then parked Andy's car beside the Essex County Air Services hangar. Pidge's car sat under a layer of light snow. The hangar lights cast a glow through high-mounted windows. Sparkling snow continued to fall, but the flakes had become tiny and dust like. Colder air, sweeping down from Canada, had been promised and it kissed my cheek as I stomped my shoes and pulled open the hangar door.

She sat gleaming in the harsh halogen hangar lights.

"Holy shit," I said. "How did I not know about this!"

"Right?!" Pidge called out to me from the driver's seat on the propane-powered tug that would pull the gleaming airplane out of the hangar.

"Mojave?"

"Fuckin' A!"

White overall, with the same gold and red stripes Earl favored on his fleet, the airplane stood on long legs, coiled for flight, sleek and silent.

"Turbocharged. Pressurized. What's it cruise? Two forty?" I strolled forward, admiring the seductive lines of one of Piper's crowning creations.

"'Bout that," Pidge nodded, taking a moment to admire it.

"They only built a couple hundred of these." I touched the fuselage below the pilot's side window. "This is the Cheyenne without the turbines. When did Earl—?"

"Some guy bought One Nine Alpha, sight unseen, and sent Earl a fat check. Earl turned around and found this. It was delivered last Monday. Fucking beauty."

I knew very well that Earl had received a check, seemingly out of nowhere, for seven hundred and fifty thousand dollars for the Piper Navajo that Pidge had flown to my rescue in Montana and seriously damaged in the process. The check came as a shock to Earl, who had just started gearing up to fight with an insurance company that refused to fix the airplane. Earl had no idea the new owner of the old Navajo made his decision to purchase when I put a gun to his forehead.

I had not heard that Earl reinvested the windfall in a Mojave.

She felt cool and restless under my fingers.

Reading my thoughts, Pidge asked, "So when are you going to get your shit together with the feds?"

I looked at her. Cute. Petite. A pretty blonde you should underestimate only at your peril. One of the few pilots I ever knew who might actually be better than she shamelessly claimed to be.

"Gettin' there," I lied.

"The old man gripes about you all the time," Pidge said. She sounded a little jealous.

"Not as much as he flat out bitches about you." The comment made something sparkle in her eye.

"C'mon," she said. "Let's launch this bird." She cranked over the starter on the tug and I headed for the switch that opens the hangar doors.

PIDGE PULLED the airplane onto the snow-covered ramp. The city had not yet cleared the airport surfaces, and probably wouldn't until morning.

After she disconnected the tug and parked it, I closed the hangar door. I followed her up the air-stair door into the cabin. She flopped into one of the passenger seats, but I tapped her on the shoulder.

"Get your ass up front."

"Not me. I've been drinking."

"Yeah, and I'm not doing this alone. Move it."

She flashed me a grin and slid into the co-pilot's seat.

"I want to roll before we build up snow on the wings," I said, sliding into the pilot's seat. "Gimme the start-up checklist."

Drinking or not, Pidge was sharp. She took me through the checklist step by step, pointing at things when I couldn't find them in the unfamiliar cockpit. In short order, we had both engines running, blowing snow off the wings, which made me feel better. Even a small amount of contamination on a wing can cause a serious deterioration in lift.

We rolled across the ramp. Pidge pulled up her iPad to review a weather briefing she had obtained. She gave me the highlights. I warmed up the radios, collected the AWOS automated weather for the field, and tuned the field's Unicom frequency. I clicked the mic five times and brought up the taxiway and runway lights. Pidge fiddled with the cockpit lights, dialing things down to a level that gave us the best night vision. We lit the navigation lights, red on the left, green on the right, white on the tail, but left the taxi and landing lights off. With the snow still flying, it was easier to see without them. The wind favored a departure on Runway 13, so it was a brief roll across the ramp to the taxiway and the runway hold-short line. Our world consisted of a cockpit lit in night-vision-protecting red light. Beyond the Plexiglas windows we had a confusing mix of runway lights, flying snow, and the flash of the aircraft beacon, all of which required careful interpretation to form a positional reality.

I spoke to Pidge through the headset intercom.

"We're just going to slide all over hell if we try to run 'em up here," I said. "You take the throttles and the rudder on takeoff. Anything looks wrong to you, pull 'em."

"Roger that."

"Call out all the speeds, too. I haven't read the manual." I assumed she had.

"Roger."

"Pre-takeoff checklist."

Pidge read it off to me. I checked each item. The routine felt comfortable. I flexed my fingers and felt a familiar electric charge at the back of my neck, then down through my arms. A tension that confirmed I was all in with what I was doing.

We completed the checklist. I released the brakes.

"Essex County traffic, Mojave One One Kilo, back-taxiing for takeoff Runway 13, Essex County," I radioed to warn anyone stupid enough to be out flying tonight.

We rolled onto the runway. I back taxied to where a set of runway end identifier lights marked the very edge of the asphalt. Trying to stay off the brakes, I used one engine to turn the big airplane around. I aimed it down the center of two lines defined by white runway lights. Except for the lights, the white, snow-covered surface of the runway had no defining edge. Snow and darkness obscured the horizon.

Pidge knew the drill. She held her gaze on the windshield and the cues offered to us by the runway lights. Her job was to bring the power up on the twin turbocharged Lycoming engines, and to work the rudder pedals, which controlled the nosewheel steering. With slippery runway conditions, it was vital that she bring the engines up evenly, avoiding asymmetrical power, and the possibility that it could pull us to one side or the other.

I locked my eyes on the instrument panel.

"Power," I said to Pidge.

She pushed the throttles forward, slowly, working them, keeping an eye on the power gauges, and an ear on the harmonic hum of the two engines. We surged forward.

I watched the directional gyro, set to our magnetic heading. It wiggled but held steady on 130 degrees. Pidge worked the rudder pedals. I checked airspeed, power, and the engine gauges. With a flick of the eyes, I assured myself that the oil pressure and oil temperature gauges read properly. I listened for any hint that the engines weren't performing perfectly. They sang.

The airspeed needle came alive. I checked the vacuum gauge. Peripheral vision gave me a sense of building speed as snowflakes etched horizontal lines past my window.

"Rotate," she commanded. I eased back pressure onto the yoke and saw the nose rise on the artificial horizon instrument. I felt the nose free itself from the runway. The mains followed.

Flight.

Pidge issued crisp commands.

"Hold her."

"Gimme five degrees up."

"Blue line." She called out minimum controllable airspeed, the speed below which we would lose directional control if one engine failed and the other continued to run. If that happened, her job was to kill the good engine.

"Gimme ten degrees up."

"Positive rate."

"Gear up," I ordered. She pulled the handle. I felt the aircraft shrug off the aerodynamic awkwardness of extended landing gear. The Mojave tucked her wheels in and shot forward, clean, and free to fly.

"Cruise climb, one-thirty," Pidge advised me. "Props at twenty-five. Power is yours. Runway heading. You're up on Center."

I settled in to hold the speed and heading. Pidge had already copied our clearance into controlled airspace via her cell phone. I now made the connection through the aircraft radios.

"Good evening, Chicago Center." I gave them our full call sign. "Climbing to three thousand." We were damn near there. This bird could fly.

"Mojave One One Kilo, Chicago Center, radar contact, turn right one seven zero, climb and maintain one nine thousand."

I repeated the instruction and eased the airplane into a shallow turn. Pidge fiddled with the power settings to maintain climb power. I glanced at the vertical speed indicator. Close to two thousand feet per minute. Nice.

The windows offered nothing but black. Snow flew past the colored wingtip navigation lights at more than one hundred and thirty knots. Flying on instruments, we climbed away from Essex County Airport.

Pidge managed the Garmin navigation system. She had already programmed our flight plan. The vector given us by Chicago center showed us tracking to the left of our intended course, on a line that would eventually intercept the magenta course line on the moving map screen.

I scanned the panel. Attitude. Power. Engines. All good.

Navigation. Good.

"Mojave One One Kilo, cleared direct West Bend, proceed on course."

Communication. Good.

Flying.

In this bubble of technology, sound, and speed, I felt at home again. The engines hummed and massaged my soul. At a little more than twelve thousand feet we broke into a star-filled sky above a layer of moonlit vapor. A world of white cloud tops sprawled away in all directions. The Piper Mojave, solid and strong, pulled us higher, granting us a breathtaking view made more magical because it belonged exclusively to Pidge and me. I marveled that millions of people below us slept, oblivious to the magnificent skyscape over their heads.

I thought about the appointment on Tuesday with Stephenson, and Earl's insistence that I pilot the plane to Madison. Earl's no dummy.

He knew I missed this.

13

"**I**s that him?" Pidge pointed at a figure standing alone, framed in the glass doorway of Signature Aviation. I taxied toward the building. Thanks to a giant-sized snow removal budget and dozens of pieces of equipment conducting an attack on nature beneath flashing amber lights, the taxiways and ramps at General Mitchell International Airport were clear. The same light dusting I noticed on entering the hangar at Essex County continued to fall through my taxi lights, but there would be no further accumulation. The storm system had moved on. By the time the airlines began their morning rush hour, this airport would operate as if nothing had happened.

"That's him," I confirmed. I recognized Detective LeMore's wiry, five-five frame. Bundled in a heavy down coat and knit cap, he waited beside two hard-shell roller bags. "I'll shut down the left side. You load him up. Put him on the intercom."

Pidge unhooked her seat belt and doffed her headset. She maneuvered her small body out of the copilot's seat. I rolled the Mojave to a stop near the general aviation terminal. A ramp rat with lighted wands had been signaling me toward tie-down parking, but I flashed my landing light at him to indicate I wasn't interested. This would be a quick turnaround.

Winter reached through the cabin and touched the back of my neck when Pidge opened the cabin door. Even with the left engine shut down, the slipstream and noise from the running right engine swirled around us. I felt the airframe bob lightly as Pidge climbed out, then again when she loaded LeMore and secured his bags. She put him in a forward-facing club seat on the right side of the plane and secured the door. By the time she slipped back into the co-pilot's seat, I had copied our clearance back to Essex County.

"Hello, Greg," I turned in my seat and extended my right hand. He reached up and shook it. He spoke, but it failed to transmit through the intercom. "Move the mic close to your lips. Almost touching," I told him.

"Better?"

"Yup."

"Good to see you again, Will. How's the hip?"

"I know when the weather will change," I said, not bothering to correct him. Last time I'd seen Detective LeMore, I had been on crutches, nursing my healing pelvic bones. "Let me get this show on the road, and then we'll chat once we're in the air."

"Sounds good," he said. He settled back to watch out the window.

Pidge fired up the left engine. I told Ground Control we were ready to roll.

LEVEL AT FOURTEEN THOUSAND. Cruising at two hundred fifty miles per hour. The autopilot held us on course for home.

LeMore had slipped off his headset. I turned around and gestured for him to put it on again.

"How did you find the camera?" he asked.

"Remember Lane?"

He did. I explained Sarah, and Lane's involvement, and from that, Lane's analysis of the image.

"Clever girl," he said.

"Is she right about the way the images are transmitted?"

"It's the way I would do it."

"Then, does that mean we can follow the trail to the perv's computer?"

"Maybe. Depends on what we're dealing with here. Is this some garden-variety pervert who has graduated from putting mirrors on his shoes to look up girls' skirts? Or are we dealing with something more sophisticated?"

"How 'more sophisticated' do you mean?"

"Organized."

"As in organized crime?"

"Maybe." I'd only known LeMore for a few minutes during the search for Lane, but his caution remained consistent with my initial impression. "If the guy is using a photo for internet extortion, and his goal is physical contact, rape—as bad as that sounds, it might be the good news."

"With organized crime being the bad news? I don't get it. What interest would organized crime have in shooting pervert photos in a girl's locker room. Hasn't the porn industry got everything covered—and I mean *everything*? What's a few non-erotic photos in a locker room to all that?"

"If it's just photos, you're right."

"What else could it be?"

"Streaming video. Ever watch action movies?"

"I do."

"Some guy gets his leg ripped off. Some other guy gets cut in half. Shit like that. My wife won't watch it, but I can eat popcorn and drink beer while it's happening. I love action movies, as long as they're not cop movies."

"Uh-huh."

"Okay. Did you ever see the NFL footage of Joe Theismann getting his leg broken?"

I knew the clip. Lawrence Taylor of the New York Giants snaps the Washington Redskins' quarterback's leg during a sack.

"I can't watch it," I said.

"Neither can I. Because it's real. I can watch that movie shit until my wife tells me to go to bed, but I can NOT look at that clip. Or any other video of some guy on a football field getting his knee bent, or his ankle turned around. Can't do it."

"Because it's real."

"Right."

"And innocent, unsuspecting girls taking a shower is real."

"Yup. I need to find out if this camera is streaming video. If it is, then this situation might be something...more elaborate."

"Like what?"

"Like being sold as an event."

"A what?"

"Look, you can download porn all you want, any variety you want, and watch any combination of men and women you want. But it's all staged. Actors and actresses having phony orgasms, 'scuse my language, miss," he said, considering Pidge.

"Fucking phony fucking," she said.

"Uh, okay. Anyway, there's a culture of sick puppies that will pay to see something real. Live. Like Pay Per View. Some versions of it are scheduled, set up, promoted. Sold in advance and then broadcast to subscribers."

The uneasy sensation I felt when I first considered the camera location returned.

"Don't get me wrong. This could just be a one-off, mirrors-on-the-shoes kind of pervert, and let's hope it is. But it's a public facility, an institutional pool, with scheduled events involving underage girls. Maybe a lot of them. And it's real. I need to see what we're dealing with. How many cameras in the locker room?"

"Who knows." *Shit.* "Can you find them? Scan for them or whatever?"

"Maybe."

THE COLD FRONT pushing snow through Essex County brought with it a shift in winds. By the time we landed, gusts blew out of the northwest, dictating a landing on Runway 31, in the direction opposite our takeoff on Runway 13. Instead of falling snow to obscure our vision, we had blowing snow on a runway that had not yet been cleared, and with the blowing snow came challenging crosswinds. On top of that, I'd never landed a Mojave. And while the airplane is kin to the Navajos in which I'd accumulated hundreds of hours, it's not the same. Add to that the critical appraisal of my former student and co-pilot, Pidge, and several months of not flying, and I'll admit my pucker factor elevated slightly.

I nailed it. And if asked again, I'll happily repeat that I nailed it.

After rolling out the landing and shutting down in front of the hangar, I checked my phone for messages and the time. Four-forty-seven.

"Andy says to meet at the station," I told LeMore after reading a text from my wife.

"Go," Pidge said, waving me off. "I got this. I'll put it back and Earl will never know we touched it."

"Good plan," I said, pointing at the hangar door, which now rose slowly. As it exposed the lighted interior of the hangar, it did a slow reveal of Earl Jackson's fireplug form, standing like a conqueror's statue on the empty concrete. "Better yet. You can tell him yourself."

"DID you break my goddamned new airplane?" Earl demanded as we disembarked. To anyone who doesn't know Earl, the encounter might have been terrifying.

"She's a beauty," I said, answering the true question he asked. A fissure in his permanent scowl told me I hit the right note.

"So's the King Air," he stuck it in and twisted. "Andy get you squared away about Tuesday?"

I didn't want to discuss the subject with Earl, so I gave him a hasty Yes and turned to LeMore.

"Detective Greg LeMore of the Milwaukee Police Department, this is Earl Jackson, our benefactor for the rapid transit tonight. Owner of Essex County Air Services," I said.

"Marine?" Earl asked. I have no idea how he knew.

"Semper fi," LeMore shook hands with Earl.

"We don't suffer from insanity, we enjoy every minute of it," Earl said.

"Well then, we'd best get moving," I said. I was anxious to get clear of Earl. Pidge took the same tack. I heard her start the tug and throttle it up, scooting out of the hangar onto the ramp.

"Tuesday, buddy," Earl clamped one of his calloused claws on my shoulder. "Wheels up at six a.m."

"If I'm not here, start without me."

"Don't make me call your wife."

As if he hadn't already.

I ushered LeMore to my snow-covered car, leaving Pidge to her fate.

14

"We have a variety of scenarios."

LeMore stood at the whiteboard in the Essex PD conference room. The scene reminded me of the war counsel at the Milwaukee Police Department headquarters when Lane had been abducted. This time I had a seat at the table instead of spying on my wife from a vantage point near the ceiling.

Andy sat beside me. Across from us, Tom Ceeves sat next to Al Glower, the school superintendent. To Glower's left, Chet Allison. I warmed my hands around a mug of fresh coffee. Someone seemed bent on meeting the city's budget by eliminating heat from the police department.

Between Chet Allison's house and the station, Andy had insisted on a stop at home. Her blue velvet dress had been replaced with blue jeans, a white sweater, and a dark blue blazer. Her new Detective shield hung from her belt, along with her service weapon. The elegant date night hairdo had been converted into a conservative police ponytail. I felt out of place beside her in my date night black suit, black shirt, and a red tie I dug up in honor of the coming holidays.

The coffee was okay. It wasn't LeMore's. The detective might look like he just came from two years of undercover work with a drug cartel, but he has an angel's touch with a brew. I also could have done with some breakfast, considering our dinner last night had been gifted to Robert and Donna Lewis. My stomach made rude comments.

"From what Detective Stewart—"

"Andrea, please."

"From what Andrea said, the image matches up to the location in the women's locker room. The nozzle that isn't working aligns perfectly with the photo. Your young friend Lane got a match to the background using the Gausian Blur effect in Photoshop. So, we know our perp used the effect on Sarah's image. That means he probably has a Mac or PC with Photoshop." LeMore made a note on the whiteboard.

"Like most of the population," Glower muttered. I didn't like the man. More politician than educator, I disliked his glad-handing style. I expected his contribution to the proceedings to prioritize covering his ass first, the district's ass second, and Sarah's interests a distant third.

"Scenario One," LeMore ignored Glower. "Our perp is a lone wolf, has some tech skills, and was able to gain access to the facility or possibly has regular access to the facility. The camera takes and stores images. He retrieves the images and cherry-picks photos." LeMore blushed suddenly and glanced at Andy. "Sorry."

"But he's not a simple peeping Tom," Andy said quickly, brushing off the word slip. "Or he never would have reached out to Sarah. He's a potential or perhaps already-registered sex offender. I asked Mike to run the statewide database, then organize them by distance to Essex."

Tom Ceeves nodded.

"No, he's not passive. His texts to Sarah are aggressive," LeMore wrote the word *Aggressive* on the board under Scenario One. "So, within this framework, let's look at possible transmission methods. First possible scenario, he has a fixed unit that shoots and stores the images. He has access to the facility on some regular basis and retrieves the images manually, plus ensures that the unit has power—probably battery. If the camera is self-contained in the nozzle, he might have a twin—a pair of camera-nozzle units—and he swaps them out. Quick and easy."

"If he's male, which is an assumption," Andy said, "then he has to be someone with approved access to the women's locker room. Which also means limited access. Someone coming and going when the locker room isn't in use. That narrows it down. Coaches. Maintenance. Faculty."

"Assuming," Tom Ceeves interjected, "he's accessing during acceptable hours. Hours when his coming and going might be seen by others. He could be an outlier, slipping in and out without authority."

"The school is secure," Glower declared.

"Reasonably secure," Allison said, drawing a disapproving glance from his boss, but scoring points with everyone else for his truthfulness. "We know it's not perfect. He may have a key. Or coded access. We're not the E ring of The Pentagon, for God's sake."

"All of which is relevant if the photos must be retrieved manually," LeMore said. "However, I rank Scenario One a long shot. Which brings us to the more-likely Scenario Two. The camera is transmitting. The device is motion-sensitive and shoots when a subject enters the frame. Or worse, may be remotely controlled—but that's complicated, and I'd rather sideline that thought until I can examine the hardware. If the images are transmitted, it requires no physical retrieval. Which then removes our perp from the narrow confines of people who have access."

"But he had to get the camera in there in the first place," I said.

"True," Allison conceded. "But that could be anyone. A contractor. A maintenance worker. A citizen attending the winter orchestra concert who wandered down the north corridor into the pool lobby on a night when everything is closed and empty. The locker rooms are not locked."

"Something we need to review," Glower said.

"And if the camera is a self-contained module in a shower nozzle, it's a simple matter of unscrewing the original and screwing in the camera," LeMore added. "No technical expertise required."

"Is it possible, then," Andy asked, "that the installer and the owner are two different people?"

"Certainly." LeMore agreed.

"A drone. Someone completely disconnected from what's going on," Andy thought out loud. "Which could make all of this—" she gestured at sheets of paper laying on the table; the pages bore lists of names "— largely irrelevant. The person installing the camera might have no idea it was a camera."

LeMore squinted an expression of equivocation. "I dunno. First off, the dynamics of a second party doing that for our perp get complicated. Second, I made it sound simple, but the camera needs to be aimed properly. Maybe tested. I wouldn't throw all that out yet."

Tom Ceeves spoke up. "What about this perp becoming aggressive?"

Six-foot-six and upwards of two hundred eighty pounds, Tom is an imposing figure in any setting. Seated at the conference table, he looked like an adult visiting an elementary school classroom. He wore a gray hoodie over dark gray work pants, and no sign of a badge or gun. No one would ever mistake him for the chief of police.

We all looked at him.

"He made contact. He's pushing to have sex with an underaged girl. He's not just some voyeur jerking off in front of his computer. Or if he was, he's graduated to the next level. He's either already a violent offender, or about to become one. What I want to know is how does that fit with someone sophisticated enough to build and install this device? My gut tells me that's not the same personality profile." Tom looked at LeMore and challenged him to answer.

"I agree with that assessment. The two don't fit. The discovery of this camera...it was highly unlikely. This camera could have gone unnoticed for a long, long time, giving a voyeur a steady stream of self-gratification material. He took a risk contacting Sarah."

I raised my hand.

"You don't need to raise your hand," Andy said.

"How?"

I got blank looks.

"How did he contact Sarah? How did he get her number, her cell phone number?"

"Good question." LeMore nodded.

"It is a good question," my wife agreed. "Simply obtaining a photo of a girl in a shower room isn't enough. He had to bridge the gap between a photo of a naked girl—and in that context, a girl with no identifying clothing—and someone whose phone number he was able to text. This could be significant. He may know her."

"Maybe," LeMore balked at the flow. "If you're in a locker room, where is your cell phone?"

"Locked in a locker," Andy replied.

"So, under what circumstances could it be accessed?" LeMore prompted us.

"Probably a variety of circumstances," I said. "But now you're talking about someone of the same sex, especially if the locker room was busy at the time. And someone who can get into a locker. Don't they use personal padlocks?"

"They do," Allison confirmed. "But maybe Sarah left her phone lying out? Or lost it. Kids mishandle those things all the time."

"So, this could all be some kid with a crush on the girl," Glower interjected eagerly. "Misguided high school hijinks."

"Jesus, Al," Tom shook his head. "Nobody says 'hijinks' anymore."

"Sexting, yes," Andy said. "Sending lewd photos, yes. But I get the sense that this camera is at a higher level of sophistication. The two don't mesh. High-level technology and some kid hitting puberty too hard?"

We all took a moment. The permutations were growing fast.

"I want to go back to the retrieval system," Tom said. "Detective, you're more familiar with the tech. Walk me through that."

LeMore tapped his board.

"Two options. Bluetooth or Wi-Fi. The school has a public access Wi-Fi system. If I were setting up a camera like this, it would have motion detection, video and still image capability, and would transmit encoded bursts via the Wi-Fi system. Or—long shot—maybe streaming video."

I caught a quick glance from LeMore. On the way to the station from the airport, he asked me not to bring up our conversation about organized crime and streaming. He suggested it was a big reach, and that it might misdirect everyone with a distracting theory. I said nothing.

"You would have to know the Wi-Fi password," Glower said defensively.

"Essex2018," LeMore said. "I had it before I left Milwaukee last night. Not that hard."

Glower made a sour face.

"Of course it's available," Allison said. "That's the whole point."

"So, which is it? Bluetooth or Wi-Fi?" Tom Ceeves wanted to know. LeMore smiled.

"Big difference," he said. "Bluetooth is designed for device-to-device communication. There are three different levels, but they're all short range and low power. That's how you can use Bluetooth with your phone and not blow the battery. I doubt this is a Bluetooth connection, because that just gets the camera to deliver the photos to another device."

"Like a cell phone?" Andy asked.

"Or laptop. Or just about anything," LeMore said.

"The images are being transmitted only when the other device is in range?"

"If it's Bluetooth."

"That means the perp could be visiting the locker room regularly, carrying a cell phone that wakes up the connection to the camera, and downloading the stored images," Andy said.

"Right," LeMore repeated, "but we don't know the photo resolution. We could be talking about a lot of data. I mean *a lot* of data."

"But if he's doing it the way Andrea suggested, does that mean he's *not* using the school Wi-Fi?" Chet Allison asked.

"Possible," LeMore answered. "But if I were to guess, between the two, I'd say it's the Wi-Fi. More powerful. Much more data capacity. Public. Encrypted. Unnoticed."

"But we can turn it off, can't we?" Glower asked Allison. "Throw a net over it?"

Allison nodded. "We have the capability. It's available for emergency situations when we don't want every kid in the school broadcasting."

LeMore looked for Andy to field this one.

"We don't want to do that. Not yet, if we can avoid it. Shutting the system down may tip off the perpetrator."

"Well, we can't just leave things the way they are, Detective Stewart!" Glower protested. "In less than twenty-four hours we have young women using that facility. If it gets out that we allowed them to step in front of a camera in that shower room, knowing they were being photographed—!"

"Al," Tom Ceeves put a huge hand on Glower's forearm. "Don't have a cow here. Nobody's going to let anyone get in front of that camera. But Andrea is right. We have a shot at finding this pervert perp. We're not going to blow it by sending him a message that we found his camera."

LeMore minced his feet. "Just the same, I really, really need a look at the hardware," he said, steering us back to the whole reason he had come this far. "If I can see what components he used, what power supply it's using—it will tell us a lot."

Tom waved his worries aside with the same big hand he used to settle Glower. "Andrea's got a plan for that." He nodded at my wife.

"Actually," she poked a thumb in my direction, "it was his idea."

All eyes settled on me.

"Target fixation," I said.

15

Chet Allison drove to the high school alone. He parked in his reserved spot, entered through the district office door, and went to his office, just like any other Sunday when he put in a few hours unnoticed by the taxpayers.

Andy persuaded Al Glower to go home. She told him we couldn't be sure the perpetrator wasn't watching the high school, and a caravan of officials could tip him off. The rest of us recognized Andy's ploy to get him out of our hair.

Tom Ceeves announced his intentions to monitor the situation from Sully's Pub, where he also planned to watch the Packer game. He trusted his newest detective to execute the plan and told Andy to keep him informed.

Andy drove Greg LeMore and me to the high school, where we entered at the far end of the parking lot, drove around the back of the building past the football field, and parked in a slot near a door accessing the science wing. We waited in the car until Chet Allison opened the door and let us into the building.

"It's not really target fixation," I explained as we hiked the empty hallway through the building. "That's the phenomenon of a vehicle operator, usually at high speed, becoming fixated on an object, thereby increasing the chances of hitting the object. The name comes from training fighter pilots not to lock themselves onto the target to the point of flying right into it."

We turned and started down another long hallway.

"It's more accurately called Fixation Error. The most famous case of that was probably Eastern Airlines flight 401. They had a landing gear light malfunction, and ended up descending into the Everglades after becoming so fixated on the problem they failed to see—"

Andy touched my arm. "No one cares, dear."

LeMore smirked. "It's a good plan, Will. If it gets me the hardware without tipping them off."

Damn right it was a good plan.

WE MUSTERED IN THE LOBBY. Allison unlocked a maintenance closet and produced a mop, bucket, tray full of cleansers, and a set of coveralls.

"Hope they're your size," he handed them to LeMore. "If not, I can find another set."

The coveralls hung loose but worked once LeMore rolled the pants cuffs up. Sporting a heavy beard shadow and unruly black hair crushed in a wild array of directions by his knit cap, LeMore pulled off the weekend janitor look well.

Andy produced her police notebook and a pen. She handed both to me, and we huddled.

"Here's the shower room," I drew a rectangle. "This is the end that opens to the locker room. These—" I drew twelve circles "—are the pillars, or whatever they're called. There are four nozzles on each. Here. Here. Here. And here. We think this is the one—first pillar, second row."

"Wait," Allison stopped me. "You were the one that found it?"

"No, she did," I lied and pointed at Andy. "But she can't draw worth a darn. Never team up with her in Pictionary."

LeMore's cast me a skeptical expression. "Then they saw you. If you were in there, they saw you searching for the camera."

"Searching for this," Andy said quickly, touching the tiny stud earing on one lobe. "I went in searching soap dishes for a lost earring. I made a big deal of finding it after I spotted the lens." LeMore absorbed the lie with a solemn nod. Andy pointed at the sketch. "Based on the photo, and

Lane's analysis, we think this is where Sarah was standing when the photo was taken."

"That's your target," I pointed at the sketch.

LeMore studied it. "Okay. I'll work my way around to it. If they're live, and watching, or if I set off any motion detection, all they'll see is the image of a janitor. It's going to take me a while, because I want to show them that I'm really scrubbing these things down. That should give me a chance to examine each one. If there's a lens, I should be able to see it. When I get to the camera, I'll rub some soap into the nozzle, like I'm cleaning it. Shake it around a little if I can. Try to obscure the lens. When you hear me whistle, kill the Wi-Fi. If this works, they'll think it was me."

"I have to do it from the office."

"You and I will keep an open line," Andy pointed at Allison and held up her phone. "I'll relay the signal to you. You kill the Wi-Fi. When it's done, confirm that it's offline. When you do, tell me."

"Oh! Hey!" I held up a hand. "Hang on a second!"

I turned and ran across the lobby.

"What?" Andy called after me.

I ducked into the men's locker room. A few minutes later, I jogged back out again and rejoined the huddle.

"Here," I handed LeMore a shower nozzle. "Replace the camera with this. In case we decide to wake up the Wi-Fi and they have other cameras watching."

I got an appreciative nod from LeMore. "You must be good at planning surprise parties."

"He's the worst," Andy dismissed the notion quickly. I couldn't argue.

"Are we all set?" Allison asked.

"What's your number?" Andy held up her phone. Allison gave it and she dialed. His phone rang. He poked his screen to open the line.

"All set. You're on!" She pointed at LeMore.

Adopting a bit of an I-don't-give-a-shit slouch, LeMore picked up the tray of cleansers and pushed the rolling mop bucket into the women's locker room. Allison headed in the opposite direction toward the principal's office.

Andy and I positioned ourselves in the doorway to the women's locker room. We heard LeMore guide mop bucket across the tile floor. The sound changed when the hard-plastic wheels hit the smaller tiles in the shower room. Faintly, we could hear him squeezing the spray bottle of cleanser and brushing the stainless-steel pillars.

Andy stood with her phone to her ear.

"Stand by."

"I'm here," Chet Allison said. "Ready."

LeMore acted out his role. We heard the tray of cleanser being nudged across the tile floor. We heard the spray bottle squeak.

A light whistle, enhanced by the acoustics of the locker room, sang out. Something classical. I couldn't place it.

"Now." Andy spoke into the phone urgently.

"System off," Allison said. "Stand by ..."

We waited. LeMore continued whistling, scrubbing and spritzing.

"Confirmed," Allison said. "The Wi-Fi net is down."

"We're offline, Greg!" Andy called out to LeMore.

The whistling stopped. We heard nothing for a few moments, then the sound of the mop bucket rolling toward us.

LeMore appeared seconds later. In his hand he held the shower nozzle.

"Gotcha!" he said proudly. He unzipped the coveralls and reached into one of his own pockets. He pulled out a silver, Mylar-like sack, and dropped the nozzle into it. "This will shield any transmissions."

Allison trotted into the pool lobby.

"Now what?" he asked.

"I don't suppose you have a Faraday cage lying around," LeMore asked.

Allison grinned.

"Who doesn't? Follow me!"

LeMore wore an expression of unvarnished wonder.

"Your kids built this?" he walked around the cage. Roughly the size of an upright commercial freezer, the wire construct sat in a crowded storage room in the science wing.

"Not just this, they built a whole lightning show. You should have seen it!" Allison said proudly. "Part of something we call Project Pursuit. Amazing program for our Gifted and Talented kids."

"Incredible," LeMore said. "If we can get some light and a table set up in there, I can get to work."

"Do I dare ask?" Andy ventured.

"If I can block the electromagnetic fields, and isolate the device, I might be able to create a counterfeit network for the camera to talk to. Make it think it's phoning home when it's really talking to a device I control. It's a big maybe. I have to test this cage. This one is wire mesh. Solid metal would be better, but we'll see." LeMore spoke with the excitement of a kid unleashing a new toy.

"I don't mean to slow things down," I said, "but am I the only one starving here? It's been a long night and we have another long night ahead if the pervert really does set up a date with Sarah at midnight. Anybody else want to get some breakfast?" I looked at my watch "Or brunch?"

LeMore shook his head. "I'm fine. I really want to dive into this."

"Tell you what," Allison offered LeMore, "I'll have my wife bring something for us. You can get straight to work."

"You two don't need to hang around here for this. It's going to take a while," LeMore gestured at his hard-shell cases. "I have all my tools. I'll call you when I know something."

I didn't need to hear any more, but Andy went through a round of "Are you sures?" before I pulled her away.

As we were leaving, LeMore called after Andy.

"Detective, as long as the network is down, you should have someone go through both locker rooms and test every shower nozzle. We might not have the only one."

Allison offered to call in the maintenance staff, but Andy declined. She wanted it done by the police, to keep word of the investigation confined to a tight circle. She told LeMore she would return with a team.

IN THE CAR, Andy derailed my expectations for a trip to the Silver Spoon Diner and a nice meal together.

"I'm dropping you at home," she announced.

"What? No!"

"You can join up with us later. I know what you're going to say, and before you launch your argument—*I agree with you.* I want you there tonight. Ready to do your thing."

That raised my eyebrows. "Really?"

"We'll try to put together a surveillance plan, but frankly we're not set up for it. And if it means having Sarah on the move, it will be blatantly obvious if some minivan or unmarked car is following her. I may need something subtle. Aerial surveillance."

"Yes!" I pumped a fist. She gave me a tolerant smile.

"But first, go home, eat. I'll get something on the way back to the station. I need to get things moving. LeMore is right about searching the facility. We don't have much time. I need to get Sarah out of the house and Pidge in position."

I got it. Pidge. The same size as Sarah. Blonde. Petite. A coiled cobra.

"Does Pidge know the plan?"

"I talked with her after you landed. That girl is going to burst, she's so excited. But I need to get this in motion. It's possible our pervert is watching. I'll have Sarah's mom take her out of the house—grocery shopping or something. She'll drop Sarah at the station, exchange her for Pidge. They can trade clothes. Pidge goes home with mom. Then mom and dad make a show of leaving. Pidge—Sarah—is home alone. *Et voila!*"

I love a good plan. Knowing Andy, she had pieces in place I couldn't begin to consider.

"Hey, what's 'The Candy Store'?"

"Oh," Andy said. "Lane filled me in. Some phone app. Something the kids use to flash mob themselves, I guess. A combination of geo-locating and social broadcasting, like Instagram, where kids log in or tune in to find out what's happening and when and where. You can create exclusive groups, cells. Only those included can log in. The digital age version of 'the in crowd,' I guess."

"One more way to exclude people." I'm not a fan of social media.

"Probably."

"At midnight Sarah is supposed to check in with The Candy Store and find out where she's supposed to go?"

"That's what it looks like."

"Great plan. Except the girl is fourteen. She doesn't have a car or a driver's license. Is she supposed to use a designated driver to get to the pervert's basement lair?"

Andy shrugged. "Lane rode her bike all the way out to Sarah's house."

"Christ, I hope that's not what this asshole has in mind."

"Now you see my problem with surveillance."

I did.

16

Andy dropped me off at the farmhouse. She pulled away without me. The house looked picturesque in a newly snow-covered yard. Entering alone reminded me that our date night evaporated when Lane texted her SOS.

Getting intimate with my wife wasn't the only thing on my mind last night. I had planned something for Andy besides bedding her.

I had two pairs of ski goggles stashed in a kitchen cabinet. Not exactly the sort of accent you expect to find on a romantic dinner date, but my experimentation with *the other thing* had given me an idea—and the first fresh snowfall offered the perfect opportunity.

I slipped my overcoat off and took out one pair of goggles. From another shelf in the same kitchen cabinet, I pulled down a trio of small, custom-built propulsion units. The body of the device resembled an ordinary flashlight, containing C-cell batteries. On the side of the cylinder, where a thumb would rest, I had attached a slide control. Instead of a light, the end of the unit sported a small electric motor and a hobby-airplane propeller.

I tested each unit. Pushing the slide control forward, the propeller began to turn, slowly, clockwise. Pulling it back to neutral, it stopped. Pulling farther, it reversed. Perfect.

"Ladies and gentlemen, I give you the FLUB," I said aloud. "Flight

Launching Unit B-Model." I couldn't wait to tell Andy the new name.

I dropped two units into the pocket of my suit jacket and stepped out the back door of the house. I slipped the ski goggles over my head and pulled them over my eyes. The tinted plastic warmed the snowy world with hues of amber, accented by the low angle of the December sun.

It was damned cold outside. During the night, dense, high-pressure air from Canada dropped in a vast heap onto the upper Midwest. The bitter air brought clear skies, temperatures in the low twenties, and hustling winds out of the northwest.

My suit offered almost no protection from the cold. The pants and jacket were distressingly light. Perfect for my experiment.

I grabbed the doorknob with my left hand and pushed the hand holding the third FLUB unit into my jacket.

Fwooomp! The familiar sound I heard in my head told me what I saw for myself. I vanished. I felt a momentary disorientation as gravity abandoned its governance of my body.

In the early stages of discovering *the other thing*, I harbored a deep fear of entering this state in an open space. I worried that I might float free of any tether or grip, be unable to stop, and might rise to a height from which I could not safely fall. Because falling is the only option. When I reappear, gravity takes over. Too high, and the result would be serious injury, or worse.

Now, with the FLUB for propulsion, the open yard, and in fact the whole sky, became my playground.

I noted the cool sensation on my skin, on my body. It made me smile.

When I slip into the vanished state, *the other thing* coats my body with a cool sensation. Not cold. Not uncomfortable. The equivalent of easing into a farm pond on a summer afternoon. Of feeling a sweet evening breeze on a veranda.

I laughed. Not for the first time when alone, I laughed out loud at the effect I felt on my skin. Despite the icy Canadian winds clawing into my thin suit, I felt perfectly comfortable.

"Son of a bitch! It's like long underwear!"

I had gained an inkling of this over the last few weeks as the temperature changed. But our first real blast of winter had been slow in coming. A few days ago, I did a test flight in the early morning, with the temperature hovering in the low forties. The test confirmed what I suspected.

Wrapped in *the other thing*, coated by the cool sensation, my body did not feel the chilling wind.

This is what I had hoped to show Andy last night. I had hoped to take her in my arms and make us both disappear, and then take her out into the snowy night for a flight across the wintry fields. The ultimate sleighride. A pair of human snowflakes, gliding across the newborn landscape.

I am the god of romance.

Some god. Here I was in stark morning light, flying solo.

I pushed off. Almost immediately, the steady breeze took me, pressing me back toward the side of the house. I aimed the propulsion unit toward the open yard and eased my thumb forward on the slide. Unseen, the propeller spun, blowing a light breeze back over my hand.

I slid the power control forward and picked up speed. With a gentle adjustment, I tipped the axis of the power line upward and began to climb. I crossed the backyard, cleared the garage roof, and accelerated out over corn stubble that stretched for half a mile in three directions.

Faster. I felt the wind generated by my speed. It tugged at my clothing. But what should have been a killing wind chill failed to touch my skin. I felt the temperature of the air as I breathed it into my lungs (note to self: wear a scarf or a mask of some kind) but my skin remained cool and comfortable.

"This is freaking great!"

Flight.

Climbing slightly, accelerating over an open field, feeling the thrill welling up inside, I suddenly felt ashamed of my self-pity. The whole business of moping around, feeling lost without my pilot's license seemed trivial. I owned the air, the sky, in a way anyone who isn't a bird could only dream of.

I eased my wrist left, then right, then left. The movement redirected me in a series of slalom-like curves. Except for the wind, the only sound in this winter landscape came from the FLUB unit and my own laughter.

I shot across the cornfield, picking up speed. A thickly wooded area approached. By the time I reached it, I had accelerated to at least thirty knots. The last time I tried speed like this, the wind watered my eyes and made it hard to see. The ski goggles eliminated the problem. I found it interesting that although the amber goggles had vanished along with me, they still colored my vision, turning the landscape to gold.

I sailed over the trees, struggling not to hoot and holler and laugh like a maniac. I thought of how Andy would have marveled at this, and how beautiful this would have been in the night, sweeping through the sky amid the falling snowflakes.

I skimmed the treetops. I followed an icy creek and chased across the fluffed-out tips of cattails. I zoomed low above a railroad track as if perched on the front of a locomotive. I dipped my toes to brush the tops of tree branches and shook loose crystals of snow that glittered in the sunlight. The freshly powdered landscape flowed beneath me as if I stood still and the world had become a fluid white river. When the first FLUB began to lose power, I shut it down and let myself glide on the northwest wind, reveling in the silence and the sweep of the land passing beneath me. After a while, I pulled a second unit from my pocket. I fired up the fresh FLUB, made a wide turn back toward the farm and set sail for home.

I made a kamikaze run toward the barn, then swerved around it at the last second, skimming past the single standing silo, around the red-painted side of the barn and into the yard, thinking I would do a quick power reversal, and bring myself to a perfect hover at the back door of the house.

The woman stepping out of a silver Mercedes blew my approach plan straight to hell.

I killed the power. The FLUB works well, but it is anything but silent. At full power it sounds like an angry wasp. Momentum carried me on a line straight for the gravel driveway behind the house. I faced a choice. Fire up the FLUB and risk being heard, or splat in a heap on the snowy driveway.

The woman walked carefully across the slippery snow, following our unshoveled walk toward the back door—the very spot where I had planned to reappear. In a moment she would be standing on the back steps, about to witness a grand and unexplainable entrance.

Having no real choice, I aimed the FLUB skyward and shoved the power to full. My course altered immediately, but the sound carried. The woman turned her head toward it. I shot upward on a new vector over her upturned face.

That's when I experienced the otherworldly sensation of seeing Andy dressed in clothing I'd never seen, stepping from a car we could never afford.

About six months pregnant.

17

I shot over the roof, curling my legs to avoid hitting the snow-dusted shingles. My course resembled a shuttle launch. The roof fell away below me.

A pang of worry stabbed me, dead center, as it always seems to when I make a sharp climb. If the FLUB failed now and the spare didn't work, I wouldn't stop. Period. Given my assumptions about *the other thing*, unless I reappeared and dropped to my death, I figured I would be dead of asphyxia before I got high enough for my blood to boil in the upper stratosphere. My corpse would continue into black space, sailing frozen, forever.

"Yeah, let's not do that," I muttered. I aimed the FLUB downward and pushed the power slide, holding it to a low growl to keep the woman from hearing the device.

The effect broke my trajectory. Instead of continuing skyward, I scribed an arc, like a gravity-affected projectile running out of energy. I estimated my altitude to be several hundred feet, the highest I'd yet ventured, as the trajectory flattened and began downward. I angled my wrist and added a turn to the path. Slowly, now descending, I circled back toward the front of the house and the silver Mercedes in the driveway. I assumed the woman still stood on the back steps, rapping on the storm door. We don't have a doorbell.

I wove a path down through the maple trees, pulsed a couple shots of reverse thrust into the FLUB and settled on the front lawn. I let my feet skid through the snowy grass and tried to stabilize.

Fwooomp! I reappeared a little too soon. My weight dropped onto my feet. Both legs acted surprised by gravity's repossession of my body. One went one way, one went the other, slipping on the slick snow. I landed on my ass with a sharp jolt of pain that reminded me I had broken my pelvis just six months ago, and it wasn't quite ready for rugby yet.

"Shit!" I cursed as the back of my head hit the frozen lawn.

I lay sprawled in the snow. "Great," I said aloud. I pulled off the ski goggles and shoved the power unit in my pocket.

"Making snow angels?"

I looked up. The woman stood by the fender of her Mercedes.

Andy.

Not Andy.

Damned close to Andy. The same stunning looks, but with a little less underbite. The same rich dark hair, tucked under a cashmere knit cap. Brown eyes, not green. Pregnant. Really pregnant.

"I thought the yard could use a little artwork," I replied, working myself up to a sitting position. Sudden exposure to the cold cut razor lines down to my leg bones.

"You're not doing it right. You have to swing your arms up and down. To make the wings."

In for a penny...

"Okay." I laid back in the snow and flapped my arms.

"Legs, too. It makes a skirt. Angels are always women."

"But not vice versa," I said.

I complied and swept the snow with my legs. Finished, with cold seeping through the thin fabric of my suit and snow starting to melt into my underwear, I stood up and walked toward her.

She appraised my creation.

"That looks good. How did you manage to get out there without making tracks?"

I turned around. The only footprints were the ones I just made. I looked at the woman. She looked at me. It was eerie, seeing Andy—and not Andy.

She didn't wait for me to answer.

"If you're just some stranger who goes around making snow angels on people's lawns, I feel obligated to tell you that the woman who lives here is a cop."

"I'm married to the cop who lives here."

Her face lit up and the eerie sensation magnified as I saw Andy's bright, guileless smile. It glittered up into not-Andy's brown eyes.

"Then you would be Will!" She reached a leather-gloved hand toward me. "I'm Lydia!"

"I figured." I took her hand.

Andy's sister. Three years older than Andy; they could have been twins. The few photographs I'd seen didn't do justice to the resemblance. In photos, Andy's older sister always looked aloof, remote. Stuck up. Rich, and aware of it. And blonde. The photos showed none of the mirth dancing on her face now. Maybe seeing me sprawled on the lawn was the first thing that ever struck her as funny.

"Pleased to meet you. Can I interest you in coffee? Or shelter? Because I'm feeling the onset of hypothermia."

"Please," she gestured for me to lead the way.

INSIDE, the cold and wet staged a final assault on my body. We stood in the mud room at the back of the house. I tried to shake the snow off my suit.

"Let me," she offered. She brushed my back, my arms. She started on my legs, but it got a little strange.

"I got this," I said, finishing up. My pants were soaked through.

I pulled off my jacket and ushered Lydia Taylor Bates into our kitchen. The warmth only seemed to emphasize the cold on my skin.

"Go," she said, shedding her coat. "Go put on something dry. I take it Katie isn't home?"

Katie?

"Uh, no," I must have looked bewildered.

"Sorry. Andrea. I called her Katie growing up. Go."

"There's coffee…" I gestured at the kitchen countertop and the Mr. Coffee machine.

She gestured at the baby attached to her abdomen.

"Right. I'll be back."

. . .

I RETURNED after a few minutes in dry black jeans and a long-sleeved pullover shirt. She stood in the dining room.

"Your wedding pictures?"

She pointed at Andy and me, hanging in stasis on the dining room wall. Me in the same suit I had just soaked with snow. Andy in a flower-accented summer dress. For our wedding, Andy didn't opt for a wear-it-once dress that would have cost more than my car. Andy married me in a light, yellow and white summer dress that she still wears, and it still steals my breath.

"Uh-huh."

Lydia turned to me abruptly and took both my hands.

"I am *so sorry* I wasn't here for her. Truly, truly sorry, Will!" The damp glitter in her eye surprised me.

She abruptly hugged me. It was awkward, with the baby bump between us and the fact that we were almost complete strangers. And the fact that this was nothing like the older sister image I had fostered.

"Well, honestly," she backed away, rubbed her eyes, and looked down. "This one is number three and I think she's got me on more of an emotional rollercoaster than the other two combined!"

"Can I get you anything? Excluding alcohol, caffeine, sushi—anything else?"

"A glass of ice water, please. Yeah. I know. On a day like this? But this one is also a little heater." She patted her belly.

"Please, sit down. Be right back."

After fetching the water, we sat in the living room. She took my favorite recliner. I perched on the end of the sofa.

For an uncomfortable moment, she simply stared at me.

"What?" I finally asked.

"I shouldn't tell you. But Katie said it was your eyes. She said they were always *right here*, and a mile down the road at the same time. She called them mystifying. Something to do with being a pilot, she said. Oh! Now you're blushing."

"I turn red at the drop of a hat. I can't lie to your sister."

"Nobody can lie to my sister," she allowed. "Katie always knows."

"Why 'Katie?' I mean, obviously, her middle name. But I never knew she was called that."

"She wasn't. Except by me. When she was, oh, I guess about six or seven, she announced that she didn't want to be Andrea. She wanted to be Katie. For the longest time, she wouldn't answer to anything else. I thought it was fun, and let her have what she wanted, but my parents and our brother flatly refused. I guess that was the first of the great wars."

"You should know, everybody calls her Andy. I call her Dee, some-times." I didn't explain that 'Dee' came from D.E. which stood for Deeply Embarrassed, which is how she introduced herself to me when we met, what with the vomiting.

Now it was my turn to stare. She read it and blinked back at me.

"What?"

"Well, I guess I'm going to be a little blunt with my sister-in-law who I never met. But you're not what I expected."

She gave me the same open expression her sister uses when she wants me to keep talking—or digging a hole for myself. I knew the trick and countered by saying nothing. She caved first.

"Does she talk about me?"

"Honestly? We don't talk about—"

"The War?"

"We call it The Shitstorm."

"Yes. Of course."

The Shitstorm. In four years of knowing and three years of marriage to Andy, I never met her family. Andy had grown up with money and a father who had expectations. Andy, at the top of her high school class with a pile of Ivy League acceptance letters, rejected those expectations to follow the dream that pumps blood through her heart and pushes air through her lungs—law enforcement. But, as Andy puts it, nobody rejects her father's wishes. It led to six and a half years of cold war between Andy and her family, most of whom took her father's side. Including, as I understood it, her older sister Lydia.

"So, I must ask, Lydia. Why are you here?"

She looked at her hands, resting protectively on her unborn child. My reality flickered back and forth as I saw Andy's long lashes drop and a stranger's eyes appear when they rose again.

"There are two answers to that question. One is simple. To tell my sister I'm sorry. I want her back in my life. I miss her."

Again, not what I expected. Andy portrayed her older sister as the trophy wife of an anything-for-money Washington lobbyist. A woman whose only functions were to appear on her husband's arm at the right business moment and pump out babies. The latter seemed a little on the nose, given her condition, but the way she carried herself, the mirth in her eyes and the way her smile radiated genuine warmth told me that I'd unfairly adopted a caricature description of Lydia.

"The second answer is a little more complicated. I came here, to Essex, to rent a house for the month. For Christmas. I want to end the war between Andrea and our parents. And that will not be easy."

"You might want to practice on the Palestinians and Israelis first."

"I know."

"Andy's not here, of course. She's on a case. Probably won't be back until after midnight—or even later."

"I guess I should confess. I knew she wasn't here. I called the station house and asked for her. They told me she was on duty, but out of the station. I didn't say who I was or leave a message. I came here to talk to you first. I'm...somewhat terrified of my sister."

I leaned back, physically demonstrating the wariness I felt.

"I sense a mine field here. As much as I wish for Andy to have everything be right with her family, you're barking up the wrong tree if you try to enlist me to do something behind her back."

Lydia shook her head vigorously. "Nothing like that, Will."

"Good. I won't keep secrets from her."

"I won't ask you to."

We seemed to have the ground rules in place.

"Oh..." She said suddenly, wearily. "Crap."

I watched her face shed something, a pretense. She shook her head at herself.

"Crap. Crap. Crap," she said with resignation. "That's not why I'm here. No! It really is. But—but it isn't." She shook her head angrily at herself. Then blew out a long breath. "Look, I know, or I think I know, what you think of me. I know what I am. What I became. My marriage. My life. I was the obedient older sister. I married the way our father wanted me to marry. Did you know he actually encouraged me to drop out of college to marry Davis?"

"I did not."

"I lived the way Dad wanted me to live. You probably don't see it in me, but I was always the silly one. Katie was the serious one. Our father didn't like silly, so he did his best to hammer it out of me, and I did my best to please him. Katie was stronger and said No, which is a word our father reserves for his own personal use. They were always at war. I got along. And to get along, I went along. And I put up—"

She stopped abruptly. Tears welled up. Baby hormones? Or manipulation? I felt ridiculously uncomfortable. I had no idea what emotional engines govern a pregnant woman.

"Sorry," she said. She put her hands out, flat, and worked them up and down to suppress the emotional swelling. "I put up. I put up. I put up...and I put out," she said and laughed abruptly. She gestured at her belly. "Boy, did I ever!"

The laughter mingled with a sob.

"I warn you right now, Will. We Taylor women are crazy when pregnant."

I handed her a tissue box.

"Okay. Buck up, Liddy," she commanded herself. "Here's the deal. I meant what I said. I miss Katie. Andy. We trade e-mails occasionally, but it's not real, and I've been covering up. Pretending to be my father's daughter—when I should have been my sister's sister. Does that make sense?"

I held my tongue.

"I read about Ka— er, Andy. About Senator Stone. I have this remarkable sister doing amazing things—and do you know what my father and husband had to say? She should have stuck to writing traffic citations and stayed out of the way of the money that makes government work. Davis told me some of his associates—not friends, because there are none in Washington—some of his associates lost big contracts because of my sister. Because she took down Pearce Parks. Do you know what I said to that?"

I pressed my teeth together.

"Nothing," she said. "Nothing. I toed the mark as usual."

She blew her nose.

"Okay, cut to the chase, Liddy," she told herself. "There's more. I can't believe I'm telling you this—I can't believe I'm doing this—but I'm leaving my husband. He's a lying, cheating ass—but that's not why. I bet if I went back and looked it up, philandering was probably in his wedding vows. Guess what? This isn't his only bun in the oven. Our nineteen-year-old nanny is pregnant, too! We can take birthing classes together!" She laughed. One short pregnant-crazy burst that stopped sharply. "I'm taking the kids and I'm taking everything he owns, and that is a fuck-load of money, because—well, my lawyer says that me and the nanny aren't the only ones who are now royally screwed. Anyway—all that—that's not why I'm leaving the bastard. Oh, God! I can't believe I'm dumping all this shit on you."

"It's okay."

"Bullshit. But nice of you to say."

She let the compliment hang for a moment, looking at me like I was something rare she had never seen close-up. Maybe, as husbands go, she hadn't.

"So...why...? Why *are* you leaving?"

I expected her to need a moment, but she answered immediately. "I need my sister. I need her strength. I need her to forgive me for taking sides with our father, and my fuck-anything-in-a-skirt soon-to-be ex-husband who would do anything to suck up to Dad. And by anything, I include getting me to treat my sister like shit all these years. I am *so sorry!*"

She wept. Lip quivering. Shoulders shaken by silent sobs. Her voice went high and tiny.

"And...I need my sister...to help me see...if I actually still exist."

I sat like an idiot with no idea what to say or do.

She blew her nose loudly, then blinked through big wet tears, sending them down her cheek. With a flourish, she held out her hand.

"Nice to meet you, brother-in-law!" she laughed, and it was genuine, with perhaps a touch of pregnant-crazy, but not so much as before. The laughter sparkled with release of a truth suppressed for a long time.

I couldn't help but smile.

"Hiya, sis!" I took her hand and shook it.

18

I settled into one of the squad room chairs with a fresh coffee, hoping LeMore had brewed it. He hadn't.

"Okay," Andy said. All eyes locked on her. "Mike's got his pickup. Jeff, you're in your Subaru. I'll be in my car. Paul, you're in twenty-one, and we've got three sheriff's squads on a rolling perimeter, here, here and here." She pointed at the big county map on the squad-room wall and the county roads which formed a large square around the general area anchored by Sarah's home. "Pidge—er, Miss Page—is already in place in the house, with the Chief."

I looked around the room. Serious faces broke into smirks. Everyone had been amused when Mrs. Lewis showed up at the station with Sarah. The plan was to exchange Sarah for Pidge. Mrs. Lewis would return home with a petite blonde stand-in. Chief Ceeves declared he would take up station in the house by riding back with the two women, hidden in the back seat. An excellent plan, except Mrs. Lewis showed up in a Toyota Prius. The chief folding himself into the rear of the tiny car had been a comedy.

"I hope they had a can opener," Jeff Parridy, Essex PD's other detective, said.

"And some canola oil," Mae Earnhardt, the regular evening dispatcher, added.

Andy let the laughter ripple through the squad room, then returned to business. She looked at me. "Will has volunteered to ride with me so I can drive and have an extra pair of hands to work a phone and work communications with all of you. Strictly phone and text tonight. If this guy is tech-savvy, he could be monitoring the radios. Make sure your phones are charged up and on. We have extra charge packs in the back cabinet."

"Any progress with the camera?" Jeff asked.

"Only that Detective LeMore seems to think the Faraday Cage works for whatever it is he's trying to do. He's been deep into it all afternoon," Andy replied.

"This app—this Candy Store—is there any way we can see what he's telling her?" I asked.

"Not without joining in as part of a group, or mob, or whatever it's called. There's a function that allows you to log in as a private cell. We expect him to use that, which isolates him with her. Tom will relay his initial instructions to us. Once Sarah—Pidge—is on the move, she'll relay the instructions to us via text if she can."

Mike spoke up. "Best guess is what? He tells her to get on her bike? Damned cold out for that."

Andy gave a who-knows shrug. "Or sends an Uber. Or shows up himself in a vehicle."

"An Uber would be great. Easy to track down the client," Jeff said.

"Fine, but if it's an Uber, do we want her to take the ride? And lead us to him?" Mike asked.

"We do," Andy said,

Mike protested. "But if it's him, we're putting her in serious danger if she gets in a vehicle with him. How are we supposed to know the difference?"

"We might not," Andy allowed. "Jeff?"

"She'll have an alert medallion, hidden," Jeff Parridy explained. "My mother carries one of those medical alert medallions. It's like that, but this one sends a signal to Mae in Dispatch. Our Sarah will have it. If anything is out of whack, she hits the silent Panic button. Mae will get a signal and relay it to us."

"And we'll have a rolling tail on her," Andy reminded everyone. "If she hits the alert, we close in. Remember, if we take him down, get him out of the vehicle and keep his hands away from anything tech. Phone.

Laptop. iPad. Get his hands secured first," Andy said. "I'm less worried about him having a weapon than having a chance to erase files or crash his computer or run any kind of program that destroys evidence. Does everyone have one of these bags?" She held up a silver drawstring bag. LeMore provided half a dozen of the special Faraday Evidence Bags.

Everyone except Mae nodded or held up a bag.

"If you see any kind of device, toss it in the bag immediately. Tie it shut and just hold it. The bag prevents signals from entering or leaving."

The instructions seemed clear enough.

"This is going to be fluid. We'll call it as we see it unfold. I've got my phone set up to conference all of you when things start moving. I'll hit it so we're all on a conference call. The location isn't the best for surveillance. Stay off the radios. We have excellent cell coverage. The subdivision only has four houses, and we can't be rolling through there at midnight or parking cars on those empty roads. I'll be here," she pointed at the map, "in this driveway across the road from the subdivision entrance. I'll have a view of the Lewis house. Jeff, you'll be here, parked at the BP station to the east. Mike, you're west, here, at the Mason farm. I spoke to Lee Mason, so they know you'll be sitting in their yard. The three of us are the inner ring. The marked cars are the outer ring."

Andy stopped. She looked around.

"Any questions?"

"Only the ones we haven't thought of, Sarge," Mike said. Andy ignored his use of her former rank.

"That's it then." Andy studied the faces of her fellow officers, searching for the piece of the plan she had missed.

19

We sat in Andy's car with the heater blasting. A digital display on the dashboard reported that the outside temperature had dropped to seventeen degrees. Cold stars in the sky gave the white landscape a ghostly glow.

Andy had backed into a private driveway that joined the highway two hundred yards from the subdivision entrance. She eased the car in as far as possible, keeping the Lewis house, roughly a quarter mile away, in sight. Running the engine wasn't ideal, but she hoped by putting the rear of the car slightly behind our host's house, the exhaust wouldn't be obvious.

"He sounded juvenile." Andy's comment sailed out of the blue. We had been sitting in silence. I couldn't connect her statement to anything. She does that sometimes.

"Who?"

"The pervert. That thing about 'be my sex bitch.' That sounds juvenile."

"I don't do much sexting, so I couldn't say."

"Doesn't it? I mean, sound like something someone—I don't know—less worldly would say?"

"I guess."

"Like someone who just learned new swear words."

I had no opinion. After the intensity of planning and conferring at the station, we had slipped into the doldrums of waiting. My mind wandered back to the visit from Andy's sister, Lydia.

I planned to tell Andy. Everything. I told Lydia so. However, a strong instinct told me that this wasn't the moment. For one thing, Andy was on duty. For another, she was running on coffee and adrenaline. I stole a much-needed nap during the afternoon. Andy swore she had grabbed a nap in the Chief's office on the only sofa in the police department building, but it couldn't have been much.

Time ticked by slowly. The clock on the dash said eleven forty-five. If our pervert kept to his schedule, we were still fifteen eternities away from something happening.

Lydia didn't go much deeper into her story, other than to say she had a meeting with a real estate agent at a house on Leander Lake. The property was furnished and available for rent month-to-month. If she liked it, she planned to sign for it today, then fly back to Washington tonight. In the coming week, she expected to return with her two girls and enough clothing to get through December. She said she wanted to use the month to make decisions.

She said she chose Essex because she wanted—no, *needed*—Andy.

"You're putting me in the position of making first contact," I said to Lydia when she put on her coat to go. "Which Andy will take as me acting the intermediary."

"I guess."

"Did you mean to do that? Coming here?"

"I'm lucky if I can pull my thoughts together long enough to put my left shoe on my left foot, Will. And I have a mountain of decisions to make. But...maybe I did. I'm sorry."

I shrugged it off. "Andy will see it however she sees it. But be prepared to apologize for not reaching out to her first."

I didn't intend to throw Lydia under the bus, but I sure as hell intended to get out of the space between the two sisters.

It frustrated me that we were sitting in a car, alone, with little to talk about, and I couldn't bring it up.

"It's nice that Rosemary II and Lane asked Sarah and her parents to stay over tonight."

"Way better than sitting at the station all night," Andy agreed.

The silence folded around us again.

"We have fourteen minutes. Want to make out?"

"No."

AT THREE MINUTES TO MIDNIGHT, Andy initiated a conference call on her cell that included the Chief hiding in Sarah's house with Pidge, Jeff and Mike in their cars, Paul Ebersol in squad twenty-one, and Mae at dispatch. I envied Mae, sitting in the relatively warm station office. Everyone checked in on Andy's speaker phone. Mae confirmed contact with the Sheriff's deputies loitering on the perimeter roads.

We waited.

At midnight, Tom announced, "She's logging in to the app now. Stand by."

We waited.

Snow-covered, the subdivision, which had a slight slope to it, appeared luminous in the starlight. The four homes that had been completed were black except for yard lights and weak all-night interior lights. One of the houses had neither. To all appearances, the occupants of all except the Lewis house were asleep. Sarah Lewis's bedroom remained illuminated.

Three minutes passed.

"Nothing yet," Tom reported quietly. As if someone might be listening.

Five minutes passed.

"Has he texted?" Andy asked.

"No."

We waited. Each digit change on the dash clock seemed to mark an hour. I found myself remembering a similar interminable wait in a billionaire's bedroom, also lit by cold starlight.

A quarter hour passed with no contact. I thought about Sarah, sitting with Lane, holding her breath. Sarah knew about the midnight deadline, and the net poised to drop on her tormentor. I wondered if she was pondering the possibility of failure. Of seeing her friends downloading and trading the image of her naked body.

We couldn't fail.

"Andy," I broke the silence in a low voice. "Ask Pidge to go to the window in Sarah's bedroom. Tell her to stand there, like she's waiting. Have her hold the phone and look at it."

"Copy that Tom?"

"Got it."

A quarter of a mile away, a lighted upstairs window cast a glow down across the front yard of the Lewis home. Something moved in the frame of yellow. Andy raised a set of binoculars, studied it, and then handed them to me. A petite blonde filled the window frame, holding a cell phone, just as I suggested.

I swung the binoculars away, across the landscape.

Nothing. Black on black.

I reached down and touched the Mute button on Andy's phone.

"I think he knows we're here," I said.

Andy considered the possibility.

"That means he's watching. I want to take a closer look," I released my seatbelt.

She made a face to protest, but I pulled one of the propulsion units from under my coat.

"Once around the neighborhood. I want to see if anyone's lying in the weeds somewhere."

"You'll freeze to death," she argued.

I pulled a balaclava from another pocket and worked it down over my head until only my eyes showed. Then I slipped on the ski goggles.

"Nope. By the way," I held up the propulsion unit proudly. "Flight Launching Unit B-Model. FLUB."

"Absolutely not." She reached up and flicked the overhead light off so that opening the car door would not illuminate the interior. "Make it quick and come right back. I have no way of communicating with you. And if something happens and I have to leave you just follow me."

"Not a problem." I had three more power units packed in my pockets. "Be right back."

I slipped out of the car into the cold and closed the door behind me.

Fwooomp! Instantly, cool replaced cold. Weightlessness replaced gravity.

I pulled the propulsion unit from inside my coat and aimed it straight up. Power lines and telephone wires ran along the highway between me and the subdivision. I wanted to be well clear of them before starting toward the Lewis house. Andy's car fell away below me, along with the house and yard of whoever had allowed us to park there. I located one of the powerline poles spaced evenly along the highway. A helicopter pilot once told me that wires are the helicopter's deadliest enemy. You can't see the wires, but you can see the poles, so always fly over the poles and you'll clear the wires. I took his advice and angled the propulsion unit forward.

The house slipped under me. The highway followed. I crossed the power lines over the nearest pole, then flew over open, undeveloped lots in the unfinished subdivision. I noted that the powerlines here had been placed underground, so I lowered my trajectory until I skimmed just above the ground, rising and dipping in harmony with the terrain.

I passed the first two houses, skirted a third on my left, and headed toward the last, on my right. The Lewis house. As I approached, I saw Pidge more clearly in the upstairs window. Sarah's bedroom lamps bathed her in soft incandescent light. Pidge played the Sarah role in Sarah's bright clothing—tight leggings and a loose sweatshirt. She balanced a phone in one hand. She wore a floppy knit hat to suppress any obvious differences in hair style. With her back to the light, her face was dark. Dark enough, I hoped, that a watcher couldn't see that Pidge wasn't Sarah. Putting her in the window had been a risk.

I swung myself across the front of the house, cut the power, and held a silent glide past the window. Instead of looking in at Pidge, I looked outward.

Three other houses occupied the landscape. Beyond them lay unfinished out-lot. Then to the west, the perimeter of the subdivision property edged a span of dark, wooded acreage. Plenty of hiding places.

Adding power, I curved west, to the perimeter. I made a wide turn. I began a run down the line of trees. I cut the power and continued forward on a silent glide.

From fifteen feet up, I had a clear view into the woods. The snow created a white carpet between the trees and the scrubby buckthorn. I studied patterns in the white as I floated by. I expected a body to stand out. Anyone hiding here would have planned on a long wait and would have to be dressed heavily. Even if they wore all white, tracks and a silhouette would stand out on the snow, seen from above.

I reached the end of the woods, where the highway ran east and west. I saw nothing. I added power, climbed back up over the power lines and started a turn back to where Andy had parked.

Oh, well. It was an idea. And I was in the best position to investigate it. That it had come to nothing matched our other efforts this night. I began to feel despair for Sarah, and for any hope of protecting her.

Not even old enough to drive, and she could wind up a piece of porn traded on the internet. The idea sickened me.

Just before reaching a point where some reverse thrust would have dropped me down in the yard beside Andy's car, I had another thought.

Not old enough to drive...

Instead of reversing thrust, I added power.

I swung left, back over the power poles, back over the highway, and down into the subdivision again. This time, instead of aiming for the Lewis home, I aimed for the first house.

Nearly identical in construction, but with different accents and different siding, the first house illuminated its driveway with two soft lights on the attached garage. Pulsing the power back, I vectored myself past the front of the house. A light glowed somewhere inside. I flew on a path around the building, checking each window. The interior lay dark except for a light above a kitchen sink. Nothing unusual about that. Nearly all the first-floor windows offered a view inside. The second-floor windows were shaded.

Nothing here.

Following a line across the property's front yard, I flew to the second house, also on the west side of the street shared with the Lewis home. This was the house in full darkness. Either no one was home, or they chose not to keep a light on for security. Because of the darkness, the building had an abandoned look, yet fresh tire tracks in the snow entered and departed the garage.

I slowed myself for a closer scrutiny, working around the first-floor windows. Again, most were not curtained or shaded. The view inside offered nothing but darkness. After completing a circuit, I aimed higher, and moved closer, and reduced my speed. At barely a crawl, I worked my way past the second-floor windows facing the Lewis home.

He watched from the upstairs room on the right.

A standard double-hung window. Shaded. The shade hung to within a few inches of the sash.

Two huge lenses peered out—binoculars on a tripod. Something glowed, bathing the room in weak light. A dark figure sat behind the binoculars.

Gotcha! You pervert son of a bitch!

Once again, I found it hard to fix my mind on the fact that someone could look directly at me, and not see me. I held myself perfectly still and floated past the window with the silent power unit in hand.

I continued my glide past the corner of the house, over the open yard. I advanced the slide control on the power unit. It produced a low growl, but I felt certain that it could not be heard. The window had not been open and wouldn't be on a night like this.

Now what?

I knew what Andy would say. Report back, allow her to muster her law enforcement forces and formulate a new plan. But based on what? *Oh, Will flew past the window and spotted the guy.*

Even if some version of that could be sold, what then? She couldn't exactly storm the house. A polite, inquisitive knock on the door might not bring an answer. And if it did, one click of a mouse or press of a button could launch Sarah's picture onto the internet, where nothing ever disappears.

I had another idea.

I turned myself around and aimed for the back of the house. I maneuvered to the rear of the garage, then around the corner to the side of the garage farthest from the interior of the house. A double-hung window occupied the center of the wall. I pulled up close, examined it, and found what I needed. A single latch locked the window at the center.

I secured the propulsion unit in a pocket. Fixing a grip on the window frame with one hand, I worked myself into a position that allowed me to aim an elbow at the glass above the window latch. One swing shattered the upper pane. Half of the pieces dropped into the dark garage and produced a ridiculously loud tinkling sound. The other half remained in the frame. I carefully plucked them out and dropped them in the snow. When I had enough room, I reached in with a leather-gloved hand and flipped the latch. The lower half of the window slid up easily.

At this point, an alarm would have blown my plan to pieces—if the house had an alarm system.

Silence held fast.

For anyone else, climbing through a half-open window would have been a challenge, having nothing to stand on and nothing to land on inside the garage. For me, it was a simple matter of extending my body horizontally and floating through.

I bumped into a parked car, adjusted my trajectory, and floated over the car to a far corner of the garage. The amber ski goggles, meant for sunny ski slopes, made it too dark to see. I shoved them up on my forehead.

The door to the interior of the house had a standard doorknob and lock, and a deadbolt lock. This might have stymied me, if not for another trick I learned from *the other thing*. I can extend *the other thing* to make ordinary items, even other people, vanish along with me. But if an item, in particular a metal item, doesn't vanish entirely, the borderline between what is gone and what is not tends to *fray* the material. I don't know another way to put it. Once frayed, metal or not, it will break under pressure. That's how I separated Lane Franklin from a chain holding her to a wall.

I wasn't entirely sure it would work, but I found the doorknob and clapped one hand around it. Then I wrapped my other hand around the deadbolt lock. I *pushed*. In my mind, I put an imaginary hand on a pair of cockpit power levers, like the controls found in the Piper Navajo I had flown to disintegration. I pushed those levers forward, extending *the other thing* beyond my body, into the door, into the metal of the lock.

At the same time, I pulled on the doorknob. I felt a tug, a snap, like a soft strand of yarn separating. The door swung toward me.

Andy's not going to like this.

The house lay in darkness. Starlight streaming through the windows provided the only light.

Directly inside the garage door, a short hall ran forward to what I guessed to be a family room or media room. Several LED lights dotted the far wall. The odor of recent cooking lingered, faint, in the air. Spaghetti sauce.

Immediately to the right, I found the front foyer, the front door, and the stairs to the second floor. I made the glide up the stairs, found a hallway, and a typical array of upstairs bedroom doors. At the mid-point of the hallway, a full bathroom. The door I wanted was the last on the left, opening into a bedroom that corresponded to the window containing the eyes spying on Sarah. All the upstairs doors except this one stood partially open.

The same glow I'd seen from outside could be seen faintly beneath the door. The only sign of life in the house, although I couldn't be certain that the other bedrooms weren't occupied.

I used hand pressure on the walls to propel myself forward until I reached the door.

I closed my hand slowly around the knob.

New, like the house, the doorknob felt firm, the mechanism, smooth. Not locked, it turned silently.

I may have taken thirty seconds to turn the knob. Or three minutes. Either way, I moved it at a glacial pace. When I was certain the latch had cleared the face plate, I pushed. I felt no resistance. Again, thirty seconds. Or three minutes. I have no idea. I moved the door slowly, listening for the first hint of a squeak. When it parted enough for me to slip through, I performed a slow glide into the room.

He sat on a low plastic stool, hunched over the binoculars, watching.

On a desk beside him, an iMac screen cast thin light across his shoulders, which were covered in a dark sweatshirt. Inexplicably, or perhaps acknowledging his criminal intent, he wore a hoodie over his head. It came to a point that looked stupid to me.

After assessing his location, the position of a bed to my left, and the possibility that others slept across the hall, I turned and eased the door closed again. It took forever. The latch finally slipped into place, giving out a painfully loud click at the end. It stopped my breath.

He didn't flinch. That's when I noticed a pair of wires dangling from the sides of the hoodie. His head bobbed almost imperceptibly.

He likes his perversion set to music.

Growing more confident in my plan, I pushed across the room toward him. He remained affixed to the binoculars. I noticed a cheap phone on the desk. The screen was open to the Candy Store app. A series of messages filled the screen.

I'm here.

Please.

Where are you?

Andy must have instructed Pidge to start sending.

He sat and watched 'Sarah' beg.

I stopped directly behind him and pulled a propulsion unit from my pocket. I flipped it around so that the round end of the battery pack stuck out of my fist instead of the propeller.

Deep breath. I pulled the mirrored ski goggles down over my eyes. The balaclava covered my head. A black leather jacket covered my upper body. Black jeans covered my legs, which I positioned on the floor behind his chair.

Fwooomp! I reappeared.

I braced one foot against the back of his stool. I hooked my left arm around his throat and yanked him backward. The stool remained static, but he didn't. He tipped and dropped to the carpet with a heavy thud. I heard him gasp but didn't give him time for words. I swung a leg over and dropped onto his chest, pinning his arms down with my knees, pressing the air from his lungs with my weight. I threw my left hand around his throat.

I pushed the end of the power unit into his forehead, holding it like a gun.

"Don't move." I said it in a menacing half growl, half whisper. "Or I blow your head off." A good movie line, I thought.

In the darkness, I saw wide, white-ringed eyes. He couldn't focus close enough to his head to see that I was holding a flashlight body, not a gun. That part of the ruse worked. But I realized he hadn't heard a word.

I released his throat and yanked the ear buds out of his ears. Tinny heavy metal music tumbled away. I jerked the wires out of whatever device he had in his pocket.

"Don't move. Or I blow your head off." I delivered the line again. This time it sounded lame to me, but to someone lying on a floor under a black specter, it played to good effect. He froze, every muscle tense under my full body weight.

I reached up and pivoted the computer screen.

Sarah filled the screen. Full frontal. Skin sparkling and wet.

I left the image alone but pushed the screen away until it faced the wall.

We stared at each other for a moment. Me looking at his terrified eyes; he fixed on my mirrored goggles, black head, and the 'gun' at his forehead.

I felt a strong urge to pound on his pale face with the metal flashlight body. Instead, I reached onto his desktop and pulled down his phone.

"Make a sound and I kill you," I said. The wide eyes blinked.

I used my left hand, awkwardly, to change the screen on his phone, keeping the app open, I hoped.

"Very quietly, whisper, say the street address of this house," I told him.

"Huh?"

"The street address! The fucking street address for this house." I had no idea.

Choking on the words, he gave me the address.

"Now shut up. Make a sound, and I kill you."

I thumbed the phone. After a moment it rang. Rang again. Rang a third time.

"Nine-One-One, what is your emergency?"

I held the phone to my head. Whispering urgently, I said, *"There's a guy with a gun! He's in the house! Please, hurry! He's coming up the stairs!"* I gave the address before the operator could ask. *"I'm in the back bedroom on the left! I'm hiding but he's coming! Please! Hurry!"*

I touched the Mute button on the screen and leaned down.

"Who else is here? In the house?"

"Uh—my parents—my sister."

Shit!

I flicked the Mute button off. Again, whispering, I said, *"My parents and my sister are sleeping upstairs. I'm in the last bedroom on the left! He's coming in here! Hurry!"*

"Stay on the line. What's your name?"

"Can't talk!"

I left the line open and tossed the phone up onto the bed in the corner of the room. I dropped my left hand back onto his throat. He gasped.

"Don't move."

I hadn't completely thought this through. If the Essex PD showed up in full hostage response mode, I might have to reconsider my whole approach. For the moment, I sat still. The white-ringed eyes stared up at me. I felt his whole body holding itself rigid beneath me. I tensed, waiting for some effort, for a fight. It never came.

After several long minutes, a loud bang broke the silence in the house.

I heard heavy footsteps and a deep voice shouting, "Police! Police! Everyone stay still, get down! Police! Police!"

I readied myself. I moved my hand from his throat and covered his eyes. He began to shake. I fixed my eyes on the bedroom door.

It opened explosively. A flashlight beam swung into the room.

Fwooomp!

I vanished, kicked off and rose to the ceiling, leaving the hooded figure on the floor. The flashlight beam found him and held him, a face frozen in terror.

"DON'T MOVE!" Tom Ceeves bellowed, out of breath. His giant frame and enraged voice filled the room.

"Police! If you live here, call out your name!" Andy's voice broke out in the hallway. A light flicked on. Voices, calling out first names, responded from other rooms. Heavy footsteps pounded up the stairs. The new sound of sirens joined the confusion.

"DON'T MOVE!" Tom repeated. He slapped at the wall, found and turned on the light in the room. He loomed over the figure on the floor, and for the first time in my life I saw the Chief of Police with a weapon in his hand. The standard issue revolver appeared toylike in his massive grip.

"What's going on!?" someone cried out.

"Police! Stay where you are! Stay where you are!" Andy commanded. She appeared in the doorway behind Tom, searching. Her eyes studied the dimensions of the room, including a glance at the ceiling where I floated.

She took in the figure on the floor, the binoculars mounted on a tripod at the window, and the shape of the iMac on the desktop. She pushed past Tom and reached for the desktop computer. She pivoted the screen just as I had.

She and Tom looked at the screen, then down at the figure on the floor.

"Don't you fucking move," Tom growled harshly.

The kid on the floor looked like he would pee in his pants.

20

"How about pizza and beer for breakfast?" Andy asked, smiling down at me.

"Am I dead? Are you an angel?" I blinked sleep out of my eyes.

"No, but there's a snow angel in the front yard. What's that about?"

I levered the recliner into an upright position.

"What time is it?"

"Four-thirty." Andy wriggled her weapon and holster out of her belt, then shook herself out of her blazer. Still in her jeans and white sweater from yesterday, she confirmed her off-duty status by breaking her hair loose from her police ponytail. She shook her head and ran her fingers through it.

"What day is it?"

"Monday! Go start the oven, love. I'll be down in a minute." She took the stairs two steps at a time. I tried to tally up her sleep in the last forty-eight hours but gave up after the fuzz balls clotting my brain kept erasing the math.

Pizza and beer for breakfast. Something to focus on.

Oh, and the snow angel in the front yard. That was for your sister.

"On it!" I called up the stairs.

I fired up the oven and dug out a frozen pizza. Pepperoni.

I pulled two cold Coronas from the refrigerator. We were out of limes again. Sunday had slipped past without a run to the grocery store. I popped open the two beers and stole a slug from one of them.

ANDY TREATED herself to twenty-some minutes of whatever women do alone in a bathroom at the end of a really-really-long day. She descended the stairs in a fuzzy robe wrapped over sweatpants and a t-shirt, her hair brushed out.

"Did anybody ask where I disappeared to?"

"Not really," she said, lending it a note of wonder. "I said something about telling you to call for an Uber after the excitement began."

"Your hero."

She folded herself into a corner of the couch and pulled a big blanket over her lap. The farmhouse is cold in the winter, and our budget cuts it close on the heating bill.

"Hold on a sec!" I yanked the blanket off her lap.

"Hey!"

"Hang on!" I dashed off through the kitchen, into the laundry room. A few minutes later I returned after running the blanket in the dryer to heat it up. I threw it over her, and she pulled it up to her chin, moaning deeply.

"Oh lord," she uttered in ecstasy, "will you marry me?"

"Sorry, I've got a hot girlfriend, and I'm just a wild stallion who can't be tamed. A free spirit who can't be—" She reached up and pulled me down into a long, energetic kiss. As it ended, she slipped her hand around the back of my head for another.

"I do," I said when our lips broke apart.

"Me, too."

The stove timer interrupted. I pulled away and dashed off to the kitchen for a second time. I returned with the pizza divided onto two plates, and cold beer under my arms.

"Napkins?"

"I'm a guy. What's a napkin?" I made another trip to the kitchen and returned flying a paper towel flag. "C'mon, Dee, you're killing me. What happened?"

"After you disappeared?"

"After I flew off into the night sky like Batman." The scene in the house caused a lot of bodies to crowd into the kid's bedroom. It took me a while to slip out of the house. Once outside, I couldn't come up with a way to simply reappear, so I launched using a propulsion unit and took a night ride across Essex, across the farm country and home.

"Batman can't fly like you. Usual disclaimer?"

"Usual disclaimer," I recited, verifying secrecy between us. It reminded me I hadn't told her about Lydia's visit.

"First, may I just say, what you did—and I know it was you—was *not* part of the plan. Not part of any plan. Not part of anything I expected in any scenario tonight."

"What makes you think it was me?"

She gave me a don't-be-stupid look.

"Aside from the obvious, there was that rub on my shoulder I got from some poltergeist as we were handcuffing the kid. How did you find him?"

I explained the circuit I flew, and the fruitless search of the woods.

"I was about to return to the car when I thought about something you said. About the text sounding juvenile. And then I thought about how Sarah doesn't have a driver's license. That seriously limits her mobility. What if the pervert never expected her to go anywhere? What if all he wanted to do was look? Make her sweat and obey—and watch her do it."

Andy took a long pull from her beer, letting the pizza cool, and appraising me with cop eyes.

"Breaking and entering," she said.

"Who? Me?"

"I figured it out as soon as the Nine-One-One call came in. I told Tom that the call had to be connected—that it might be our guy, breaking into another house. He ran down the street from the Lewis house. Jeepers, that big guy can move fast when he wants to."

"So? Who is he? The kid. What's his deal?"

"Adolescent hormone chemistry gone terribly wrong it seems. I feel a little bad for the kid. He's a junior at Essex High. Has had a crush on the cute girl across the street since middle school. It explains how he knew her number. When we called Sarah to tell her what happened, or as much as we were willing to share, she said she gave Terry, the kid, her number so he could call her when the school bus was coming. He can see the highway from his house. She can't."

"Whoa! Whoa! That's all sweet puppy love, but let's not forget planting a camera in a public shower room, taking involuntary photos, making extortion threats, essentially conspiring to commit sexual assault."

Andy nodded. "Right. There's no question that the kid is in deep trouble. But here's the deal. We can't interrogate a minor without his parents present, and his parents—once they got their bearings—divided their time between screaming at the kid and telling us nobody is saying anything until their lawyer gets there. Or they find one."

"You can't beat it out of him?"

"Mwah bwumph," she chewed and swallowed, taking a second to savor her first food in a day. She sipped her Corona. "My bet is that this kid doesn't know anything about the camera. LeMore quit for the night after all this went down, but he said he'd have a go at the kid's computer —after we get a warrant—tomorrow."

"And what's the latest from his cage match with technology?"

"He said he'd give us a report tomorrow—er, today—but he did say that we're dealing with highly sophisticated tech. Did I tell you we found three more nozzle cameras in the women's shower? None in the men's."

"I suppose at this point, it doesn't matter whether or not someone knows we found them," I said.

"Maybe. But Chet Allison is keeping the Wi-Fi network down. He put a notice on the school website that it's down due to a router failure and won't be repaired for a couple days."

"Clever."

"Will, that kid didn't have anything in his room except his personal phone, a burner phone, and the iMac he used to retouch the photo. What I'm getting from LeMore is that the tech is way beyond this kid. That's all I know. We'll know more this afternoon. By the way, this may throw a wrench in my going with you to Madison."

"I'll call Stephenson's office and postpone." I tried to act disappointed.

"No. Not an option."

Dammit.

I sat back and thought about the turn of events. "This is not good news for Sarah."

"Right," Andy said solemnly. "It means we didn't get to the origin of the photo. Only a copy in the hands of a kid. No! No! I get it," she anticipated my interruption. "The kid played out a pretty sick scheme on an innocent girl. But in a way, the kid committed the digital age version of calling up some girl and hanging up when she answers. Tell me you never did that."

"C'mon, Dee, it's way more serious than that. Given the chance, he might have committed assault."

Andy put her hands up. "No question. It's serious. My point is that this is not one, but four cameras. Multiple angles. And we don't know how long they've been there. Or what they've captured. I don't think the cameras were there so that this kid could blackmail the girl across the street into...whatever."

"Then you should know something LeMore said on the way up here. He asked me not to toss it out, you know, as a theory, because he thought it might dominate everyone's thinking. I should probably let him tell it— and I'm sure he will. But ..." I went on to explain LeMore's deduction that the camera might be part of a broadcast event.

"That's—Jesus, Will! That's disgusting!"

I offered an I-don't-make-people-act-this-way shrug.

"Organized crime?" she asked.

"Organized pornography, at the very least." I explained LeMore's example of Joe Theismann's broken leg.

"Wow."

Andy gets a look when her gears are turning. She adopted that look now. I took advantage of the pause and devoured a slice of pizza.

"You're going to Madison tomorrow morning..." she said after a few minutes. She said it in a distant, distracted way.

"That's the rumor. I estimate I have about twenty-three hours to talk you out of it."

She paid no attention.

"Do you think Earl would let us go today? And by let us go, I mean lend us Pidge and an airplane?"

"Ooooh, I don't know. We have a habit of taking his airplanes and breaking them."

"Once," she delivered a playful backhand to my chest.

"Well, I've got two to my credit. On the other hand, he did get a nice new airplane out of it. You haven't seen it yet. Why do you want to go to Madison a day early?"

"Not Madison. Escanaba."

"Michigan?"

Andy nodded. I waited. She bit off a mouthful of pizza. I found myself watching. Even when she eats, she has a flow, a smoothness that makes me want to touch.

She said, "Allison pulled the files on the construction of the pool, and the locker rooms and shower rooms. The plumbing came from a company called Reichenbach Builders."

"So?"

"In Escanaba."

"Okay, but anybody could have swapped the shower nozzles."

"True, but three weeks ago, the company called and told the district they needed to upgrade some of the components. No charge. A courtesy recall of some defective parts. They didn't say which, and nobody asked."

"How terribly convenient!"

"Maybe, or terribly stupid. I mean, they're our first suspect."

"You want to fly to Escanaba today? Why not just call them?"

"We did. All we got was a recording. Leave a message. Message mailbox full. People can hide behind a phone. Sometimes it's better to show up in person."

"What about sleep?"

"We grab a couple hours. Leave at noon. See what we can find in Michigan, then fly down to Madison direct tonight or first thing in the morning."

I started to knock back my remaining Corona—then stopped, considering that I might be flying in just under eight hours.

I slid my hand under the blanket, onto her thigh. "You know what would help us slee—"

"No."

"Damn," I said. I pulled my hand back and tried to pout. "Never should have said 'I do.' They say marriage kills the romance."

"Oh, stuff it, love. I'll show you romance—you won't be able to handle it." She ran her fingers through my hair. "When I'm not running on two hours' sleep in the last forty-eight."

She tipped her beer. After a couple swallows, she asked, "So what's with the snow angel?"

21

"You never told me that you went by 'Katie' when you were a kid."

Andy stopped cold, holding her Corona in mid-flight between her lips and the coaster on the end table. She blinked twice, causing the gold flecks in her green eyes to glitter. Behind those eyes, dots connected.

I tried to maintain a casual demeanor. I took a bite of pizza.

"How...?" she started to ask but paused. More dots connected. Then her expression hardened. "When did you talk to Lydia?"

Direct hit. The pizza in my mouth suddenly seemed dry. I chased it down with beer.

"You did," she said. "You talked to Lydia. It wouldn't have been my parents. They never call me..." She trailed off again, following a memory somewhere.

"Lydia stopped here."

"Here?"

"Uh-huh."

Andy moved her plate to the end table. Breakfast was over. That fast, her guard went up. That fast, mine went up, too. Two people on their guard means it only takes one spark to turn a conversation into an argument. Exactly what I feared. Not for the first time since meeting Andy's sister, I wondered how much of Lydia's unabashed personal sharing was manipulation.

"Dee," I began slowly. "I am going to give you the facts, and only the facts. Okay? I'm not advocating for—"

"When was she here?"

"Yesterday. She—"

"And you're just telling me this now?"

"We were a little busy."

"We were sitting in a car last night for half an hour talking about the weather, Will."

In my head, I ducked and let that one sail past, letting it explode somewhere behind me. Deep breath.

"I thought you would prefer to have a chance—"

"What did my sister want?"

"Well, some things have apparently changed—"

"I know my sister. Lydia wouldn't come here unannounced unless she wants something."

"For starters, she's pr—"

"Did she call you? Did you set this up with her?"

"Hey!" I reached out and put a firm hand on Andy's knee. "If you're going to interrogate me as a suspect, I want my lawyer. If you're going to ask me questions as a neutral, unsuspecting witness, I will tell you what happened. Unvarnished. Okay?"

For a split second, her tension escalated. Her jaw locked, and her lower lip warned me of the mine field this conversation represented. Then a hint of hesitation flickered in her eyes. I took the opening.

"Your sister, a woman I never met before, showed up in our driveway yesterday after you dropped me off. I know how matters involving your family can be intense, so I chose not to dump this on you while you were absorbed in your professional responsibilities. If that was a mistake, we can deal with it later. Right now, I just want to give you the facts."

Andy gave me a five-count without moving, then lowered her lashes briefly—the signal to proceed. With caution.

I told her everything that happened, including my crash landing on the front lawn and the origin of the snow angel. I told her about the pregnancy —both pregnancies—and about Lydia leaving her husband. To my ear, I sounded like Andy herself, the few times I visited a courtroom when she testified as a police officer. Curt. Crisp. To the point. I labored at not giving the slightest hint of an endorsement to Lydia or her motives.

"Why didn't she come to me with this?"

Because she's scared of you. "I have no idea."

"Is she expecting me to—what?—meet with her?"

Preferably unarmed. "I have no idea."

"Six-and-a-half years, Will! Does she think I can just write that off?"

It's not like you can get it back. "I have no idea."

That was one too many. Andy gave me a cold look.

"Okay," I said, "there's one more thing. This blow-up with Davis—she's taking the kids, and she's looking to move here."

"Here? To Wisconsin?"

"To Essex."

"What? Why?"

Because she needs her sister. "I have no idea."

Andy pushed my hand off her knee and shoved the thick blanket to the floor. She bounced up off the sofa in one lithe move and paced across the living room floor to the French doors that opened onto the porch. She whirled and wild hair fell across one eye.

"I was her maid of honor. That summer. The summer I graduated from high school."

I waited. She took and released a breath. Then another.

"I put my heart and soul into that monstrosity of a wedding for my sister, and do you know what she did? The night of the rehearsal dinner?"

I had no clue.

"That was the night my father told me in no uncertain terms that he had arranged for me to accept admission to Harvard. Sixty days before classes began and he pulled strings—no, he pulled fucking steel cables—to get me in. I had already made my plans for the fall semester—plans I had to make with no help from my loving parents—after a running battle with him for the better part of the year."

She paused. She studied something distant.

"A year when I was also supposed to be excited about graduating and going to college. A year I instead spent waiting on my marrying older sister hand and foot as her maid of honor. And that night my father told me my plans, my dreams, were shit."

I knew part of this story, but not the cold details.

"Over shrimp cocktail and champagne, he told me how it was going to be. Period. And it broke me down. After all that, after losing fifteen pounds out of sheer stress, after breaking my back for Lydia, it broke me."

She looked deep into me.

"I came apart," she said, faintly, just above a whisper. "And do you know who I turned to? I turned to my sister—"

Andy's voice hitched. She steeled herself. But her voice was high and thin.

"My sister. Who counted on *me*. For her fittings. And her lists. And her shoes and her appointments. I turned to her, and I counted on her. And do you know what she told me?"

I thought for a moment that tears might come, but what came wasn't tears, it was cold and hard.

"Live with it."

I wanted to do something, say something. I wanted to go to her and take her by the shoulders and say, *Hey! It's me! I'm here!* I wanted to take her in my arms and melt the wall I could feel going up around her.

I put the pizza plate on the sofa cushion and rose.

She crossed the room on a line for the stairs.

"I'm going to bed."

22

Earl said Yes because he can't say No to my wife. He threw in Pidge and his brand-new Mojave because he thought letting me fly it would stoke a desire to get back on the flight line. I think he would have given me the keys to his new turbine-engine Beechcraft King Air 90 if he thought it would do any good, except I wasn't checked out in the airplane. He told Andy she should pull her gun on me if I balked at seeing Stephenson.

Andy and I managed to get a couple hours of sleep. It would have been more, but Andy's snow-angel question and the conversation that followed induced the equivalent of a straight shot of caffeine to Andy's blood. I slept fitfully. I'm not sure she slept at all.

Pidge met us at the field shortly after noon, with the airplane fueled, the flight plan filed, and the weather briefed.

We rolled on Runway 31. I lifted the airplane into the cold, crystalline sky and logged wheels-up at twelve twenty-seven. Pidge refused to sit up front with me. She curled up under a blanket in the club seating, claiming she'd been up all night fighting crime. Andy took a seat across the aisle from Pidge. I have enough husband training to know that the sullen mood she radiated, and the fact she wasn't speaking to me, had nothing to do with me.

I made the most of taking the pilot's seat, having the cockpit to myself, and doing what God meant me to do.

AT THE DELTA COUNTY AIRPORT terminal, I gave Pidge instructions to secure the airplane and line up an engine preheat whether we decided to depart later in the afternoon or early in the morning. The air temperature hovered just above fifteen degrees in Escanaba. Andy told Pidge to hang loose at the FBO, and that if it looked like we would stay overnight, she would call her.

"Let's get a rental," I suggested, figuring the expense would go to Essex PD. Andy said nothing, but started for the Avis counter in the tiny terminal. Pidge gave me a look meant to ask a question: *What the hell did you step in?*

Andy stopped suddenly. She stood frozen for a moment. Then she turned around and took three quick steps back to me. She put both hands on my face and pulled me into a kiss.

"Sorry," she said, pulling away. "This thing with Liddy. It's not about us."

She probed my eyes, looking for confirmation.

"You never told me," I said.

"I know. Sorry."

I kissed her.

"S'okay."

23

"This looks like the place." Andy turned into a broad, snow-covered parking lot. An *empty* parking lot. "Seems quiet for a Monday."

"Seems deserted."

The building, a one-story office fronting a much larger construction warehouse, showed no interior lights through tinted glass running the length of the façade. We parked directly in front of glass double doors and walked across squeaky-cold snow on a sidewalk that had not been shoveled. Ours were the first footprints since the last snowfall. Locked doors prevented entry. A notice on one door told anyone interested that Deliveries Should Call The Following Phone Number. Andy pulled out her phone and snapped a picture of the notice.

I cupped my hands around my face and leaned into the cold glass under the Reichenbach Builders lettering. A reception area and office showed empty cabinets, desks without equipment, no sign of desktop computers, and a rolling printer stand with no printer. File drawers hung open, empty.

"Dee, this place looks like it's been cleaned out."

"Weird." Andy pressed her own face to the glass. She pulled away and started around the building. I followed. We found a security fence surrounding the property. A gate had been wrapped in a heavy chain and padlocked. Inside the gate, trucks, assorted construction equipment, and rows of building materials lay under a coating of snow. Upper Michigan gained three or four inches more than Essex over the last few days. The yard showed no sign of tracks. Nothing had been plowed. Nothing moved.

"When did these guys come down to Essex to do that courtesy installation?" I asked.

"Allison said it was three weeks ago."

"Doesn't look like anything has been going on here for longer than three weeks. I know construction slows down in the winter, but not this slow."

"Allison made it sound like these guys were busy all over the Midwest," Andy said. She pulled her coat tighter against an icy low-velocity wind. "C'mon. Let's go talk to the owner. I think I know where to find him."

24

Andy had done her homework. She drove, I navigated, following a path on the map app in my phone. We followed US Highway 2 out of Escanaba, working our way north and east, occasionally within sight of a back bay to Lake Michigan. The winter landscape looked nicely snow-covered to my eye, but I knew the season had yet to mature. Much more snow would pile up before spring. The main roads had been plowed and sanded, but not salted. We crunched over a thin layer of packed snow.

At Highway 495 we turned right and drove toward the water. Approaching the shore, we found a narrow road called Beil Way. It took us through wooded land to a clearing immediately on the bay. In the cold winter sunlight, the surface of the water reflected a crisp, cobalt blue. It might have been pretty, but what I saw looked more like hypothermic death to my eye.

The house seemed small for a lake property. Bigger than a cottage; smaller than a beachfront McMansion. Where Andy and I come from, lake property means big money.

We stepped out of the rented Chevy Malibu into a silence undercut by the sound of weak waves kissing the shore less than fifty yards away. The house commanded a stark view of the water. Winter-naked trees formed a ring around a small yard. The cold air seemed cleansed by a combination of the temperature and the proximity of the lake.

The homeowner stepped onto the front porch as we approached the door. The last time someone met us like this, in Montana, the greeter carried a rifle. At the time, Andy didn't think much of that effort and plowed ahead. This time she stopped.

"Can I help you folks?" It wasn't a friendly question. We could see both hands, thumbs hooked into the hip pockets of blue jeans, but that didn't mean he wasn't carrying a concealed weapon under his thick down jacket. Andy unbuttoned her coat.

He looked old to me. Fifty or sixty seems like a long way off to someone working his way through thirty-three. But this gentleman wore fifty or sixty like eighty. He looked worn, and troubled.

"Mr. Reichenbach?" Andy asked.

"Who wants to know?"

"Detective Andrea Stewart of the Essex Police Department."

Using gray eyes under thinning hair, he fixed a wary stare on Andy.

"City of Essex, Wisconsin," Andrea said. "May I have a few minutes of your time?"

"What can I do for you?" It wasn't an offer.

"Could we talk inside?"

"Nope."

Andy considered the impasse, studied him now as an adversary, and adjusted her demeanor.

"Mr. Reichenbach, are you the owner of Reichenbach Builders?"

"Nope."

"That's not what my information says."

He didn't answer. To be fair, it wasn't a question.

"*Were* you the owner of Reichenbach Builders?"

"Once. Not anymore."

"When did you sell?"

"None of your business."

"Mr. Reichenbach," Andy said, taking a step forward. "I'm here making a general inquiry in an investigation that might have nothing to do with you or your company. But if you aren't a little more helpful, you will pique my interest and suddenly you and your company will become a much more focused part of my investigation. Now, I have a few simple questions. And so far, your reluctance to answer them is far more interesting to me than your answers. Care to try this again?"

"I told you. It's not my company. I'm retired. Sold the business two months ago. My wife and I live here alone. I got nothing to do with the business anymore. If you have questions, ask the new owners."

"And who are the new owners?"

He tipped his head back slightly, working his jaw but not speaking. If he'd been a man chewing tobacco, he would have spit.

"It's a simple question."

"Go look it up." He turned halfway, then looked at us one more time. "We're done here."

"No, we're not," Andy took another step closer. "Did your company install plumbing for schools? Public pools?"

"Talk to the new owners."

He showed us his back, pulled open the door to the house, and disappeared inside.

Andy stared after him for a minute—at the vacant glass between us and him. Long enough to let him know, if he looked back out at her, that this wasn't finished. His face did not appear at any of the windows.

Andy turned and flashed a let's-go gesture my way. We headed back toward the car.

From the corner of the house, a woman marched across the snow. She wore a skirt over heavy boots. A thick, gray woolen coat wrapped her upper body, and a scarf covered her hair. She wore no gloves against the cold. She used her hands to hold her coat together. Her general fashion statement said post-World War II refugee. She trudged across the snow on an angle that intercepted us near the car.

"Do you know the Meijer store?" she asked urgently. Her face, like his, wore years beyond her years.

"Yes," Andy lied.

"Buy some bananas at three o'clock."

She turned around and hurried back the way she came.

Andy and I watched her disappear around the edge of the house.

"Okay, that's the weirdest damned thing yet," I said.

"We better call Pidge. I think we're going to be here overnight."

Yes! I liked the idea. Because an overnight left little chance of making it to an eight a.m. appointment with Stephenson.

I pulled out my phone as we climbed into the car.

25

"Did you know these are locally grown bananas?" I pointed at the pile of yellow fruit. "That's what the slogan says."

"Right. Just like the mangos and pineapples. Grown right here in the tropical forests of Upper Michigan."

"Advertising can't lie, right?"

We pushed a cart through the produce section of the store like a married couple. I resisted the impulse to grab some limes, an impulse driven by the memory of breakfast Corona's that had suffered their absence.

"Is that her?" Andy asked. I followed her gaze up the aisle.

The store sprawled; a big box solution to shopping for anything and everything from bananas to car parts. I'm not a fan of the big box. It spawns images in my mind of billionaires sitting in darkness, grinning. The woman powered an empty cart down the wide aisle toward us.

"Looks like her," I said. If we had any doubt, it evaporated when she locked eyes with Andy. As soon as she did, the woman shot a worried look over her shoulder.

"Seriously?" I asked Andy out of the side of my mouth. "Are we passing secrets through the Berlin Wall?"

We waited by the bananas. She rolled up and stopped. If she reached five feet tall, it required heels. Her hair hung gray and lifeless beneath a scarf. Her face wore the same tortured look as her husband. Retirement did not look good on either of them. Desperation tugged at the lines on this woman's face.

"Mrs. Reichenbach?" Andy asked. She nodded. "I'm Detective Andrea Stewart. This is my husband, Will."

She shook hands with each of us. Her fingers felt fragile in my hand.

"Are you here about Caroline?" she asked urgently.

"Possibly," Andy said. The woman's desperation turned to tortured hope.

"Please, tell me, is she alright?"

Andy took a surprisingly harsh tone. "Ma'am, I'm not answering any questions until you answer mine." The tough tactic struck me as a gamble, but it worked. The poor woman shrank a little, but did not flee. Andy said, "Let's go somewhere and talk."

"Oh, no! I have to do the shopping. This is all the time I have." She looked over her shoulder again. "Allen is here. Allen will not like it if he sees me speaking to you."

Andy shifted gears.

"Fair enough. First question; why did your husband sell his company?"

"They made him."

"Who made him?"

"I don't know! People came in September. They wanted to buy the company. Allen wouldn't sell, of course. He loved his company and all his employees." Her eyes lingered on a memory. "Now it's all gone. They're all gone."

"How did they make him sell his company?"

She looked at Andy as if she should already know the answer. "Our granddaughter! Isn't that why you're here?"

"Answer my questions, Ma'am," Andy ordered her. It jarred the woman.

"When Allen wouldn't sell, they told us Caroline worked for them. They hired her."

"Doing what?"

"As a hostess at a restaurant. In Chicago," she said. "Caroline was so excited about it." She made it sound sad.

"These people, the ones who bought your husband's business—they own a restaurant? Where your granddaughter works?"

"I don't know! I guess! They came to our home. One day after Allen told them no, some men came to our home. With pictures. Hor—horrible pictures. Of Caroline. They said they gave her that date drug—that rape drug. And they took pictures. They told us if we told anyone, the next time they would do things to her. Or she wouldn't wake up. They said if we told Caroline, they would take her and put her to work doing—doing —" The woman put a fist to her lips, unable to speak the words. "All they wanted was to buy the company. Sell it, they said, and they would leave her alone. Leave us alone."

"Why didn't you tell your granddaughter to quit? To leave?"

"Oh, they thought of that! Go ahead, they said. Talk to her. Take her away. Tell the police. They said they would wait find her. No matter where she went, no matter how long it took. They said they were watching us and they would simply wait and then do everything that they promised."

"Did you have an attorney involved in the sale?"

She made a sound that was meant to be a laugh but didn't get past her lips as anything more than a choked moan.

"Our attorney called us and told us he had a conflict of interest. Thirty-five years of paying him and he said he had to drop us. The coward told us over the phone. They scared him off. Or paid him off. They made Allen sign everything by himself."

"There has to be a record. Names. Documents. Filings. Does your husband have copies?"

She shook her head. "They gave us a bill of sale marked Paid."

"Did they pay you?"

"Practically nothing! Not even enough to cover our debts."

"A check?"

"Cash. Cash all wrapped up in plastic."

She stood on the verge of tears.

"They told us if we ever said anything—what they would do. To Caroline. To us."

"What about Caroline's parents? Did you warn them?"

"Our daughter—Caroline's mother—she passed six years ago. Her father, he's been—distant. He doesn't speak to us. Caroline is all the family we have."

And easily isolated, I thought.

"What was the name? The name of the company making the offer. There has to be something."

She shook her head.

"They were always confusing about it. M Engineering one time. Then M Construction, it said, on the bill of sale."

"Was there an address?"

"Allen looked them up on the Google. And the maps. The Google had no information, and the address was fake—just an empty nothing in Illinois. Allen found pictures. But there was one time…" she fought with herself, deciding whether to tell this part or not. "There was one time, when Allen signed their papers, one of them called somewhere. I wear hearing aids, and sometimes I turn them up, and I can hear better." She gave us a look that told us she meant eavesdrop. "One of them called their office and a woman answered and said 'something Midwestern Central something.' That's all I remember. Midwestern Central."

"What about the land? The building and the land?"

"No. They didn't want it. But the bill of sale includes a thirty-year lease of the building and land. What are we supposed to do?"

She dug into her purse. She pulled out a folded piece of paper and clutched it, struggling to decide whether to surrender it to us or not.

"Now you answer my questions," she demanded, finding strength.

"I'll try." Andy softened her tone.

"Why did you come to our house?"

I thought Andy might evade the question with vague on-going-investigation talk, but instead she said, "There's a young girl. She was threatened, in a way very much like your granddaughter. We made a connection to your husband's business, but we had no idea what you've gone through. We didn't know anything about your husband selling the business."

"You don't know anything about Caroline?!"

"Not until you told us."

"If you don't know anything, then what good are you?" She jammed the paper back in her purse and tried to push the cart around Andy. "I have to do the shopping. Please leave us alone!"

"Have you talked to the police?" Andy grabbed her sleeve.

She shook Andy off.

"Yes. Just now. See what good it did!"

She launched her cart forward. Andy side-stepped like a matador, but then closed her hand around the woman's arm in a harsh grip. Mrs. Reichenbach uttered a squeaky gasp. For a moment I thought she might scream and create a scene. Andy flipped back to the harsh tone.

"Listen to me." She held the woman's arm. The woman cowered. Andy relaxed her grip but didn't let go. Leaning closer, in a much softer tone, Andy said, "Listen carefully to me. We don't know anything about the sale of the company, or who extorted you, but what they did was criminal. The people who did this to you are people we're after for something entirely different. We intend to destroy them. That's the only way to ensure your granddaughter's safety—and yours."

"NO! You can't! They'll think we sent you!" She struggled to pull her arm free.

"We can. And we will. We will destroy them. A moment ago, you were going to give us information about your granddaughter, weren't you?" Andy gestured at the purse. "Weren't you?"

"I thought you were here because you already knew. But you don't know, and you need to leave us alone!"

"That's not going to happen. We're going after these people no matter what. When we do, they will think you sent us, and they will hurt Caroline. So, my advice to you is that you tell us where to find her. We will get her out of the way. We will keep her safe. And we will make certain they never go after her, or anyone else, ever again. But if you don't tell us—they could hurt her before we can get to her. That will be your fault, not mine."

The woman stared at Andy, wide-eyed, terrified. She held her hand clamped over the top of her purse.

"Let us get Caroline away from these people. You would have done it yourself if you could have. But they're watching you."

Mrs. Reichenbach nodded firmly.

"Let me get to Caroline. Without them knowing. They're watching for you to try. They will never see us coming. *You* didn't see us coming."

Andy pointed at the purse with her eyes.

Mrs. Reichenbach's lips trembled. Her eyes fell as Andy's had, and she released her grip on the purse. She reached in and pulled out the folded paper and handed it to Andy.

Andy unfolded it. Inside, she found a photograph, a small head shot, a school picture. The paper had notes on it. An address.

"*This—this is Caroline,*" the girl's grandmother whispered. "This is where she is working. This is her address. Please get her away from them! She won't want to go. She thinks she has a good job. She doesn't know what they did to her. You have to make her leave!"

Handing the photo and notes to Andy took the strength out of the woman. Andy tightened her grip on the woman's arm to steady her.

"*Oh—oh what have I done? Oh—I—!*"

Andy leaned close to her ear and spoke. "You gave us the best chance of saving your granddaughter's life."

No moment is as terrifying in a crisis as the moment within reach of salvation. Fear lit the woman's sunken eyes.

Andy released her arm. Mrs. Reichenbach pushed the cart forward but could not stop turning her head to look at us. Not until she moved out of sight.

"What the hell?" I looked at Andy.

Andy folded the paper over the photo and slipped it into her pocket.

"We have to go."

26

I n the big box lot, behind the wheel, Andy's thoughts bubbled up.

"Why does anyone extort someone to sell a company, a building and plumbing company, and then simply shut it down? It sounded like the thing was a profitable going concern."

"They wanted something. Got it. And dumped the rest."

"The rest being all the equipment, supplies and employees? What else is there?"

"Shower nozzles? Maybe they needed the parts, so they could install the cameras."

Andy shook her head. "Those were stock parts. American Plumbing Supply catalog part number—oh, crud—I had the part number memorized. Trying to impress you. Anyway, you can buy them online. It makes no sense. Anybody can do that. Buy a bunch of shower nozzles, gut them, stick in some circuitry and a camera, and there you go."

"I see your point. And what's that business about a thirty-year lease?"

"It means there's no record of a property transfer with the Register of Deeds office," Andy explained. "It means the tax bill goes to the Reichenbachs."

"Would any of this stand up in court?"

"None of it. But if Reichenbach makes any move to attack the sale, his granddaughter pays the price. It's pure extortion, but it works because the only people who can report it won't."

Andy's phone buzzed loudly. She uses a ring tone that sounds like a transmission eating itself from within. Hard to miss.

"Chief," she put it on speaker as she drove and handed it to me to hold up between us.

"I just spent the last hour with the kid's mother blubbering in my office. I'm going to have to clean the carpet, fer chrissakes," Tom Ceeves growled. His voice reminded me of Andy's ring tone. "Guess what she gave me?"

"Carpet mold?" I offered.

"Hey, Will. No. She came in here to try and make a deal for her baby douche bag. She told me her kid got the picture from his cousin."

"I thought they hired a lawyer," Andy said.

"They did," Tom said. "They got that guy on TV. The one who's always on the morning news. 'Forget the rest. Call the best.'"

"I hate that guy," I said.

"I hate those 'Billion Dollar Boys' more."

"Yeah, they suck, too."

Andy ignored the two of us.

"Chief," she said. "Where's the cousin?"

"I think you already have that figured out, Detective."

We looked at each other.

"Can you text me the name and address?"

"Yup. But it might not do you much good. The mom told me she had a huge fight with her husband about coming to see me. The husband is the one who wants the kid to shut up and let the lawyer do all the talking. When the mom stopped crying long enough, she told me that her husband got it out of the kid last night that the picture came from the cousin, who comes from hubby's side of the family. His brother's kid, or some such."

"Doesn't matter, as long as we got the guy," I said.

"Except mom also told me that her hubby called the cousin and warned him someone would be coming."

"Shit!" Andy spat the word out. "He'll destroy any evidence. When did he warn him? How long ago?"

"Best guess is around ten, this morning."

"Shit!" Andy rapped the steering wheel. "Text me what you have."

27

"Justin Erickson! Open up!" Andy pounded on the apartment door. The numeral 8 hung in brassy plastic above the peep hole. The plastic wiggled when Andy pounded. "Police!"

I had offered to check the windows first. Erickson lived in a second-floor apartment. A little exterior reconnaissance would have been easy.

"Don't bother," she said. "We're long past hoping to find anything, unless the guy is an idiot—which I really shouldn't rule out." Anger undercut her tone.

"Any thoughts on calling in local law enforcement."

"It's the Delta County Sheriff's office and that would be a brilliant idea, and proper protocol, and just down-right courteous—exactly the thing I would want someone doing, instead of marauding around in my jurisdiction—Justin Erickson! We know you're in there! Open up!" She hammered the door. "Except this is all going to do us ZERO good—because that dumbass dad gave the guy a hundred-mile head start."

A voice behind us interrupted Andy's rant. "He's not in there."

We both turned.

"He's not in there," the woman repeated. Young. A little on the heavier side. She wore a nice dress under a thick sweater. She looked like someone who either just returned home or was just about to leave for work. I checked the time. Just after four. I guessed the former. She stood in the open doorway across the hall. "Are you really cops?"

Andy flashed her badge, but not for long enough to read the Essex Police Department embossing.

"Do you know if he's been here in the last few hours?"

"I just got home from work, but he's been in the process of moving out for weeks now. I don't know why it's taking him so long. He keeps talking about it. Once in a while he loads up a bunch of stuff in his car and he'll be gone for a few days. He's all—*I'm getting out of this dinky town* —and all about—*I'm going to live in Chicago.* Like I'm supposed to be impressed. You know, there are people who like Escanaba," she insisted. "How many murders are there in Escanaba, I ask you."

"Was he here today?" Andy repeated the question.

"I don't know. I had to work," the young woman said. "I think he's almost done packing. Last time I went in to feed his cat, it was almost bare in there."

"You can get in?" Andy asked.

"Sure. I feed his cat when he's gone. Hang on a sec."

She disappeared, then reappeared a moment later with a fat wad of keys in her hand. "I teach music in the school district," she said. "I need forty different keys to get in all the different buildings and rooms and cabinets."

Wad notwithstanding, she deftly pulled the right key, inserted it in Erickson's lock and twisted. The lock released. She pushed the door open for us.

"Is he in some sort of trouble?"

"Do you know him?"

"I guess so. We date. A little. Not much lately. Just a friend thing."

"What does he do?"

"Computers. I think he does freelance IT work. Network engineer, I think he said."

"Would you wait out here, please?" Andy pressed the young woman back into the hall and moved to enter first. She unbuttoned her coat but refrained from drawing her weapon.

Cat smell announced itself at the threshold. Erickson, if he was moving, wasn't getting his security deposit back.

The apartment was a studio. The neighbor's assessment seemed accurate. Except for a few pieces of worthless furniture, next to nothing filled the available space. An open box of books lay on the floor. A pile of clothing occupied one end of a cheap sofa. Andy probed the living space and kitchen, checked the bathroom—including a swipe of the closed shower curtain. She searched the empty bedroom. She returned with a scowl on her face.

I pointed at the top of a cheap, scarred desk in the corner of the apartment. A surge protector sat on the wood surface. Its cord snaked behind the desk. A coaxial cable lay under the desk, connected to the wall.

No computer.

"He might not be coming back." The neighbor's voice came from behind us again. She had followed us into the apartment.

"Why?" Andy wanted to know.

"He took Muggle," she said. "His cat. The cat box is gone."

28

"Nuts!" Andy muttered.

"Language, Dee."

She steered the rental car out of town and drove to the Comfort Inn adjacent to the airport.

I let her marinate her thoughts. After a while, her expression softened. I know how my wife processes adversity. She chews on it, mauls it, knocks it into a shape that takes new meaning and points her in a new direction. When it yields a new path, it is forgiven for being adversity.

Pidge texted Andy that she had booked two rooms, and that she could now be found at the Texas Roadhouse across the street. By the time Andy and I collected our key card and marched to our room, she seemed to have moved on from the missed chance to find the cousin.

Our overnight bags waited in the room for us.

Andy used the bathroom first, then let me. When I finished, I found her sprawled on the bed with her cell phone on speaker, looking like a teenaged girl talking to her bestie. She reminded me of Lane and Sarah.

Greg LeMore lectured on the benefits of a Faraday Cage.

"... fully protected so I can set up a complete Wi-Fi simulation and got it thinking it's talking to the school Wi-Fi, and hence to the web. Phoning home. Of course, it's not getting through, but I wrote a log program to track its efforts. I'm logging and back tracking the IP addresses it's trying to contact. Persistent little shit."

"Can you get a geographic location on whoever it's trying to talk to?"

"No. And yes. And no. The short answer is that the internet isn't quite as anonymous as people think. Everything has an address. Somewhere. The long answer involves the nature of IP addresses, the service providers who shield them from law enforcement like us, and different ways people mask addresses, or hide them. I don't want to make any promises, but I'm working on it. I can tell you one IP address. I found it in some of the code —I think it was used for testing."

"Let me guess. Escanaba, Michigan."

"Bingo. But that's old code. Commented out."

"What about the hardware? Anything interesting?"

"No, but that's what's interesting about it. It's not custom made. Nothing but off-the-shelf components."

"Is that good?"

"It is good. Off-the-shelf means we can find the shelf. Your department can cook up a warrant for shipping and order records. The source probably sends out a zillion of these things, but you know how it works. From a list we might find somebody connected. Like a building supply company in Escanaba."

"Maybe. But I would also be interested in shipments going to Chicago."

"Chicago..." LeMore didn't ask why. "Listen, we might want to put these puppies back where we found them and turn on the Wi-Fi again."

"Um, I know at least one school superintendent who is going to launch some serious resistance to that suggestion. May I ask why?"

"Two reasons," LeMore said. I slid onto the bed beside Andy and ran my fingers up and down her spine. From the way she flexed her shoulders, I knew she appreciated the effort. "First, having them pop back online will put the owners at ease. They're probably getting paranoid. Our broken Wi-Fi router bit may not last long. I'm not sure how long our target misdirection—"

"Fixation," I chimed in.

"—is going to keep them from thinking we know," LeMore finished.

"And second?"

"Well, I might know a guy, who knows a guy, who might be able to give me a little code I can introduce to the software running these cameras. A little worm that can do some traveling, hitch a ride with the images, maybe nest somewhere, and maybe report back to me when it gets all comfy. It's above my skill set, and the sort of thing that requires a court order if you ever plan to use it in court, but like I said, I know a guy…"

"How long would that take? Once you move them back to live?"

"Nanoseconds. As soon as we turn them back on, it would do its thing."

Andy considered the scenario. "Could we turn them on, let them send a few more shots of our janitor, and deliver the worm?"

"Yes."

"How long do you need for the 'guy' to do his thing?"

"He's working on it now. I may have something tonight."

I liked LeMore. Better to ask forgiveness than permission.

"Do it. I'll have Tom run interference with Superintendent Glower. Maybe we can shut down the locker room for a day or two. Clean for mold, or something."

"Andrea," LeMore said. "If what I suggested, about a broadcast, is correct—well, Principal Allison told me the school has a swim meet this Thursday. That sounds like a deadline, but it might be an opportunity."

"I hear you."

I made a you-can't-be-serious face but held my tongue.

"One more thing," LeMore said. "I might have bogarted your investigation. I called Chief Schultz and brought him up to speed."

"I don't have a problem with that," Andy said. "He was kind to loan you out to us."

"I asked him to involve Crimes Against Minors. You did some good work with them on the Franklin case, and they respect you. I asked him to ask them to see if there have been any sex crimes against young, female athletes. Local, statewide, and beyond if they can. Just testing the profile."

"Greg are you thinking this is bigger than Essex?"

"Just a hunch. I hope you're okay with that."

"I'll take all the help we can get. And speaking of…there's something I need."

"Shoot."

"Who do you know in Chicago?"

Andy gave LeMore the abbreviated version of Reichenbach's business sale and the meeting at the banana stand. She pulled the folded paper from her pocket and read the details as LeMore took them from her.

"Any chance of getting someone to find her?"

"Deputy Chief Schultz has more pull with Chicago PD than I do. He's got a brother there."

"I'll send you the photo. I don't know, Greg, even if Reichenbach had nothing to do with the cameras, if half of what the woman told us is true, we need to get this girl out of the path of whatever is coming. After that, maybe we can get Delta County in on this. Maybe they can open an investigation into this extortion business with Reichenbach."

"Right. Lemme see what I can do."

She clicked off the call. After a moment of contemplation, she rolled onto her back and propped one arm behind her head. Her hair formed a rich, dark frame around her face. I got a smile, which spun off a thrill inside me.

"You hungry?" she asked.

"For what?"

"Food," she shook her head at my one-track mind.

"And after?" I stayed on my one track.

"After, Pilot, a little breaking and entering."

29

"SCRAM," I said.

Andy looked at the propulsion unit in my hand and the pride on my face. Her expression could only have been more skeptical if the propeller had been mounted on my head.

"Special Creation Rendering Aerial Maneuverability," I said proudly.

She filled her lungs, counted to ten, rolled her eyes. I'm not sure what else she has in the repertoire, but if we'd had more time, I think she would have shown me.

"No," she announced. "I'm not calling it a SCRAM. And just so you know, I'm *really* not looking forward to this. It's cold out there!"

I flashed her a grin and handed her the ski goggles. I pocketed the SCRAM and two of its twins for backup. When I plan for a flight, I like a healthy fuel reserve.

She looked around the Pizza Hut parking lot. The lot lay at the edge of town. Measured as we crows fly it was the public lot nearest to the Reichenbach Building property. Even at that we had a solid mile to cover. Parking in Reichenbach's big empty lot would have made the rental stand out unacceptably. She might be a cop, but that didn't give her a pass for breaking and entering. Being out of jurisdiction added icing to the scoff-law cake.

We slotted the rental among half a dozen cars. The lot seemed clear of potential observers. I checked my watch. Almost six-thirty.

"You ready?" I asked.

"No," she said unhappily. "Let's do it anyway."

Andy slipped her badge off her belt and tucked it in the small shoulder satchel she used for a purse.

"Give me your wallet," she held out her hand. I complied, pulling the small collection of cash from it first and stuffing the bills in my pants pocket. She dropped the wallet in the satchel and slid it under the front passenger seat. We climbed out of the car, and I jogged around to her side. We locked the rental and double-checked the parking lot. All clear. She adjusted the ski goggles over her eyes. I pulled her into an embrace. We traded a kiss. Our goggles bumped awkwardly.

Fwooomp! We disappeared. My insides shifted as weightlessness took effect. My feet lost contact with the ground.

"Eeee!" I heard her say, close to my ear. She pulled herself tighter.

"Did you just say 'Eeee'?"

"Shut up."

I pulled a now-vanished SCRAM unit from my pocket, held it vertically and pushed off with my toes. Andy pulled even tighter.

"Dee, I still need to breathe. And you're not heavy. In fact, you've lost a lot of weight. To be precise…all of it. Just keep a grip on me."

We rose slowly. I thumbed the slide control on the SCRAM unit. I opened the power to a low growl. We immediately accelerated upward.

"*Ohmygodomygodomygod…*" Andy chanted urgently in my ear.

I wanted to laugh, but held it in.

"Why are you going so high?" she demanded.

"We're not even above the Pizza Hut roof yet!"

"That's high enough!"

I continued the climb. "Wires, Dee. We need to get higher than the power lines or you and I might acquire a sudden suntan."

She made a noise merging a muted scream with an angry growl. I ignored her. She tightened her grip.

We rose. The streets fell away. The streetlights dropped below us. I had my eye on a set of power lines running along the highway. I watched them sink below our level. At that point, I angled the SCRAM unit and shifted to forward motion. The propulsion unit buzzed. Andy faced me with both arms around my chest. Her fingers dug into my shoulder blades. I held a light grip around her waist with my left arm.

"Hey!" she said suddenly.

"What?"

"I'm not cold!" I felt her head move beside me.

"We're flying like a couple of fairies, and you're amazed because you're not cold?"

"Did you know about this?"

We flew parallel to the highway. Cars followed cones of headlight in both directions. The winter landscape caught the spilled glow of street-lights, but we were nearing the end of public light. Beyond it, the white spread beneath stars, seeping into forest. Black leafless trees extended infinitely into the Upper Michigan peninsula.

"I did," I said. "I planned to surprise you with it Saturday night. I thought we'd go for a flight in the snow."

"Aww," she cooed appreciatively. "You really know how to scare the shit out of a girl."

She poked her face in my direction until it made contact, then kissed my cheek.

"I don't think making out under these circumstances would be very easy," she noted.

"Oh, beg to disagree!" I'd been thinking about that—trying to find a way to broach the subject.

"Forget it," she read my mind.

We cruised on.

The streetlights ended. We followed the highway another half-mile, then made a turn. Reichenbach Builders slid closer, a black rectangle nestled beside a much larger black rectangle. The parking lot spread out white and empty, virginal except for the tire tracks Andy and I made earlier in the day, and maybe one or two other sets, which I took for vain attempts at deliveries.

The chain-link fence we peered through on our first visit confined a square roughly two acres in size. Vans, trucks, equipment, and stacks of building materials covered most of the property. Even at fire sale prices, there had to be several million dollars' worth of equipment. I understood someone stealing it from Reichenbach but couldn't fathom it being left to rust.

"I want to get into the office. I think the best way is through the warehouse," Andy said. I felt her turning her head, examining the property as we approached.

"Let's do a circle and see what's in back."

I checked for power lines, antennas, and other obstacles. Finding nothing threatening, I angled the SCRAM unit into a descent. We dropped out of the night sky and scribing a slow circle around the structures. The north side of the building had solid walls. Curving west, around the back, we found two loading docks, each with overhead doors pulled shut. A man-sized entrance stood between the big doors atop a set of concrete steps.

The south side of the building bordered the utility vehicle lot with a wall containing two large overhead doors. Bigger than hangar doors.

All openings to the building were closed. I had expected outdoor security lights at the front and back, but the property lay dark.

"Back door," Andy said. I agreed. We swept around again, but this time I slowed as we descended. Trying to show off a bit, I made a nice gliding approach to one of the loading bays. I gave the SCRAM unit a shot of reverse thrust. We stopped perfectly. My toes touched the concrete.

Fwooomp! We reappeared. Andy dropped a bit more than I did, but neither of us lost our footing on the snow.

She gathered herself, then stood gaping at me for a moment.

"What?" I wondered, as I often do, what I had done wrong. She should have been impressed as hell with our perfect landing.

"I don't know if I can wrap my mind around what we just did, Will." She shook her head. "Is this starting to feel normal to you?"

I shrugged. I pulled off my ski goggles and reached out. She handed me hers. I stuffed them in my flight jacket pocket.

"A little."

She said nothing. She turned and considered the warehouse door.

The loading dock extended as a lip from the building. Andy went to the man-sized door and studied the deadbolt lock.

"Can you do your lock trick on this?"

"Step aside, young lady."

Fwooomp! I vanished and grabbed the door handle. The handle had no lock, but a deadbolt above it ran through the jamb. I put my palm over the deadbolt and *pushed* the levers in my head forward. Like liquid, the effect spread outward from my palm, over the deadbolt and over part of the metal door. As it spread, we could see through the door to the dark interior of the warehouse—like opening a porthole. When the effect reached the jamb, it created a frayed border where the bolt penetrated the faceplate. I pulled on the handle. A soft tug and snap, and the door swung open. The bolt, severed, fell out of the faceplate, and tinkled across the concrete floor into darkness.

Andy made an educated guess where I was and clamped her hand on my arm.

"Let me," she said, edging past me. She held her right hand on the grip of her service weapon.

Fwooomp! I reappeared and fell in step behind her.

The warehouse loomed above and around us, black corners filled with black objects. The center lay open and empty. Starlight, filtered by snow-covered skylights, produced shadows. I made out toolboxes, cabinets, and parked vehicles. Again, I wondered about the value of the assets in the building, and why it seemed the new owners had simply walked away from a thriving business.

Because there's more money to be made.

At what? I wondered.

I thought Andy might pull out her phone and use it as a flashlight, but she didn't. My eyes adjusted to the black. We crossed the floor, stepping over thick compressor hoses that snaked their way over the concrete. We found a door to the front office. The smell changed from steel and oil to musty carpeting as we entered a short hallway. In a few steps, we stood in what was left of the front office.

It had been stripped bare. File drawers hung open. Desktops were cleared. I saw shoebox-sized computer battery backup units under the desks, but the cords that ran from them lay unattached. Bulletin boards still held notices and cards. A map with pins occupied one wall. Shelves lay empty and cupboards, the doors ajar, hung barren.

Andy stood in the center of the space, turning slowly. After a moment, she spotted a door, went to it, and opened it. I followed. The room beyond the door was black and felt empty. I heard her jacket rustle, then blinked when she turned on the flashlight app on her phone.

A single empty server rack stood against one wall. Knots of Cat 5 cable lay on the floor. Pieces of cellophane wrap lay underfoot.

"Server room," Andy said, looking around. "A lot of server rack space for a building company. And look." She pointed at indentations in the carpeting. "This wasn't a server room until recently. This was an office."

I stood in the doorway as she checked the empty rack. She took interest in a rough hole cut in one of the walls, where cables snaked in and out of the room.

As she peered at the hole, a heavy hand clamped down on the collar of my flight jacket and jerked me backward. Something hard and metallic poked me in the back of the head. From the pressure on my skull and the cold, metallic touch, I took it for the barrel of a gun.

A flashlight, stronger than Andy's phone, lit up the room. Andy jumped to her feet. Her hands moved on instinct. She pulled back her jacket and reached for her service weapon.

"Stop!" A voice behind me said. "Pull it out with your fingertips and drop it to the floor." To emphasize the point, the heavy hand jerked my collar.

Andy put her free hand out flat, in a gesture of compliance. She could see what I couldn't, which I presumed to be a pistol pointed at my head.

She eased her Glock from its holster, using her fingertips. She crouched and lowered it toward the floor. Instead of dropping it on the floor, she slid it onto the bottom shelf of the server rack. She gave it an extra push.

"This way," the voice commanded. He pulled me backward out of the room. Andy followed slowly. I saw her flick her phone light off.

"Drop the phone, too," the voice told her. She crouched and let it fall to the floor. I thought of mine, still in my hip pocket.

He pulled me backward into the center of the main room. My nerves tightened. My breath felt choppy in my chest. Andy stared at whoever stood behind me.

The notion of disappearing ran through my mind. It might confuse the guy long enough for me to move aside, turn, get a grip on the gun, or poke his eyes. Or he might just continue to hold me by the neck of my jacket and pull the trigger. Shoot first, figure it out later. My wife repeatedly tells me people are only faster than bullets in the movies.

The hand on my collar released, but the weapon remained pressed to the bottom of my skull. I heard nylon rustle, then a phone beep, then a phone ringing.

"What?"

"Somebody's poking around in here. I got 'em."

"We're on our way in. Bring them to the loading dock."

Another beep as the connection severed. I tried a turn of the head to get a look, but the hand returned to snag my collar, and I received another jerk of the neck and poke from the gun barrel as a warning.

"You first, through there, outside," he said. A man of few words. Andy followed whatever gesture he gave her and led us back down the short hallway to the warehouse door.

Back in the warehouse, we formed a processional across the floor to the loading dock door. Andy opened it for us. We stepped onto the snow-covered platform.

Headlights washed the yard, projecting geometric shadows from the chain-link fence. A silver SUV nosed up to the gate as someone dressed heavily against the cold pushed the gate open. The SUV pulled through and parked at the steps beside the dock. The man who opened the gate jogged across the work yard to a larger vehicle, a flatbed truck. He climbed aboard without clearing the snow from the vehicle. A few seconds later, a diesel engine cranked over and fired. Holding the door open to see, the driver maneuvered the truck forward, did a Y-turn, and backed up to the dock, briefly bathing us in brake-light red. The flatbed stopped a foot and a half from the dock wall. The deck of the truck bed aligned slightly below the lip of the dock. Brakes squealed briefly.

Both vehicles killed their lights. We adjusted to the starlight again, a world rendered in black and white with only gray shades between.

The driver of the flatbed hopped up on the dock and disappeared inside the warehouse. I heard the latches snap on the roll-up door. A moment later, the door clattered open.

Two men emerged from the SUV. I still couldn't see the one behind me. He held a tight grip on my collar and seemed to want to push the muzzle of his pistol through the knotty vertebrae at the base of my skull. Andy stood to my right. We both faced outward. I've seen her tense before. This looked worse. Her hands hung at her sides with her fingers splayed slightly, looking like claws ready to rip something. Her lower lip extended, telling me she had her jaw locked. She worked her eyes from one man to the next, imprinting their faces in her mind.

One of the two men from the SUV wore a suit, tie, and overcoat. He stepped onto the snow-covered lot and surveyed the yard. He looked up at us. Medium build, with neatly trimmed short, light-colored hair. He studied Andy and me with pale eyes and lines creasing his brow.

After a moment he climbed the concrete steps and stood facing me. I smelled peppermint. He worked a candy around in his mouth. Early forties, I guessed. Bad acne as a kid, and now at a station in life where he didn't give a crap if you noticed it or not—or maybe if you did, you would wish you hadn't. His eyes were cold, and I hated him for moving those dead orbs up and down Andy.

"Who the fuck are you?" he asked in a voice that carried an accent not found at anchor desks on the evening news.

"Collections," I spoke up quickly. "These guys owe us a ton of money and it's been weeks with nobody answering our calls. We thought we'd come and have a look for ourselves."

I glanced at Andy. Her expression gave no hint of her thoughts.

The man in the suit squeezed his lips together, making shallow mounds at the corners of his mouth. He nodded at the story, looked down at his shoes, and then back up at us.

"Justin!" he called out.

Someone new slid out of the SUV. Overweight, greasy haired and looking self-important, Justin Erickson responded quickly to the man facing me.

The man with the accent asked, "Who the fuck are these people?"

"Cops!" Justin called back to his boss. "That's gotta be the two cops my neighbor told me about." He heaved himself up the concrete steps. "She called to tell me two cops—a man and a woman—were poking around my place. Gotta be."

I guessed that the neighbor wanted to remain more than friends with Justin. Thanks a lot.

We got pursed lips and a nod from Suit and Tie.

"Cops doing collection work," he mused. I expected a clever remark, but he didn't offer one.

The driver of the flatbed, a powerful-looking man, appeared in the dock doorway. He added to the impression of strength by carrying a fifty-five-gallon steel drum in his arms. He passed between me and Andy and hopped across the gap between the truck bed and the dock. He dropped the drum onto the snow-covered flatbed. It landed with a hollow *bong!* Empty. He looked at Suit and Tie for instructions.

"Open it," Suit and Tie ordered.

The barrel carrier worked the rim clamp loose and pulled off the cover. A second man in Carhart overalls joined him. I did the math. Two on the truck. Mikey behind me. Suit and Tie to my left. The overweight, out-of-shape computer geek cousin behind Suit and Tie.

"Mikey, did you search this moke?"

Mikey, holding onto my collar, hesitated.

"Well, don't you think you should?"

Mikey moved fast, having been caught in a rookie mistake and wanting to make amends. He held the pistol to my head but released my neck and worked his hands around my chest, down my sides. When he hit my pockets, he jerked out the SCRAM units, looked at them, and tossed them to the concrete. He pulled my phone out and I heard it clatter and break somewhere. He tossed both pairs of ski goggles to the ground. He stroked up and down my pants legs looking for a weapon.

"Good. Now her."

Suit and Tie reached inside his jacket lapel and pulled a small, black semi-automatic pistol from a holster. "It's alright. I got this one." He pointed the pistol at me.

Mikey moved to Andy. He made a show of searching her, groping her, squeezing her. It drew smirks from the man on the truck. She stood frozen, impassive. Andy held her eyes on the man holding a gun on me.

I forged a white-hot hatred for Mikey as he pawed Andy.

"Hey, asshole!" Mikey paused and looked up at me. I spoke just above a whisper. "I will see you dead."

Suit and Tie said nothing. Mikey grinned and went back to pawing my wife, who shook her head at me. The one item he found, the keys to the rental, he tossed into the snow on the platform.

"Okay, okay," Suit and Tie said. "Enough. Let me ask you again, who the fuck are you?"

"FBI, special taskforce," I said. "Lead team surveilling this facility. Now might be a good time to surrender. You're being watched."

Suit and Tie stepped directly in front of me and looked at me with narrowed eyes, sending tiny clouds of peppermint into the cold air with each breath. "You're a bit of a wise ass, aren't you? I'd threaten yer girl here, if I thought it would settle you down, but honest—she looks like she's ready to claw me eyes out." I made the accent. Irish. "I've seen her type. Tougher than the lot of us together."

"You have no idea."

He smiled. "Justin!"

"Yah?" Justin stood mincing his feet, trying to look important.

"There's a piece of rope down in the bottom of that barrel. Pull it out for me, willya?"

Justin shot me a smug now-you're-gonna-get-it look and hopped from the loading dock to the bed of the truck. He stepped up to the empty barrel and squinted down into the black. He leaned over.

"Reach in there and grab it," Suit and Tie said.

Justin's belly flesh spilled over the lip of the barrel. Farther and farther in, he reached, straining. Fat pushed on stomach, which pushed on lungs, which squeezed out his breath.

"I'm not feelin—"

The strongman who had carried the barrel moved like a dancer, swift and sure. In one motion he ducked low, clasped his hands around Erickson's ankles, and heaved his legs up. Erickson flopped over the lip of the barrel and dropped. Something, probably his head, hit the bottom and issued a steel drum note, accented by a girlish shriek.

Erickson tried to kick, but the man on the truck, joined by his companion, punched the back of his knees, causing his legs to fold. Both men put their weight into it and drove Erickson's feet down. The shriek turned to full-blooded screaming, then choking sounds as the compression emptied Erickson's lungs. The second man, the one in coveralls, leaned over the barrel, holding the feet down. The other picked up the steel cover and slid it in over the opening, eventually snapping the cover into place while his companion put his weight onto it. He slipped the locking ring around the cover and snapped it shut. I had the chilling feeling these two had done this before.

From inside the steel container, we heard muffled screaming, pleading, coughing. The barrel wiggled a little, and weak knocking sounds came from the sides, but with no room to swing an arm or fist, the knocking turned to scratching.

Suit and Tie turned to us.

"I know what yer thinking. Seems a bit cruel. Put yer mind at ease, because we poked a few holes in that barrel to make sure he has plenty of air. We're not monsters. If we hadn't, he might go ten, maybe fifteen minutes. This way, who knows? He could last a good long time." He smiled. "Of course, all that fat, all that compression, and being upside-down like that. 'S got to be hell."

The screaming and scratching continued, making the point.

"Bring out the other two drums, lads."

Suit and Tie looked at me, then Andy.

"I'll make you an offer. Tell me everything you think I'd be interested in hearing, and I'll put a bullet in your head before we shove you down into one of those. I'm a bit claustrophobic myself. The idea of it—I have to say, I'd rather take the bullet."

The two men ignored the muffled high-pitched noises and clawing-on-steel sounds in the drum. They hopped up on the dock and disappeared inside. A moment later, they each returned with an empty barrel and placed them back of the truck, on either side of Erickson's. They worked the covers free.

"Why don't you start with who the fuck you are?" Suit and Tie looked past me at Andy.

"You're here to clean up after him," Andy said. "Because of the picture he sent."

"Aren't you the sharp one. I never saw it, myself. Sounded a lot like child pornography to me. Makes me feel like we just did a community service, shoving his fat ass in that barrel. You know those sick perverts can't be cured, doncha?"

"They say," Andy answered coldly.

"I still want to know what you're doing up here in fuckin' frozen-land, askin' about the lad."

"Did he swear to you that he only sent one picture?"

"He did, and I believed him, and you won't convince me otherwise. He confessed all his sins. Felt bloody awful about the whole affair, but we forgave him, didn't we boys."

The boys grinned in the affirmative.

"We patted him on the back and made him feel much better for being honest with us. What with him being indispensable like he is."

This brought a laugh.

"Did I mention she's my wife?" I stepped closer to Andy.

"Kudos to fuckin' you, but I don't give a shit," Suit and Tie snapped at me. "And I'm not interested in standin' around out here in this cold all night."

"I mention it because she's hot. Look at her. Mikey here, dipshit that he is, couldn't keep his hands off her. She's voracious, too." I reached a hand toward. She met it with her own but kept her eyes on Suit and Tie. Mikey had stepped back to let his boss have center stage. During his search of Andy, he had stuffed his weapon into his pants. Suit and Tie still held his gun in his hand, but let it hang low, casual, aimed at the concrete —confident that nobody was going anywhere.

"Know what I mean?" I winked at a face growing harder and colder with each word I spoke. "She can't get enough of it."

I pulled Andy close, turned and put my lips to hers. Her eyes went wide, but I played out the act of kissing her. Parting, I muttered, "Bend your knees, dear."

"Get the fuck away from her!"

Too late. I dropped. Andy dropped with me.

FWOOOMP! I pushed *hard.* The cool snapped over us. To the eye, we dipped downward, then vanished. A split second into the cool sensation, even before full weightlessness overtook us, I kicked hard with both legs.

We shot upward.

Suit and Tie fired his weapon. I heard the shot and waited to feel searing pain. The muzzle-flash lit up the side of the building and I realized I was seeing it from above. Too late. He missed. The loading dock fell away rapidly.

"WHERE THE FUCK—?" Suit and Tie shouted. "FIND THEM!"

"Look under the dock!" one of the men on the truck shouted. "They dropped under the dock!"

We rocketed away. Below, figures scrambled off the flatbed, dropped to the snow and disappeared under the truck thinking we had slipped through the gap between the flatbed and the loading dock. Mikey lit his big flashlight. The beam swept back and forth over the snow beneath the truck.

The shouting ended. Serious searching continued. We climbed higher and higher. The scene below became small and remote. Tiny figures fanned out in the yard. I realized I'd been holding my breath. I tried to pull in air. I had trouble.

"Dee," I squeezed out the word. "Ease up a little. You're not going to fall. I gotcha."

She let out a full breath. Her grip loosened—just a little.

"Will," she said, "that's enough."

The landscape spread around us, falling. The Escanaba city lights spread on the horizon, defining the limits of civilization. Beyond the lights, the black expanse of Lake Michigan reached for infinity.

"Please, that's enough! That's high enough!" Andy said urgently.

"I know. But we have a problem. Just—just hang on for a sec—"

I needed to think.

"What?"

"Just give me a second, please."

I patted my jacket, feeling for a SCRAM unit. I patted it again. Like someone looking for their keys and reaching in the same empty pocket over and over. They weren't there. They were on the snow-covered loading dock.

Five hundred feet. Easy to estimate. I'd seen it ten thousand times, turning base to final on a landing approach. Five hundred and climbing. I felt wind, but it was vertical, the relative wind generated by the speed of our ascent.

The hypoxia will knock you out before the lack of atmospheric pressure boils your blood.

Andy figured it out. "Can you stop us?"

"I don't know." It felt like a lie.

"What about that thing? That thing you did in Montana? That *Up!* thing you did?"

Seven hundred—eight hundred feet. The Reichenbach Builders property and the men searching for us had become tiny. I noticed something else. Wind drift. We angled east, over the city.

"I haven't been able to do it again. I've tried."

I had. I went to the barn several times and tried to replicate what had happened twice. When emergency situations caused me to simply think a direction—pure, non-verbal messaging between my consciousness and *the other thing*—it resulted in a pull, or push, or something that changed my direction. In a room filling with toxic smoke and heat, it pulled Lane

Franklin and me out the only escape route possible. In a motel room in Montana, it shot Andy and me to the ceiling half a second before someone filled our bed with automatic gunfire.

A thousand feet and rising. Light relative wind flapped our clothing, and I hoped it would slow our ascent, but knew it would not be enough. The air would grow thinner eventually, reducing its drag on us.

Focus. I concentrated on the idea of *Stop!*

Nothing.

"Will…"

"Hush."

I tried again.

STOP!

Nothing.

"I don't know," I said, frustrated. "I don't know how to do it!"

She pulled me closer.

"What if we just—reappear?" she asked.

"We'll drop like two people without parachutes. It will not end well."

"What if we reappear, then disappear again?"

"We still drop. I don't think I can do it fast enough. Not before we build up speed at thirty-two feet per second per second. Even if I can disappear us again quickly, we'll be coming down hard. Too hard."

Falling.

We had substance. We took up space. If someone walked into us, they would feel us. But to gravity, we were nothing. I once compared it to a dandelion fluff, but a dandelion fluff has weight and gravity pulls it to the earth just like anything else. We didn't. Falling in a vacuum, a dandelion fluff will accelerate at the same speed as a bowling ball. The only reason it doesn't fall when you blow it off the stem in summer is wind resistance. And we didn't have anything to create enough wind resistance to stop us from falling. That's what parachutes are for.

Two thousand feet.

"Andy." My voice against the silence of the empty sky around us sounded terribly alone. "I'm going to try something. Hang on to me."

She pulled me close and held on tight. I caught the scent of her hair. If my heart hadn't been hammering a new hole in my chest wall, I might have found the moment intoxicating. Andy. The starlight. The earth below. Our bodies locked together.

It might have been beautiful if it wasn't scaring the shit out of me.

"I'm going to ease up my hold on you."

"WHAT?"

"You'll be fine. Relax." I lightened my hands on her back, on her waist. She tightened her embrace.

"Don't you have to maintain a grip on me? What if I suddenly fall out of this?"

I'll admit, the idea horrified me. But I had confidence in what I was doing. On a few of my flights with Lane Franklin, taking her on excursions through the barn, I had released my hold on her, letting her maintain the contact. I wasn't entirely comfortable hugging a fourteen-year-old girl who had a crush on me. I found that she could hold on without me putting my hands on her.

"You won't. I've tested this." Still, I remained vigilant. At the first hint that she might reappear or fall, I was prepared to grab and push the levers in my head to full power.

Andy adjusted herself. She wrapped her legs around my hips and locked them behind me.

My hands eased away from her body.

"I've got an idea."

I reached into my pocket and pulled out the folded cash I carried. Behind Andy's back, I unfolded it and felt for a bill. Extracting one, I clamped it between two fingers, then closed the rest and put them back in my pocket.

Three thousand feet. The wind pushed us over the city. Lights spread beneath us like embers from a finished fire. Christmas lights decorated what must have been the main street, spreading additional glow on the snow. Individual homes blazed with bright colored lights and strings adorning rooftops.

With both hands behind Andy's back, I folded the still-vanished bill into smaller and smaller squares. After turning it into a tiny, firm rectangle, I pinched it between the thumb and forefinger of my right hand. I cupped my left hand somewhere directly under the bill.

"What are you doing?" Andy wanted to know.

"A trick I learned when I was still on crutches."

I felt her twist her head around.

"Don't do that. I need both hands close together." She returned to a firm embrace, facing me, her body pressed against mine. "Okay, here goes."

In movies, the first attempt fails, just to build tension. I frankly didn't need any more tension. My nerves screamed. My muscles had drawn tight throughout my body, down to my fingers.

I tried hard not to think about the drop below us.

Hand cupped below the folded bill, I released.

My fingers felt a cool, electric sensation. In the glow of the city lights below us, the tiny square of folded currency reappeared as it dropped away from my touch. It fell, but only for an instant. It landed in my cupped hand. Resting there, the folded bill remained visible, and now it had weight.

I have seventeen years of watching the world rise and fall around me as I navigated the sky. With a student pilot in an airplane, I can tell from the tiniest shift in the horizon whether we're holding altitude, climbing, or descending.

The instant the paper landed in my cupped hand, I sensed that our climb diminished, then arrested. The wind marking our ascent stopped. A moment later, the wind reversed. The paper lay in my hand, easily seen, catching the light from below. And it was now falling. And we with it. I felt the shift in the air around us. In a few seconds we would accelerate to terminal velocity. Killing velocity.

I flipped the bill out of my hand as if it would have burned me. For a shaved second, I feared it would hang with us, telling me that I had waited too long, that I had allowed us to accelerate downward to a velocity far greater than we could survive. But the paper square tumbled away, racing below us toward the city lights.

"I feel it! Will! I feel it!"

"Yup."

We descended. I couldn't guess how fast. I had a feeling the landing was going to be ugly. But maybe it wouldn't kill us.

She pulled me tight and kissed my cheek. I squeezed back. We held on for the ride, feeling relief and reaffirmation in the body we each held close.

We weren't going to die in the stratosphere.

I looked down.

No, we were going to die of hypothermia in Lake Michigan.

30

"Will, are you seeing this?"

Escanaba lies not on Lake Michigan, but on a bay formed by a finger of land extending from the north into Lake Michigan. Descending now and driven by winds aloft running out of the northwest, a quick estimate of trajectory, rate of descent, and wind drift told me we were not going to land on solid ground. It would be close, but that meant little. My estimate of survival time in the water at this time of year, and this temperature, came to less than three minutes.

"Yeah."

We dropped. We tracked over the center of town. The evening remained young, but the streets appeared deserted. I thought perhaps, as we got lower, we could start yelling for help. Get someone to launch a boat. A fine plan, except the slips along the waterfront were all empty. Maybe Escanaba had a Coast Guard station, or the fire department had a boat.

"Can we increase our rate of descent?"

Death by drowning or death by impact.

"I'm thinking," I said. Of what, I had no idea. "There are two reasons I wish I had Lane with me instead of you."

"Lane?"

"Yeah. First, I think she might come up with something, because she's smart as hell, and I'm coming up with jack."

"Second?"

"Second, I just wish you weren't here."

She gave me a squeeze.

"Aw, you say the nicest things."

I kept thinking. It didn't help.

We dropped below one thousand feet. The shoreline approached.

What would Lane tell you? About inertia. About weightlessness.

We reached five hundred feet. A road, a parking lot, some waterfront walkways and piers lay between us and the water.

"We'll drop as soon as its safe. As close to the shore as we can. As soon as we hit the water, kick off your shoes and jacket and swim like hell. DO NOT look for me, because I won't be looking for you. I need you to swim like there's a goddamned shark on your ass."

"I can't leave you."

"You can't save me, and I can't save you. We save ourselves, or we both die. Don't worry about me. All you'll see of me is my cute butt. Follow it."

"That's what got me in this mess."

Two hundred feet. We passed over the parking lot.

Over the walkway.

Over water.

A hundred feet. Still too high. We'd die hitting the water.

"Get as much air in you as you can on the way down," I told her.

Seventy feet. We continued drifting over the bay. Ten yards. Twenty. Thirty yards from shore. Too far.

How high was that pool platform? The one I thought I'd never dive from?

We were at twice that height.

"We're getting too far out, Will. We need to drop!"

Too soon.

"Will!"

We drifted and continued the slow descent. City lights reflected on the surface of the water, but now we were fifty yards out. In warm water, the swim would have been easy. I'm a good swimmer. Andy's better. But the cold would kill us.

I fixed a grip on her, prayed, and—

"Wait-wait-wait-wait-wait!" I cried.

"What?! We have to go now!"

"Hold on! Lane!"

"What about Lane?"

We dropped below the diving platform height. I smelled the water. I held on.

"Physics! No weight! Volume with no weight!"

We dropped. We seemed to accelerate, the way a train approaches slowly until it's only a few hundred feet away, then it rushes. The water rushed up to consume us.

"Will!"

"Buoyancy!"

We hit the water. Our feet sank, and it was like stepping into a springy, mossy swamp. We sank to our knees, then popped back up again. Now we were rising again.

"Ha!" I cried out.

"What just happened?" Andy wriggled in my arms, trying to look down. Drops of water materialized out of thin air, falling off us, creating a trail of ripple rings.

"Buoyancy! Volume! We take up space, but we have no weight. That's why the wind blows us. We're like a beach ball. Empty space. We couldn't sink if we tried." The bay, glassy smooth, spread all around us. I hardly noticed that once again we were space-bound, although this time we rose at a much slower pace.

"*Oh—my—God!*"

"No kidding."

I felt Andy tremble, and thought for an instant she might be crying, but then I heard sparkling laughter, helpless and life-affirming. I joined in.

We floated to a height of probably fifty feet before the two of us could calm down enough to talk.

"Now what?"

"Now I pull out another piece of genuine American currency, only this time we hang on to it, and let it take us down to the water. We displace way more water than the weight of a dollar bill, but it will hold us down. Maybe we can—I dunno—run on the surface."

Although still straddling me, I could feel Andy's tension ease. I reached in my pocket and extracted another bill. I repeated the trick of dropping the bill, this time unfolded, into my cupped hand.

"Shit!" The bill fluttered past my hand and fell to the surface of the water. "Dammit! That was a Twenty!"

Andy broke into another laugh. It seemed to bounce away on the glassy surface of the bay, an escaped, playful spirit. I grinned despite the monetary setback.

The next bill—in the light reflecting off the bay I confirmed it was a One—fell from my right hand into my left. It detached from *the other thing* and remained visible, but being the heaviest thing about us, the only thing subject to gravity, it pulled us down.

"Turn around," I told Andy. "Hook your arm in mine, like we're in a processional. Like we're off to see The Wizard!"

I felt her move. Not trusting me entirely and knowing she would drop like a stone if her connection with *the other thing* were severed, she kept both hands on me as she maneuvered. I tried to reassure her by keeping my right hand around her waist. After a moment, she hooked her left arm inside my right. She still held a death grip on me with her right hand, and she pressed her breast into my upper arm, but now we were side-by-side, facing forward.

The water came up quickly again. Our feet touched. We sank less this time. We began running.

And laughing. I couldn't help myself. I pictured the two of us, arms hooked, pumping our legs, splashing forward on the surface. The water offered no friction, so we didn't gain much, but the result was, in fact, forward motion. Combined with the wind at our backs, we propelled ourselves forward. The spring action from sinking and buoying back up again sent us airborne into a moon-walk sort of leap. We drifted thirty or forty feet forward, then sank by the weight of our dollar bill. When we touched the water, we jogged, and repeated.

"Should we try to turn around?" Andy asked.

"I don't think it will work, because of the wind. I think if we turn around, and try going into the wind, we'll end up in the same spot, bounce, gain a little, and then lose ground. Look. Lights on the other side of the bay. Care for a stroll?"

"My feet are wet," she said. "But they're not cold. What on earth—?"

"You got me. All I know is—" I brought my voice up, strong, proud, projecting like a stage artist, "I HAVE JUST PROVEN TO MY WIFE THAT I WALK ON WATER!"

The words boomed across the glassy bay.

An empty silence fell between us. I waited for Andy to speak.

We rose. Dropped. Jogged and splashed.

"You're never going to let me hear the end of this," she said.

"Nope."

I squeezed her arm, and thanked whatever gods were in charge of our lives.

Again.

31

I put the woman's age around eighty. She pulled her back door open far enough to poke a big black semi-automatic pistol at us.

"What are you doing in my yard at this time of night?"

Andy smiled warmly.

"Ma'am, that's a Beretta PX4 Storm, and…" she reached through the door and put her hand on top of the pistol; in one quick twisting motion she pulled it out of the woman's hand, "…this is the safety, here," she pointed, "on top, and the way you have it now means it's on. You have to flick it this way if you want it to fire." She showed the woman, who stood aghast. "Also," Andy pulled the slide back slightly, "you don't have a round in the chamber, so nothing is going to happen unless you do this," she racked the slide and chambered a round, then pulled the slide back to show the brass glinting in the chamber, "and now it's ready to fire."

Andy dropped and caught the magazine, ejected the round from the chamber, and handed the pieces back to the woman.

"May we come in? Because if we meant you harm, it would all be over by now."

Stunned, the woman backed into her kitchen and gestured for us to enter.

The warmth felt good, although we had only been exposed to the full depth of the cold during our walk to the house from where we made landfall. Our feet were wet, and once we dropped out of *the other thing* the cold began to dig into our flesh.

The house, a simple Northwoods waterfront cabin, sat on the eastern side of the bay we had just crossed. Across the water, the low barrier of Escanaba city lights created a shimmering horizon. On this side, structures were few, and the land nestled dark and quiet. The woman may have had good reason to be suspicious of strangers in her yard, but answering the door armed clearly wasn't the answer.

"That thing was my husband's," she said. "I never liked it, but he insisted we have it around here."

"Well, if you intend it for self-defense, may I suggest you get some training? And never get that close to someone you're pointing a gun at. Or they can do what I just did. Now, please put that somewhere safe. May I borrow your phone?"

32

"Andy, you can't," I said.

She put her hand up between us. "Will, I have to. You heard the man. Erickson is still alive. I have to call this in."

She was right, of course. I leaned against the kitchen counter without another word. The old woman handed Andy her cell phone and took a seat at her kitchen table after extracting a largely empty bottle of bourbon from a cabinet. She offered us each a drink, but we refused. She poured herself a stout shot and downed it.

Andy put the phone to her ear and looked at me.

"We talked about this."

We had. A life on the line trumped all other considerations.

I heard a voice answer her call but couldn't make out words. I listened to Andy's side of the conversation.

"Chief, it's me."

"No, it's a civilian phone."

"Escanaba."

"No. He was gone when we got there. That's why I'm calling."

"No, I didn't talk to the Sheriff's office."

Andy squeezed her eyes shut as Chief Tom Ceeves dominated the line.

"I know."

"I know."

Ceeves continued. Andy nodded.

"I know, and it's all on me, but now I need to alert the Sheriff and—"

Ceeves upped the volume. I made out a few words. Andy winced.

"I understand. But if I call, they're going to want to get ankle deep in protocol and apologies and explanations before I can get them focused on the situation. Plus, I might have been a little off-the-books on this."

"Uh, breaking and entering. Illegal search. Trespassing."

"Right."

"Kidnapping and attempted homicide."

"I was hoping you would call them and tell them our department received an anonymous tip."

"I realize that."

"Yes, sir.

"Okay. And thank you. About an hour ago," she began, and she went on to give Tom Ceeves a filtered version of what happened, omitting details that involved me and her and *the other thing*, focusing on the abduction of Justin Erickson by three armed men.

"A flatbed truck. GMC or possibly International. Red cab. Michigan plates. Also, a Silver Chevy Tahoe. I didn't catch the plates. Tell them to look for a steel barrel strapped to the back of the flatbed."

"No, they put Erickson in the barrel. Alive. They meant for him to stay alive. Until he isn't."

"Yes, it is."

Ceeves asked questions. Most of Andy's responses were the same.

"I can't tell you that." She grimaced each time she said it.

"I will. I'll explain everything."

"Thank you."

She lowered the phone, shaking her head, her eyes meeting mine.

"I'm sorry," I said.

I meant it.

Andy turned to our hostess.

"Ma'am, is there any chance you could drive us to Escanaba? I know it's late, and cold outside, but the situation is urgent, and," Andy reached in the inside breast pocket of her jacket to extract a card, "it is police business."

The woman pulled glasses from her sweater pocket and put them on.

She read the card. "Sergeant Andrea Stewart. Pleased to meet you. I'm Mary Biggeman."

Andy held out her hand and offered a fresh smile. "It's Detective now. I got promoted, but the city can't afford to reprint the cards."

"Oh! Congratulations, dear!" she said brightly, taking Andy's hand. "Would you like to take my car? I don't drive at night anymore. Plus, I'm quite shitfaced."

33

"The old girl drives stick!" Andy marveled as she bounced the Jeep Wrangler out of Mrs. Mary Biggeman's snow-covered driveway onto a snow-covered road.

"Another damned Jeep," I muttered, rubbing my legs to keep warm. The last time Andy and I borrowed a Jeep, we left it burning beside a highway in Montana. I wanted to light this one on fire, too. It rode stiff and ran cold. "Where's the heat?"

Andy applied effort to warming up the vehicle by stomping on the accelerator. The speedometer wound up to sixty on the winter-slick road. We blazed a trail under an archway of leafless tree branches. I expected to see a deer come through the windshield at any moment. Compounding my anxiety was the fact that Andy looked sharply at me, instead of the road.

"What?"

"Voracious? Can't get enough? Is that any way to talk about your wife?"

"Dee, for a split second—a vital split second—the sight of you and the thought of it drained a little blood from their brains, weakening their synaptic connections and quite possibly cutting their reaction times by the millisecond we needed."

"You're so full of it."

"Would you please watch the road?"

She did, if reluctantly.

"That was clever of you. I didn't know you were going to call Tom. I thought you were calling 9-1-1."

"It's only a short-term solution, but if it gets results, maybe no one will ask hard questions. Who do you suppose those guys were?"

"Willing to kill us, whoever they were."

"Yes. But think about that. What kind of scheme or investment justifies murder?"

"Whatever's at stake, they aim to protect it. We stumbled into their path. They were there to get rid of Erickson."

"He certainly walked right into it, poor soul."

"It's a lot less work, getting your victim to walk over and stick his own head in a barrel."

Andy fixed her gaze on the distance and began thinking out loud. "Erickson had access to images shot in the shower room at Essex High School. One of which he gave to his little cousin. Erickson was the source of the photo. But what's his source? And how did he get it?"

"Computers. Network engineer, like the girlfriend told us," I suggested. "He must have access to the collected images. Maybe he helped build the system. Maybe the camera thing was his idea in the first place, and he found some partners."

"If he was so important, why would they come here to kill him?"

"Well, he's obviously not the lynchpin to their plans that he thought he was. They can simply hire another engineer. Even so, it seems extreme."

"He stirred up unwanted attention. If he hadn't given away the photo—"

"JESUS, ANDY!" I grabbed the dash.

She swerved around a raccoon the size of a small bear, sitting in the road like he was waiting for a bus.

"—his cousin Terry wouldn't have tried to extort sex from Sarah, Sarah wouldn't have threatened suicide, Lane wouldn't have intervened, and we wouldn't have come poking around."

I peeled my grip off the dash and restarted my heart.

"We know about the cameras," Andy continued. "We know Reichenbach Building has something to do with them. And now they know we know."

"Obviously. They were willing to commit a triple homicide over all of it."

"Triple disappearance."

"What?"

"It's only a homicide if you have a body and a police investigation," she pointed out. "The three bodies tonight—two of them very dear to me —were never going to be found. I just hope they can find him in time. First and foremost, to save a life. But second, after what they did to him, he might be in a talkative mood."

I felt a chill and it wasn't because the heater in the Jeep wasn't working yet. I imagined Erickson's abbreviated future if he wasn't found.

I shook the thought away.

"How?" I asked.

"How what?"

"How did they find out Erickson gave away a photo?"

Neither of us spoke for the next mile.

"Oh my God!" Andy exclaimed. "He confessed!"

"That's what they said..."

"No! No!" Andy rapped her palm on the steering wheel for emphasis. "Erickson himself told them what he did! He got the call from the kid's dad early this morning. It must have been a shock. I think he drew the conclusion that we found the cameras. He may have seen that they were offline. He reported it!"

"He brought this on himself?"

"He panicked. Called in the cavalry."

"Wow. He puts out the alert that something hit the fan way up here in Escanaba and O'Bannon shows up to put him in a barrel. Surprise!"

"Who?"

"The Irish guy. Whatever his name is. In the suit."

"... way up here..."

"What?"

"You said, 'way up here,' meaning Escanaba. You're thinking it, too, aren't you?"

"That those guys are not from around here?"

"Yes. This whole thing might have started with Reichenbach, and Erickson, but it's moved on."

"Erickson was moving."

"To Chicago."

"Where Reichenbach's granddaughter lives."

We rode in silence for a moment. Then I asked, "Do you think there's any possibility they'll find him alive?"

Andy glanced at her watch. "If not, it would be a horror."

"O'Bannon was right about one thing," I said. "I would have asked for the bullet."

MARY BIGGEMAN'S instructions said to take County 513 T Road north to Highway 2, which we knew from our trip to Reichenbach's home. She said it would take a little under an hour. The county road threw a series of curves at us as we followed the contours of the bay. Andy swept through each without batting a lash or letting up.

I asked, "Do you think we should pay another visit to the Reichenbachs? I'd like to know if Reichenbach knew Erickson. Or if one of the people threatening him has an Irish accent."

"I thought about that. It's not far—on the way. But the wife said they were being watched. And if they're watching, someone might also be listening. If that's true, we may have put the Reichenbachs at risk simply by showing up there this afternoon. I don't want to make it worse. Not until we find out if the granddaughter is safe."

"On the way?"

"What?"

"You said, 'on the way.' On the way where?"

"Back to Reichenbach Builders. I'll bet you anything Mikey forgot that I dropped my gun and my phone in the server room."

"Anything? Anything?"

"Well..." She flicked me a teasing look.

"You said, 'Anything'!"

One track mind, hell. It's a freakin' monorail.

34

I lost the bet.
Andy drove through Escanaba and went directly to the Reichenbach Builders warehouse. We both expected the place to be lit up with units from the Delta County Sheriff's Department.

It remained deserted.

"What the hell?" Andy asked.

We parked in the work yard near the loading dock.

Getting into the Reichenbach Builders warehouse posed no problem this time. The gate hung open. The loading dock door would remain unlockable until someone fixed the deadbolt. I looked for my SCRAM units in the snow on the loading dock. They were gone, along with the pieces of my phone.

"They have my phone."

Andy gave me a grim look. "Then we can assume they know, or will know, who you are."

Andy found the rental car keys. Small favors.

Before entering the building, Andy pointed across the back lot. The flatbed had been returned to its spot in the snow. All three barrels were gone.

"Over there," I pointed. A spot on the lot showed where another vehicle had been parked. Footprints disturbed the snow around a rectangle of dry ground. "They switched vehicles. Putting out a description of the flatbed didn't work."

We trooped back through the warehouse, into the cold, empty offices.

Mikey was the idiot Andy assumed he was. Her weapon remained on the server rack shelf, and her phone lay on the floor. Andy retrieved both.

"Missed call from Tom," she said. She dialed him back.

"It's me, again. What happened?"

She put her hand to her forehead and closed her eyes.

"Dammit."

"No, we're back at Reichenbach Builders. We saw the truck sitting here. They switched to another vehicle."

"No idea."

"Right." The call ended.

"What?" I asked.

"Tom made the call. Got a reasonably good response. Until they called him back and told him that they sent a unit out here and the missing flatbed is sitting right where it's supposed to be."

"Because they switched vehicles."

"They told Tom that Erickson appears to have moved to Chicago. Their take on it is that the tip was a hoax. They were not happy about the whole thing. They're not stupid. They're going to figure out that we sent an investigator and didn't pay a courtesy call."

"You tried. And even if you try again and can figure out how to alert the cops here without putting the two of us in jail, it will take hours to figure out what they're driving and which way they went. By that time, they could be dumping the barrel in the Chicago river or anywhere in between."

Andy poked around the office space. We found boot prints in the carpeting and an empty Cheetos bag on a large desk in what must have been Reichenbach's personal office. If Mikey had been dropped off to keep watch, he selected the most comfortable chair for the job. I kicked myself again for not reading the snow tracks in the parking lot correctly when we did our aerial survey of the building.

"What's missing here?" Andy asked.

"Everything," I replied, not being helpful.

"Right. Everything. Every shred of paper. Every computer. Every file and receipt. Why the hell do that? Most of that was probably just business records. Invoices. Shipping. Contracts. Receipts for tax records. Payroll. Who cares about any of that? Yet someone came in here and loaded it all up and hauled it away—and left hundreds of thousands of dollars-worth of equipment. Why?"

I had no clue.

Andy's eyes, which had been searching every corner of the empty space, rose and focused. She stared at the wall in front of her.

"What?"

She pointed.

I looked at the map we'd seen earlier. Someone had affixed a laminated map of the United States to a wide cork board. Colored pins protruded from the plastic map surface. The largest number of pins populated the upper Midwest, but pins reached as far as south Florida, Vermont, and the little squares in the corner of the map containing Alaska and Hawai'i.

Andy followed her outstretched finger until it touched a blue pin in Wisconsin. She turned and looked at me.

"Essex."

35

Andy dropped me off at the Pizza Hut where we retrieved the rental car. She made an immediate point of pulling her small satchel from under the seat where she'd left it. From inside, she pulled out her badge, looked at it, then returned it to the clip on her belt. She gave it a pat. I think it made her feel whole again. She handed back my wallet. I resolved to keep cash in my pants pocket.

We parked Mrs. Biggeman's Jeep at the Sheriff's department and left the keys under the front seat, as we had promised the old woman. She told us her daughter would come by to take her shopping in a day or two, and she would pick it up then.

I lost all track of time. My watch read almost ten p.m. when we reached the Comfort Inn. Andy had two missed calls from LeMore. Andy chose to wait until we slipped into the room to dial him back. She put the call on speaker.

"Crimes Against Minors called me back," LeMore dove right in. "Nothing definitive..."

"But?" Andy asked. She sat on the bed, staring at the phone in her hand.

"Might be connected...one missing girl. Swimmer, like Sarah."

"Where?"

"Monroe, Indiana. She's a junior on the high school swim team. It might be completely unrelated. I'll reach out to the local authorities in the morning. See what I can find out. And I'll send you a photo."

"See if you can find out what facilities the girl used."

"Will do."

"This might help. I'm sending you a couple images. A map we found at Reichenbach Builders, in the office—which was completely cleaned out, by the way. But somebody didn't notice this map or didn't think it was detailed enough. They put pins in it—my guess, to celebrate sales or jobs. We found a pin for Essex. I bet you'll find a pin in Monroe, Indiana."

"How many pins are there all together?"

"A hundred? More? I didn't count."

"Damn. Can you get a list? Something more specific?"

"No." Andy spoke slowly, thinking out loud. "That's what I mean...the...the place was...cleaned out...all the records gone...and I think...I think that was the whole point."

"Of what?"

"Of buying Reichenbach Builders. The business has been cleaned out. The company history is gone. Sales records. Customer lists. Job locations. The former owner is being terrorized and is no help. It might be impossible to put together a list of jobs they've done unless we find and interview former employees, but that could take—who knows?"

Andy didn't speak for a moment.

"I feel like that's the whole point. To make it impossible to know what jobs they did, and where."

She stopped for a moment, thinking. LeMore waited.

Then she said, "Did the Chief tell you? The cousin is dead. Justin Erickson."

"What? How?"

She gave the edited version of Justin Erickson's death and gave descriptions of the men involved. She described the abandoned server room. She explained that she'd already given a version of this story to the chief. "My bet is they were here doing cleanup, and Erickson was part of a trail somebody didn't want left behind. Plus, he was punished for screwing up."

LeMore asked, "Did you give this information to the locals?"

"I can't." She stroked a hand through her hair.

At length, LeMore offered a simple, "Okay." He said nothing for a moment, then he asked, "Do you think they know we know—about the cameras?"

"I don't know why they wouldn't assume it. It's too much of a coincidence that they have this screw-up with Erickson, and the cameras have gone offline. Why wouldn't they jump to the obvious conclusion? But that doesn't change what you're doing. You can still try and ping their location, right?"

"Right."

"This missing girl," Andy said. "If she's connected…"

"I know…" LeMore said. "It changes the whole vibe on this. The cameras. A missing girl. You know what I mean?"

Andy glanced at me, and I nodded.

"You mean the broadcast thing?"

"Maybe worse," LeMore proposed.

"What's worse than that?"

"An auction."

PART II

36

"What the fuck!" Pidge met us at the door. It might have been the middle of the night in the dead of winter, in a hotel that wasn't spending much money on heat, but she pulled the door open and confronted us wearing nothing but a fierce, interrupted-sleep expression and her bra and panties. I double-checked to see if she was alone. Her last text to us said she was hanging in the Texas Roadhouse bar with a couple of Cessna Citation pilots.

"Suit up," I said. "I already called for a preheat. We're heading for Chicago."

Pidge checked her watch using eyes still pinched with sleep. "Do you two ever do anything in daylight?"

"Madison," Andy corrected me.

"We gotta go," I said.

"Where?" Pidge snapped.

"Chicago," I said, thinking of the missing girl in Indiana—and of how I didn't want Caroline Reichenbach to become another one.

"We're going to Madison. You have a doctor's appointment." Andy said.

"Chicago. We can grab up Caroline Reichenbach, then have the cops up here get Mr. and Mrs. Reichenbach into protective custody and start shaking information out of the old guy."

"So where are we going?" Pidge asked.

"Madison," Andy told her, firmly. "Will, Greg already has Chief Schultz working with Chicago PD to find the granddaughter. It's all being taken care of by professionals. We're going to Madison. There's nothing we can do in Chicago."

Dammit.

"Yet," Andy added.

"Fuck. You people are the worst!" Pidge slammed the door in our faces.

37

Escanaba, Michigan to Madison, Wisconsin measures two hundred ten nautical miles. A little over an hour in the Mojave. Back-time ten minutes to start the engines and do the run-up, fifteen minutes to load, thirty minutes to preheat, and another fifteen to get from the Comfort Inn to the airport and take care of the rental car, plus twenty minutes to roll out of bed, get dressed and get to Pidge's door—and you come up with the three-forty a.m. wake-up call that pulled Andy and me out of another short night's sleep.

Cumulatively, that put us on the ramp in Madison at six in the morning, and in the Jet Room diner a few minutes later. We ate an unhealthy high-butter, high-salt breakfast, then told Pidge to kill time in the pilot's lounge while Andy and I went to see Dr. Doug Stephenson. The meal fortified us, but the coffee saved our lives. We both ran on Empty from three nights of abbreviated sleep. The adrenaline kick that caught up with us after we got back to the room didn't help.

We had come close.

The ending—splash-running across the bay—may have seemed comical after the fact, but our laughter had been terror-inspired. I knew if I wanted to stop my heart, all I had to do was picture Andy being pushed toward one of those empty steel barrels. Or slipping out of my grip at three thousand feet. Or succumbing to hypoxia at twenty thousand feet and climbing.

We had come *close*.

Thinking about it on the cab ride to Stephenson's office, I felt my pulse pounding again. Not the best idea when you're on your way to see a doctor.

"You're sure about this?" I asked Andy for the tenth time, the other nine having been in my head.

"Yes." She dished out a deeply meaningful look and squeezed my hand. I realized that for every one of the horrors I pictured involving Andy, she had one of her own. Little gray blobs on a brain scan. The word "Tumor." She had her own heart stoppers, and I found traces of them in the worry overlaying her face.

I decided to stop arguing about seeing the doctor. We were almost there, and I do know when I'm beat. Sometimes.

"WILL, Mrs. Stewart, good to see you again!" Doug Stephenson met us in his office lobby almost immediately after we were announced, an act that brought a look of surprise to his stoic receptionist. I wondered if the doctor often greeted patients personally.

"Andrea, please."

Andy shook hands with and looked up at the tall, self-assured neurologist, assessing him with cop's eyes, and reaping reassurances with worried-wife's eyes. Stephenson had to be in his seventies if, as I'd been told, he rioted in Thai brothels with Captain Earl Jackson during the Vietnam war. His tanned skin, fit physique and athletic movement challenged any age assumption, however. He seemed to brim with life.

"Thank you for seeing us again," Andy said.

"What? No Earl?"

"Not this time. Something about having to work for a living," I said.

"The man would vibrate if he tried to stop. This is an early appointment slot for me, so I had Ann bring a carafe of fresh roasted coffee up from the shop downstairs. Care to join me?" He gestured toward the gap in a glass panel behind the reception desk, the route to his office.

"Sounds like good medicine to me," I said.

We settled in his office, where I'd visited the doctor alone less than six weeks ago. Nothing had changed, although I noticed a framed photo of Stephenson that I hadn't seen the last time; he stood on a golf course with two former presidents. The image underscored the magnitude of the favor Earl pulled in by persuading him to see me.

Andy and I took chairs facing the doctor's desk. He poured us each a mug of heaven. I took a long sip of coffee, savored it, and said, "Okay, I'm good. Thanks, Doc. Let's go." I started to rise.

"Sit!" Andy commanded. Stephenson slid into his seat behind a desk with almost nothing on it.

"I surmise you're here under duress, Will," he said.

"Tell him," Andy urged me.

"Hold on," I put up a hand between us. "Before I open the discussion, I'd like to hear your thoughts, Doctor. I know we discussed this last time I was here, but if you would, please, run it down for my wife?"

Stephenson nodded his doctorly nod. I think they teach that gesture in the final year of medical school. I've seen it before.

"Alright," he said. "But let me throw a few questions back at you first, Will. Is that okay?"

"Shoot."

"Any nausea?"

"Nope."

"Vomiting? Dizziness?"

"Nope."

"Headaches?"

"Nope."

"Vision changes? Double-vision? Spots? Coronas?"

"Only with lime."

He smiled and considered my report.

To Andy, he asked, "Have you noticed any mood swings in your husband?"

"Aside from the usual? No."

His gray eyebrows jumped slightly, the face's version of a shrug. He picked up a small remote control and turned in his chair, gesturing at a flat-screen TV taking up most of a side wall of the office. I guessed fifty-five inches.

Instead of HBO or Netflix, the screen faded up from black to show a panel of brain images. My eyes jumped to the data boxes at the bottom.

Along with patient file number, date and a technical description of the machine parameters when the image was made, a box in the lower right held the patient's name. These images said John R. Smith.

Good! I thought. *If the FAA ever asks, I was never here.*

"Here you are, Mrs. Stewart."

"Andrea, please," Andy repeated. She studied the screen intently.

"Andrea. Proof positive that there is something between your husband's ears."

"Vindicated!" I said.

"I'm going to guess that one reason you're here today, Andrea, is because your husband scared the living daylights out of you by using the word 'tumor' when he reported to you that I found something. Am I right?"

Andy nodded.

"Well, I take some of the blame for that," Stephenson said. "I did tell Will I found something on his scans. And I did use the word tumor, but to be clear, I said it looks nothing like any tumor I've ever seen. I hope he conveyed that to you."

"He did," I said.

"That said, the images do, in fact, reveal an anomaly. When that happens, I go to my playbook and see what we're dealing with. The answer is not always clear. In fact, the answer is rarely clear. Tumor describes an abnormal growth of cells, and brain tumors come in a wide range of specific types. Some benign, some not so benign. I won't run down the list because that's just going to unnecessarily scare you. But you can be assured that I've had some practice at this, and almost always eventually guess correctly what we're dealing with."

I realized he made a joke and wanted us to laugh. Or at least smile. We let him down.

He gave it a beat, then aimed a laser pointer at the screen.

"Okay, so what did I find? Will, you probably remember me pointing it out. But here, here, and here—do you see these fine lines? Over on these images, they appear as tiny white dots—because this image depicts a horizontal slice of the brain. Tu—or rather growths usually appear as white blobs on this kind of image. Do you see them?"

We did. On the profile image, they appeared faintly as wires running roughly up the center of the brain where they blossomed like a star-burst formation of air show jets, all going in separate directions. On the other end, they clustered and ran down toward the spine. At both ends, they seemed to fade into nothing.

The lines were far from obvious. You had to look closely to see the pattern. If Stephenson hadn't pointed, I doubt I would have detected them.

"Let me jump to the questions you want to ask me, Andrea. Can they be removed? No. They're tiny. They're deep. They're intertwined with lots of stuff in your husband's head that he probably needs. Do I know what they are? No, not with any certainty. As I said, they're like no tumor I've ever seen. Do I know if they are malignant? I do not."

"You do cut to the chase, Doctor," Andy said grimly.

"It saves time and gets us to the next question, which is—what do we do now? The answer to that is not in my hands. It's in the hands of the anomalies. Will they grow? Will they begin to disturb things up there? Will they start to affect Will in ways we cannot anticipate?"

"Such as?"

Stephenson flicked off the monitor, appreciating the power the images had over people. A train wreck you can't stop watching.

"Does pecan pie suddenly smell like gasoline? Do you no longer remember how the dishwasher works?"

"That assumes he ever knew in the first place," Andy said.

"Or how to fly an airplane when you're in the middle of a landing approach," Stephenson, to my dismay, stated the FAA's position.

"Or nausea, vomiting, dizziness?" Andy asked.

"Yes." Stephenson sat back. "The point is, the answer to the 'what-do-we-do-now?' question is—we monitor. These things don't grow overnight—"

I wasn't so sure about that.

"—which is why it's best to schedule regular intervals to look at what's going on. It's possible this is it—and they're done doing what they're going to do. And nothing more will come of it." I didn't need to guess that, in Stephenson's experience, such an uneventful scenario ranked as a long shot.

He paused, offering an opening for questions. We had none.

"I suggest we start by taking pictures to gauge any change since the first images were recorded," he offered.

Andy, sitting beside me, said, "Tell him."

"Okay".

"Tell me what?"

"I have another theory to offer," I said. One last chance to back out. I looked at Andy, who gestured me onward. "Doc, you're going to want to sit down for this."

Stephenson looked down at himself, already seated.

"Uh...okay."

"I told you about the accident. I told you that, from all indications, I hit something. Or something hit me. It tore the airplane apart. It landed me in a marsh, sitting in the pilot's seat. I have no memory of any part of what happened. None."

I felt a nervous need to stand. I slid out of the office chair and paced a line behind it. "How many people do you know who pop out of a disintegrating airplane at five hundred feet, going a hundred and forty miles per hour, and who survive without a parachute? Frankly, at that height and speed, you might not survive *with* a parachute."

"True," he said.

"Something made that possible. And I have a pretty good idea what it was. You asked about any weird effects such as dizziness, vomiting—there's been nothing like that. But since the accident, there has been *something*."

He stared blankly.

Andy looked at me. Looked at him. Looked at me.

"Before I tell you, I really, really, *really* need to confirm with you that we have absolute patient confidentiality here."

"We do."

"You can't un-see this, once you've seen it," I told him, thinking of something Earl once told me. "I'm offering you an out. Down the road, there may come a time when you wish you hadn't seen this."

More likely, I'm going to wish I hadn't shown you.

Stephenson offered a humble shrug. "I think I've seen just about everything once or twice."

"Oh no, you haven't," I said. "Doc, that thing on the screen, that 'wiring' in my head—I think it came from what I hit. I think it's the reason I survived—and the reason for what you're about to see—or not see."

He glanced at Andy to determine if she followed all this. What he saw told him she not only followed along but felt anxious to move forward.

"Okay. Here goes."

I stood still, behind the office chair, facing his desk. I made sure I had his eyes locked on me.

Fwooomp! I vanished.

Stephenson blinked. Blinked again. Stared at the space where I had been standing.

"I'm still here."

The whites of his eyes expanded. His mouth dropped.

Fwooomp! I reappeared.

He twitched in his chair.

His mouth hung open. I thought for a moment he had gone speechless, but he found words.

"Okay, you're right," he said slowly. "I haven't seen that before."

38

Being a man of science may have rendered the revelation harder to absorb. At the top of his profession, Stephenson probably *had* seen everything once or twice before. Even the strange cases eventually found a slot within his experience. I took Stephenson for a man accustomed to finding answers. Encountering the impossible strained him. His demeanor became unsettled. He couldn't stop staring at me.

"Weightless, too?" he asked after I explained, in brief, *the other thing.*

"And no mass or inertia, or unaffected by the normal rules regarding inertia," I answered. "I haven't explored all the effects yet."

"But still—solid?"

"Yup. You can reach out and touch me. I can't go through walls."

"And you think those—wires—are the mechanism that makes this happen for you? That you got them during the accident?"

"Right. That's why," I said this to Andy more than to Stephenson, "I don't think it's a brain tumor. Or an anomalous growth of cells like the kind you deal with day to day. Look, Doc, to be honest, I don't want to be telling you any of this. I—we—don't want you—or anyone—to know about this. But we didn't expect something to show up on those images. It did. And now, she—and I, too—needed to know this isn't one of yours. You know. One of the things you've seen a thousand times."

Andy spoke up, "We have a lot to figure out. You added a disrupting variable when you reported these anomalies to Will. It's crazy, but I can accept that he has something in his head that makes him do what he does. But I can't accept the possibility that it's a medulloblastoma or pineoblastoma."

"Well, someone's been on Web MD," Stephenson smiled.

"I'm a detective. I need facts."

"So, you're here—"

Stephenson stopped abruptly. He stared at me.

"Holy shit!"

The expletive popped out of him unexpectedly. He shook his head and waved his hands in apology.

"Sorry, I had that building up. So, you're here to give me the fixed parameter. The thing I didn't know. And now it's up to me reevaluate based on this new information—"

He stopped again. Blinked.

"HOLY SHIT!" He grinned like a little kid. "Will, you're like something out of a comic book!"

"Don't try to dazzle me with technical medical talk, Doc."

Stephenson stood and paced to his window, then back to his chair, running his hand through his neatly coiffed hair and making a mess of it.

He stopped.

"This is—this is—I'm sorry, could you do that again for me?"

Fwooomp! Gone. *Fwooomp!* Back again. He gaped at me.

"Have you used this? Done anything with it?"

"I'd rather not say," I answered before Andy could, stating the position we agreed on in advance.

She said, "We think it's best to share with you only what you need to know."

"I get that," he resumed pacing. "My god, you could get into the office of the director of the CIA! The White House!"

"Easy there, Doc," I said. "Let's keep this down to earth." The irony was not lost on me that his suggestions were pedestrian compared to walking across part of Lake Michigan.

"Right, right," he said. "Okay, so you want me to reconsider what we're dealing with in light of—"

He froze again.

"HOOO-LY SHIT!"

I began to see the teenaged orderly Earl Jackson knew fifty-plus years ago. The man, the very picture of dignity and a nationally known master of neurology, stared at me like a preteen boy seeing his first naked breasts.

He dropped back into his chair, pulled open a panel on his desk and extracted a laptop. He flipped the top open. Simultaneously, the big wall screen lit up, this time displaying an administrative log-in screen. He typed a quick sequence and opened a complex record keeping program.

"Doc," I said, "hold up there a second." I looked at Andy for support. "You can't keep a record of any of this. It's bad enough that you're going to walk around with the information in your head. You can't tell anyone. You can't write any of this down."

"I'm not," he said, busily chasing screens on his system. "When Earl booked your appointment in September, he insisted it be under the name John R. Smith. You may have seen that name on the images."

I had.

"I get what he was doing. Hedging his bet so that if the images came out bad you could claim you were never here. I'm familiar with FAA regulations requiring medical and treatment disclosures. It probably wouldn't have worked, by the way. But the situation has changed. You need to consider the possibility that someone, perhaps entirely innocently, knows you came here, which means someone less innocent could also find out. Which means I need to have a record of your visit."

"No!" I said. "That's the whole point!"

He waved his hands at me.

"It's not what you think," he said. "I'm creating a record for William Stewart—what's your middle name?"

"Er—Stanley—after my grandfather."

"For William Stanley Stewart and I'm attaching to it a set of perfectly normal images. And an utterly boring, absolutely normal report."

Andy leaned forward, concerned. "Are you afraid someone might get into your records?"

Stephenson stopped typing. He looked Andy in the eye. "Andrea, I was in southeast Asia at the end of the Vietnam war. I saw things which, to this day, if I told anyone, I might disappear faster than your husband. Paranoid? My generation invented paranoia. Let's be safe. If someone comes around here, or forces their way in, all they'll find are some pictures of a healthy thirty-three-year-old male's brain. I have a few of those on file."

He went back to typing. I'll admit, I hadn't worried much about someone taking an illicit interest in me. On the light side, Andy and I joked about government laboratories and super villains. On the serious side, we struggled with the conflict between secrecy and enforcing the law —with the Erickson murder hanging close behind us as a prime example. But the idea of someone getting their hands on my images had not occurred to me. Now Stephenson's urgency and his rapid trip to the conclusion that someone might poke into his records worried me.

However, before I spoke up, something else jumped in front of the fresh concern.

"Doc," I said, forcing myself to sound casual, "the government is already poking around this."

"What?" He stopped typing.

"The feds. I'm the subject of an accident investigation. The FAA is waiting for me to send them a set of images. It's the last step in the process of revalidating my medical certificate. When those images—" I gestured at the screen where my wire-head images had been "—came back the way they did, I just let it hang. I gave up. But doing nothing doesn't look right. I kicked and screamed about them taking my medical away—and pissed and moaned that I had to go through all the testing. Suddenly, I stop showing an interest? That's not going to look right. It fails to complete the investigation."

"Someone might start asking questions," he said thoughtfully.

"Someone might start asking questions," I repeated.

"And if I have these harmless images, the ones I just attached to your formal, real record, but don't submit them—it could look suspicious," he said, stroking his chin.

"Exactly!" I pointed at him. "Good thinking!"

"Will," Stephenson dropped the pretense and smiled slyly at me, "I once stole a helicopter. I once adjusted the medical records of an entire platoon, so they got sent to Hawai'i instead of Da Nang. I once helped get a full bird colonel reassigned stateside due to pregnancy—and *he* was eternally grateful. This is not my first rodeo, son."

I turned a shade or two of red.

"On the other hand, falsifying a record as security against someone poking around here is one thing. Submitting a counterfeit set of images to the FAA Aeromedical Branch is something entirely different. They have investigators who do nothing but track down false records. And—!" He shot a finger in the air to make the point. "And, I have to consider the possibility that you're wrong. That it is an abnormal growth. Being complicit in putting you at the controls of an aircraft, when you might find yourself incapacitated...that's serious business."

He gave me a long, solemn look to cement the point.

"So...you're not going to send the fakes to the feds?" My disappointment ran to the obvious.

"Oh, hell yes! I am!" he announced proudly. "It's been a while since I stuck it to Uncle Sam. Still feels good! Had you going there for a moment, didn't I? HOLY MOTHER LOAD OF SHIT!" He pressed his hands to the sides of his head and stared at me again.

I could have kissed him. Instead, I pulled Andy out of her chair and kissed her. After all, this whole Stephenson thing was her brilliant idea.

39

S tephenson settled down, poured a fresh round of coffee, cancelled his next appointment, and announced that there was a catch—actually, two.

"I'm pretty sure I'd go along with anything," I said, feeling giddy over the idea of surmounting the impasse with the FAA.

"First, I want to continue testing. Will, you came here with a theory, and—I must admit—it's compelling. Perhaps undeniable. But let's be sure. Let's be sure this isn't a cellular anomaly. I meant what I said about not wanting to be a party to putting you behind the controls of an airplane if you have a—shall we say—more conventional issue at hand. Let's do more testing. Monitoring. That's what you were about to ask for anyway, Andrea, wasn't it?"

"Yes."

"And second...there's someone I know—someone I'd like to bring on board as a consultant."

"Whoa, whoa," I said. "I retract my offer. I'm not prepared to go along with *anything*."

Stephenson nodded and said, "I hear you. I completely understand. But Will, this person is much more paranoid than I am, so your secret will be safe. This person's research has been dismissed by the authorities any number of times, which means she's not likely to be taken seriously, or cause government eyebrows to rise if her name comes up—which it won't. And lastly, she's the only person I consider qualified in this—er, area of science."

"Can you do it blind?" Andy asked. "Not reveal who Will is to her?"

Stephenson considered the notion. "Possibly. I suppose she could know you only as John R. Smith."

"What, exactly is her area of expertise? Neurobiology? Oncology?" Andy wanted to know.

"Not really," Stephenson hedged. "Her original discipline was astrophysics, but her interests have taken her farther afield, shall we say? I see her being less focused on the neuroscience—my bailiwick—and more able to address the question of what you hit, and the question of how it produced a bio-interface that appears to have given you *the other thing,* as you put it."

"Oh, my God! She's a UFO buff!" Andy frowned and folded her arms. Her defenses went up quickly. "One of those paranormal types. Am I right?"

"That's not how she would put it. She's a researcher, but...in the main..."

Andy rolled her eyes and sank back in her chair. "Seriously?"

"Andrea, I find your skepticism surprising. You are aware that your husband can vanish and can fly—without a license or an airplane? I should think your mind would now be open to any possibility."

I thought I'd try. "Andy, as an investigator—"

"Do not try to turn my own words, my profession, on me. Really, Will? You want to let some crackpot—I'm sorry, Doctor—into a circle of trust that until about ten minutes ago you were dead set against expanding? We only let *him* in to confirm that you're not dying of a brain tumor!"

For a moment, I couldn't fathom how my argument had become hers, against me. She looked at me with jaw locked and lower lip prominent, a warning I fully intended to heed.

"Let's try this, Doc," I said, feeling for the middle ground. "As long as it doesn't have an adverse effect, we'll keep testing. You can take some pictures today, and you will monitor the situation. Andy and I will take it under advisement that we may, at some point, want to explore the bigger questions of what, how, and from where—with outside help. And we will consider your recommendation."

I looked at my wife who wasn't about to endorse anything.

Stephenson slowly produced another of those doctorly nods.

"Meanwhile, to avert suspicion, you'll send the 'clean' images to the FAA. I'll get my life back on track and try to make things look normal. And I swear to you, and to you—" I took Andy's hand "—if I detect any changes, any of those symptoms, I'll turn myself in, and voluntarily stop flying." I turned to Andy. "Do you trust me?"

She gave me an eye lock, the deep one that sees truth, however thin or veiled it may be. I may have oversold the bit about averting suspicion, but that's not what mattered to her.

"I do trust you." The way she said it secured me in a promise I knew I would keep, even if it meant never touching another aircraft.

"We have an accord," Stephenson said. "Shall we take a few pictures?"

STEPHENSON CANCELLED a second appointment and dismissed his technicians, announcing he would be running some CAT scans himself. I thought the move might arouse curiosity among his staff, but they took it in stride. He eased my concern when he told me he often operated the machinery himself, preferring to fine-tune the settings, especially in difficult cases. The hands-on approach made sense to me and added to my understanding of why he was considered one of the best in his field.

We moved to his imaging lab, a spotless white environment containing the big donut-shaped computerized axial tomography machine. Stephenson handed me a flimsy gown and told me to strip down to my skivvies and remove anything metallic.

We started with CAT scans. It seemed routine initially, but then I got a first-hand look at what he meant when he said fine-tuning. Stationed with Andy behind a protective wall, Stephenson fiddled with the machine controls on a computer terminal, taking long periods between images to examine the previous scan on the monitor, sometimes muttering to himself, sometimes sharing his thoughts with Andy. He let her ask questions, while telling me to remain still in the big white donut. The two of them began to irritate me. The more they worked, the more they chatted back and forth like conspirators while I lay on a cold cushion in my underwear.

"Will, come see this!" Andy finally called out to me. I heard a note of joy in her voice.

I scooted out of the ring, off the bed, and ducked around the radiation protection wall.

Stephenson pointed proudly at a screen, at a three-dimensional image of my head. Using a track ball, he was able to rotate the image. He used other controls to zoom in and out.

The 'wires' could be seen with slightly greater clarity. To my eye, they looked no bigger or more threatening than the original image.

"Doctor Stephenson says there's no growth." Andy confirmed my impression. She beamed at me. I felt a little less irritated and left out.

Stephenson gave me a rundown of the areas of the brain adjacent to, and involving, the 'wires.' He used a dizzying array of names, none of which I committed to memory. He detailed the functions each area controlled. There seemed to be no specific pattern, at least none that was obvious to me.

Andy wrapped her arm in mine as we listened to Stephenson. Giddy energy powered his voice.

"It is, as I originally noted, like no tumor I've ever seen. There's one more thing I'd like you to try," he said. "Would you let me shoot a set when you're—you know—?"

"Gone?" I hesitated. "Doc, we had a situation recently. I can't give you the details, but I was 'gone' and tried to fire a pistol. The pistol was inside *the other thing* with me. Yeah, I can do that. I don't know what happened or why, but something backfired. Some sort of energy feedback from the discharge. It kicked my ass. I'm afraid if you run that machine after I disappear, it might be a problem."

Stephenson pushed his hands into his lab coat pockets and took a moment to think. "I see what you're saying. We don't know the properties of *the other thing* or how it would respond to energy. Obviously not well in the instance you described. I would never consider doing it with an MRI. On the other hand, a CAT scan is an array of x-rays. And we're exposed to low levels of x-ray radiation all the time—which doesn't seem to affect you. Also, what you described was an energy charge within *the other thing.* We're applying the x-rays externally."

He let me think about it.

"It's your call, Will. My estimate is that there will be no effect, not like the one you experienced. But I'm not the one lying in the donut."

"What's to be gained?" Andy asked. "If he does this?"

"Knowledge," Stephenson replied. "The full extent of that knowledge, we won't know until we try. But we might learn one thing that could make all of us sleep better. If an image reveals activity in the anomalies when you're in the disappeared state, it will confirm we're not dealing with what you called 'one of mine.'"

They both looked at me. Andy wore her vote plainly on her face, but held her tongue, leaving the decision to me.

"What the hell. But if this kills me, I'm coming back to haunt the both of you."

I crawled back on the bed and Stephenson slid me into position.

Fwooomp! I vanished. He stood for a moment shaking his head in wonder. I grabbed the sides of the bed to avoid floating.

"Go ahead. Touch my leg."

He reached hesitantly, palm out. A grin broke across his face when he bumped into my knee.

"Holy shit," he muttered, pulling his hand back.

"Just one," I said. "Just one picture."

"Affirmative."

A few minutes later, after the machine did its thing without killing me or jolting me across the room, I heard him call out, "Remarkable!"

Fwooomp! I reappeared, hopped off the bed, and hurried around the barrier wall.

Sculpted in electronic contours on the screen, a three-D image of my head, with my eyes closed, gave the appearance of a plaster statue.

"It can see me!" I said. "That's what—x-rays?"

"Yes," Stephenson said, rotating the image, showing me the back of my head. "More interesting, the x-rays don't penetrate. They map the contours but give us no look inside."

"Well," I said. "Looks like we've found an Achilles heel. Something that can see me."

"Or another property you were unaware of. In the altered state, you seem to be impervious to radiation, at least in this spectrum."

Something about the image made me uneasy. Andy said it before I did.

"Doctor, I want you to delete that image. There can be no record of this. Not even for John R. Smith."

"I agree." Stephenson somberly tapped his keyboard to delete the image. The system asked if he was sure. He told it Yes.

"One more," I said, heading back out to the bed. "I want you to do one more. Can you shoot it when I give you the word?"

"Yes," he said.

I slid back into the donut and fixed myself in place.

"Ready?"

"Ready."

I closed a grip on the sides of the bed.

"Now!"

Fwooomp! As the machine triggered, I vanished. When I was certain the doctor had his picture, I let myself float off the bed, gave myself a push and shot over to the wall. I grabbed it, rounded the corner, and positioned myself behind Andy and the doctor.

Fwooomp! I reappeared.

"Jesus Christ!" Stephenson jumped. I grinned.

"I know," Andy said. "It freaks me out, too."

Stephenson shook his head but went back to his screen. He brought up the image captured as I transitioned into *the other thing.*

"Oh my God," Andy said slowly. I felt her hand squeeze mine.

At the center of the image, the 'wires,' quadrupled in size and prominence, seemed to glow.

"Now we know," Stephenson said. "That's no tumor."

40

"Do you want the bad news or the worse news?"

LeMore spoke through Andy's phone speaker, which sat on a conference table in the pilot lounge at Wisconsin Aviation. Andy and I leaned over the table. Pidge curled up in a fat lounge chair. She flipped through an *AOPA Pilot* magazine.

"Is there a third choice?" Andy asked. Her elegant fingers slid up into the rich layers of her auburn hair and disappeared.

By the time Andy and I cabbed back to the airport, noon had come and gone. Stephenson cancelled his schedule for the morning. He poked and prodded me a bit further, studied the images we shot, and made a show of deleting all but the original images related to John R. Smith. Those, he said, we keep for comparison. He took us back to his office and we reviewed my new medical record at Neurology Associates, the one under my own name, the one with the healthy brain scans. We checked the dates of my two previous visits, dated the false records, and doctored his notes. With each energetic contribution Stephenson made to the false records, I felt a surge of renewed hope. Stephenson took to the task like someone reliving the electric days of rebellious youth. While he worked, I popped in and out of *the other thing* several times, just to make sure the scans didn't disrupt anything. Each time I did it, Stephenson marveled.

The doctor eventually finished the process by printing the phony scans and writing a brief report to the FAA. He signed the report with a flourish and sealed the works in an envelope addressed to the FAA Aeromedical Branch in Oklahoma City, giving my name and pilot certificate number as a reference.

"Just like stealing scotch from a Navy supply depot." He winked, hinting at another untold story from his misspent military past.

We left him wearing a look of wonder after I did the trick one last time in his office.

While we waited for the cab outside Stephenson's office building, I pulled Andy close. We held on silently for a moment, each working hard to make the moment real. The energy I felt centered around putting my pilot's license back in my wallet. For Andy, however, the moment was a step back from the unthinkable. I tried to let her know that I understood, but could only express the message with my arms, wrapped around her, holding on.

Back at the Madison airport, Andy dialed LeMore and we listened to his choices. I recognized a strange incongruence. Bad news comes with a next step, something to do, even if only to fight in vain. Good news produces a void. An empty-feeling sense of disbelief, as if the road you've been traveling suddenly disappeared and you're left wondering which direction to go.

"I'll give you the bad," LeMore said. "Remember me telling you about a guy who knows a guy? And a little worm? Well, we came up with our worm last night, and your chief somehow persuaded Glower to let us reinstall the cameras and turn on the Wi-Fi, which we did this morning. As soon as we turned on the Wi-Fi we sent our janitor in to trigger the motion sensor. The idea was to have the cameras upload the image, transporting our traveler with it."

"But?"

"But it didn't. We went live, but before any images could be sent, the cameras checked in with home base, and somebody or something sent out a kill message. I haven't been able to get into it, but I can guess. They killed all of the cameras."

"What do you mean 'killed?'" I asked.

"As in murdered their own devices with malware. Like I said, I haven't been able to get back into them, but everything went dark. I rigged some code so that whatever the cameras sent out would be copied to me—to monitor. Even the code I added isn't responding. They're no longer drawing power. They're dead."

"That kid's idiot father tipped off Erickson, so they wrote off the cameras in Essex!" Andy slapped her palm on the table which rattled the phone.

"Seems like. I'm sure they put two and two together after Erickson spilled his guts, and it was confirmed by us shutting down the Wi-Fi network. Too much of a coincidence."

Andy drew herself erect and propped one hand on her hip.

"What about the IP addresses you collected?"

"Working on it. Don't hold your breath. They will probably all come up in Slovenia."

"Crap," she said. After a moment she said, "What's the worse news?"

LeMore hesitated.

"Chief Schultz had his connections in Chicago find Caroline Reichenbach."

"Is she okay?"

"She's fine. Didn't know anything about anything. They have her in protective custody. They're putting together background on the restaurant she worked at, to see if anything pops out of the woodwork. As soon as they had her, Chief Ceeves called Delta County and asked them to bring in Mr. and Mrs. Reichenbach."

I didn't like where this was going.

"And?" she asked.

"No sign of them. Deputies went out to their place. Said nothing was out of order. No sign of trouble. But they're gone. Car's still there. They're gone. Locals put out a call statewide. If nothing pops, they'll issue a Silver Alert."

Andy closed her eyes.

"Did you give Delta County the rest of it?"

"They already figured it out. The anonymous tip. Erickson. The description of the men you saw and the truck. They were not delighted. They would like to chat with you."

"I can imagine" Andy said. "I should have—"

"No!" I interrupted. I wasn't about to let her take this on herself.

She looked at me and held up her we'll-talk-about-this-later hand. I made a mildly threatening face at her.

"I'm afraid they're in a barrel somewhere," she said to LeMore.

"Oh crap!" I blurted.

"What?"

I looked at Andy, helpless to hide the horror on my face.

"What, Will?"

"O'Bannon. He said, 'Bring out the other two barrels.' They didn't just go for Erickson…"

"Oh, Lord," Andy said. "They were there for all three. Erickson. The Reichenbachs. I should have—"

"You didn't know," I said. "There's no way you could know."

It didn't help.

LeMore, unable to see the look on Andy's face, chimed in. "Cleanup crew. For the record, I'm with Will. You didn't know. Nothing you could have done about it. It's not like Reichenbach tried to save himself from these thugs. I think they were done for when Erickson panicked. For all you know, they may have been taken before Erickson got his." I nodded, glad that LeMore offered the possibility.

Andy wasn't buying it, but she moved on. "This makes it that much harder to find out if any of the other pins on that map are involved."

"Harder, but not impossible."

"What about Indiana?"

"Monroe, Indiana is a pin on the map."

"What about the missing girl? Any more information?"

"Yes, and no. We spoke to the cops there and got the general gist of the case."

"But?"

"But they're uncharacteristically tight-lipped. There's a big civil thing wrapped around it. Nobody wants to say anything about anything to anybody. Lawyers are all over it."

"I thought this was an abduction. How is that a civil action?"

"The cops are working the girl's disappearance as an abduction. But there's some sort of lawsuit tying everything in knots. I asked about cameras and photos, and they got pretty cagey about it. Wouldn't say."

"Not even off the record? For a brother in blue?"

"No. They said everyone around this thing had clammed up because of the lawyers and court orders. Besides, the case is four months old."

"Four months? That's before Reichenbach sold out. Maybe the

missing girl really doesn't have anything to do with anything. This civil action—is it the parents? Who are they suing?"

"No idea. We checked state and federal court dockets. Nothing jumped out at us."

"That makes no sense."

Andy and LeMore let silence fill the connection for a moment.

"That's a shitload of bad news, Detective," I said.

"Tell me about it."

Andy picked up the phone. "Greg, I can't thank you enough for all you've done—and I hate to keep asking for more. Is there any chance you can stay another day or so?"

He laughed. "Funny. I just told Chief Schultz I needed a couple more days. If nothing else, I need some sleep. No problem. I can stay. I want to work on these dead cameras, and on those pins you sent me. Also, I'm hoping to violate some federal law and get a hit on those IP addresses. Don't ask."

"Would you do something for me? E-mail me the notes you took on the Monroe case?"

LeMore agreed, but warned, "There's not much. I'll send it. And a photo of the girl."

"And one more thing?" Andy asked.

"Name it."

"Essex is out of the picture. The cameras are burned. We had a swim meet scheduled for Thursday. I thought that might be their target."

"You're thinking they will look for other targets."

"We need to find out what other schools have meets scheduled, and when."

"Where?"

Andy may have seemed like she was staring off at nothing, but I knew her eyes were fixed on the map in Reichenbach's offices.

"Everywhere."

That ended the call.

"Is that it? Are we screwed?" I didn't mind a dead end if the consolation prize meant firing up the Mojave and flying back to Essex in time for dinner, a long shower and a longer sleep.

Andy shook her head.

"How long will it take to get to Monroe, Indiana?"

41

A ndy made calls while Pidge prepared the Mojave for another flight. She called the Monroe County Sheriff's department and told them she was coming to talk to them about the abduction case. She called Delta County, but couldn't reach the sole detective in the department, so she gave her name and number, telling the dispatcher she was about to board a plane and would call back later. She called Tom Ceeves to tell him her plans for charging ahead—although it seemed more like sideways to me. She called Earl to ask his blessing for keeping the airplane a little longer, and I know she candied that request with a version of good news from our visit with Stephenson.

The weather, still under the dome of Canadian high pressure that dropped on the U.S. during our long-gone date night, provided us with clear air stretching to the eastern seaboard. Pidge and I opted not to file an instrument flight plan. The most direct route to Monroe, Indiana from Madison, Wisconsin skirted the Chicago area. Filing an IFR flight plan would have meant obtaining an ATC clearance. ATC tends to route you needlessly wide of the busy Chicago area. Flying under Visual Flight Rules allowed us to choose our own route, use our own eyes for traffic separation, and adhere to our choice of VFR flight altitudes—all of which let us cut much closer to the Chicago Class B airspace, shaving ten to fifteen minutes off the flight.

A little after one p.m. we taxied for takeoff. I gave Pidge the left front seat and pilot-in-command position. She handled the big twin-engine airplane like an artist, taking us skyward smoothly. Well before reaching our cruising altitude of eleven thousand five hundred feet, I slipped out of the co-pilot's seat and moved back to the cabin.

Andy faced forward on the left side of the plane. She fingered her laptop keyboard on the fold-out table. I slid into the rearward-facing seat in front of her, directly behind Pidge. Andy reached for her headset, but I waved it off. The cabin was far from silent, but it was quiet enough that we could talk, without having Pidge listen in on the intercom.

"Are those LeMore's notes?" I asked.

She folded the laptop and shook her head. "He has almost nothing. No, this? I asked the Montana AG to send me copies of their investigation into Parks. They've been generous, although I think some of that is designed to make me a well-informed witness."

"It was your investigation. You handed it over to them." I tend to advocate for my wife's accomplishments.

Pearce Parks remained in a Montana jail, having been refused bail owing to his wealth, his ownership of a jet aircraft, and the absolute certainty that he would bolt if given the chance.

"Anything interesting?"

Andy shrugged. "They're taking their time and doing it right. Very thorough. I need to go out there at some point. To work on my statements with their prosecutor. If Parks takes it to trial, I may be deposed by his attorney—although if that's the case, they can come to me."

The idea of sitting down with lawyers working for Parks disgusted me, but Andy took it in stride. Another day at the office.

"Let's hope that doesn't happen until summer, and maybe we could make a vacation out of it. I'd like to see the west. Or a little more of the west than we've seen so far."

"Richardson, the lead prosecutor, sent me copies of some of the Evergreen records." Evergreen Reform was the name of Parks' prison enterprise. I believed the "green" in the name referred to money, and the name itself referred to a constant flow thereof, thanks to Parks' partial ownership of our state governor and the lucrative contracts he championed. Andy gestured at the laptop. "It looks like Foyle and Tyler weren't the only recruits."

"How many more?"

"I found four men fitting the profile. Lifers. Murder convictions. All four listed as Death In Custody. Tyler, we know, died in custody. Foyle, we know about—then there are two more possibles. One is still alive for certain. He showed up on facial recognition crossing into Mexico last summer. But being dead took him off the detain list. He hasn't pinged anywhere since."

"Wow. An actual graduate of the Parks Reform Program."

"He predates Foyle," she noted.

"The other?"

"He could be anywhere. Or he could really be dead. The records for all four men indicate their remains were cremated and disposed of—we know that's a lie for two of the four."

"Going to Mexico sounds like someone wants to spend the rest of his life on a beach in anonymity. The other guy might be doing the same. Has Parks given up anything on these two?"

"He's not chatty. He has an army of lawyers around him." Andy flipped open the laptop and turned it toward me. "Here."

The screen displayed two sets of mug shots. One looked familiar. Prison tattoos adorned the man's neck, cheeks and forehead. Nazi symbols and code made up most of the artwork, just like Garret Foyle. Andy pointed at him.

"That's the one who crossed over the border."

I wondered how all that white supremacy ink played in Mexico.

The second man seemed mild in comparison. Hollywood might have cast him in a bit part as the friendly hardware store owner or the congenial postal carrier—if they could get past the cold, dead eyes.

"Two dead men. The Nazi is apparently sunning himself in Mexico. The other one—who knows?"

Andy pulled the laptop back and closed it again. She drummed her fingers on the silver casing and looked out at the hazy sky. The southern end of Lake Michigan curved away to the horizon. It looked cold. Talk of dead men made me think of the wisps of ice steam rising off the water as the spirits of dead mariners. I read once that the American Great Lakes claim more than ten thousand shipwrecks. I found it hard to believe there were ever that many ships on the lakes to begin with.

Thinking of the missing made me think of a girl, a swimmer, cute and full of life, gone for four months. The best outcome after that much time often seems limited to finding her remains and bringing closure to a family burdened with loss. Putting a restless spirit to rest. The more likely outcome is no outcome, an endlessly open question.

"Why did you call ahead to the cops in Monroe? That's not your style."

"Really? Do you see me as some blunt force, bursting in on people?"

I laughed. "Anything but! You're more of a ninja. Appearing out of nowhere. Surprise is your ally. Of course, it helps you have a sidekick who can make you disappear."

"Ninja, eh?" The image aroused an amused smile. "I called ahead for precisely the opposite reason. We're not going to learn anything about the girl disappearing that LeMore wasn't able to get already."

"So why go there? Other than the joy of all this..." I gestured at the cabin of the airplane and the sky outside the window.

"Sometimes—no, oftentimes—you learn more about people or a situation from the way they try to hide something. LeMore said the Monroe cops are stonewalling him. That's way out of the norm. That's TV bullshit, you know. All that interdepartmental turf crap that writers use to keep a plot going. That just doesn't happen. Yet here we have a sheriff's department that's been unable to resolve a missing girl case—turning away a fresh angle from the outside. And I don't understand how it became a civil case. Something's not right. I'm not going to get a read on that from a phone call."

"Okay, but all this seems to have happened long before Reichenbach met the goons that forced him to sell. It might have nothing to do with Reichenbach, or cameras, or Erickson. Could just be coincidence."

She spread a patronizing smile across her lips. Dimples appeared in full bloom.

"Yeah, okay," I said, acknowledging her well-established stance on coincidence.

"We can't assume that the sale of Reichenbach's company is the zero point on this timeline. We still don't know Erickson's relationship to Reichenbach. Or the Irishman. Or his role in the installation of the cameras. Time is a character in every drama, too. A suspect we...have...to ..." Her gaze slipped off my face and focused on infinity. She stared ahead for a moment, then reeled her focus back again and looked at me, startled.

"How long does it take to drive from Chicago to Escanaba?"

"Five, maybe six hours?" It was a guess. Guesses don't sit well with Andy. She opened her laptop and tapped the keyboard hurriedly.

"Five hours and thirty-one minutes. Assuming perfect traffic, which never happens—and good road conditions, which we did not have." She thought about it. Her lips parted and moved forming silent numbers as she calculated. "That's tight. It's doable, but awfully tight."

"What is?"

She explained. "Sometime around ten in the morning Erickson gets a call from his uncle. The pervert kid's dad. Probably denies everything, but that's not relevant. What does he do after he gets off the phone?"

"Panic?"

"Yes. Panic. Freak out. Worry. Pace. Then eventually conclude he must confess to someone higher up—to O'Bannon—which he did, right? With bad results, of course. The question is—how much time did he need to reach the decision to confess? How much time did he need to get up the courage to call O'Bannon? How much time did he waste trying to come up with a better idea? A better lie?"

"No way to know, but I'm guessing it could have taken a while. I think I see where you're going with this."

She threw up a finger. "Plus! O'Bannon needed time to gather his troops, get organized, conclude that he had a mess on his hands."

"Maybe he needed time to confer with someone about this loose cannon," I suggested. "Maybe O'Bannon isn't the top of the food chain. Maybe he needed time to discuss the situation in Escanaba as a whole."

Andy leaned forward. "When they went to deal with Erickson, they obviously decided to deal with Reichenbach, too. Point being, it's tight. It's tight to put all of this together in the time it takes to get there. From Chicago. Driving."

"Driving," I echoed her. I picked up the headset and gestured for Andy to follow suit. Once on, I said, "Pidge, what else did you see on the ramp at Escanaba? Transients?"

"Just us."

"Nothing else?"

"Nope."

So much for that theory. I knew what Andy was thinking. That like us, O'Bannon and his crew didn't drive to Escanaba. If they had flown in, there might be a record of the aircraft registration. Owned or chartered, we might be able to track it by the N-number.

Pidge's voice popped up between our ears on the headset.

"Except those two Citation pilots guzzling iced tea at the bar." Pidge said. "They paid for a heated hangar. I thought about hooking up, but jeez, one of them was about ninety, and the other one had this mole on his chin. I mean, he would'a been humping away and I'd be staring at that mole. No, thank you. Plus, they bugged out for Chicago around eight."

Andy smiled.

42

The snow line ended just south of Gary, Indiana. From there to Monroe, we flew over a dry patchwork of midwestern agriculture, December brown and dormant. Highways cut the patches into neat squares as far as we could see, which, from eleven thousand five hundred feet, in clear air, stretched at least a hundred miles.

Pidge made a silky-smooth descent into Monroe County Airport and greased the wheels onto the runway. Superb flying. The fat grin she threw back into the cabin after turning off the runway told us she knew it.

Monroe County offered self-service fuel, and there were no ramp rats to wave us in or throw down carpets at the foot of our air-stair door. Pidge had her choice of empty space on the airport apron for parking. She rolled to a stop and worked her way through the shut-down checklist.

We saw the Sheriff waiting for us in the fixed base operation office.

Andy and I left Pidge to attend to the airplane. We walked across the ramp in low-angled, surprisingly cold sunshine. The FBO office occupied the classic one-story annex to a larger hangar. A sign on the glass door said Monroe Aviation—Instruction—Scenic Tours—Inquire Within.

We stepped into a cramped office that smelled of old maps, engine oil, and a few decades of tobacco smoke embedded in the acoustic tile ceiling. Framed photos of airplanes randomly decorated the walls. A low counter ran through the back half of the room. Glass display cases offered second-hand flight instruments, flying handbooks, and hats for sale.

My kind of place.

"Jim Hanneman, Monroe County Sheriff." He stepped directly to us with his hand extended. Andy introduced herself, then me.

Hanneman gave me the eye, wondering why a husband tagged along with a detective, but he said nothing. Roughly my height and weight, he seemed young for an elected sheriff. I guessed early-forties. Ex-military, according to the haircut. Not a politician. Law enforcement through and through.

"Sheriff Hanneman, we're here—"

"Pardon the interruption, but I know why you're here." His stern expression ran no risk of being interpreted as friendly. "Before we talk, I need to ask one question. Can we agree that this meeting, this conversation, never took place? That we never met?"

"That's two questions, and yes," Andy replied. He chipped a faint smile from his stony expression.

"Good. Let's take a ride."

43

"The Kaitlyn Aberdeen case has just about torn this community apart," Hanneman said, starting his car. He drove an unmarked SUV. His personal vehicle, I suspected, noting the sprinkle of Cheerios on the floor of the back seat, child seat indentations in the upholstery, and the fact that I wasn't sitting behind a cage screen. "Even my own department. You know how rare this kind of abduction is, media stories notwithstanding. It hit this community hard."

"I don't have much detail," Andy said.

"No, you don't. And I'm not supposed to give you any. My department is under court orders. We're past the finger-pointing, blaming and accusation stage. Now we're in the lawyer stage." Hanneman made no effort to mask his bitterness. "We did everything. Dogs. Volunteer searches. State police. FBI. Media blasts. Social media. Amber alert, of course. Worked with NCMEC. And now—now civil action, gag orders. People taking sides. A judge deciding what is and isn't evidence. It's about as ugly as it gets."

"I don't understand."

I leaned toward the center of the back seat and watched our progress through the windshield. Based on a cursory glance at the flight planning map, I knew the Monroe city limits were northeast of the airport. We weren't headed for the Sheriff's Department. We were headed away from town on a simple county road running arrow-straight between fields of corn stubble.

"Kaitlyn Aberdeen, sixteen, junior at Monroe High School. The oldest of four girls. Perfect grades. Active in school. No boyfriend to gum up the investigation. Her friends all swear she didn't touch drink or drugs. Christ, she even volunteered on weekends to sing at the nursing home. She had a summer job at a local garden center. One night the owner closed up and saw her car still sitting in the lot. That was it. Gone."

"When was this?"

"Thursday, August ninth." The way he said it, I had a feeling Hanneman might forget his wife's birthday before he forgot that date.

"The information we have is that she was on the swim team. This happened in summer, during summer break?" Andy asked.

Hanneman began nodding his head even before she finished. "Yup. Yup. Kaitlyn was captain of the junior varsity team. And yes, they were practicing during the summer. Our district even organized a couple of mock meets with other schools. A program to keep the girls in shape. The last one was on Saturday, July 28 with one other school. That's when we think the video was shot."

"Video?" Andy, already attentive, glanced back at me.

Hanneman eased the SUV to a stop at a four-way intersection. We were well into the farmland around Monroe, with empty fields on three corners and a pasture on the fourth. Dairy cows stood in the pasture like statues, oblivious to the cold. Hanneman let the big engine idle.

"Your Detective LeMore asked us if we found any cameras. If there had been any incidents of indecent photos taken of young women, in locker rooms, related to our case. Now, before we go any farther and I start violating court orders, I need to know what you know."

Andy ran it down for him, starting with Sarah Lewis, detailing what had been found, what we knew about the cameras, and the connection to Erickson and Reichenbach. She gave him everything, excluding our encounter with and escape from the cleanup crew. She told him both Erickson and the Reichenbachs were presumed dead because they couldn't be found.

She did not mention LeMore's dark theory about the cameras.

"Detective LeMore said your office stonewalled him on the camera question," Andy said. "Why?"

"We never found any cameras. We didn't know anything about cameras or photos or a video until later. About a month after Kaitlyn went missing, a video turned up. And even though the video originates *before* Kaitlyn was abducted—because she's on it—officially, we can't connect it to her disappearance. And—we're not allowed to talk about the video or any supposed cameras."

"Why?"

"It's the subject of a civil action."

"But you've seen it?" Andy asked.

"No. I haven't seen it."

"I don't understand."

Hanneman shifted in his seat.

"The video is of girls in the showers at Monroe High School during the mock swim meet. The circumstances of it turning up are unclear. One version is that some of the girls' parents found it online. Another version is that some international cyber security outfit found it, tracked it down to Monroe, and started contacting parents of the girls they were able to identify. We can't verify it, but according to that version the same outfit pulled it off the internet. Shut it down. No telling where the original is, but I guess these guys have ways of fighting this stuff. Rumor has it this outfit also works to take down those terrorist sites. Anyway, I guess about two heartbeats after finding out about this, the parents called in the lawyers. And the lawyers reached out to more and more of the parents to put together a huge civil suit."

"Against who?"

"The Monroe School District. They hit the District like a ton of bricks. Just about all the girls who attended the mock meet on July 28 wound up on the video—according to the report we got. A potentially giant-sized liability. At roughly the speed of light, the District, their insurance company and the lawyers for the parents came to a settlement."

"How much?"

"Nobody will say, but the number I ferreted out is fifteen million. And you didn't get that from me, because I got it from someone who violated the settlement agreement by telling me."

I gave a low whistle to the figure.

"I know. Money like that, it's got power. I think it's the reason we got locked out. Nobody will talk to us. I naturally thought there might be a connection between the video and Kaitlyn going missing, and wanted to hunt that down, but the settlement agreement sealed everything up tight. We never got to see the video. We petitioned the court to provide us with a written report, but they redacted so much that it was useless in our investigation. We did our own search of the school facilities but found nothing. And given the time that passed between when it was shot and when it surfaced, it doesn't surprise me. Whoever put those cameras in place came back and took them out again. Or else the District and their lawyers took them out, which they would never admit. No way to know."

A car pulled up behind us and sat waiting. Hanneman flicked on his cop lights, rolled down his window, and waved the driver to go around.

"I don't understand you being denied access to the video," Andy said.

"We tried. Believe me, we tried. Came close to a fist fight, arguing with the attorney for the District, and the judge, and the lawyers for the parents. The parents involved say they feel bad about Kaitlyn but I guaran-damn-tee you they are more interested in making sure video of their naked daughters isn't playing on every kid's phone. I get that. I think they'd sell their souls to prevent that. And I think they may have. We went from a community pulling together to find a sweet girl, to completely turning their back on that girl's abduction."

Andy glanced at me; a check-in glance.

"We'll send you everything we have on the camera we found. You need to go into the District's records," she told Hanneman. "Look for Reichenbach Builders as contractors. See if they came in around the time of the meet—before and after—to upgrade any equipment. We think that's how the cameras were installed in Essex."

"Won't be easy at this point," he sighed. "The superintendent jumps at his own shadow. Barely willing to pick up his phone without having the District counsel on speaker phone with him. There are two camps in town. One camp says the whole video thing had nothing to do with Kaitlyn going missing—that it's an unrelated tragedy. And they want the whole issue of the video locked up tight. Picture people with their hands clamped over their ears, yelling Nah Nah Nah Nah." He pantomimed the image.

"And the other camp?"

"You're looking at half of it," Hanneman said. "Now I want you to meet the other half."

Hanneman flicked off the lights, turned right, and drove a short quarter mile to a driveway and farmhouse cut from the same mold as the house Andy and I rent. He parked and led us to the front door. He rapped lightly. The door opened quickly. Someone expected us.

"Louise," Hanneman greeted the woman who answered the door.

She may have been my age and she could be called pretty, but she wore hard times embedded in pale skin. She didn't put much effort into makeup. Her brown-blonde hair was tied back in a functional ponytail, with errant strands escaping on both sides of her face. She wore a flannel shirt and jeans and rubbed her hands on her pants automatically before shaking hands with Andy and me. Someone who works for a living.

"Louise Hartman, this is Detective Andrea Stewart and Will Stewart." Then, to the woman, he added, "She's the one I told you about."

The woman measured Andy with a guarded eye.

"Alright, come in." She pushed the door wide open and ushered us into a warm, wood-paneled farmhouse foyer. We became aware of another woman, standing to one side in what would have been called the parlor in another age. In this age, the room had a half ring of thick sofa seats facing an oversized flat-screen TV.

"This is my sister, Linda Aberdeen," Louise said.

We could see it at once. The mother-daughter resemblance. If not for the toll that loss had taken, the woman might have been bright and attractive, like the photo LeMore sent Andy of her missing daughter. She had the look of someone who had been hollowed out. Her eyes were sunken, yet overly alert, as if the discovery of one horror in life meant another lurked around every corner.

Hanneman introduced her as Kaitlyn's mother.

"Can I offer you coffee?" Louise asked.

"Please," I said. Andy concurred, but asked for use of the restroom, something she would have done after we landed had not Hanneman greeted us so quickly.

After Andy returned, we were led to a dining room, each taking a seat at an oval table. Louise poured coffee, which no one touched but me.

"My husband can't know that I'm talking to you," Linda Aberdeen said, all but glancing over her shoulder to make the point. "We do not see eye to eye on any of this anymore." Pain in her expression told me her daughter was not her only loss.

"Linda, I don't want to give you false hope. I never want to do that. But you know that I've argued until I'm blue in the face that the whole video business might be connected to Kaitlyn. Detective Stewart and her department found cameras set up to get what looks like the same kind of video that was shot in Monroe. I brought her here today to talk to you. Louise and I thought—well, there are things you can tell her that I can't—things that might help her, which in turn..."

"Damn lawyers," Louise interrupted. "This business of the settlement agreement, of taking *money* in exchange for silence! The District agreed to a settlement to keep it hushed up. Pure and simple. The terms lock everybody up so tight that nobody can talk about it. Just take the money and shut up. I told you it was wrong from the get-go, Jim. You remember. And I'm sorry I was hard on you, Linda," she took her sister's hand. To Andy, she said, "It's not easy for her to be here today. But we can't let this go. *We can't let go of Kaitlyn!*"

Mother and aunt clutched hands and let their eyes fill with tears from a reservoir still full after four months.

"It's good of you to talk to us," Andy said softly.

"No," the mother said. "It's good of you to come."

"How did you hear about the video?" Andy asked.

"That's the part I don't trust!" Louise blurted, then stopped herself. "Sorry..." She gestured for her sister to respond.

"We were approached by an attorney. He said he represented a group of parents. He came and met with us. He said he got our name from some of the other parents and had confirmed that Kaitlyn was at the meet. We were just another name on a list to him. He didn't know about the abduction."

"He said," Louise muttered.

"What attorney?" I asked.

Hanneman shaped a disgusted expression. "From that bunch that's on TV all the time. The 'Billion Dollar Boys' they call themselves. Fulton Law. Over a billion dollars in awards for their clients, they say. Can't watch the damned news without seeing that actor they hire talking about car accidents and nursing home abuse and whatever the flavor of the day is for these ambulance-chasers."

"That's a big firm. How did they get involved?"

"That's the thing!" Louise blurted again. "I keep asking people.

Nobody wants to talk. If they do, nobody knows who called them. It's always, 'I got approached because of so-and-so.' Like some sort of litigation chain letter. And that's not all. Tell 'em about the money!"

"It's not about the money," Linda said weakly. "All of the parents of kids who were on video—from the locker room—"

"Wait!" Andy stopped her. "I thought you said you hadn't seen it?"

Hanneman said, "She hasn't. Nobody has. That's their whole argument. Nobody sees it. Everything we know came from the court, who got it from the cyber security outfit, who apparently contacted parents. Or the lawyers. We don't know which chicken or egg came first."

"Folks think those people are heaven-sent," Louise said sourly. "Just because they're keeping their kids naked tushies off the internet. I get it, but now they have everything tied up in this so-called settlement agreement. Nobody can say anything, or they forfeit their cut. Nobody wants to believe it, but all this hush-hush could be getting in the way of finding whoever took Kaitlyn! What if that video was part of the reason Kaitlyn was taken? What if they were spying on her?"

Andy said nothing. I followed her lead.

"Tell 'em about the money, Linda," Louise urged her sister.

"I'm not supposed to tell anyone any of this. It's part of the settlement. Nobody can say anything to anyone. My husband—he thinks that the whole video thing is completely unrelated to Kaitlyn. That's what the lawyers keep saying."

"That's why they got an injunction against releasing it to us," Hanneman said. "They got a judge to rule that even though she was on it, the video was unrelated to Kaitlyn's case and could offer no benefit to our investigation, and therefore could not be released to us."

"And how would that old fat-ass know?" Louise snapped. "I told you, Jim. I told you he sits on the same state bar board as Fulton. *Nothing to see there, by God.*" Louise, whose face had gone red, steadied herself. "By that time the District was panicking, and the more parents those lawyers talked to, the more pressure built up to follow their advice. Make the District pay. Take the money,"

"Louise, please," Linda said.

Louise said bitterly. "It's just insurance money, they say. Idiots. It's not. Some of it is, but most of it comes from the school district's reserve fund. You can kiss decent education goodbye in this county for the next couple decades!"

Linda patted her sister on the hand, the practiced gesture of an older sibling dealing with the fiery sister. Louise calmed enough to let Linda continue.

"My husband thinks the video is just another kick in the gut, but he says at least we got some money out of it. He—he's letting go—he's letting go of our baby." Linda needed a moment. We waited. "I can't. There isn't enough money anywhere."

"Tell 'em, honey." Louise stoked her anger again.

"Eighty-seven thousand dollars. We got a check for eighty-seven thousand dollars, and a promise that the law firm would have that cyber security company monitor to make sure the video won't appear again."

"That almost sounds like—" I was about to say blackmail.

"Do the math! Do the math!" Louise reached in her pocket and pulled out her phone. She tapped the screen. "There were thirty-three girls at the meet. At eighty-seven thousand dollars per family—assuming everyone was paid the same—"

"Which we have no way of knowing," Hanneman said.

"—that comes to...two million, eight hundred seventy-one thousand dollars! So, where's the other twelve million!?"

"Louise! Enough about the money!" Linda turned urgently to Andy. "Those cameras you found—did you find the person who put them there?"

Andy said. "Not yet."

"But you think you might?"

"Linda, please, go easy," Hanneman said. "I don't want you to get your—"

"Hopes up?" she shot back. "Do you imagine I can EVER stop having hope? Do you think I can just give up like Trent has? Oh, I know the statistics, Jim. I know the timeline. The days. The critical hours. I counted them myself. I know that reason and rationalization all say that my baby girl is *dead*! But tell that to my heart. Because I can't."

Andy leaned forward and pulled the woman's hands into her own, drawing Linda's eyes to hers. I held my breath, fearing my wife would make another promise to another victim that she might not be able to keep.

"Mrs. Aberdeen don't ever give up what you have in your heart. That's where Kaitlyn lives for you." Andy's words swelled a fresh flow of tears in the mother's eyes. Andy continued, "I don't know if we will find whoever put the cameras in our school district's shower room, or if it's the same person who did it here. Or if they are at all related to your daughter's abduction. But I promise I will never stop looking."

There it was.

"Me, too," Hanneman said.

I was outvoted.

Linda Aberdeen gave Andy's hands a strong squeeze, then pulled away. She reached for her purse, sitting on the chair beside her. She pulled out an envelope.

"This is the settlement agreement. It states in here that the making public of this agreement to any persons other than the signatories shall void the agreement for all parties, and can result in forfeiture of all funds paid to *all* parties in the agreement—"

"Excluding attorney fees and expenses!" Louise shot out. "In other words, the twelve million those lawyers took from the taxpayers of this district!"

Linda waited for her sister to finish.

"I'm giving this to you," she handed it to Andy. "I don't know if it will help you, but I would pay the whole fifteen million myself if it brought Kaitlyn home to me."

When the front door closed behind us, we walked back to Hanneman's SUV without speaking. December grew dark around us, as dark as our thoughts. You can't brush up against that kind of pain without letting its shadow into your soul.

After clicking his seatbelt and starting the vehicle, Hanneman said, "If it gets out that I was party to violation of that settlement agreement, they'll have my job."

"It won't," Andy assured him.

"If it means finding that girl, they can have it."

"I have a question," I said from the back seat. "When those 'Billion Dollar Boys' showed up, how many were there?"

"Seemed like a goddamned army, but maybe it was only four or five."

"They're out of Chicago. How did they get here?"

Hanneman turned in his seat and looked at me.

"Same as you."

AT THE AIRPORT, Hanneman let the engine run. He reached in his pocket and pulled out a flash drive. Holding it up, he said to Andy, "This is everything we have. Forensics on her car. Phone dump. Interviews. Every tip, every nutball that called, everything. No reason you can't have this much." He handed it to her. "the rest of it..."

"We never met. We never talked," she said without needing to. Hanneman returned an appreciative nod just the same. "One question. Did you ever get a name for that cyber security company?"

Hanneman shook his head. "Lots of double-talk from the lawyers about a need for secrecy because of their international work. Always followed with a, 'but they're happy to have been of service' line. Like they were doing us a favor during their lunch break."

"But the lawyers know," Andy said.

"Yeah, the lawyers. Big fucking heroes around here. Except this settlement bankrupts the school district. Twenty percent of the teaching staff will be furloughed next semester. Class sizes will run in the fifties. Just about anything extra is being cut."

"I thought insurance covered the settlement," I said.

Hanneman laughed. "One million. That's it. The rest comes out of the general fund and assessment. It's going to take years to restore the level of education we had. People who got the big payout are fighting over slots in the private schools, which just hiked their rates, by the way."

"Jesus," I said.

"Lawyers," he said.

He turned and shook Andy's hand, then mine.

ANDY STOOD and watched him drive off, holding the flash drive in her closed fist, thinking.

I didn't wait. I hurried inside. This time, the office was not empty. A retiree anchored an office chair behind the counter, bellied up to an old wooden desk, flipping through the latest issue of *Trade-A-Plane*.

"Hi!" I said. I skipped the pilot small talk. "Do you have a sign-in book?"

"Right-yar," he gave me a look and pointed at a ledger-style book spread on the counter, which I should have seen.

"Thanks!"

Pidge, who had been cooling her jets on an old sofa, stood up and dropped a magazine onto a pile of back issues. She strolled over.

"We going?"

"Yup."

"Where?"

"Midway."

"On it."

She spun on her heel while I looked at the ledger.

Most small airports keep a Guest Book, a ledger to record visits by transient aircraft and pilots. No requirement or regulation governs the practice. It simply honors the fact that You Were Here. I've seen books dating back to the 1930s, and once had an airport owner show me a Charles Lindberg signature.

Pidge had already signed us in. The entry showed the date, time, aircraft type, registration number, home base, and pilot's name. She simply wrote "Pidge" in the final column.

I began flipping pages, and quickly realized that I overestimated the number of visitors to Monroe County Airport. After turning only a few pages, the entries were more than a year old. I backtracked.

Andy stepped up behind me and slid one hand around my waist. She pressed close for a look.

"What are you looking for?"

I scanned the listings since July.

"Cessna Citation. Chicago." After a moment, I returned the open book to the current entries. "Nuts. Not there."

44

Ever since Mayor Daly ripped up the runway at Meigs Field, there's nothing easy about flying into Chicago. O'Hare is strictly for the big busses. That leaves Midway or one of the northside executive airports, both a fair distance from The Loop. Pidge filed an IFR flight plan for Midway. We caught the tail end of evening rush hour. Even with good weather, we were delayed on the ground for twenty-five minutes before ATC issued a release to enter controlled airspace. I flew the left seat. After the third routing change involving waypoints I never heard of, I muttered thanks to Pidge for flying co-pilot and programming the navigation system.

We touched down at Midway a little after ten. Even though I knew the field well, I asked for and took progressive taxi instructions to Signature Aviation. The ramp was crowded. The wand-waving ramp attendant slotted us between a couple of business jets.

Shutting down, I hit a familiar wall of fatigue. Long charter-flying days can knock the stuffing out of you, especially when crew call comes at three forty-five a.m. Andy showed signs of it, too. We both moved stiffly through the motions of disembarking, securing the aircraft, and paying the ramp fees.

The hostess at Signature Aviation arranged a cab for us.

"We need to find a hotel," Andy sighed. "Something cheap."

"Screw that!" Pidge lit up an impish grin and held up one hand. "I have the company credit card!"

"We can't," Andy protested. "Pidge, no. I'm going to expense this with the city as much as I can, but we have to be frugal."

"Fuck frugal. Where are we going?"

I decided to let Andy handle Pidge, but her reply was aimed at me.

"I want to talk to those lawyers," she said. "I looked at the papers Mrs. Aberdeen gave me. Everything about that cyber security company is cryptic. If the lawyers can connect us with the cyber people, maybe they can give us a lead on who put in the cameras."

"What lawyers? Where?" Pidge asked.

"They're on south Michigan, just below Wacker."

"Hyatt Regency, baby! It's fucking right next door!" she pumped a fist. "Cheap hotel, my ass! Seriously, girl. You have no imagination. Let me show you how it's done."

Andy was simply too tired to argue.

My watch hit eleven just as the cab dropped us under the Hyatt Regency portico. The doorman, bundled against the cold, offered bell and bag services. We declined and followed Pidge inside. Andy and I were dragging, but something pumped a shot of energy into Pidge. She bolted ahead, up the escalator.

We caught up with her on the second floor, where check-in desks lined a wall of windows divided by vertical blinds.

"Hang back," she instructed us. She bounced up to the only manned check-in station and engaged in an animated conversation with a young man wearing his name pinned to the breast pocket of a dark suit. I occupied myself by studying the skyline outside and the vast lobby inside.

I see space differently now. The interior of the Hyatt Regency offered plentiful room for flying. Grid structures above the café looked useful for maneuvering. Open space and high beams beckoned. I made a note of wires hanging a large array of lights from the high ceiling. A hazard. They were nearly impossible to see. I found myself calculating vectors from one point to another in the expansive atrium.

"Here," Pidge returned in short order and handed us a pair of key cards. "You're in thirty-two oh three. That'll get you club access, too. You have to swipe the card in the elevator to get to the floor and the club up on top."

"How much did this cost?" Andy held up the card.

"Next to nothing. I once dated a guy who worked the desk at the Hyatt in Milwaukee. Unsold rooms. You just have to know what to ask for. And how to ask."

She beamed at us, whirled, and strolled toward the skybridge to the West Tower.

HUNGER TRUMPED FATIGUE. After dropping our overnight bags in the room, Andy and I headed down to street level to see if they were still serving at the Sweetwater Tavern and Grill a block over. Pidge said something about finding the workout room, then the bar—or finding the bar and seeing if she could get a workout. I'm not sure which.

Andy and I left the West Tower lobby and cut through the space between the Hyatt and the Midwest Center, a trio of identical high-rise office towers. The stroll might have been romantic, if most of the courtyard between buildings weren't cordoned off for remodeling and if we hadn't been shivering thanks to a typical Windy City breeze. I wanted to catch a look at the Christmas lights on Michigan Avenue, but Andy insisted on scouting the Midwest Center.

Three office towers stood in a cluster, constructed of steel and glass as orderly vertical rectangles, gray and unimaginative against the skyline. Each of the three stood above a cold, empty-feeling lobby of polished granite without a single curve or obtuse angle. Whoever designed these towers used a T-square and right triangle, period.

A lighted Christmas tree stood alone in a corner of the center tower lobby. One other splash of color broke the cream and tan color scheme. A pop-up display panel, at least fifteen feet high and twenty feet wide, proclaimed this tower to be the new home of the Billion Dollar Boys. With an eight-foot-high head, the firm's has-been actor spokesman asked if you got your share of the payout yet. The pitch made civil litigation sound like a lottery. A row of bullet points at the bottom listed some of the tragedies that could make you rich.

As we passed the glass exterior of the lobby, Andy studied the security station. A young woman sat on a stool behind a twenty-five-foot-wide counter, facing the interior of the building. She wore an ill-fitting black uniform. Bored senseless, she did not manifest the image of serious security. Behind the woman, we could make out a set of monitors, a control panel of indeterminate purpose, and a hand-held radio on the counter. I looked for a tenant listing board and spotted it on the far side of the lobby. I asked Andy if she wanted to go in and see what floor the Fulton Law juggernaut occupied. She said no.

"I don't want to show up on their security cameras yet."

"I can take care of that," I offered.

She shook her head, hooked her arm in mine and hurried us forward.

We ate a midnight meal of sandwiches and french fries, nicely accented with Corona and lime. I thought Andy might want to chat about the hunt we were on, but she didn't raise the subject and I knew her well enough to let her thoughts percolate.

Instead, we talked about Stephenson, his child-like reaction to seeing me disappear, and the rather amazing leap he made to willingly falsifying my medical records. We speculated on how long it would take for the FAA to process my medical in Oklahoma City.

Andy fiddled with her food. I know when she has something on her mind. When she looked up at me, her green and gold eyes were like diamond bits, drilling for an answer to a question she hadn't asked.

"What?"

She hesitated. Then, "I'm happy about Stephenson. God knows, I'm happy it's not a brain tumor."

"Amen," I picked up my glass and we clinked and sipped. "But…?"

"And I'm happy for you, if this all goes through with the FAA."

"But…?" I repeated.

The eyes again. Looking at me for an answer before the question crossed her lips.

"Is it what you really want? Flying charters for Earl?"

"It's what I do. God knows, we need the money."

"Aside from that."

I didn't answer. I rotated my beer on the coaster. I thought about a decision I made a little more than a month ago—about what I wanted to do with *the other thing*. That had not changed.

"Don't get me wrong, Will. I know what flying means to you. It's just...I was wondering, after Litton and all that, and all we talked about...I was wondering if you really want to be flying charters again."

I wasn't ready to concede that she bared a truth I remained unwilling to confront. She always arrives ahead of me in matters with weight.

"The only thing I know for certain is that I need to be a pilot."

She packaged deep and complete understanding in one brief look, sugared with a dimpled smile. She picked up her glass again. We clinked them.

"My pilot," she said.

"My girl."

She let it go at that.

I thought about bringing up Lydia but decided to let her find her own time and place for that discussion. Sometimes my husbandly genius awes me.

After that we talked sparsely about how bone-tired we were, which I also took as a signal there would be no marital mischief on the Hyatt sheets tonight.

On the walk back, she steered us up Michigan, then along Wacker, avoiding the shortcut past the Midwest Center towers. I caught her smiling at the blaze of holiday lights extending north on the Miracle Mile.

When we reached the room, I entered first, patting the wall for the lights.

"Don't," she said, touching my arm. I thought for a moment she changed her mind, that a meal and a beer restored her energy. No such luck. She pushed past me in the dark room and went to the window.

Directly across from our room, we could see the middle tower of the Midwest Center. Late hour or not, a few of the floors containing tenants were well lit and occupied. Half a dozen floors glowed with reduced lighting and were utterly barren. Directly level with us, the thirty-second floor lay empty. We had an unobstructed view through the entire floor and out the other side of the building. Higher up, above another empty floor, the top floor showed ranks of vertical blinds on all the windows.

"That's a lot of unoccupied office space," I said.

Andy hummed a reply, studying the building. I wished now that we had checked the tenant board. We might have been able to see into the floor recently infested by the Billion Dollar Boys.

After a few minutes of reconnaissance, Andy pulled the thick curtain shut, wrapping full darkness around us until she found a light. She then took the desk chair, rolled it into position just inside the room door, and tipped it on its side. It reminded me that the last time we spent a night in a motel, someone blew into the room in the middle of the night firing a machine gun. I double-checked the deadbolt. The Hyatt hardware felt significantly better than the locks at the Sioux Valley Motor Court.

"You go ahead," Andy said, gesturing at the bathroom. "I want to make a call."

When I finished a quick bedtime routine and reentered the room in boxers and a t-shirt, I found Andy on her stomach, on the bed. She propped her chin in both hands and listened to the phone laying on the sheet. She looked like a teenaged girl trading Friday night schemes with her BFF.

"...three possible locations," Greg LeMore told Andy via the speaker on her phone. I had a moment to feel jealous that this was the second time I found my wife in bed with the swarthy Milwaukee detective. I slid onto the bed beside her and began rubbing her back possessively. "One in Iowa, two in Minnesota. All three have swim meets starting at three p.m. tomorrow. All three are pins on the Reichenbach map."

"The deadline," Andy sighed.

"Seems like. Your chief has been in touch with departments in all locations."

"Please tell me they didn't rush in looking for cameras."

"No, they're all playing ball with us. But that's only good until tomorrow. Before they let anyone into those locker rooms, they're all doing searches. We bought as much time as we could. They won't go in until right before the meet. But if they find anything, they're going to take them out right quick."

"So, if we don't come up with something before three tomorrow, there's an excellent chance we'll spook these people for good," Andy sighed.

"'Fraid so." LeMore gave it a moment. Then asked, "What are you thinking?"

"What am I thinking...?" Andy rolled on her side and looked at me, shrugging with her eyebrows. "Erickson was a pervert who worked for or was connected to Reichenbach Builders. Maybe he did freelance IT for the little construction company. Whatever—he saw an opportunity in their public shower construction business at schools with easy Wi-Fi access. Maybe he started out with crude homemade cameras. Got some photos for his own self-stimulation...but then what? Somebody found him on the internet? Somebody approaches him? O'Bannon? Or he approached O'Bannon? I don't know. They get together and turn it into something bigger. The broadcast event. Then somebody wants to make it even bigger. They buy up Reichenbach and take the show on the road. Now it's big enough that when Erickson screws it up with an amateur move, they eliminate him."

"You think they extorted Reichenbach out of his company just to get his list of customers and to gain access?"

"Possibly. On the upside, we may not be the only ones after them. There's also this cyber security outfit."

"Yeah," LeMore said, "who are those guys?"

"All I know is that they're working with the lawyers and they might be our best way of getting to O'Bannon. We have a physical link—we've seen his face. They may have a cyber link. Put the two together, and who knows? I want to get in to talk to the lawyers tomorrow—" She glanced at the clock on the nightstand. "—er, this morning. If I can get the name out of them, maybe we can find out how they found the video and shut it down."

I chimed in. "Don't you think the lawyers are going to be tight-lipped? Client confidentiality and all that crap?"

"Hey, Will."

"Greg."

Andy said. "We need to get them to understand that we're trying to save another group of girls from being photographed. If we can get them to see that it's an emergency..."

"Ha!" I laughed. "More likely, they'll want to let it happen and start passing out business cards after the fact. Sounds like they just made a major score on the Monroe settlement."

"Either way, I need to talk to them ASAP. I wish we had more time to confirm that there really are cameras in those three locations. Maybe we could get your software bug into one of them, Greg."

"Whew! That would take some magic, a mobile Faraday cage and somebody willing to fly a fast airplane all over the Midwest tonight," LeMore said.

"Oh, no," I said. "I'm done for the day. Exceeded crew duty hours and all that crap. I'm dead on my feet."

Andy said. "If there are cameras at any of the three locations you've identified, I want to leave them alone until the last possible moment. If I can get in touch with the cyber guys, and get a lead from them—well then, having the bad guys think their system is still working right up to the last minute could help."

"Long shot," LeMore said.

"The longest."

Andy passed along the new question of a Cessna Citation that had been in Escanaba, and asked LeMore to check it out. I told him how to track down the information through the fixed base operator at Delta County Airport. I told LeMore that the crew paid for a heated hangar during their short stay.

At that, Andy killed the connection and pushed her phone aside. She looked up at me for a moment, then pulled me into a kiss.

"That's all the dessert you get for tonight, love. I'm beat."

Twenty minutes later we both slept soundly.

45

"Wake up, Divisible Man, I need you."

I felt long fingers running through my hair. Light pried at my eyelids. I squeezed them tighter.

"Then crawl back in here and you can have me," I said.

Andy's gentle scalp massage ended. A moment later she yanked the warm coverlet off my body. The room had gone cold during the night.

"Let's go."

"You're an evil sorceress. You know that, right?"

Fifteen minutes and a fast shower later I followed her out the door. She punched the lobby button inside the elevator. My watch read just short of ten in the morning. Not a bad night of catch-up sleep.

"Do you have everything you need?" Andy asked as we began the drop to ground level.

I patted my leather flying jacket, which bulged around my midriff. "Balaclava. Goggles. Three DOLTs."

"Three what?"

"DOLTs. Discrete Operational Lift Transmitters."

The door opened on the Hyatt West Tower ground floor.

"No," she said, and walked out of the elevator.

Andy had showered and dressed before waking me. How she managed to live out of a single, carry-on-sized overnight bag and look so good mystified me. French braid in her hair. Snug-fitting slacks with calf-length boots. White sweater that accented all the best compound curves. She stepped forward toward the bridge to the Hyatt lobby with her leather jacket folded over one arm and her duty satchel slung over her shoulder. I guessed correctly that her badge and weapon were in the satchel.

"Seriously? You don't like DOLT?"

"Not a chance."

"You crush my creative soul," I said, catching up after treating myself to a quick appraisal of her from behind.

"Come up with something better, love," she said. "I talked to LeMore this morning. He ran down the registration on that Citation Cessna."

"Cessna Citation," I corrected her. "Business jet."

"Well, the number they gave the FBO was Nine Eight Seven Alpha Lima. Greg ran it through the FAA database and got a hit." She got points for using the aviation phonetic alphabet, instead of the police version.

I had time to think what complete idiots O'Bannon and his team had been to miss the fact that the aircraft they owned or chartered might lead us to them. Then Andy popped the bubble.

"The number is registered to something called an RV-6 in Alaska."

"Shit. RV-6 is a single-engine home-built. Kit-built."

"Not a business jet, I take it. So, they gave a fake number. You'd think someone would notice. Wouldn't the tower notice?"

"There's no tower at Escanaba."

I thought about it. If they didn't buy fuel, it meant no ramp rat took down the tail number on a fuel slip. If they signed a visitor book, they could write whatever they wanted. If they paid cash for the hangar, there would be no credit card record. And if someone at the front desk at the FBO asked for their tail number, they could have said anything. On top of all that, an FAA program allowed aircraft owners to register so that their tail number didn't show up online in publicly available programs like Flight Tracker.

Not quite the idiots I hoped they would be.

Andy led us across the bridge. The expansive Hyatt lobby hummed with activity. A low rumble of continuous conversation echoed off the glass and granite above an undertone of piano music. People waited in checkout lines on the second floor. More people occupied tables at the café on the first floor. And more stood in various stages of departure at the front door as parking valets shuttled cars from a remote garage.

The day looked cold and clear outside the glass. I caught sight of crystalline blue sky above the Wrigley and Tribune buildings. Andy pulled her coat on, drew a scarf from one pocket and gloves from another.

"Are we storming the bastion of the Billion Dollar Boys?"

"Not yet. You need a phone. There's a place in Nordstrom's, just up Michigan."

"Do they have coffee?"

She hooked one arm in mine and pulled us toward the door.

"I've heard rumors, just rumors, mind you—that there might be a Starbucks somewhere in Chicago. No promises. But if we see one, we can stop."

I took back the evil sorceress comment.

WE SCORED A HALFWAY-DECENT COFFEE FIRST, then a cheap phone with cheap minutes at a store in the Nordstrom mall, just outside the department store proper. Women standing at makeover stations inside the Nordstrom's perimeter cast longing looks at Andy as we marched toward them. Andy paid no attention and dashed their hopes when she steered me into the phone shop. In addition to the phone, she bought a pair of Bluetooth earpieces, the smallest she could find. With the help of the store clerk we powered them up and put them in our ears, then tested a call between her phone and my new burner. We'd done this before when she sent me on a reconnaissance mission and wanted constant contact.

"What if we lose the connection?" I asked as we headed back to Michigan Avenue.

"I'll call you back. You won't be able to see your phone, but you will hear it ring and you can take the call by touching here," she took my hand and raised it to my ear, then guided my finger to the button on the earpiece. "See?"

"Got it." I looked at my watch. "We're coming up on eleven. I thought you'd be in more of a hurry to get into Fulton Law."

She talked as we walked.

"I was," she said. "I called them at nine sharp this morning and asked to speak to Joe Treppany, the attorney listed on the Monroe School

District settlement papers. I used that term specifically to shake the tree a little. They put me on hold for a while, then some associate answered and wanted to know all about me. I told the young lady it was police business, and she better put me in touch with Attorney Treppany right away or there would be serious problems in Monroe."

"Did you strike fear into a heart?"

"No, but I did find out that Mr. Treppany would not be in the office until one-thirty, and apparently no one else associated with the case is available."

"Christ, we're running out of time!"

"I know. But the more I pushed, the more I felt a wall going up. And when lawyers want to stonewall, nothing budges them. At which point I hung up on the underling. Which means we have time for a bite of lunch."

"Did I mention I love you?"

WE CROSSED BACK over the river and stuck to what we knew. The Sweetwater Tavern and Grill was busy with a lunch crowd and Christmas shoppers and I feared we might not get a table. The hostess knew better and found a booth near the window. I kept my jacket on, trying to regain some warmth and trying not to draw looks at the old fishing vest I wore. Jammed with propulsion units and ski goggles, the pockets took on the appearance of a bomb vest. I didn't think that would go over well in the heart of Chicago during the first full week of the holiday shopping season.

Over a bowl of superb chili and a salad for Andy, we discussed the plan.

"I'll go up to the law offices. You wait in the lobby," Andy explained. I felt myself formulating a protest. She saw it coming and held up an index finger stop sign. "There's no need for your services in a bunch of law office cubicles. We're up against a tight clock. We'll only have an hour and a half before those swim meets start and those locker rooms have to be swept."

"But—"

"Hang on! If I can get the name and location of their secret cyber security people—and if they're here in Chicago—you might be able to get to them a lot faster than I can. As the crow flies. Way faster than the two of us catching a cab and trying to get across town or wherever they might be. If you can get there in time to tell them what we know, maybe they can tie into the Wi-Fi at one of the locations. Or trace the IP addresses. Or something. At least put them on the phone with LeMore. Maybe the nerd force can come up with a break in all this. I mean, these guys supposedly found the Monroe video, right?"

"Why not just call them?"

"I have Sarah's phone in my carry-on, up in the room. If we can get her phone to them...I don't know, maybe they can do something with the photo. Maybe they can work some magic and point us at O'Bannon."

"Any sufficiently advanced technology is indistinguishable from magic," I said. Andy questioned me with a look. "Arthur C. Clarke."

I got dimples for that one.

I bought into her premise, and her endorsement of me as a fast way of getting where we needed to go. Assuming we could figure out where I needed to go.

"If you get the name, hustle down to the lobby. We'll grab Sarah's phone and I can get us both there in a hurry," I said.

She stabbed at her salad.

"I was okay with our excursion to Reichenbach's place," she said. If by okay, she meant digging her fingernails into my body, then yes. "But there are a lot of tall buildings here, and—I don't know—that makes the height seem more real. I'm not sure I could handle being up there like that."

This was hard for her. Andy doesn't like defeat of any kind.

"Dee, it's fine. I get it. Want to know something weird?"

She looked up at me with just a touch of little-girl-looking-for-comfort.

"When I fly, in an airplane, I can go to any height—ten thousand feet, whatever—and tip that thing on its side and look straight down at nothing but empty air between me and the earth—and I feel *nothing,*" I touched my chest. "In here. Not a twinge. But last night, when you went to the window in our room, and I stood with you and looked down...I got a knot. It spooks me, too. Even knowing what I can do. Something about being on a structure, up high like that. It freaked me out when I climbed up to Andre's penthouse. But I can zoom all over Essex County above the tree-tops without feeling it. Weird. So, I get it. If you get a name and address,

I'll fire up the—um, propulsion units—and get there as fast as I can. I'll let them know you're coming."

"Maybe we can get Chicago PD in on it," she said. "I can call Chief Schultz's brother on my way to you."

She reached her left hand across the table. I folded my right hand into hers.

"Worst case, we don't get anything in time today. At least we shut down the cameras we know about. Either way, we'll still ask the cyber security nerds to run a search on that image of Sarah Lewis. See if it's out there. They might have a way of removing it from the internet, making sure it doesn't show up anywhere. And we can put out a bulletin to schools, anyplace with a pool, nationwide. We can shut down O'Bannon and his asshole crew. Then we investigate from another angle. Sooner or later we'll find them."

46

I finished the chili and savored the warmth it contributed to my body.
Andy left half of her salad untouched. She couldn't stop looking at her
watch. We had another twenty minutes to kill before the clock struck one-
thirty, but Andy wanted to be waiting for the lawyer when he arrived at
his office.

Andy waved for the server when we heard the grinding ringtone from
her phone. She picked it up and waved me to lean in and listen.

"Pidge?"

"Where the fuck is Will? I've been trying to call him."

"He doesn't have his phone. He's here with me," Andy said.

"What the fuck?"

"Where are you? What's going on?"

"What do you mean where am I? I'm here, waiting for Will. He texted
me. Emergency. Meet up. Car waiting in the parking garage."

Andy sat bolt upright.

"What? No! Pidge—!"

"It's fucking cold down here and—"

"Pidge! Wherever you are, get out of there now! Get to where there
are lots of people, NOW!"

"Andy, what the fuck—?"

Andy listened.

"Pidge?"

Nothing.

"Pidge!"

She looked down at her phone. I saw her screen. Call Ended.

Andy shot out of the booth and pulled on her coat. I skidded after her.

"How could she get a text from me? My phone—*shit!*" Andy met my stare.

"O'Bannon has your phone!" she said sharply. "Only we never told Pidge!"

She stabbed a finger at her phone screen and called Pidge. I heard it ringing. No answer. She stopped the call after it went to voice mail. She pocketed her phone.

"Shit!" I said loudly enough to draw reproachful glances from families seated nearby.

"They know we're here," Andy said, throwing a glance at the windows around us. "How do they know we're here?"

It hit me.

"They tracked us. Shit! They tracked us!"

"What do you mean?"

We hurried to the door. I spoke to the back of Andy's head. "The same way we were going to try and track them. Aircraft. They have our airplane tail number. It's a simple matter of going on Flight Tracker. Online. Anything that's on a flight plan can be tracked if you have the flight number or the N-number. Goddammit! They've had us since Escanaba. We flew IFR to Madison. Then they would have lost us after that because we didn't file to Monroe. We flew that leg VFR."

Andy yanked the door open and we hurried out.

"But then we flew IFR from Monroe to Midway."

She looked back at me and did a quick deduction. "Which told them two things. It told them we found Monroe. And told them we were on our way here. But how did they know about Pidge? How could they know to text her?"

"Because Pidge is in my contacts as 'Pidge.'" I said. "And that's how she signed the book at the airport in Monroe."

"They had someone watching in Monroe? What the hell?"

I felt a cold punch in the gut as the image of a steel barrel came to mind.

47

The courtyard between the Hyatt and the Midwest Center second tower lay largely empty, despite the lunch hour. Cold wind, driven between the buildings, dug into our already iced blood.

"We stick to the plan. The cyber people are still our best link to O'Bannon. And he's here. Somewhere nearby," Andy declared as we reached the entrance to the Midwest Center tower.

"Bullshit. I'm going up there with you. If that asshole doesn't cough up the name with his first sentence, I'll—"

She spun on her heel and put a firm hand on my chest.

"Do you think for one second I won't get him to tell me?" Fury ran beneath her clipped words. Her eyes flared. She reached for her hair and pulled it free of the neat French braid, setting it loose with strands that flew in the wind and fell over one eye. "I need you ready to move as fast as possible—if we're going to have any chance of getting to Pidge in time."

She arranged her hair over her ears and covered the earpiece. Then she pulled out her phone and dialed my burner number. I left the phone in my pocket. When it rang in my ear, I reached up and touched the earpiece to complete the connection.

"We're on." I said.

Andy nodded and bent at the waist. She unzipped the top of her calf-length boot and slipped the phone in at the side of her leg, then zipped up the boot tightly over it.

She stood and put her hands to the side of my face and pressed home an urgent kiss. Then she turned and hurried into the building.

"Dee!" I said after the door closed behind her, leaving me outside the glass. Her voice came up in my ear.

"I'm here."

"I want running commentary. I want to know what floor you're on and what side of the building. I'll be outside." She glanced back at me and I pointed up. I got a firm nod. She broke into a trot that took her to the security desk. After a quick exchange she hurried to catch an open elevator and was gone.

"THIRTY-SIX," she said in my ear.

"Got it."

I looked around the courtyard. What had been empty a few moments ago, now teemed with people returning to work from lunch. For an instant, a black fury ran through me and I honestly didn't care if someone saw me disappear or not. *So what? Try and explain it.*

I pulled out the balaclava and slipped it over my head. Then I put on the ski goggles, easing them down over my eyes. The gold tint rendered the world around me in shades of amber. A few people looked at me. One man, shivering, pointed and said, "Good idea!"

I stepped back and considered the task.

The Midwest Center tower rose to the sky with glass rectangle windows separated by I-beams that began at the first floor and ran arrow-straight to the roof. I couldn't have asked for more perfect structure. The windows ran from floor to ceiling on each floor, with a horizontal span of steel delineating the floor itself.

"I'm on thirty-six. Looks like the reception desk is on the south side."

"Roger that."

Andy had entered the building from the north side, leaving me at the entrance. I hurried around the building footprint. At ground level, black pillars met the concrete surface of the sidewalk. I saw my opportunity. It wasn't perfect, but again, I was past caring what people saw or didn't see.

Reaching the corner of the building, I cut inside the pillar, turning south. Adjacent the pillar I—

Fwooomp!

—vanished and immediately pushed off with my feet. The cool sensation wrapped around my body. Strangely, it felt both cool and warm as it replaced the frigid winter wind that had been cutting through my clothing. A cluster of people walked north toward me, too absorbed in clutching their coats against the cold, or staring at their outstretched phone screens, to notice a man disappearing.

Rising, I angled toward the bottom edge of the building. The rows of I-beams were easily in reach. I caught one and pulled myself from under the edge of the building, starting up the side. I stopped at a point where a person standing on the first floor would have faced me.

With my left hand on the I-beam, I pulled a propulsion unit from my vest. I found the switch and slid it forward. A low growl and tug on my arm told me it was working.

Once, I would have made my way up the building hand over hand, never daring to release my grip for fear of floating out of reach. Now, I quickly let go and pushed the power control forward until the unit hummed strongly. I instantly accelerated, moving along the glass panels toward the corner of the building.

At the corner I turned right. I aimed the unit up and started counting.

Andy was right. Something about the tall building closed a grip on my chest. Flying near structure and seeing people on the other side of thin glass barriers felt dizzying.

Eight. Nine. Ten. I increased the angle and climbed within arm's length of the glass façade. Empty floors sank past me. Busy floors followed. People at desks facing the windows worked oblivious to my passage.

Fifteen. Sixteen. Seventeen.

The perspective of the entire city changed all around me. Buildings much higher than the Midwest Center towered overhead, yet seemed less remote, more within reach. I had become more a part of the air and less a part of the structure. The knot in my chest eased.

Twenty-six. Twenty-seven.

I concentrated on the numbers. Empty floors passed by. People went about daily routines oblivious to the precipice on the other side of thin glass.

Thirty-six. I stopped. I closed a grip on an I-beam between two of the windows and looked through the glass at the offices of Fulton Law.

Andy stood with her back to me, facing a broad reception desk. Above the desk, gold lettering spelled out the firm's name. A ridiculous floor to ceiling panel off to one side showed the giant scale head of the actor paid to sell the lottery-like concept of litigation to scared, injured people glued to late-night television and local news.

The woman behind the desk gestured for Andy to wait while she answered the phone. Through the earpiece, I heard the receptionist say, "Fulton Midwest Center." Something about that sounded familiar.

A moment later, after redirecting the call, the woman looked up at Andy.

"I'm here to see Mr. Treppany," Andy said.

"Yes, you can wait over there," the woman said. She gestured at expensive-looking uncomfortable furniture occupying a broad expanse of the thirty-sixth floor near the elevators. The woman made no move to pick up a phone.

"Are you going to call him?"

"His secretary will come for you when it's time for your appointment."

"I don't have an appointment," Andy said.

Now the woman looked up. "If you use that phone over there, you can dial his office to make an appointment. There's a directory on the card."

"No," Andy said.

"I'm sorry?"

Andy leaned over the desk, held up her badge and lifted the phone from its cradle. "Get on your damned phone and tell Mr. Treppany that Detective Stewart is here to see him. Tell him it is a police emergency, and if I am not in his office in the next two minutes a judge is going to shut down the entire Monroe District settlement and freeze every penny paid out. And immediately on the heels of that, we will open a justice department investigation into Fulton Law's role in trafficking child pornography. And I will personally ensure that you," she glanced at the name on the desk plate, "Miss Glazer, are named in the investigation."

Andy thrust the phone forward.

The woman's eyes opened wide. She grabbed the phone and punched the keypad. A moment later she muttered something urgent and unintelligible. She held the phone to her head, nodded, nodded again, and said, "Yes, sir."

She stood up. "Follow me, please." It was not a friendly entreaty.

Andy fell in step behind the woman who hurried out of sight from where I hovered

"Corner office. Northwest," Andy said in my ear.

I pushed off and fired up the propulsion unit, heading west to the edge of the building. As soon as I reached the corner a stiff northwest wind caught me. The force of it, channeled between Chicago towers, pushed me hard, away from the building. I shoved the propulsion unit control forward and stopped the drift, then accelerated into the wind. My clothing flapped. Directly below, Michigan Avenue sliced the city, flowing south into a sea of lower structures, and north across the river to become the Magnificent Mile.

Against the wind, I regained the Midwest Center tower and continued along the west face of the building, just as Andy instructed. But she had been wrong.

The office on the other side of the glass wasn't a corner office. It took up the entire west end of the floor. Except for lacking a giant-sized bed, it reminded me of a billionaire's bedroom I visited not long ago. It had a kitchen, a fake fireplace, a sitting room area, a conference table, and a vast, empty glass desk in one corner. The wall dividing it from the rest of the offices on this floor stood just shy of the elevators. A set of private doors gave access to the elevators through a keypad much like the ones used by the Hyatt. Expensive-looking artwork hung at intervals across the entire wall. Trinkets representing wealth dotted coffee and end tables throughout the room.

The man waiting for Andy stood at the center of his opulent workspace. I arrived in time to see Andy enter the room through a set of floor-to-ceiling double doors. The receptionist did not follow or announce her.

"I'm outside, Dee," I said. I saw her head nod.

She took several steps into the room and faced her host.

"People who use threats to intrude on my time come to regret it," he said as Andy entered. He was stout, shorter than her, and wore his hair in a greasy comb-back that arranged thin black lines on his skull. His age, upward of seventy, meant his hair was way past having pigment of its own. The dense black color he applied bore no relation to the age on his face.

"I don't have time to spar with you, Mr. Treppany—"

"Fulton."

"What?"

"Ellery Fulton," he said. "Mr. Treppany is retired but allows us to use his name in certain matters which require discretion. And I don't have time to spar with you either, Detective Stewart. After today, I will have nothing further to do with you. You, on the other hand, will spend the rest of your life regretting the way you approached me today."

Andy took a step forward and adopted a milder demeanor. It took effort. "Look, Mr. Fulton, I apologize for my tactic for getting in to see you, but a life is in terrible danger, and there's no time to be polite. A young woman has been abducted. To go directly to the point—I need to get in touch with the cyber security firm you contracted with in the Monroe case. And I need them right now."

Fulton turned and strolled to the mesh-back chair behind his glass desk. He sat down.

"Under other circumstances, Detective, I might have been more than willing to assist law enforcement. But aside from my anger at your utter disregard for proper etiquette here, there are serious matters of confidentiality that outweigh your needs."

"Sir, in a matter of minutes, it's possible that an associate of mine may die. The only chance we have of finding her is through your contacts. It's a long story and I don't have time. I just need a name and address," Andy pleaded. "Look, I exaggerated. There is no threat to your settlement in Monroe."

"The fact you are aware of a settlement is in and of itself a threat. I don't know if you realize the degree of confidentiality involved, or the ramifications of breaching that confidentiality."

"Fine!" Andy snapped at him. "You can have my job! You can have my career! You can make sure I never work in law enforcement again, or whatever draconian threat gets your rocks off, but I NEED THAT NAME NOW!"

I expected to see Andy draw her weapon.

Fulton raised his hand slowly, palm toward Andy.

"Please, Detective, there's no need to become disruptive. I am not unsympathetic, but you must recognize that I have obligations to my clients. I am deeply concerned that you seem to have information you should not have regarding the Monroe matter. Information that could jeopardize a delicate situation, and many, many more lives than the one you speak of."

Okay, now I genuinely expected Andy to draw her weapon and shoot this sanctimonious bastard. She didn't.

He said, "But you seem like a lovely young woman." He let his eyes wander.

Oh, you didn't, I thought. I now bet less on Andy drawing her weapon and more on her simply clocking the old bastard.

"We both share a duty to the law. Clearly, you need my help. I can't give you the name..." He gave the declaration a dramatic pause. "However, my head of security can."

Andy's hand, coiled at the flap of her shoulder satchel, relaxed.

Fulton reached in his pocket and pulled out a cell phone. He made a slow show of opening the screen, tapping through several icons, then raising the phone to his ear.

"Sean, would you join me in my office please?"

Fulton lowered the phone to his desk.

"Thank you," Andy said.

I shifted in position on the I-beam and looked for a clock. My watch disappears with me. The same with my phone. In the disappeared state, I find it hard to determine the time, and time was short. If O'Bannon and his crew had Pidge—

Christ!

The thought of what they had done to Erickson all but stopped my heart.

I abruptly let go of the I-beam I had been gripping and let the wind carry me to the next in the line, closer to the center of the office. There had to be a clock somewhere. On a wall. Above the fake fireplace. Fulton's desk was a joke. I wondered what possible sense it made to have a glass desk with nothing on it. Not even a phone.

The sitting area had an array of low sofas and coffee tables. Oversized color photo books occupied most of the tables. A lamp stood here and there, the cords disappearing discretely into the floor.

My eye drifted magnetically to one of his trinkets of wealth.

"Shit!" I said. "Andy, look at the coffee table. Far left. Your left."

I saw her casually scan the room.

"That's a Cessna Citation. The kind of model owners have. The tail number is...hang on ..." I let the wind carry me two more I-beams south "... Nine Eight Seven Foxtrot Lima. Not Alpha Lima. *Foxtrot Lima!*"

An easy cover. The last two letters of the registration were FL, standing for Fulton Law, no doubt. But it would be easy to sign a book or give a distracted FBO clerk the letters AL. Even if they glanced out the window at the jet, the mind would see what it had been told.

"Andy, it was their jet!"

She stiffened.

"What did you say his name was? Your head of security?" she asked casually. "Did you say Sean?"

"I did," Fulton answered.

"I think we've met. Irish gentleman?" Andy's hand slipped under the cover of her satchel. She moved away from the double doors toward the center of the room, looking for a vantage point that covered both Fulton and the door.

Fulton watched her. He tensed.

She didn't wait. She pulled her weapon from the satchel and fixed it on the door. Fulton didn't seem terribly surprised.

"I need to get in there with you." I said.

She shook her head but didn't speak. She held a firing stance on the door.

The door clicked and opened.

He walked in grinning. Bastard.

"Hello Detective Andrea Stewart," O'Bannon said. He slowly raised his hands, a move I trusted about as far as I could throw this building.

"Get on your knees," Andy ordered him.

"I don't think so," he said. "Sends the wrong message."

"Where is she?"

"Yer friend, Pidge? Cute name, that. A fuckin' tigress, that girl. My boys almost couldn't get her into the barrel."

O'Bannon stood with a smug smile on his face. Andy took a step closer and lowered her weapon until it pointed at his right knee.

"You're going to tell me where she is, right now, or I'm going to start with the knees."

"God damn it, Sean!" Fulton barked. "You swore to me!"

"Shut up, Ellery," O'Bannon said out of the side of his mouth. The dynamic between the two men changed. O'Bannon took command. "Detective, before you cripple me, may I?"

He plucked at his lapel with two fingers and pulled his coat open, exposing a cell phone in his shirt pocket. Andy brought the weapon back to bear on the center of his chest. From fifteen feet away, it would only be a question of which icon embroidered on his tie she aimed for.

O'Bannon used his other hand, again with two fingers, to lift the phone from his pocket. He spoke into it.

"Mikey, are you there?"

"Yes, boss."

"Hold the phone down by the hole." O'Bannon extended his arm and held the phone toward Andy. "Say hello to your girlie friend."

"Pidge?" Andy called out.

"Andy? WHAT THE FUCK!" A stream of invective sounding hollow and distant came through the phone. It faded away as Mikey pulled the phone from Pidge.

"Girl has the mouth of an ironworker," O'Bannon pulled his phone back. "Now, Detective, I want you to lay your weapon on this fat fuck's desk and raise up yer hands. Or you can shoot me. And Mikey starts pouring acid into that barrel. He'll fill it up about half full and let her slosh around a bit."

"You bastard," Fulton said. "You swore to me! You fucking greedy, ignorant son of a bitch! You swore you wouldn't! If you think—"

O'Bannon turned sharply to Fulton. "Please!" he snapped. Then drawing a calming breath, he said, "Just a moment more, Ellery, and I'll see to your needs."

"Andy, do what he says," I said into her ear. "I'm coming in for you."

"Wait!" she said. To me. Not O'Bannon. She made a show of tipping the muzzle of her Glock up and took it to the glass desk. She laid it down, raised her hands clear of the gun, and backed away.

Fulton marched around the desk, away from Andy and her surrendered weapon as if they might stain him.

"I will NOT be a part of this! We had a deal!"

"Much better," O'Bannon said to Andy. He lowered his hands, then reached behind his back and drew a similar Glock from his belt. His version carried a long suppressor. In one swift motion he formed a grip, raised the weapon—not at Andy, but at Fulton—and fired.

The window behind Fulton developed a tiny, frost-fringed hole, painted all around with blood and brain matter spray. Chunks of skull slid down the wet glass. Fulton, late of the Billion Dollar Boys, dropped unceremoniously to the carpet, spilling the rest of the contents of his head onto plush fibers.

O'Bannon lost no time swinging the weapon toward Andy.

He heaved a long sigh.

"If I've learned anything in my travels, it's when to fold up the tent," he said. "I hope you'll bear with me, lassie, but his death makes sense, with what's about to be learned about the Billion Dollar Boys. Terrible symptom of this litigious society. How this firm went around puttin' cameras in little girl's shower rooms just so they could come back later and force school districts and insurance companies to pay out big settlements, most of which the good lawyers kept for themselves, as I am sure you learned on yer little trip to Monroe yesterday. Thanks to that fucking idiot Erickson, a well-crafted and very profitable scheme seems to be coming apart. This poor fella just couldn't bear what was coming and decided to take the honorable way out. But the thing is, finding you dead here, too, might confuse the authorities. Better you should simply disappear. So, I'm offering you a choice. Come with me and I'll let you say good-bye to yer little girlie friend, and I'll promise to put a bullet in both yer skulls before we seal you up."

"Or?"

"Or I shoot you here and now and tell Mikey to start pouring. Either way, as you can see, my days among the Billion Dollar Boys have come to an end, as have your days among the living."

Andy gave a calculated shrug.

"Lead the way."

O'Bannon eyed her for a moment, weighing how easy that had been. Then he backed up. He twisted the knob on the door to the office, locking it. He went to the desk and slipped Andy's weapon into his belt. After that, he went to the private elevator. He pulled a key card from his pocket and swiped the reader.

"You know, we had you on camera all the while. Comin' here today. Saw you casing the place last night, too."

"Clever you."

"Oh, and yer hubby, too. Nice of him to lend us his phone. The boys have probably picked him up by now. He'll be joining you. We saw him with you down on the street. I don't think you'll get to perform yer little disappearing act this time, but I'd love to know where you went the other night."

"Fuck you," I said to O'Bannon, although it went into Andy's ear.

O'Bannon stepped away from the private elevator door. He bobbed his head from side to side in a silly tick-tock gesture. "Takes a while. The elevator sensors wait until it's empty, then locks everyone else out so it can come up and that fat shite won't have to rub elbows with his employees."

"How did an operator like you hook up with a nerd like Erickson?" Andy asked.

O'Bannon smiled. "Right. This is the part where I, the villain, proudly explain the whole fucking scheme to you, giving you time to activate yer homing device or disarm me or some of that movie house shite. I don't think so."

"But tell me this much. We traced an IP address to this location," Andy lied. "You're running the servers out of this building, aren't you? I had a bet with my husband."

"I'm sure you did. I'll tell him to pay up. This hulk has more empty space than renters. And half the renters are in default on their rent. That stupid shite was over the moon when I told him I could get him a deal on space here, and then save him a small fortune in server farm fees. He doesn't know a server farm from a trout farm. Bastard was all about appearances. Parading that actor around on his arm like a trophy wife. Look at this ridiculous room. But no matter. All I cared about was the T-one and a couple empty floors—once we shut everything down in fucking frozenland."

"Erickson made cameras and used his job at Reichenbach to launch the idea. You took it to the big leagues."

"Erickson was makin' cameras to peek at little-girl pussy, the wanker."

"Fifteen million in Monroe doesn't seem like something to sneeze at," Andy pressed for more.

"Jesus, nobody can keep their mouth shut. Fulton and his fucking scheme. Fucking litigation, that's risky. I prefer a sure thing."

Kaitlyn Aberdeen. LeMore had it right.

"So...Monroe...that was Fulton's idea?"

O'Bannon said nothing.

"Monroe was proof of concept," Andy said. "All this...this was just infrastructure. Servers. After you outgrew the little room in Escanaba."

"Who fucking wants to live in Escanaba? Or Chicago, fer that matter. Someplace warm. Servers run just as well where the ocean is blue and the sand is white, lassie."

The elevator door opened and stayed open.

"Now, Mrs. Detective Stewart, I think you're the same kind of wildcat that yer friend is, so I want you to step into that box, go to the corner and get on yer knees facing the wall, and put yer hands behind yer head, please."

Andy moved slowly across the room. The closer she got to O'Bannon, the more he stepped back. His hand never wavered.

I frantically searched the windows, thinking I might smash through. I considered breaking into the one with the bullet hole. But the hole showed me that the glass was half an inch thick. Even if I crashed into it at full speed, the likely outcome would be me injured—or worse, popping out of *the other thing* and taking a long fall to the sidewalk.

"Hum once if you go up. Twice if you go down," I told Andy as she slipped out of my sight.

My heart hammered. I wanted to tear my hair out.

O'Bannon stepped into the elevator after her, moving to the opposite side, also out of sight. In a moment the door closed.

"Hmmmm." Andy signaled.

Up.

I aimed the propulsion unit vertically and let go of the I-beam.

48

The floor above Fulton's office contained offices full of busy-looking people in tightly packed spaces. The bulk of the Fulton Law firm, I guessed. The floor above that was empty. The next above that was the top floor and had vertical blinds hanging inside all the windows. The vertical blinds may have kept out prying eyes using cameras with zoom lenses at a distance, but up close I saw through the gaps.

The same three banks of elevators stood at intervals at the core of the building, but here they did not open privately on the side facing me. This end of the floor looked empty. However, beyond the block of elevators, cables snaked across the carpet.

I pointed the propulsion unit sideways and flew along the glass to the northwest corner of the building. As my perspective changed, a cluster of haphazard workstations came into view, looking isolated in a broad empty space on the east half of the open floor. At least a dozen flat screens formed a semi-circle above the workstations. The screens were lighted and active, showing simple login graphics. Easily recognizable from a distance, each of the screens had a box for a username and a box for a password. A monolithic rack with multiple servers stood at one end. Heavy cables ran from the server rack into a utility panel in the floor.

At the center of the semi-circle, at one of the workstations, a thin figure hunched over one of four laptops. All four laptops were open, displaying boxes of code or moving colored bars. The figure at the laptop, a young man wearing glasses, seemed to be alone on the entire floor, absorbed in his work.

I saw no sign of Andy or O'Bannon. I didn't think he would have prodded her at gunpoint into the main Fulton Law offices. Too many witnesses. They should have been here by now.

Down one.

I caught hold of an I-beam and worked my way down, hand over hand. The second-from-the-top floor came into view.

Andy moved across the wide-open floor space. Behind her, O'Bannon followed holding his suppressed weapon. I saw what I had missed from my perspective on the west end of the building.

Mikey stood waiting for them beside three steel barrels. A flat freight cart sat nearby.

"What is your deal with the barrels?" Andy asked.

O'Bannon laughed.

"Ah, it's an old trick from my days in Dublin. Much better than plastic wrap or old carpeting for bodies. You can move 'em in broad daylight. Slap a label on—make it for something truly frightening—and nobody asks to open 'em." O'Bannon sounded enthusiastic. "And you can get creative. Put a fella in upside-down like Erickson. Throw in some rats for fun. Acid. Cement. Whatever yer fancy. And at the end of the day, we'd take 'em out into the North Sea and chuck 'em overboard. Sometimes we'd let 'em float for a while. Shoot some holes in and let 'em sink, slow-like. Great fun! That lovely lake over there works just as well."

"Andy! Is that you?!" Pidge cried out, muted.

"I'm here, Pidge!"

"Good! Would you please rip this fucker's balls off and drop them in here, so I can smash them to paste!"

Mikey flinched.

"I'll be honest, I am truly inclined to try and sell her. I know some fellas in Africa who would pay a lot for her kinda spice," O'Bannon said. He looked at his watch. "But I'm afraid there isn't time. Thanks to you. Speaking of which, I have hosting duties to attend to. I promised you a chance to say yer good-byes, so in you go and you can chat away. Yer husband will be joining you shortly. I'll come down in about an hour and give yer both the bullet to the head I promised."

Mikey lifted the lid on one of the barrels. He stepped behind my wife. My guts froze. He clamped his hands around Andy's arms and lifted her. Instead of fighting, she lifted her legs over the lip. Once inside, Mikey pressed on her shoulder. She crouched, and Mikey put the lid in place. The lid had a screw-in plug, which he removed.

I swore I would see the bastard dead. I added his boss to the list.

The sound on my earpiece became Andy's breathing.

"I'm here, Dee," I said. "I see you. I'll be there for you in two minutes."

Distantly, I heard O'Bannon's voice as he gave instructions to Mikey. I watched O'Bannon step over to the barrel and heard him as he leaned over the open top hole.

"Sorry, lassie. I lied. Ye should be dead in about ten minutes. But I hear it's a peaceful way to go."

Mikey stepped up and began screwing the plug in.

"You there, Pilot?" Andy's voice, tight, came to me.

I wanted to scream.

"One minute out, Dee."

"I love you."

"One minute."

I couldn't speak. I turned and searched the street and courtyard three hundred feet below me. *There!* I saw what I needed.

I took one last glance at the scene on the vacant floor. O'Bannon hurried on long strides toward the elevators. I didn't wait to see him go.

I dove for the earth. I've never pushed a propulsion unit to full power in a dive. The acceleration stunned me. The Hyatt West tower and the Midwest Center raced upward on either side of me. Halfway down, I flipped the unit around and applied full power to arrest the fall. I feared I'd overdone it. Failure flashed through my mind. Crashing into the earth. Injured. Lying there while Andy and Pidge suffocated.

A construction fence came up fast, offering to impale me. I twisted my wrist and let the propulsion unit scream until it brought me to a halt. I cut the power a split second before it tried to take me skyward again. People hurrying busily across the courtyard stopped and searched for the angry insect sound. Some scanned the sky for a drone.

I pulsed the unit and aimed myself into a work area. Scaffolding reached up to a new skybridge being built for the Midwest Center. A work truck had been parked near an area of the courtyard that had been torn out of the earth. Slabs of concrete, large and small, lay where a jackhammer had smashed them, waiting for a loader to lift them away.

I saw two pieces that fit my needs and eased myself down onto the first. Looking closer, I spotted a piece of rebar running from the concrete chunk deeper into the pile. No good. I used the corner of the slab as a grip and pushed myself over to the next piece, a slab roughly the size of a kitchen sink.

Two workmen in heavy Carhart overalls stood nearby. One operated a cutting tool, slicing lengths of rebar. He cast an inverted V-shaped spray of sparks to the ground around his feet. The other examined something on an electronic tablet.

I didn't have time to care.

Fwooomp! I reappeared over the concrete and dropped onto it. A sharp edge bit into my right knee.

"Hey!" The man with the tablet startled. I can only guess where he thought I came from, or what he thought I was doing, hugging a piece of concrete.

I pointed behind him. "He's got a bomb! Get everybody outta here! He's got a bomb!"

The startled worker turned quickly to see where I was pointing.

"Get outta here!"

I spread myself flat over the concrete slab and *PUSHED* harder than I've ever pushed.

FWOOOMP! The sound thundered in my head. The cool sensation didn't flow, it *snapped* over me. I looked down and saw concrete, and for a moment thought I had failed, but the slab engulfed in my arms had disappeared.

Vaguely aware of the workers now scrambling to act on my warning, I held the weightless concrete slab and pushed away from the earth. Up. Holding the propulsion unit in my right hand.

"Will, please hurry," Andy said softly in my ear.

"I'm coming!"

I rose above the construction site. I fired the propulsion unit and shot skyward. Full power. The acceleration caused the Hyatt West Tower and the Midwest Center tower on either side of me to sweep past. Faster, faster I climbed. The city spread out around me. Lake Michigan, a cold blue horizon, appeared beyond the towers to the east. I shot past the top of the Hyatt, past the floor where Andy's breathing reached out to my ear. I climbed over the Midwest Center rooftop and saw the Chicago Loop sprawl in cold sunshine.

The concrete slab had no weight or mass, but its bulk required holding it with both hands. I clutched it like a waiter delivering a tray of food to a table. My right hand held both the slab and the power unit. I turned the propulsion unit to scribe a tight arc over the river. I applied a down angle and dove toward the Wrigley building. Skirting its towers, I swung to the right, crossed Michigan Avenue, and sped past the Tribune building and three stoic medieval knights who didn't seem to give a damn what I was up to.

If I had to guess, I would have put my speed at over forty knots. Add in the northerly tailwind and I may have hit fifty knots crossing back over the river, skimming the rim of the Hyatt West Tower. My target lay beyond the Hyatt, but to do what I needed meant cutting as close to the lip of the hotel's roof as possible.

Target fixation.

I let nothing intrude on my vision. I fixed the glass panel in my mental crosshairs. The Midwest Center tower grew larger and larger. I shifted my grip on the slab, holding it out like an offering to a glass god.

"Will, hurry…" Andy whispered.

God damn O'Bannon.

I angled downward. The Hyatt roof shot under me. Below me, I was vaguely aware of people running and shouting, but the split second that followed offered no time for anything but—

Release!

I threw the slab forward and instantly shoved the propulsion unit to full power.

A cold electric snap bit into my hands as the concrete slab slipped my grip. Jagged gray stone appeared out of thin air. Gravity closed around the concrete and yanked it earthward, but my forward speed sent it hurtling on an arc toward glass.

I flicked my wrist to the right; the propulsion unit screamed.

The glass wall surged forward as if to slap me out of the sky. I curved right, diverging from the trajectory of the now hurtling, falling concrete slab.

I heard glass shatter as I hit the wall and for an instant thought I'd broken through the window to the right of my target. Not so. I hit hard with my left shoulder and hip. My six-month-old pelvic break screamed at me. Worse—

Fwoo—

"NO!"

The propulsion unit escaped my grip, appeared, clattered against the glass as the prop spun, and fell away.

I bounced off the glass and saw my arms and hands reveal in front of me. I felt gravity reach for me. I fell, tumbling and spinning toward Michigan Avenue.

I frantically *pushed.*

Fwooomp! My arms vanished again. The horizon changed places twice. My downward trajectory took me toward the street. In seconds I would hit pavement.

I stabbed a hand into my jacket, found a vest pocket and yanked free a fresh propulsion unit. In the same motion I found the slide and shoved it full forward, raising it above my head, like someone using an umbrella as a parachute. The unit screamed.

The street rushed up. Cars and busses shuttling up and down Michigan Avenue offered a whole new selection of ways to die.

A bus bore down on me. A lighted bus banner proclaiming Ontario Street its destination swept under me. The trajectory bottomed out. My feet, unseen, hit the top of the bus and I found myself running, banging loudly on the roof. After several steps, I soared again.

I hooked hard left, directly in front of the Sweetwater Tavern where lunch seemed like a distant dream. S-turning, I cleared the tavern building and cut the corner back over the courtyard. People transiting between buildings below me ran. I climbed frantically for the top of the Midwest Center.

On the concrete below the building, I saw debris. For one terrible moment I assumed the glass had been stronger than I imagined, and the slab had merely bounced off. But then I saw sky reflecting in bits of the debris. I looked up and saw a rectangular gap in the glass façade where my targeted window had been.

"I'm almost there, Dee! Almost there!"

I widened my vertical trajectory to make room for a turn. Coming even with the floor where Andy and Pidge were breathing their last, I leveled off and snapped a hard turn toward the building.

The missing window left a hole. Glass fragments lay on the carpeting beyond the gaping rectangle. The concrete slab lay thirty feet inside the building. It left a trail of torn carpet and chipped concrete. I shot through the hole as Mikey strode wide-eyed past the concrete, toward the broken window. He blinked and searched for the wasp sound closing in on him. Behind Mikey, I saw the barrels. One of them wobbled side to side under its own power. The moment of each wobble cycle grew until the barrel slapped down on the rug. With a loud clang, the lid broke free of the clamp. It hurled across the floor, kicked away by Pidge's feet. She slithered out after it.

I raced through the space between floor and ceiling.

Too fast! I reversed thrust to halt before hitting the windows on the south face. Pidge found her feet and charged past me, unaware of my arrival. I touched down and—

Fwooomp! I reappeared, stumbled forward, and fell flat on my face. My speed exceeded my legs' ability to run.

I heard a feral scream that stabbed ice into my heart. Thinking the worst, I turned my head in time to see that Mikey had reached the hole. He stood cautiously peering out, trying to figure out what insanity sent a chunk of concrete through the glass. A screaming Pidge hit him in the center of his spine with the full force of her small body.

Mikey lunged for a desperate grip on the edge of the opening, on the I-beam running skyward. His fingers connected, but only served to spin him around. He pinwheeled and dropped out of sight.

"FUCK YOU!" Pidge screamed after him, perilously close to the edge. She sucked in great gulps of air and staggered backward.

I scrambled to my feet and rushed to Andy's barrel. At first, I couldn't figure out the clamp. I clawed until my fingers found the release. I threw the top aside. Andy rose into my arms, gasping.

I lifted her bodily from the round horror chamber. She staggered a step and I held her upright, letting her fill her lungs and clear her head.

She looked at me, looked at the slab, and looked at Pidge who now turned around and faced us.

"That—guy—" Pidge gasped "— really—*pissed me off!*"

49

"We have to get out of here," Andy said.

"What about O'Bannon?"

"We go after him. With reinforcements."

"Oh, I'm pretty sure reinforcements are already on the way." I said to Andy. Distant sirens warbled through the hole in the glass wall.

Pidge strode toward the elevators. She pointed at the concrete slab. "How the fuck did that get in here?"

"He's one floor up," I said. "O'Bannon is one floor up. That's where he has his servers. I think he's about to launch his auction there."

"I don't think he can get out of the building." Andy started for the elevators.

"Guys!" Pidge called out.

Andy and I hurried to join Pidge. She stood with her hands on her hips, flexing a perturbed look at us.

"What?" I asked.

"None of these buttons work. I've been pushing them, but none of them work."

I stupidly stepped past Pidge and pushed one of the call buttons. She gave me a perturbed look.

"I told you!"

"They must have the elevators locked out for this floor. And probably the one above. We need a key card. And I think Mikey took his with him."

"Wait! You said he's one floor up? How do you know?" Andy asked.

"I saw the setup. Servers. Monitors. He's running his auction up there," I repeated.

"You saw it?"

"Pretty sure," I said. I checked my watch. Two-fifty-five. "Looked like login screens. Let's hope LeMore shut him down."

"If he did, O'Bannon's clients are going to get a big surprise," Andy said. "We need to get up there. More importantly, we need to get off this floor. That broken window is a beacon for the police. I don't want to be around to have to explain Fulton or Mikey."

"Wow," I said, appraising my wife. "Look at you, bending the law."

"I'm not bending anything. I just don't have time to start from scratch with the first officer on the scene."

"Who's Fulton?" Pidge wanted to know. "What auction are you talking about? And what's with the fucking get-up, Will?"

I was still wearing the balaclava and goggles. I lifted the goggles and touched the earpiece so that I stopped hearing Andy twice.

Andy jogged to the stairwell door. She pulled it.

"It's locked."

"Fulton's the dead guy down on thirty-six. The Irishman who stuffed you in the barrel put a bullet through his head." I went to the stairwell door and studied it. "This is a magnetic lock, Andy. I don't think I can do that trick I do. There's no bolt."

"Wait! That fucking lawyer guy? The one on TV? Seriously?"

"The same."

"FUCK! I would have paid to see that!"

"Easy, kiddo. One messy homicide per day."

"So, if that's locked, and the elevators are locked out, how do we get off this shitty floor?" Pidge asked. Then she looked at me. "How did you get here?"

"Hang on," Andy paced, hand to her brow. I eased into position to intercept her after she turned.

"You and Pidge stay here. They'll take you both into custody and you can explain everything."

"No! By then, O'Bannon will be gone."

"I'll find a way up there. I'll go in the same way I got in here if I have to."

"You?"

"Me. You're unarmed, remember?"

Her jaw locked. Her lower lip swelled. The gold flecks in her green eyes became sharper, penetrating.

"It's what we said," I reminded her. "In California. For those times when you can't. Or it's too messy. This is one of those times."

She didn't answer.

"For people who need something the law can't give them."

She still didn't answer.

"You know I'm right."

Pidge stood to one side watching and listening.

"Okay, now you guys are really starting to freak me out."

"Really?" I turned to Pidge. "*This* is what freaks you out?"

She flipped me an impish shrug.

Andy let her face fall to stare at the carpet between us. After a moment, I saw movement, the slightest nod.

"You're right about how we finish this. But we do it together, which means we can't leave her up here by herself."

She looked up at me, and then we both turned to Pidge.

Andy said, "Pidge, honey. How much do you trust us?"

50

"Oh! You are fucking kidding me!" Pidge cried into my ear.

"Stop shouting. I'm right here."

"*You are fucking kidding me!*" She dug her hands into the back of my ribs and tightened her thighs and legs around me. I was honestly glad Andy couldn't see this. We skimmed over the carpeting.

"Pidge! Relax!" Andy followed the sound of her voice and tried to calm her.

I aimed the propulsion unit toward the hole in the wall.

"Oh shit *oh shit oh shit!* SHIT! YOU'RE REALLY DOING THIS!" Pidge saw the hole coming, the edge of the floor, the empty space.

I would have said, "Hang on" but she had that all worked out, and I didn't think I had enough air in my lungs for the words. With the grip she fixed on my torso, I had little hope of drawing more air. I prayed my oxygen would last until we touched down.

We shot out the hole and she screamed. It echoed off the buildings around us and took a dozen years off the hearing in my left ear.

A moment later, as we soared into empty space outside the building, she went silent. I think she held her breath. I wanted to get her down fast and get back to Andy, so I aimed the power unit at the sidewalk east of the Midwest Center, on Stanton Street. We skimmed the south face of the Hyatt West Tower and dropped.

Below me, uniformed police hurried to take control of the courtyard and the space around the building. Several took up a position to channel people out of the lobby, away to the south, away from the body on the pavement. Occupied with crowd control, I couldn't be sure they had dispatched anyone to the thirty-eighth floor yet.

"Now be quiet," I said. "I don't want the whole world hearing you."

She chanted her favorite word, over and over, beneath her breath.

East of the Midwest Center tower, a series of steps dropped below sidewalk level to an underground mall. A sign directed visitors to The Shops of The Midwest Center. A few people milled around above the steps on the sidewalk. They fixed their attention on the scene in the courtyard. Not for long. Police pushed toward them, shouting orders. A cop car angled toward the sidewalk, lights strobing.

I eased us down, pulsing the power unit to slow the descent. The steps to the underground mall were vacant, so I let us float down until my feet touched the last step before a set of glass doors. We landed unseen, below sidewalk level.

Fwooomp!

Pidge's pixie face and short blonde hair appeared in front of me. The look of stunned wonder enlarged her blue eyes. Her mouth opened, but nothing came out. A wonder of its own. I tried to peel her off me, since gravity had a say again.

"I gotta get back up there," I said, pulling her arms away and attempting to get her legs back under her. She finally settled onto her feet. "Go this way, through the underground. Back to your room and stay there," I ordered. "Don't let anyone in who can't recite the definition of Class B airspace."

She stood frozen.

Fwooomp! I vanished, and a fresh look of shock washed over her face. I kicked off the step and shot skyward as she found speech again.

One word. It burst out and echoed in the concrete stairwell, rising to spread into the busy street in my wake.

51

I had developed a touch with the power units. I had a working, muscle-memory understanding of what pilots call accelerate-stop distance. How much room you need to stop in proportion to your acceleration. I hurried back up to the broken window on the thirty-eighth floor, but not so fast that I'd wind up doing another face plant trying to stop inside.

To enter the window space on a level flight path, I climbed in an arc that took me first toward the Hyatt, quite possibly toward the room Andy and I occupied on the thirty-second floor. Just short of the brick and glass façade, I hooked left, along the south face of the buildings, past rooms with curtains open and rooms with curtains closed. I slowed the climb and veered away from the Hyatt, back toward the Midwest Center, lining up with the open rectangle.

The line for entry looked good until I gained a view of the interior.

Three people blocked my path.

O'Bannon's barrel-handling associates from the Reichenbach loading dock, large and rough-looking men, created a formidable human wall not far from the open window. Between them, being dragged on her knees, kicking and fighting—

Andy.

The men held her arms. She curled her legs and stomped at their shins.

She threw her weight, less than half that of either of the two men, into her elbows and jabbed. Unaffected, they jerked her forward.

I had no time to guess where they had come from or how this struggle developed. I only knew that they were about to hurl her out the open window.

"Dee, I'm coming!" I called out, but then realized I had killed the Bluetooth connection. If I hadn't, I would have known.

I slammed the power unit to full and accelerated toward the opening. I couldn't take them both, so I aimed to my right, at the larger of the two.

He stood three or four inches taller than me. He had at least fifty pounds on me. His arms were the size of my thighs. Another three steps, he and his ugly companion would be able to toss Andy out like a helpless child.

I shot through the gaping hole.

Fwooomp! I dropped short of the beast, landed one foot in a full run on the carpet, and threw my right fist forward at his startled face.

In that fist, the propulsion unit screamed at full power. It may have been a hobby-plane propeller, only six inches in diameter, but the carbon-fiber blade was razor sharp and spinning at thousands of revolutions per minute. It hit somewhere near his left eye, tearing into flesh and spraying blood.

He didn't scream. Because a fractured second later my full body hit him dead center, with one knee pumping upward in time to catch him in the groin.

The snarling electric motor and propeller chattered and stopped. Air and blood burst from his open mouth.

My one hundred and eighty-three pounds slammed into his unprotected body mass. The momentum carried in my favor and we both went over. We fell away from the window. His grip broke, releasing one of Andy's arms.

He hit the floor on his back with me on top of him. I kicked to keep the momentum going. I skidded over his head. One knee slipped across the goo that was left of his face. Behind me, I heard Andy cry out fiercely.

I rolled clear and fought to regain my footing. I had hoped my target would stay down, but shock must have numbed my blows. He also rolled, thankfully away from me. He found his way to his knees and struggled to his feet as I did the same.

Andy's attacker still had the upper hand. He spun around behind her and clamped his huge hands around her biceps, forcing her legs away from his own. With his back to the open window, he dragged her to the edge. He lifted her off her feet. She shook and twisted. Wild hair flew around her head.

Andy's attacker poised to give her body a powerful swing and send her out the opening.

Suddenly, the man in front of me staggered away to my left, arms out, fighting and swinging at empty air.

Blind!

I ran.

Straight for Andy.

Three steps. Two.

I threw myself at her. The floor, littered with shards of glass, passed beneath me.

I landed on my wife and grabbed. My weight dragged her down and my momentum carried us forward into the large man's knees. They snapped backward, unbending, tipping him out the opening like a tree.

He kept his hold on Andy and took us with him.

I felt more than saw the flat face of the building shoot past us as we exited. The empty expanse of thirty-eight floors opened beneath us. Andy screamed. She tore at his grip. He had her upper arms. If he held on, he would take us all to our deaths, no matter what I did.

I joined the effort

He screamed. We twisted and tore away his hands.

His instinct to grab at the building—at something, anything—finally caused his hands to release Andy's arms.

FWOOOMP! Once again, for the love of my life, I pushed as hard as possible. I felt the cool sensation snap into place around Andy and me.

I caught a look at the man's face as he dropped away.

He saw us vanish and looked comically surprised, then terrified.

I took great satisfaction in seeing his expression, until I realized I was getting a splendid view of it for far too long.

We fell with him. Fast. Andy threw her arms around me and held her body tightly against mine, against my jacket, against the vest inside my jacket and the last charged propulsion unit inside.

I would never pull it out in time.

Enough!

STOP!

We stopped.

O'Bannon's goon accelerated away from us. He dropped toward his friend Mikey, who lay at the center of a circle cordoned off by the police. Shrieks came from the crowds lining the sidewalks.

Andy pulled me tight. I breathed in her scent. I felt her hair on my face. I felt her chest heaving against mine.

I felt something else, too. Something at my center. A firmness. Like a muscle. Using it as I would have used a grip on a beam, I rotated us to a vertical posture. Far below, I heard what sounded like a sack of seed hitting concrete. More screams.

We remained fixed in space, less than half a dozen floors from the plaza.

Breathing. Holding each other. Alive.

Stopped.

A breeze blew past us. I had time to realize that we weren't a dandelion fluff on the wind. We were *stopped,* and the wind slipped around us.

"Hey," I said softly.

"What?" She sounded angry.

"You okay?"

"I'm done with tall buildings for a while," she said hoarsely.

52

We gave ourselves a moment. We hung in space. I felt her shiver. It wasn't the cold.

As carefully as I could, maintaining my hold on to her, I squeezed my right hand between us and pulled out my last power unit. I pushed the slide forward and we rose. After a few minutes we eased back through the opening.

"Stay with me," I said. I flew us to the center of the open floor, as far from windows as geometrically possible.

Andy's other attacker staggered in a choppy circle near the elevators. His pain caught up with him and he moaned, holding his palms to his face, to his eyes. I didn't want to see under those meaty hands. I had a strong feeling both eyes were gone. After colliding with the elevator shaft structure, he fell to his knees howling.

Fwooomp!

I gingerly lowered Andy to the floor.

She held me for a moment, face buried in my shoulder. Then she swallowed hard and looked up at me. She took in air the way she took in the sight of me. Deeply.

I didn't have words. I stroked her cheek. She closed her eyes to concentrate on the sensation of my hand on her skin.

"They came in almost the second you and Pidge went out," she said. "They were sent down to grab you but couldn't find you."

"How did they get here? Stairs or elevator?"

"Elevator. They saw me, saw that Pidge was gone and Mikey was gone, and when they saw the broken window and saw Mikey down below, they figured I had done it. They were not pleased."

"No shit."

I gave her a quick embrace then broke free and walked over to the man now moaning loudly with his hands pressed to his bloody face.

"Shut up, asshole," I said.

"Help me!" he cried at the sound of my voice.

"Sure. I'm a doctor. Stay still." The idiot believed me. That or desperation gave him no choice. "I need to check your pockets. Stay still."

He wore a nylon jacket with stripes and a sports logo I didn't recognize. I checked those pockets first. Things were getting bloody, so I was pleased when I found what I was looking for. I pulled a key card out of his right-hand pocket and a small semi-automatic pistol from his left.

"Okay, you've got a flexible oracle hemophobia. Do NOT move or you'll make it worse, understand?"

"What?"

I stood up. "Someone will be here for you in a moment. Stay still."

"Okay," he said, dribbling blood. "Please! Hurry!"

I was glad to turn my back to him. He was a mess.

I waved Andy to join me.

"Come on, we need to go. This floor will be full of cops any minute."

"I don't think so." Andy said. I handed her the pistol. "A second body just hit the pavement down there. It's going to be chaos for a little while."

"Or they counted the floors and are on their way up here to find out why it's raining men."

Andy ignored me.

"O'Bannon is one floor up. We need to get up there before he uses the chaos to get away." I glanced at my watch.

Andy saw the time, too. She said, "By now, if LeMore did his part, O'Bannon knows his whole scheme is finished. He made it sound like this was the last hurrah for Chicago when he ended his partnership with Fulton."

I held up the key card and we hurried to the elevators. I swiped the card across a reader that winked a tiny green light of acknowledgement. A moment later, one of the elevators dinged. I half expected to see a contingent of cops come out of the box, weapons high, shouting orders. Then I remembered that the private function sent an empty elevator car.

The doors opened.

We stepped in, waved the key card over the reader, and pressed thirty-nine.

Andy checked the weapon. She ejected the magazine, counted the rounds, and then slammed the magazine back in place. She pulled the slide to load the chamber. The pistol had a conventional safety, so she flicked it Off. She eased the hammer back for single action. After pushing me to one side of the doors, she took a firing stance and waited for the door to open.

I don't know if the dramatic weapons exercise was necessary, but I know the familiar routine calmed and centered her.

We arrived on thirty-nine, where I'd seen the workstations, the cables snaking over the floor, and the semi-circle of login screens.

The elevator doors opened.

We were too late.

53

"Where is he?"

The semi-circle of flatscreens had gone black.

The thin man I'd seen earlier scurried to pack up gear. He stopped in his tracks at the sound of Andy's voice. He carried not one ounce of extra flesh on a wiry frame. A scruff of beard shaded his chin and cheeks against an otherwise pasty, boney face. He wore glasses that tucked into greasy brown hair pushed behind his ears.

He froze in the act of pulling wafer-like drives out of servers blinking in a vertical rack.

Andy approached with her weapon fixed on the space between his eyebrows. His hands shot up. He began to shiver.

Andy said nothing. She moved to the workstation table and picked up her service weapon. She checked the magazine and confirmed a round in the chamber, then secured the spare in her belt. The weapon O'Bannon used to kill Fulton, suppressor still attached, had been abandoned along with Andy's. My phone, held together with a strip of duct tape, lay on the table as well.

"Where's O'Bannon?!" I demanded.

"Who?" The technician blinked, confused.

"Sean," Andy said. "Where is he?"

"Gone. He's gone. He told me to pack up. All the drives. Burn the code. Run a scrub program on everything!" His high voice quaked.

"Are you doing that? Are you running it?"

"I swear! Tell him I was about to!" He reached for a keyboard.

"Touch that and I'll blow your hand off," Andy snapped. He pulled his hand back as if the keyboard glowed red hot.

"What?"

Andy pulled back her coat and showed her badge.

"Oh, shit!" A new realization swept across his face.

"Andy, look," I said. I pointed at the three laptop screens, still open on the table.

Video images, divided across multiple windows, originated from at least a dozen cameras. Several different tiled shower rooms filled the frames. In them, uniformed police moved from station to station, checking the shower heads just as I had.

"Man, I know what they were into here was fucked up, but I just handled the eye-tee, you know. I didn't do anything. I was just hired for tech, you know. Freelance," he pleaded. "It's just code, man. That's all. No harm."

"Kidnapping. Murder. Assault. Child pornography," Andy said methodically.

"Whoa! Whoa! No way, not me! I was just hired to set up some servers, some streaming video!"

"You're not that stupid," Andy said. She took a step forward holding the pistol just inches from the man's face. "What's his name? Sean. What's his name?"

"Seavers. Sean Seavers."

"Where is he going?"

"I don't—"

"Dude," I said. "She's a human lie detector. I wouldn't."

Andy took a step closer.

"He's on his way to the parking garage! Underground! The private elevator!"

Andy pushed him backward into a desk chair. He landed hard. The chair rolled away from the workstation. Something caught my eye.

"Where's the fourth laptop?"

"He took it!"

Andy holstered her weapon and handed me the pistol we acquired from the bleeding hulk down on thirty-eight. She leaned down, putting her face inches from the shivering programmer. She said, "I'm a cop. He's not. I can't be here to witness what he's going to do to you if you don't cooperate."

A fresh sheen of terror covered his face.

She turned quickly.

"I'm going after him," she said. "See what you can get from this idiot. Don't get any more blood on your clothes." She pointed at my knee, which carried a dark stain.

"Get help. Don't do this alone," I called after her.

"I will. I'll call you." Just before she ducked around the elevator bank, she pointed at her ear. I waved acknowledgement.

54

"Give me your wallet," I said. He glanced after Andy, searching the empty space she left behind as if he expected the police to protect him. I started to think this guy *was* that stupid. I waved the gun at him. He pulled his wallet from the front pocket of his pants.

"Drew," I said after checking his driver's license, "what's on that fourth laptop?"

"I don't know, man," he said, but with a hint of hesitation.

"Did you miss the part about her being a human lie detector? That works for me, too."

"I swear, man! I don't know!"

"Wait here," I said. I jogged back to the elevators. I found what I was looking for in a metal cabinet tucked in the wall. Taking it in hand, I walked back to where Drew sat. His eyes grew wide.

"Hold on! Hold on! I want a lawyer!"

"There's a bunch of them downstairs. I'll send one up to pick up the pieces when I'm done."

"You can't do that!" He cringed.

I swung the fire ax at my side as I walked.

"She told you. I'm *not* a cop. And it's like she said, Drew. She can't witness this."

"Wait! Wait!" he rolled the chair backward as I approached.

"No, Drew, I'm not waiting," I said. "Those hands of yours, you used them to program this shit show. You knew perfectly well what was going on here. So, I think it's only right that you never touch another keyboard again. Put your hands on the desk."

"C'mon! No!" He tucked his hands in his armpits. "Wait! I'll help you!"

"Don't worry, Drew. This won't kill you. I was a boy scout," I lied. "I know how to apply a tourniquet. You'll live, and you can learn to eat with a fork between your toes. Hands on the desk now."

"WAIT! WHAT DO YOU WANT?"

"Tell me everything. Tell me way more than I want to know. Run your mouth as fast as you can because you do NOT know at what point you will have told me enough to keep me from cutting off your hands. You need to fucking babble, Drew. *Now tell me what was on the laptop he took!*"

I poked him in the chest with the tip of the ax blade.

"WAIT! Okay! He had the financial shit on his personal laptop. For the logins. The money. Transfer protocols. People—I don't know who they were—logged in and they paid up front. He handled the money trans-fers on his laptop. Once the money transferred, he allowed the user to stream."

"How many people? How much?"

"Eight of them this time. Two million each."

"This time? How many times have you done this?" I asked.

"Nev—! Once! In July! And I wasn't here for that *I swear.* July was like this test run. It was cheesy. That other guy was an amateur."

"The buyers. What do they get for their money?"

"You know…" He squirmed.

"I don't know! Spell it out! What is all this?"

"This is everything at full scale. Gone live. Eight buyers logged in and paid two million up front. Then they were supposed to—you know—watch the show and—"

"And what?" I demanded.

"Look, I know what they were doing is wrong, but it wasn't my idea! *Please! I just work here!*"

I shook my head. "Sorry, Drew, you haven't told me enough. The hands are coming off."

He jammed his hands deeper into his armpits.

"I swear man, I'll tell you everything you want to know. Just don't hurt me! The buy-in got them a ticket to the show. Then we assigned numbers to the—er, participants—with overlay graphics, you know, like NASCAR does? Then, if someone wanted to bid—you know."

"I don't know!" I snapped, pressing the ax against his chest.

"They were supposed to bid on what they saw! Okay? If they saw something they liked, they could bid. Seavers told the users they could all bid on anyone they wanted, but there would only be one sale. The highest bidder wins—you know. But only the one. Seavers said it would keep them hungry for more. Make them bid higher next time." Drew kept his hands pinned under his armpits. His expression pleaded. "Look, I know it was wrong, okay? I get it! I didn't know what they wanted when I started and once I was in, like, Seavers was scary, man! Some kinda ex-Interpol badass. That's how he knew people to invite to log in. That was his thing in Europe or some shit. People with money who have these kinds of— tastes. People—buying and selling—girls like that. But it never got to that! It never got to that!"

"Got to what?"

"You know…the merchandise," he said. "He never delivered the merchandise. From the test in July. And today it all broke up before anybody could bid. We switched on and there were cops at all three loca- tions. *Seavers had a fucking cow!* There was no show. No bidding. Just the buy-in and it all went to shit after that. The buyers started screaming for their money back, but Seavers bailed. I swear. *Nobody saw anything!*"

I poked the ax at his face.

"What happened to the girl? Last summer! What happened?"

"I DON'T KNOW!" he cried. "I swear! I don't know! All I know is something went wrong."

A cold knot formed in my gut. Kaitlyn Aberdeen. Any hope that she might be alive disintegrated.

"What went wrong?"

I touched the ax blade to his forehead. His eyes, locked on the blade, crossed.

"Dude!"

"I'm not your dude or your bro' or your man. What went wrong?"

"I don't know, man—er, Mister! She got hurt. That's it! That's all I know."

"Make an educated guess, Drew."

I pulled the ax slowly from his forehead. He swallowed hard.

"Alright! She got hurt. The buyer wouldn't take her like that."

"Did they kill her?"

"No! I don't think so! She—they—I think they were waiting. For her to get better. That's it, man! That's all I got. They don't tell me shit."

"Until she healed up? They're letting her heal up?" I asked, feeling a spark of hope.

"I'm just guessing, man! Just guessing! Seavers wanted his money. The buyer won't pay up. Until the product was—you know—whole again."

I took a long breath.

"Drew," I said. "I take it back. I'm not going to cut your hands off. I'm going to cut your balls off. With this ax." I took a batter's stance in front of his chair. "You might want to pull them out and hold them for me, otherwise I'm just going to start whacking until I get 'em. Spread your legs, you son of a bitch." I waved the ax at his knees, which he clamped tightly shut. "Unless you tell me where she is."

"I DON'T KNOW WHERE SHE IS!" he screamed, clutching his groin.

I shouldered the ax.

"WAIT! PLEASE!" he began crying. "The files! I can give you all the files! All the video! All the images!"

"What are you talking about?" I heaved the ax back to take a swing.

"EVERYTHING!" he shrieked.

"Show me," I said. "Do it so fucking slowly that if I were a kindergarten child, I would understand perfectly what you're doing. Got it?"

He slid up to the laptop again, gingerly extending his shaking hands and touching the keys.

After a few seconds he explained that he was opening cloud storage and then opening encrypted folders. He was asked for a password and I made him stop and write it down, then read it to me as I typed it in. When the folders opened, he pointed at the screen. A list of folders appeared. The folders were named by location and date. I saw Monroe. Essex. Half a dozen other city names I recognized.

"Are these backups for what's on those drives?" I pointed at the hard drives he'd been extracting from the machines on a rack.

"Uh-huh!"

"Does O'Bannon have copies on his laptop?" I asked.

"Too big. Too much risk carrying it around on a laptop," Drew said. "Man—sorry! Mister! Mister, there's no way he'd be walking around with all that. No way. He can just download them from the cloud storage."

"The hard drives and this cloud storage—are these the only copies?"

"*I swear!*"

I studied him. The sweaty brow. The quivering hands.

"Can this cloud storage be deleted?"

His head bobbed quickly in the affirmative.

"Move!" I kicked his chair backward. He slid away from the workstation but stayed seated.

I turned to the keyboard and went to work. The chair creaked quietly behind me.

Without turning to him I said, "I wouldn't, Drew. Your hands aren't all I'll take if you fuck with me."

I continued working. The chair stopped creaking.

I expected roadblocks, but it worked like Rosemary II's PC at the front desk. I highlighted the folders and pressed SHIFT DELETE. A window popped up and asked if I was sure I wanted to delete the cloud backup files. I clicked on Yes. Another window warned me they would be Permanently Deleted. I stabbed the Y key.

"This is for Sarah," I said.

"Who?"

"Nobody you deserve to know."

The files disappeared from the cloud storage folder.

I turned back to face him. He looked at me with an expression that begged, please, are we done?

"You ever pray, Drew?" I asked. He didn't reply. "If not, now would be a good time to start. Because if even one of these images or videos ever surfaces—then God will be your only hope, because nothing mortal on this earth will save you from me."

I took a moment to consider this hired programmer. It was all just code to him. Nothing but technology and a chance to show off his command of it. He had no concept of the humanity represented by the pixels.

"She's my wife," I said.

"Who?"

"The lady cop."

"Lucky you." It reminded me of O'Bannon. It reminded me that this shivering, pleading geek was more like O'Bannon than not.

"You and your friends almost killed her twice today."

Drew removed his hands from his pits and waved them between us. "Oh, no! That wasn't me! Dude, I swear, I didn't know—"

"Drew."

"I never met her! I didn't even know she was here, I swear!"

"Drew. Shut up," I said. "She's my wife. She's a cop. She believes in the law. She believes in due process."

"Yeah, man! Due process! Let the court decide! Arrest me! Take me in!"

"That's why she left." I grinned at him.

His expression shifted to renewed terror. I lifted the fire ax and touched the blade. His eyes grew wider and his hands shot back up under his armpits.

"I don't think your case is going to court," I said calmly.

"Man, I told you everything!"

"No, you didn't. You see, the human lie detector thing? It's crazy. I cannot lie to her. Neither can you. But you tried. When you did, I saw the way you looked. It's how you look right now. You're lying to me."

Beaded sweat collected on his forehead.

I said nothing for a moment. I rolled the ax in my hand. The blade rotated a slow three-sixty. Drew couldn't help but stare at it.

"Empty your pockets."

He flinched.

There it was. The lie I had been looking for. He didn't move.

"You can empty them, or I will search the bloody body parts. Your choice."

Hands shaking now, guilt etched in his face, he jammed his fingers into a small pocket in his pants and produced a flash drive. He handed it to me.

I put it on the table and said nothing. Sweat continued to bead.

"Fine!" He fished into the same pocket again and produced a second. "I swear that's it! Search me! That's it! That's everything! I just needed insurance, that's all. I'm not into that shit! I just took it for insurance! You gotta believe me!"

"Phone, too."

He tossed his phone at my feet.

"That's IT! I SWEAR! YOU GOTTA BELIEVE ME!"

"I don't."

I stepped back and heaved the ax into a swing powered by my full body. He threw his hands up over his head and tumbled out of the chair. I buried the blade in the seat of his chair, which split in two.

"WAIT! WAIT! WAIT! WAIT!" Words tumbled out of him now, a torrent delivered in a voice just under a scream. *"I ran a keystroke recording program on Seavers' laptop and set it up to transmit to a log file that I have here—I got everything—I got all his buyers and all the money transfer data and all his keystrokes including his account numbers and you can have it all you can have all the money all sixteen million I was gonna take it from him after I got outta here but you can have it if you please please please don't do it please don't hack me with that fucking THING!"*

He gasped for air.

I stood over him, rolling the ax in my hand.

"Please," he begged. "Just give me an account number. I've got access to his transfer protocol. He doesn't know. You can transfer all the money! He won't know it's gone until he logs in! You don't have much time because he'll probably move it as soon as he can connect. *I was going to take it! You can have it! I'll give you all of it!"*

"Yes, you will," I said.

I thought of the only bank routing number and account number that I knew from memory.

55

An incoming call jangled in my earpiece. I touched the button at my ear. "Divisible Man Airways. You always fly first class."

"And get the crap scared out of you," Andy said.

"Where are you?"

"Street."

"Did you catch him?"

"No. I tried the parking garage—but honestly, why would he tell that geek where he was going except as misdirection."

"Which explains why he left the little shit alive. For a guy cleaning up behind himself, I thought that was odd. I mean, he kills Fulton..."

"I think he killed Fulton because he knew that when it came down to deal-making, he didn't stand a chance against the slick lawyer connected to every judge and DA in Chicago."

"So, where do you think he went?"

"Probably merged with the crowd leaving the building. Which also explains why he didn't take his gun. He couldn't be sure he wouldn't be searched. The cops are treating this as a terrorist thing. Apparently, somebody was yelling about a bomb earlier."

"That's crazy."

"Yeah, well, the downside is that Chicago PD is more interested in evacuating than containing. He probably slipped through as one more office worker. Where are you?"

"Still on thirty-nine," I said. "Just finished up with Chatty Cathy, here."

"You do know I was being theatrical about the blood, right?"

"He's fine. Snug as a bug in a rug."

I looked over my handiwork. Drew Pogue, according to his Illinois driver's license, sat naked in the center of the vast empty space on what remained of his office chair. With the seat gone, he sat on the chair frame. It didn't look comfortable. About a hundred feet of excellent Cat 5 cable secured him to the chair and bound his hands and feet. A strip of duct tape ran around his head at eye level.

That's gonna take out some hair when they pull it off, I thought.

I acquired the cable after using the ax to sever the connection between the servers and laptops and routers and workstation equipment—and the outside world. In theory, destroying the photos and videos saved in cloud storage meant that only the originals on the server hard drives remained. I left the stack of drives on the workstation table as evidence of Fulton's and Seavers' crimes. Disconnected from the internet, I prayed the files would be safe in the hands of law enforcement.

"Did you get everything?"

"I think there's a chance Kaitlyn Aberdeen is still alive."

I explained.

Andy let silence hang in the digital connection between us. I pictured her, eyes squeezed shut, jaw locked, her expression a mix of gratitude and frustration.

I gave her a moment, then I explained the file storage, and my method of isolating the servers to preserve the evidence. She told me she appreciated me not destroying everything.

"He tried to pocket a couple flash drives with some of the images and videos. I got them. I searched him for more but found nothing."

"Did you go through all his clothing? Belts? Shoes? Look for SD memory cards? Those things can be pretty small." My girl. Double-checking my work. "Did you check his hair?"

"Yup. Can't say I enjoyed it."

"Get his phone, too?"

"Got it. He's all wrapped up and ready for Chicago PD if they ever get up here."

"I found the scene commander a few minutes ago and brought him up to speed. They were going floor by floor, but I think I got them moving your way. And Greg must be thinking fast, because it sounds like the people he's been in touch with are coming. You should be entertaining a tactical team any minute. Keep your hands where they can see them."

Click! I heard the stairway door lock release.

"Speak of the devil," I said. "Better if they don't see me at all."

Fwooomp!

"Gotta go," I whispered. "I'll find you."

I touched my ear and ended the call.

Serious looking men in tactical gear and helmets emerged from the stairway door swinging automatic rifles to clear the area. They trotted around the corners of the elevators into the open floor space and trained the laser dots from their weapons on Drew. To minimize the chance of them mistaking him for an innocent hostage I wrote "FUCKING GUILTY" on his naked chest with a permanent marker. On his forehead, I wrote "ARREST ME." I left Seavers' pistol, the one with the suppressor, taped to Drew's lap, and the spare pistol on the table.

More men arrived, some in plain clothes. They used the elevators. I pushed off the south-facing window where I'd been waiting.

Time for me to go. Since the door to the stairwell required a key card, it had been propped open by the incoming tactical team. I checked for traffic, then floated through it. I dropped down to thirty-eight where the door had also been propped open, and more cops worked the scene. Several stood over the surviving member of O'Bannon's muscle team and tried to figure out what happened to the man's face. I presumed they had called for EMTs. One officer applied a bloody cloth to his wounds.

I kept to the perimeter of the room and worked my way carefully toward the missing window. On my way, I picked up the bloody, broken propulsion unit laying on the carpet. It had been left in place to be photographed and cataloged as evidence. I folded my shirt over it until it vanished.

Then, for what I truly hoped was the last time, I went out the broken window.

56

Andy waved me off. She made eyes at me through glass and shook her head in tiny increments. The message was clear. Stay away.

I found her at the center of a cluster of men in the lobby of the Midwest Center second tower. Some wore uniforms, heavily decorated with rank. Others wore plain clothes. Two wore heavy tactical gear with helmets and headsets. She did most of the talking. Their affect oozed superiority and no small measure of anger, but Andy stood up to them. She wore her badge on her belt and her holster clipped on her hip. Her sidearm was missing, no doubt confiscated by the local authorities as a matter of protocol.

I stood on the sidewalk on Stanton. Police forced the crowd to the east side of the street. More police arrived. As their numbers increased, the blue line pushed the perimeter ever outward. The last of the building occupants were being evacuated and hustled away. A phalanx of street cops moved to clear the sidewalk where I stood. In a moment I would be pushed out of Andy's line of sight.

Just before losing visual contact, she flicked her eyes up toward the Hyatt tower, then back at me. I waved and nodded, and let myself be herded north, toward Wacker. She turned back to briefing Chicago's finest, and to showing them that the City of Essex had their own finest.

The ground floor entrance to the Hyatt West Tower had been absorbed by the police cordon and sealed off. I continued north to Wacker. I entered the hotel through the main entrance, rode the escalator to the second floor of the atrium and crossed the bridge to the West Tower. I dug my key card out of my jeans, caught the elevator to thirty-two, and let myself into our room. From the window, I looked at the gaping hole in the upper floor of the Midwest Center. Directly below it, a huge blue tarp had been spread on the concrete courtyard to cover the bodies. Half a dozen patrol officers stood on the tarp's edges, anchoring the corners against the wind. Almost no civilians could be seen. The perimeter had expanded beyond both sides of the block and Stanton had been closed. Michigan Avenue remained open and traffic flowed as twilight ignited yellow streetlights. The sidewalk on the east side of Michigan was closed, occupied by police.

I unloaded. First my flight jacket. Then the fishing vest containing my last functional power unit as well as the bloodied one I recovered on thirty-eight. The latter left blood in the vest pocket, and I saw more blood on the jacket and on my pants. I started for the bathroom when the earpiece jangled to announce an incoming call. I set the vest and jacket aside.

"Hey," I said to Andy.

"I'm going to be a while." No surprise. "Did you remember to take your phone from the table up there?"

"Got it."

"Good. I'm keeping you and Pidge out of this."

"Good idea. Any luck with O'Bannon?"

"No, but there's a whole new push to find Kaitlyn Aberdeen. They're going at the little geek pretty hard. You better go talk to Pidge."

"Yeah. I'll take her down to the bar. I could use a drink myself."

"Make her promise. Swear."

"Don't worry."

"Don't wait up," she said. She knew I would, so I didn't try to lie.

"Hey—"

A moment of silence connected us. Then she spoke.

"I know. I do, too."

The call ended. I sat down on the end of the bed and felt gravity's grip.

I sensed a different weight, one that I would carry for—as Paul McCartney once sang—a long time. I closed my eyes.

Not a split second passed before it came to me. The vision of Andy, arms held tightly, kicking, fighting. The window behind her. As if it were a dream, and not a memory, I saw what it would have been like if I hadn't reached her. I saw her thrown through that horrible hole in the wall, reaching frantically for me. I saw myself dive after her only to lose the battle with acceleration and gravity. To see her fall out of reach—to see her hit first—

"Stop it!" I opened my eyes, breathing heavily. "Jesus."

It would not be the last time the vision haunted me.

57

"I need a drink," I said as Pidge opened the door.

Like an attacking sprite, she jumped through the doorway, threw her arms around my neck and planted a kiss on my face. It lasted a second or two, then she dropped abruptly away.

"Yuk," she said. "Like kissing your brother." She stood and grinned at me.

"Well, then—what the hell!" I wiped my lips with the back of my hand.

"Can't a girl say thank you?"

"Use your words," I said. "And now I really need a drink."

"Me, too, but first get in here!" She grabbed my belt and pulled.

"Oh, no! You're already quite welcome."

"Fuck, no, I'm not going to jump your bones, Will. Yuk again. Just get in here!" She yanked me into her room and closed the door. Then she bolted around me and stood in the center of the room and looked at me, expectant.

"Do it."

I frowned at her.

"You have to do it, Will!"

"Pidge, we really need to talk."

"Fucking do it, already! Then we can talk all you want! And you better fucking tell me everything!" She bounced on her toes. "C'mon!"

I made a point of rolling my eyes, then—

Fwooomp! I vanished.

She squealed. "Jesus Mother Fucking H. Christ! Wait! Wait! Stay right there!"

She put her hand out and walked toward me. Eventually she bumped her palm into my chest. Contact made her jump backward. It also launched me on a trajectory away from her. I thumped against the room door.

Fwooomp! I dropped to the carpet.

"Pidge, I'm going to escort you down to the bar. We're going to get a couple stiff drinks and I'll tell you every detail—IF—" I held up a warning finger. "IF you can make it all the way down there and through the first drink without using the F-word once. Not once!"

She grabbed her small purse and shrugged at me.

"Shit, that's easy!"

"WHAT ABOUT STEALING STUFF? Like going into a bank vault?" Pidge asked. She was on her third rum and coke and her three hundred and third question. We had dropped anchor at a table in the bar above the Hyatt entrance. I turned my chair and leaned against a low glass wall that gave me a nice view of the lobby below. The sky had gone dark, and lights across the river sparkled through high windows.

"In theory, yes," I said. "But I'm married to a cop and she has informed me that she will arrest me herself if I ever do anything like that."

"Andy's no fun," Pidge opined. "What about going through walls?"

"Nope. And running into them hurts."

"What about punching somebody in the face?"

"I haven't tried it, but I suspect I would have very little impact. Probably bounce off and shoot myself across the room. No mass. No inertia. It would be like a baby taking a poke at Dwayne Johnson."

Pidge considered the image thoughtfully. "I'd do him."

I sipped my Corona and checked my watch. The hour hand had slipped past six. The hotel bar crowd thickened. The bulk of the early evening drinkers were convention attendees wearing lanyards with name tags. I tried to read the convention logo on one of the tags but didn't try all that hard and it eluded me.

"My turn," I said. "I saw you kick the lid off that barrel. Did they put you in upside-down?"

"No."

"Then how did you get turned around with your feet up?"

"Nine years of competition gymnastics," she laughed. "Now my turn! What about shooting someone? Sneaking up on them and shooting them?"

I smiled because the server, who hardly looked old enough to serve alcohol, stood directly behind Pidge and blinked at the question.

"You must hear the most interesting snippets of conversation," I said to the girl. She smiled.

"You wouldn't believe. Would you like another round?"

"Yes!" Pidge answered before I drew air to reply.

"Would you care for dinner? We serve sandwiches here. Can I bring a menu?"

I glanced down at the lobby for the hundredth time. I hoped to see Andy, although I knew better.

"Sure," I said. The girl nodded and moved away.

Pidge finished her drink, clearing the deck for the next round. I considered the question of when I would cut her off.

"When we were in Montana and you saved me on that highway—"

"Fucking greatest flying ever," she said matter-of-factly.

"No argument. Do you remember what I was doing at the time?"

"You were lying on your ass in the middle of the road, I presume getting a tan or taking a nap."

I laughed. "No. I was on my ass in extreme pain because I tried sneaking up on that bastard with Andy's Glock. And when I got close enough, I tried to shoot him."

The server appeared behind Pidge and laid two menus on the table. She gave me a wink.

"Snippets like that," she said and walked away again.

"Anyway, I tried to shoot him. While I was *gone*. Only it doesn't work. The energy backfires—or is absorbed—or trapped—or I don't know what. I don't know what all it did, but it made me reappear and kicked me halfway across that road. And it *freakin' hurt! That's* why I was on my ass when you came buzzing through."

"I prefer my version," Pidge said. For the thirtieth or fortieth time since finishing her first drink, she looked directly at me in stunned wonder and said, "*Fuck*, Will!"

"Pidge, I'm going to say it again. You can't utter a word. Not a word. Not to *anybody*."

"This is like a secret identity thing, right?"

"No! This is like me trying to hang on to my status as a human being and not have the whole world coming after me. Putting me under a microscope. Seriously, Pidge. Not a word."

For an instant, just a fraction of a heartbeat, I saw a look of pure adult empathy and grown-up understanding rise to the surface. Then it vanished beneath an impish grin.

"I'll keep your secret if you promise to use it to make me disappear next time Earl comes looking for me to bitch about something." She laughed.

I let loose a smile and drew from my beer.

"You're vibrating," Pidge said. She pointed at my shirt pocket.

I automatically reached for my phone, but then realized it was the broken phone. The new burner Andy and I purchased remained in my hip pocket. I didn't think my original phone still worked.

Despite a crack in the screen and a thin band of duct tape around the edges, the phone vibrated in my hand and responded when I swiped it. The number on-screen began with a Chicago area code.

"Hello," I said.

"I want my fucking money."

I stopped breathing.

O'Bannon.

I said nothing. I let electric tension settle into the back of my neck and run down my arms to my fingertips.

"Didja hear me? I want my fucking money," O'Bannon said.

"Come and get it."

"What? Right there? In the middle of fucking Hyatt happy hour?"

A knot tightened in my gut. I fought the urge to look around. There would be no point, nor did I want to give him the satisfaction of seeing me jump.

I picked up the Corona and gave it a long pull.

"Why not?" I asked after returning the beer to the table. "I'll buy the next round."

"You know that little blonde chippie with you will make a nice bonus for all this trouble. Some of those Boko Haram fellas can't get enough of blonde hair. They use fucking kitchen bleach on little girls when they can't get the real thing."

"Your tech nerd hijacked your money," I said.

"I don't think so. He practically pissed himself telling you all about his little keystroke spyware. Nice touch, by the way, that fire ax. Wasn't what I expected from a copper. Difference between you and me. I would'a used it at the end."

"Well, you certainly are one for putting cameras where people least expect them."

"You're an interesting fellow, Will Stewart of Essex, Wisconsin. You never did answer my first question to you. Who the fuck *are* you?"

"Ex-Interpol badass," I said.

Pidge stared at me, mouthing, *Who-is-that?*

"Sorry, that's my line. People love that shite."

"I bet it works nicely for a thug from Dublin. We Americans are suckers for an accent." I decided to take a chance. "Tell you what. Your money for Kaitlyn Aberdeen."

"Can't do that. She's already been paid for."

Yes!

"No, she hasn't. And even if she was, pay 'em back out of the sixteen mil. You didn't get that much for her."

"Fuck, no." He laughed.

"You make the real money on the buy-in."

"It is a glorious fucking business."

"Except, I think America might be getting a little warm for you, and I don't mean blue oceans and white sands warm. What's easier to transport across international borders? A kicking, screaming teenaged girl? Or a wire transfer? Put her in my hands, alive, unharmed, and you get your sixteen million back."

Pidge's eyes widened. I put a finger to my lips.

He said nothing.

"Look at it this way. There's the chance you could score both. Lure me in. Get the money and keep the girl. There's that."

He said nothing. Pidge stared. I felt O'Bannon's eyes on me.

The young server approached the table with a fresh round of drinks. She picked up the empties and replaced them.

I touched the side of my cold new Corona and traced my finger down through the condensation. "Come on. Let's do this. Tell me when and where."

I idly stroked my wet fingertip on the surface of the table.

"Keep the phone up at your head and empty your pockets. Now. Everything on the table."

I stood up. Holding the phone in one hand, I did as I was told. The burner phone, my wallet and some loose change dropped to the table.

"What the fuck, Will?" Pidge demanded.

"Okay, boyo, that phone stays glued to your ear. You do as I tell you. You don't speak to anyone. And don't try to give any fucking signals to little blondie or I will make her wish you hadn't."

"Yeah, yeah. Blah-blah-blah." My heart thundered. I struggled to keep it out of my voice.

"Go downstairs and get in a cab."

I looked at Pidge as directly as possible, then dropped my gaze to the table. Twice. She blinked at me.

"Move."

I turned and threaded my way through the tables and cocktail hour drinkers. I continued toward the escalators. Taking the first step down, I glanced at Pidge.

She stared down at the tabletop.

Where I had traced two four-digit aviation transponder codes.

Emergency.

Hijack.

58

The doorman waved for a waiting cab to pull up after I passed through the double glass doors and said, "Taxi." Cold wind bit through my shirt. My jacket, along with my power units, remained in the room.

The doorman opened the cab's rear door for me. I slid in and closed it, catching a sour look when no tip materialized.

"Now what?"

"Take Michigan south. And keep talking."

"Take Michigan south," I said to the driver.

"To what?" he asked.

"I'll tell you when we get there," I replied.

"Good answer. Talk to me," O'Bannon said in my ear.

"Why don't you talk to me?" I proposed as the cabbie wheeled out of the Hyatt onto Wacker. "Fill me in. Where are the Reichenbachs?"

"Fuck you," he said. "Talk. Read the street signs."

"Why?"

"So, I know you're not whispering to that black fella up front and borrowing his cell phone to call your hot, voracious wife, that's why. Now read the fucking street signs!"

I read them off. Walk signs. Green light. Yellow light. Red light.

Theater advertisements. Movie posters. Beer ads. Whiskey ads. An ad for the Billion Dollar Boys floating past on a bus. I heard O'Bannon chuckle.

"Why'd you kill Fulton?" I asked.

"Public service. Read the fucking signs, boyo."

I resumed my narrative.

The cabbie followed the flow of traffic south on Michigan. Early December darkness shrouded the city. Streetlights cast a yellow glow on the pavement. Christmas shoppers hustled along the sidewalks beneath holiday lights and decorations. We passed restaurants filled with diners. We passed cars jockeying for position in the traffic, and busses heaving themselves along their appointed routes. We swerved around delivery trucks and FedEx vans docked at the curb.

"Tell him to turn west on Rathman," O'Bannon interrupted my running monologue.

"Sir," I said, "Please turn west on Rathman."

The cabbie nodded.

"Tell him to stop at the corner of the second intersection."

I did.

After catching the red, we made the turn. We caught another red, then approached an intersection.

"Here?" the cabbie wanted to know.

"I guess," I said.

He pulled over.

"Now what?"

Before O'Bannon could answer, a lean man in jeans and a black wool coat opened the door. The scowling face that ducked down to meet me had a red scar dominating a line from above the eyebrow down the cheek.

"Really?" I said. "Where do you get these guys? Goons 'R Us?"

I slid out into the cold.

"That's twelve-fifty!" the cabbie called after me.

"Pay the man," I said to Scar Face. He drilled me with a cold look, then reached into his coat and extracted a black semi-automatic pistol.

"Whoa! No! No, not like that!"

Scar Face fixed a cold stare on me. He dropped the hand with the weapon to his side. His other hand fished a wad of currency from his hip pocket. Without waiting, I snatched a Twenty from his grip. I quickly leaned down into the back seat and looked at the driver. "Keep the change and get the hell out of here!"

I barely pulled myself free before the cab roared ahead. The door slammed on inertia.

Scar Face looked at me blankly.

"Fuck," O'Bannon said, "What is it with you and other people's money?"

The voice did not come from the phone, but the man himself, standing at what I now saw to be the sidewalk entrance to a construction site. Twin buildings in the steel and concrete frame stage rose into the night sky behind a board fence. A sign on the fence promised affordable luxury thanks to Fulton Partners.

Scar Face reached for and took my phone. I looked around. The street was dark, packed with parked cars, and empty of holiday shoppers—or anyone else.

O'Bannon strolled up to me. He squinted, studying my face while he worked a hard candy back and forth in his mouth. Peppermint drifted around his head, somehow making the night air seem colder. Shivers attacked the muscles in my arms and legs.

"Another camera? At the Hyatt?" I asked.

"Fucking amazing what you can get on the internet these days," he said. "Ol' Justin may have been a sick fuck, but he was nothing if not enlightening."

He looked me over.

"You're too damned confident, Will Stewart," O'Bannon observed. "Coming here alone. Didja bring company? That wife of yours?"

"She couldn't make it, but most of the Chicago Police department should be here any minute."

He laughed. "Fucking smartass. I know you don't have a tracker on ye, except for that phone."

O'Bannon's goon ceremoniously ripped the back off my phone and tore the components apart. He stuffed the pieces in his pocket.

"You were getting ready to get shit-faced at that bar. Never expected to hear from me, didja?"

"Wasn't in my day planner."

He studied me for a moment. "I don't know how you did that business up in Escanaba, but I wouldn't count on it working again."

"I'm just here for the girl."

"Aren't we all. Oh, I want you to meet Liam. You already met his brother, Mikey."

Before I could turn to face him, Liam smashed his fist into my gut. I doubled over and would have fallen flat on my face had he not grabbed the back of my collar and held me. The blow landed just below the diaphragm and drove deep. I gasped for air and gagged at the same time. A battle erupted between air trying to get into my body and the flood of recently acquired beer trying to leave. Hanging from Liam's grip on my collar, I convulsed.

He jerked me upright.

"Liam will want to have a few words with you, later, about his dear departed brother," O'Bannon said. "Now let's go put my money back where it belongs."

O'Bannon led. I staggered after him. We passed through the construction fence and entered a dirt lot littered with piles of steel, small mountains of rebar, and random heaps of gravel. A few security lights illuminated the perimeter, and a light hung outside a construction trailer.

I coughed and heaved and staggered forward. My eyes watered. I blinked the fluid away when details around me became blurred.

"Ho-hold up," I croaked, stopping. I waved my hand in front of my face, pantomiming the need to speak. My breath returned, ragged and whistling. I waved O'Bannon to come closer. He leaned down, blowing a peppermint cloud in my direction.

Barely able to stand fully upright, I looked at him. I whispered, "Do that again, and you can kiss your money goodbye."

He pressed his lips together, forcing ridges to appear at the corner of his mouth. "Fair enough."

Liam released my collar. O'Bannon resumed leading us.

We entered the first floor of the skeletal building by climbing a ramp where a set of steps would eventually be poured. O'Bannon produced his phone and lit the flashlight app.

"You might be thinking about picking up a chunk of steel and putting it through the back of my head," he said as he walked ahead of me.

"I call that daydreaming."

"But you're smart. You know that if you do anything to me, that little girl you seem so set on rescuing will suffer for it. You know that, right?"

"I have no doubt."

O'Bannon led us to the building's future interior stairwell. The concrete steps had been poured but were not yet lined with railings. He stopped and waved a gentlemanly hand for me to proceed before him. I doubted my stability as waves of nausea rode up my throat into my head.

Liam had vanished in the darkness behind us.

We climbed.

Between the quivering shadows cast by O'Bannon's phone light and the dizziness swarming my senses, the climb took on the quality of a nightmare. On top of that, I began shaking. The wind grew stronger as we ascended. Cold sliced through my thin shirt, through my skin, to the bone. I gave up trying to contain the shivering.

I lost count. It might have been five or six flights. We emerged on a broad, empty concrete floor. We walked toward one of the four unprotected edges. O'Bannon flicked off his flashlight app. At this height, the city lights gave ample definition to our dangerous surroundings.

"Where is she?" I asked.

"Hold up there, cowboy," O'Bannon said, raising a flat hand to my face. He worked the screen on his phone. After a moment, he handed the phone to me and said, "Routing number first, account number second. For yer banking convenience I've already entered my sixteen million where it asks for the amount."

I looked at the screen. Simple enough. Two blank boxes waited for input. When I looked back at O'Bannon, it was over the barrel of a pistol he held to my face.

"We're done fucking around," he said coldly.

"Shoot me, then. Your money stays where it is. Or produce the girl and we'll get this done." My shivering intensified, in no small measure because he might take me up on it.

"Over there," he said. He tipped his head in the direction of the second structure.

I looked across the empty chasm between the two buildings. A work light illuminated part of the matching floor of the building's twin. Liam stood on the plane of concrete near an indistinct shape. My eyes watered again. I wiped the tears away.

The shape became a person, kneeling. The hair was blonde, but backlit, I couldn't make out whether it was Kaitlyn Aberdeen or a Macy's mannequin.

"Now here's how this is going to go," O'Bannon said. He raised his voice and called out. "Liam!"

Liam waved to acknowledge the signal. He pulled the shape upright. It was a girl. She wore a medical boot on one ankle. Liam grabbed her by the shoulders and spun her around. She staggered and would have fallen, but he clamped his hands on her shoulders and held her up. He spun her again. As she whirled in the single-bulb light, I could see that a thick band of duct tape circled her head, covering her eyes. Another band of tape bound her wrists behind her back.

After a few more disorienting spins, Liam released her. She staggered.

"Let her go!" O'Bannon called over to Liam.

Liam gave her a brisk shove. She stumbled toward the edge.

"No!" I cried. "Kaitlyn, stop!"

"She can't hear you."

The concrete floor had no lip, no barrier, no low wall. It simply stopped. Kaitlyn limped forward. A few feet more and she would step off the edge.

Liam reached for her, grabbed her shoulders and spun her again. He let her go. Thankfully, this time she faced away from the edge.

"Like Russian roulette," O'Bannon observed. "So, you start entering numbers, and Liam is going to spin the little pretty around a few more times. Then tell her to run. When I have my money, I'm going to leave. Because you were right, she is a bit more burden than I need right now. If you can still stand when Liam is finished with you, and if you can get over there before she takes the high dive...well then, it's all one happy fucking ending."

He tapped the phone with the barrel of his gun.

Liam stepped close to the girl and barked in her ear. "Go!" She jumped. "Go! You're free!"

He poked her in the back. She stumbled forward. He turned and disappeared from the circle of light, ducking down the stairwell.

Coming for me.

Kaitlyn limped away on the flat concrete floor.

I began entering numbers on O'Bannon's phone. My hands shook. Nine digits for the routing number. I stole a glance across the empty space between buildings. Kaitlyn limped toward the center of the open floor. It wouldn't take long for her to reach the other side.

I worked my shivering thumbs on O'Bannon's keypad.

I checked again. Kaitlyn moved out of the light. She became a silhouette against city lights stretching to Indiana. Liam was two floors down and descending.

"Here," I said. I handed O'Bannon the phone. He looked at it. Before he could speak, I added, "You get the last four of the account number when I can see you on the ground. Down there." I pointed.

He squinted at me.

"You'll know immediately if they're correct. If the funds don't transfer, come back up here and kill me. But that's how this works. You don't get the numbers while you're up here."

For God's sake, STOP! I thought, looking at the girl, who limped blindly toward the far edge. Liam continued his descent.

"Do it now. If she goes off the edge over there, you get nothing."

O'Bannon smiled and shook his head.

"Whatever else you are, Will Stewart—and I forgive you for being a damned Scot—you've got a pair. But fuck with me and I will shove her over the side myself."

He took the phone, went to the stairwell, and began descending.

The moment his head disappeared from my sight, I bolted.

I located Kaitlyn, now three quarters of the way across the floor, perilously close to the open elevator shaft. She headed south toward the far edge of the building. I took aim for her. I had to cover fifty feet to reach the edge. The gap between buildings, another hundred feet. Another seventy-five to reach her.

"Sean! He's running!" Liam shouted. I didn't have time to figure out how, but he saw me. I ran. It hurt. The blow to my midsection stabbed me with each step.

The edge came up fast, but not fast enough. O'Bannon must have reversed course and returned. I heard a shot and saw a muzzle flash reflected on the steel structure around me. The edge lay twenty feet ahead, but my time was up. I wasn't going to do Kaitlyn any good with a bullet in me.

Fwooomp! I vanished in mid-stride and pulled my feet away from the floor to avoid kicking myself into an upward trajectory. I hadn't been running at full speed. I couldn't. But I had more than enough speed to shoot out the side of the building into the empty space between structures.

"BLOODY FUCK!" I heard behind me. "Liam! Get back up there! Fucker's doing something! I think he's crossing over!"

"How?" Liam shouted. I lost sight of him but heard his feet pounding on the concrete steps as he raced back up.

"Fuck if I know!" O'Bannon shouted.

I gauged my flight path. Not good. I was rising. At this rate, I would hit the floor above Kaitlyn. A collision meant stopping. Realigning. Killing priceless time. Killing Kaitlyn.

She stumbled toward the far edge.

The concrete floor above Kaitlyn approached level with my shoulders. I threw out my hands to meet it. It was rough and sharp. The moment my hands made contact, I used the collision to change trajectory and bounce downward.

Fwooomp! I reappeared and fell to the rough floor, inches from the precipice. One shin caught the sharp concrete edge.

I landed hard. The impact transmitted sharp pain through the body blow from Liam. My breathing hurt. To my right, from the stairwell, Liam's head and shoulders appeared as he bounded up the stairs.

"He's on your side!" O'Bannon shouted. "DON'T SHOOT HIM!"

I pushed myself to my feet and ran.

Liam emerged from the stairwell in full sprint.

Kaitlyn limped forward.

"KAITLYN, STOP!" I shouted. I know how earplugs work. I knew she could hear *something.*

She did hear. My warning prompted her to accelerate.

Shit!

I gauged her distance to the edge, then my distance to her.

No! No-NO-NO-NO-NO! She had me beat.

I pumped my legs harder. Liam matched my speed on his own angle toward the girl, but I had a step on him.

We raced.

Less than ten yards from the girl, I pulled ahead of Liam. Instead of aiming for the girl, he angled in behind me and clawed into my shirt. I expected him to jerk me back, but he stiff-armed me and shoved me forward, toward Kaitlyn, toward the edge.

"LIAM! NO!" O'Bannon shouted, seeing his money about to be thrown off a building.

Kaitlyn surged forward.

Three steps to the edge.

Two steps.

She planted her booted foot at the edge and stepped over. Liam drove me toward her. I reached back as if to push, to resist. He expected it and drove harder.

I hit her square in the back and threw my arm around her.

FWOOOMP! I released my grip on Liam and hurled *the other thing* around Kaitlyn and me.

Liam, pushing, not pulling, shrieked as all resistance vanished and his momentum carried him forward. I heard shoe leather skidding on concrete.

Kaitlyn twisted and shrieked. "Bastard! Let me go!"

Liam's body hit us from behind. We shot out into empty space.

Liam screamed. It resonated among the buildings around us. Then it stopped. Suddenly. I didn't look.

"Kaitlyn! KAITLYN!" I tightened both arms around her. She jerked her elbows back against me, landing a blow on the same spot as Liam.

I saw stars and gasped for air.

I felt her coil for another blow. She may have been small, but she was an athlete. She had strength and she threw it into me. I twisted her around as best I could to remove the threat. She brought her knee up and got most of what she wanted from the effort. I fought for air.

She tried to wiggle free. I got my arms around her shoulders and my legs to one side. She arched her back and slammed her forehead into my shoulder. I took advantage of the move and pressed my mouth to where I could feel her head. I felt the tape over her ears.

"STOP IT! YOUR MOTHER SENT ME!"

She froze.

I heaved air into my lungs. My groin throbbed. My shoulder howled at me. My guts burned. My vision grayed and sparkled.

She breathed heavily against me. Her head twitched.

It came to me that despite *the other thing* she still could not see. The blindfold over her eyes obscured her vision. The same way the gold tint of my ski goggles remained effective when I wore them and vanished. Or the way my eyelids covered my eyes when I blinked.

She had no idea we were now floating seventy feet over car-lined streets and clusters of apartment buildings.

"My mother? My mother?"

I pressed against her head and spoke.

"Yes! Don't move!"

"Are you the police?"

I looked around and took stock. I pressed against her head again.

"I'm with the police," I said. *Married three-plus years.*

I had no power unit. I had nothing in my pockets.

"Why does this feel weird?" she shouted at me.

"You don't have to shout. Your ears are plugged. I'm going to try to release your hands. Don't fight me!"

This was not good. With her hands bound, she had no way to hold me. If my grip slipped and she broke out of *the other thing* and fell, I had no way to dive after her.

"Let me go!"

"It's dangerous to release you. Put your foot down. There's no floor! We're...up high."

She wiggled and probed the space below us.

To protect myself, I had twisted her sideways. Now I pulled her around to face me.

"Okay. This is going to get weird. Trust me! If we can get through this, I can get you home."

At the mention of home, something changed. I felt her quiver.

"Right," I said to myself.

I glanced back at the construction site, now several blocks away. There was no sign of O'Bannon. I heard sirens. Between the buildings, the wind, and the city noise around us, I couldn't tell if they were approaching or chasing another emergency.

I wrapped my legs around her thighs, freeing my hands. I moved my hands down until I found her wrists, bound by duct tape. Layers and layers of the stuff.

I jammed a thumbnail into one edge of the tape and worked to start a tear. Those guys weren't kidding when they wrapped her wrists. I knew I couldn't pull it free. It had to tear. Straining, I managed a small rip. After that it wasn't easy, but it was less difficult. I ripped through the band. She felt it and pulled one hand out, then the other. I clutched the tape in my hand.

She rushed her hands up to her face and I felt her wiggling. I heard more tape tear.

"Ow! Ow! Ow!" I felt her peeling the tape away from her eyes, probably taking her lashes and eyebrows with it.

"Don't try to get it out of your hair!" I shouted into her ears. "Just uncover your eyes and ears."

She wiggled and moved. She jerked at something. I heard her gasp. Then she went silent.

"You okay?" I asked in a normal voice.

"What?!"

She wiggled again—I presume taking out her earplugs. They popped into sight and fell away as she tossed them aside.

"Can you hear me?"

"Uh-huh."

"I asked if you're okay."

"Uh-huh."

She didn't say anything. I looked down at the city flowing beneath us.

"Got any burning questions?"

"Uh-huh."

"Shoot."

"WHAT THE FUCK IS GOING ON!? I'm so sorry! I never talk like that!"

"S'okay. I have a friend who does. I'm immune."

"Holy God! How is this—? How are we—?!"

"Spit it out."

"Who are you? Where are you? I can't see you? I CAN'T SEE ME!"

"Steady. This is the part in the movies where they use the line, 'It's complicated.'"

"Ugh! I hate that stupid line!"

"Amen. So, I will explain. I'm Will. Will Stewart. This is a rescue."

"Kaitlyn Aberdeen. Pleased to meet you. *Really* pleased to meet you! And, I'm so sorry! Did I hurt you?"

"Horribly. But that's not important. Um, where was I? Oh. This is a rescue."

"I got that part."

"There's this thing I can do. I disappear. And gravity doesn't affect me. And I can take people along for the ride."

"What? You're like a superhero?"

"Yeah...no. But I *am* a pilot. I don't want you to worry. I'm going to get us down safely."

"So, you can...like, fly?"

"At the moment we're floating. Just, make sure you hang on to me, okay? I can do this, but you can't. You have to be connected to me. If you push away or let go of me, you reappear and kinda fall to your death. It would ruin your day."

"Good to know." Her fingers dug into my back. "Seriously, how are you doing this?"

"I was bitten by a radioactive butterfly."

"Really? For real?"

I took stock of our situation.

The northwest wind drove us on a southeast track. I put our position about a quarter of a mile southwest of Soldier Field. The lake waited on the horizon for us. I had no desire to splash down there. It would be a long hike to the Indiana shore.

I calculated a landing approach.

I had the wrist tape in my hand. I tore it in half and pocketed one half. Just in case.

"Switch legs with me." I dropped mine. "Wrap yours around my hips. Hold on to me, okay? Tight."

Kaitlyn was way ahead of me on that.

"Not that tight! I need to breathe," I said. "Big benefit of this: you're weightless. You don't need a death grip."

She released slightly.

With my hands free, I performed the trick of dropping a piece of tape out of one hand, into the other. *The other thing* released the tape shard and it became visible. It landed in my palm. I felt the weight and we began to descend. After we achieved an acceptable rate of descent, I threw the tape away.

So far so good.

Now all we had to do was avoid wires, trees, rooftops, cars, trucks, busy highways, and trains.

"You're BS-ing me."

"You're right."

"Then tell me."

"I would if I could."

Our path angled lower. Several apartment towers passed slowly on our right.

"What happened to your foot?"

"I broke my ankle. I tried to get away. I got out a window and jumped off a roof. I would'a made it, too."

"They gave you that boot?"

"Uh-huh. They even had some doctor look at me. I told him they were kidnapping me, but he didn't care. He was a real ass. Did my mother really send you? Is she okay?"

Railroad tracks running into the convention center slipped beneath us. We crossed heavy traffic on South Lake Shore Drive, barely clearing the streetlights. I watched for wires, but nothing threatened us.

"Your mother's fine. Worried. But she never gave up on you."

The girl hitched a sob. She tightened her embrace.

Our feet brushed the tops of the trees along the highway. The parking deck for Soldier Field passed on our left.

We floated over the South Parking for Soldier Field. No game tonight. The lot lay bare. A perfect landing zone.

The descent looked good. If it hadn't, I would have gone to my second piece of tape. We made landfall on the asphalt parking lot. As soon as my toes touched the ground—

Fwooomp!

We reappeared.

I took my first look at Kaitlyn Aberdeen as she dropped to her own feet.

She blinked at me with wide eyes, still wearing half a crown of silver duct tape stuck in her golden-blonde hair.

"Hi," I said. "Thanks for flying Divisible Man Airways."

"Huh?"

NEITHER OF US had a coat or a phone. Ten minutes of walking took us to the McCormick Place building at the south end of the parking lot, but it seemed to take forever to walk the length of the giant building to an entrance. Kaitlyn bubbled with questions. I gave her a rough outline of the path that led Andy and me to her. She interrupted with questions about what just happened. I told her what I could. For the second time today, I explained a need for discretion. I hinted strongly that she owed me that.

Both of us shivered uncontrollably by the time we found our way inside.

Kaitlyn worked on the tape in her hair but gave up when it seemed like it would pull most of it out by the roots. She tore off the loose ends and left the band running around the back of her head.

The convention hall buzzed with activity. Something to do with radiology.

I found a patrol officer who listened patiently to a rough-sketch description of an abduction, a rescue, and a link to the incident at the Midwestern Center earlier in the afternoon. My face felt frozen and I slurred my words. He asked twice if we had been drinking before allowing me to use his phone to call Detective Andrea Stewart. I didn't mention that she served the Essex Police Department, not Chicago. He insisted on dialing the number and using speaker phone, holding the device securely in hand.

Andy picked up on the third ring.

"Detective Andrea Stewart," she announced, not recognizing the number. The officer's skeptical expression softened.

"Andy, it's me. You'll never guess who I found."

ANDY MUST HAVE PERSUADED the Chicago police to surround the Hyatt Regency with a full battalion of uniformed officers. We pulled up in a patrol car with lights flashing. She came flying out the door escorted by two men who had the look of senior officers, one in uniform, one not. Pidge lingered inside.

Andy added two quick steps to her gait and hurried ahead to wrap her arms around me. She backed off quickly and looked at my companion.

"Are you Kaitlyn?"

Kaitlyn smiled and nodded.

Andy pulled her into a hug.

"I know some people who can't wait to talk to you."

"Can I call my parents?" she begged.

"Here." One of the two senior officers, the one in plainclothes, pulled out a phone. He looked familiar.

Kaitlyn scooped the phone out of his hand and dialed frantically. Andy put an arm around the girl and led her out of the wind.

Inside the hotel atrium, Kaitlyn held the phone to her ear. As it rang her face began to quiver. Tears filled her eyes. She sniffled loudly. Her chin began to shake.

The call volume was set on high.

"Hello?"

I recognized Linda Aberdeen's voice. Her daughter did, too, because she clenched her facial muscles and pressed her fist to her mouth, unable to speak. Her whole body shook. Tears spilled down her face.

Andy eased the phone from her hand.

"Mrs. Aberdeen, this is Detective Stewart. We have your daughter."

Through the tiny speaker all hell broke loose.

"YOU SHOULD CALL SHERIFF HANNEMAN," I said.

Andy shook off the idea. "I'm sure he knows by now. He doesn't need to hear it from me."

I disagreed. I thought hearing it from her was exactly what the Sheriff needed. Nevertheless, I let it go.

We stood in the Hyatt lobby. Moments after connecting with her parents, Kaitlyn was handed off to a pair of female patrol officers ordered to escort her to a hospital for evaluation.

"Will, this is Commander Paul Lesinsky," she introduced me to the first of the two senior officers who witnessed our arrival. He was a rugged-looking man who didn't seem terribly happy to be abdicating any part of his authority to a small-town cop. I noticed that Andy's sidearm had been returned. "And this is Assistant Chief David Schultz, Chief Don Schultz's brother."

The resemblance snapped into place.

"Your brother drives like a maniac," I said, shaking the man's hand.

"I won't ride with him," Chief David Schultz smiled. "Nice to meet you. Your wife has done a remarkable job here. And you, too, it seems."

The comment didn't please the scene commander, but I saw a private glow in Andy's eyes.

"Pidge raised the alarm," Andy said.

Lesinsky interrupted. "Miss Page said you were in contact with Seavers?"

I explained.

How O'Bannon called and arranged to meet. How he argued with his own man Liam over the money and the Aberdeen girl. How O'Bannon threw Liam off the sixth floor of a building under construction. How I used the struggle as an opportunity to escape with Kaitlyn, and then flag down a motorist who said he was on his way to McCormick Place. How I figured we would find police there.

I kept it simple. Complex lies tend to collapse under their own weight. This lie was constructed during the cold hike across the Soldier Field parking lot. Kaitlyn contributed the part about the helpful motorist, who, she suggested, drove off before we could get a name. I hoped that her co-conspiring strengthened her agreement to keep silent about the rescue.

Andy studied me as I told the tale, no doubt translating it in her mind to something closer to the truth.

"Why did this man call you?" Commander Lesinsky wanted to know.

"Well," I said carefully, "possibly because I swiped sixteen million dollars from him."

Andy's eyes went wide. I couldn't be sure what her story had been, other than trying to keep Pidge and me out of it. I didn't want to contradict her.

"I lost track of Andrea and went looking for her," I said. "I stumbled onto that whole business up on thirty-nine just after she left looking for Seavers. I wound up chatting with some naked guy tied up in a chair. He told me about a big pile of money a bunch of sickos paid to peek at nude high school girls and bid on kidnapping them. He said if I agreed to let him go, he would show me how to transfer the money. I made him show me first. But then I forgot to let him go."

Lesinsky looked at me with undiluted skepticism.

"We're going to want that money back," he informed me. "Evidence."

"Yeah...no," I said, shaking my head. "I no longer have it. In fact, I never did. It landed in a private education trust, and they're reaching out to the Monroe School district to discuss returning what Fulton Law took in their so-called settlement, seeing as how Fulton staged the whole thing."

Andy sent me a quick you-didn't-tell-me-any-of-this look. In my defense, some of it had not happened yet.

Lesinsky's face grew red. "That's not how things work here."

I glanced at Chief Schultz, who seemed to share his brother's sense of humor and worked to suppress a grin.

"When, exactly, were you planning on telling us this?" Lesinsky demanded.

"Exactly thirty seconds ago."

"The money gets turned over to Chicago PD," Lesinsky stated flatly.

"Well, Commander," I said. "It's out of my hands. But I'm sure the City of Chicago has attorneys who can take a very public stab at getting it back from a rural school district that's been forced to lay off teachers, cancel classes and downgrade the education it provides children just because some rich fucking Chicago TV lawyer wanted to get richer through child pornography and fraud. You might even have a shot at success. Seems to me I've seen pictures of that same TV lawyer with some of Chicago's more famous politicians. Maybe they can help you."

Lesinsky stoked a slow burn.

I started my own slow burn. I turned to face Lesinsky. I felt Andy's hand land on my forearm.

Chief Schultz stepped in. "Paul, I think we need to give Mr. Stewart credit for quick thinking. It sounds like Seavers counted on that money to run. Mr. Stewart's action disrupted his plans, forced Seavers to take risks, and that led to recovery of Miss Aberdeen."

Lesinsky wasn't buying it.

"I suggest we find him," Schultz said pointedly.

I spread a mirthless grin on my face and shared it with the Commander. He gave me a stone face in return.

"Excuse me, I've got a manhunt to run." The Commander stepped to the escalator. If it was meant to be an angry exit, it failed as he glided slowly up to the second floor behind two hotel guests with roller bags.

"He's already budgeting a chunk of that money to his unit in his head," Schultz said, watching him go.

"I don't like to judge people I just met," I said. "But..."

"No, it's okay. He's an asshole," Schultz allowed.

I looked at the developing action in the Hyatt atrium. Police stood at the doors. Police milled through the crowd in the café and the bar above the entrance. More police stood on the second-floor deck where the check-in and check-out lines formed.

"You're not going to find him here."

"No," Andy said, "but he might try to reach you again."

"He could try to get even," Schultz speculated. "Or take another stab at getting his money back."

"We are not setting Will up as bait, sir."

"Might be a little late for that," I said. To Chief Schultz I added, "Also, he threatened Miss Page. Is there any way you could assign her an escort? At least until we fly back to Essex?"

"Hey! Come on! I called in the fucking cavalry!" Pidge protested.

"Seems to me it would be a good idea to keep close tabs on all three of you," Schultz allowed. "Detective, I know Commander Lesinsky's team will want to spend more time debriefing you, and I think I'd like to tag along if you don't mind. For your own protection."

"I'll help in any way I can," Andy said, smiling warmly.

"Mr. Stewart, Miss Page, you best confine yourselves to the hotel. I'll have people stay with you. Will, at some point we're going to want to talk more about a jellied dead man in that construction site on Rathman."

"Yeah. That happened. But before all that, Pidge and I were about to have a sandwich," I gestured up at the bar. "I don't suppose you could spare my wife to get a bite? You're welcome to join us."

Schultz might have said Yes, but Andy stepped in. "We have a lot to cover and I really want to work this right now, love," she said. She gave me a quick kiss. "Don't wait up. We'll talk later."

Schultz gave me the look one married man gives another when he thinks it's wise to start digging a foxhole.

"I'll send some officers up to join you in a moment," he said.

Andy and Schultz headed in the direction of the lobby doors, notably in the opposite direction from Lesinsky. Pidge and I rode the escalator back up to the second floor to resume our post at the bar.

Halfway up Pidge punched me in the arm. I guess she had plans for the night that didn't include a police escort.

59

We got a bit drunk.

I should say, I got a bit drunk. Pidge got a lot drunk.

The two cops who joined us stuck to coffee but seemed to enjoy the duty just the same. To Pidge's dismay, they were older men, veteran patrol officers. I enjoyed their company and their stories. A detective came by and took my statement in detail. Pidge's eye wandered in the bar and she hooked a few return glances from young men in sharp suits, but they passed her over. The uniformed police officers on chaperone duty may have dampened Pidge's appeal. It put her in a surly mood. By the time we adjourned to our rooms, she barely spoke to me.

We shared the same floor but had rooms half a dozen doors apart. The officers took up station outside our individual doors.

The hotel room was lonely without Andy. With the beer buzz on, the first thing I did was draw the curtains to avoid catching a glimpse of the dizzying height and cordoned-off courtyard below.

Boots off, I fell back on the bed.

Without my phone, O'Bannon had no means of reaching me. In a movie, I supposed he might sneak behind the check-in desk, or seduce a clerk into revealing my room number. I pictured him pretending to be some stumbling drunken convention-goer and surprising one or both of our police guards with some Kung Fu—guards who, in my movie, were portrayed as less than capable and less than professional. The men in the hallway weren't athletes, but they weren't stupid either.

None of that happened.

The hotel staff did not give away my location. The room phone did not ring. O'Bannon did not infiltrate.

In the end, I pictured him in an unremarkable domestic sedan, driving through the night at just above the speed limit to get as far from Chicago as possible.

Before it grew too late, I used the burner phone to call Andy's close friend, Sandy Stone, who managed the Christine and Paulette Paulesky Education Foundation whose account number was branded in my head. I thought it might be a good idea to let Sandy know the foundation had just picked up another sixteen million dollars, and that she might be getting some angry phone calls about it.

Sandy sounded half asleep when she answered the phone. Teachers, I've learned, work damned hard and have been known to fall asleep in front of a television after a long day of herding miniature maniacs.

I traded small talk with her to let her wake up. She asked about Andy. I told her we were on a case in Chicago. She thought that was nice, which I took as a sign she wasn't entirely awake. I explained in very few words about the new money and warned her not to take any shit from anyone in Chicago.

She reminded me of the foundation board meeting tomorrow night. Thursday already. Where had the week gone? I told her I couldn't be certain we would be back in time.

Before she could ask questions, I wished her a good night and ended the call.

And there I was.

Sitting in a luxury hotel, in a vibrant city, with a nice buzz on.

Alone.

I got now why Pidge wasn't speaking to me.

60

I must have fallen asleep. Andy slipped into the room quietly, but the doors in most hotels use latches designed to wake the dead, no matter how carefully you ease them shut. She went into the bathroom and for a crazy moment I wondered if it really was Andy, or if O'Bannon had found me and planned to torture me into giving back his money—as soon as he finished brushing his teeth.

I drifted off again. The next thing I felt was movement on the bed. Andy nudged in close beside me. I caught her scent and a glimpse of her skin against the lace of her undergarments. She slid in under my arm and laid her head on my shoulder.

"I like what you did," she said. "About Kaitlyn. And the money."

"Whoever you are, you can't stay. My wife will be back any minute."

She squeezed. I squeezed back. That part wasn't about O'Bannon's money. That was about steel barrels and broken windows. We held on for a while in silence, listening to each other breathe. Counting heartbeats and adding them like coins to the treasure chest that is our lives.

Eventually I began to stroke the bare skin on her back. Her hand moved up and down my chest.

"Are you tired?" she asked.

"No."

"Good."

61

She sat coiled, humming with potential energy. If machines dreamed as Philip K. Dick speculated, this one dreamed of flight.

Earl's Mojave waited for us on the ramp, fueled and ready, nose sleek and tail high. I sat in the Signature Aviation lounge, watching the gray sky above her.

"Where the fuck is she?" Pidge looked at her watch again.

I knew better than to offer an answer.

"We're gonna be in the shit," she warned. Again.

The morning weather forecast looked troubling enough that Pidge and I told Andy we would meet her at Midway with the airplane ready to fire up and fly. Carrying a cup of coffee, Andy hustled away to police headquarters on South Michigan for more interviews and a phone conference that included the Essex Police Department, the Delta County Sheriff's Department, and the Monroe County Sheriff's office. She told me that Chief Schultz promised she would be finished by noon. I was skeptical. They had her lined up to be interrogated by everyone from Commander Lesinsky to the District Attorney.

When I spoke to her at midmorning, she said she had been treated to equal parts praise and mistrust.

"Fulton had friends in high places," she told me, speaking quietly into her phone. "Half of them want to see him portrayed as a murder victim. The other half are pretending they never met him."

"Please do not get in the way of the Chicago political machine," I warned her.

"Duly noted," she said. "I don't think there's any question that Fulton is going to go down as the villain in all this. Some of the firm's attorneys have begun negotiating for immunity. Apparently, they were already setting up two more civil actions. Pins on the map that we hadn't gotten to yet, but where videos have surfaced."

"The little geek said yesterday was only the second time. I think he meant second auction. I think they've been recording since summer."

"On the call this morning, Tom said Fulton Law rented space for an office in Essex."

"They were gearing up," I said. "Any news of O'Bannon."

"No. But I have a better idea of who he is. Less mastermind, more muscle. Suspected of human trafficking in the U.K. The Irish authorities have been looking for him for two years in connection with an abduction. I'll tell you later. Looks like they're waving at me. Love you!"

Since that call, we traded texts. I warned her about the weather. Andy promised to be on time, delivered directly to Midway after the last interview.

The cause for urgency came in the form of twin low-pressure systems marching through the Dakotas. The first system promised flurries for northern Illinois and southern Wisconsin. No real issue. But the second packed a punch with a tight pressure gradient. That meant high winds circulating around the low-pressure center. The projected path scribed a line across the Wisconsin-Illinois border. Warm air filling in from the south offered a mix of snow and freezing rain on the south side of the storm. As the air circulated over Lake Michigan and reversed itself, it picked up moisture and mixed with cold air from Canada. A full-blown winter storm was promised for most of the counties north of a line between Milwaukee and Madison, stretching as far as Lake Superior.

Essex County lay in the path of the most intense precipitation. With temperatures expected in the teens, forecasts for our little hometown predicted eight to ten inches of snow and possible blizzard conditions.

The first round of flurries began falling in Chicago at noon. The heavy-duty shit, as Pidge liked to put it, was headed for the fan starting at three p.m. in Essex.

Too much longer on the ground at Midway, and we'd be flying right into it.

My watch ticked past two-fifteen. I decided I would ground us when the time hit two-thirty.

"There she is!" Pidge pointed at the glass door entrance and the curb beyond. A drab sedan pulled up under the overhang. Andy turned to the driver, showing us the back of her head, and the ponytail she put up for the morning's officious endeavors.

"Go start the checklist," I told Pidge. "Take left seat."

She didn't question. The better pilot needed to be in the left seat for this flight, and we both knew who the better pilot was.

Andy sat chatting with the driver long enough that I finally strolled toward the entrance, thinking I would simply open the door and get her, which would not go over well. Before it came to that, she extended a hand, shook with Chief David Schultz, and hopped out of the car. I held the glass FBO door open for her as the Chief pulled away.

"We gotta go," I said. "We're up against the weather."

"Do I have time to visit the Ladies?"

"Pee with enthusiasm, please."

She made a don't-be-childish face at me but hurried down a hall.

LIGHT SNOW DUSTED the runway for our take-off. Pidge applied her usual artistic touch and made the Mojave soar. I handled the radios and stood by to program fixes into the navigation system as soon as ATC threw them at us. We ascended into the first layer of cloud before the lake came into view. The moving map soon told us we flew over water, but I found a measure of false comfort in not seeing it.

We broke through the top of the first layer at eight thousand feet. I examined the wings. The first traces of rime ice laced the leading edges. ATC cleared us to our cruise altitude of twenty thousand. Top reports near the center of the storm ran into the mid-twenties, so I knew we'd be "in it" eventually. The longer we could stay in the clear, the less chance of icing up. Pidge took us up through the next layer quickly. We broke out into blue skies and sunshine, which seemed incongruous considering the weather coming our way.

I checked on Andy. She sat with one of the cabin blankets spread over her knees, contemplating the screen on her laptop, probably pouring over more investigation reports from Montana. I wondered how much the Fulton case would demand of her time.

She must have sensed me looking at her. She looked up and cast me a warm smile, something private that carried a hint of what we had done on the Hyatt sheets last night.

I tipped a nod her way, then returned to duty, adding a bit of cabin heat for her benefit.

"Sonofabitch!" Pidge exclaimed through the headset.

"What?"

She abruptly looked at me through her Ray Bans. I didn't know whether to look at her or search the instrument panel for whatever emergency was unfolding. I strained to detect a wrong note from the engines.

"That's how you did it! The crash! That's how you got down in one piece!"

I began to breathe again.

"Seems like," I said. "The memory loss is real, so I can't say for sure. But that's the best explanation I can come up with."

"So, if the shit hits the fan, and we go down, we all jump out and grab on to you, right?" She grinned at me.

"Sure. Just follow me out the door."

I'D LIKE to say the landing at Essex County had Pidge's tender touch. It didn't. Although in the hands of a lesser pilot, it may have been a lot worse. ATC lowered us into the storm twenty minutes out and we began building ice immediately. In addition to the ice, we hit turbulence. Strong winds circulating around the center of the storm jarred the Mojave enough that Pidge reduced our speed to Maneuvering Speed, the safest place to put the airspeed indicator needle when the weather gods throw rocks in your path. I glanced back at Andy. She tightened her seat belt, folded her laptop and secured the worktable. I gave her a thumbs-up.

Aviators categorize turbulence in three levels. Light. Moderate. And Severe. We didn't hit Severe. I never want to hit Severe. Severe takes airplanes apart. But we rode that rollercoaster down the approach in almost constant Moderate turbulence. Moderate may be moderate to a pilot, but most passengers who experience Moderate turbulence jot notes to loved ones on their soft drink napkins.

During the ride down, I flicked on the landing lights long enough to see the cone of heavy snow hurtling itself past the airplane. An illusion. We were the ones doing the hurtling.

Pidge held both hands on the yoke. She didn't fight the turbulence. That only makes it worse. She did what she could to hold heading and glide path. It wasn't pretty.

Pidge never wavered. I followed her on the controls all the way down the approach and kicked the rudder to adjust our path when the runway emerged from the veil of snow. She absorbed the inputs but continued her command of the plane.

Runway end identifier lights swept under us. She pulled the throttles.

Flaring out was a luxury, and she didn't waste much effort on it. The wheels thumped down hard. It was a landing that pampered passengers might complain about, not knowing better.

Finding a set of blue taxi lights, we turned off. We blindly followed a path between the lights and rolled to the ramp. Eventually, shapes materialized out of the snow—the hangars and office of Essex County Air Services.

I glanced back at Andy. She sat in her seat with her eyes closed.

We found our way to a position directly in front of the big hangar door, which began to rise before we came to a full stop.

I pulled the mixture controls and killed the engines.

Silence gave its blessing to our successful arrival.

"THIS IS GOING to last all night," Pidge said. She heaved her flight bag onto the office counter.

"They already cancelled school for tomorrow. All evening activities are cancelled tonight, and they let the elementary school out early," Rosemary II informed us. She spotted Andy, who looked a little pale. "Honey, do you need some water? Coffee?"

Andy waved aside the notion of consuming anything.

"I'm fine," she said. "It was exciting."

Dave Peterson lounged against the counter. "I came in about forty minutes ago in the King Air. It was bad, but it wasn't anything like this. You guys are nuts." He grinned at Pidge who flipped him the finger.

"Gimme your keys," I told Andy. "I'll go start the car."

She dug them out of her satchel and handed them over, but said, "You take the car. I called the station. Tom is coming out to pick me up. I want to take Sarah Lewis's phone to her."

"Does that have to be done tonight?" I already knew her answer. It was about more than just returning a phone. All the same, I didn't like the idea in this weather. The look on Andy's face put the question to rest.

"Tom will take me home immediately after. Promise."

We'd been running hard since Saturday night. I just wanted to go home and cook a warm dinner, then sleep in my own bed. Or not sleep.

"Please tell me there's no meeting tonight," I begged Andy.

"Sandy texted me. It's cancelled. But she wants us to call her when we can. Sounds like she's been getting calls about the money."

"I hope she stood her ground," I said. "Be right back!"

I ducked out the front door and jogged through the snow to Andy's car. It started immediately. I let it run and didn't bother brushing off the snow. At the rate it was coming down, it would be covered again by the time I returned.

Back inside, I caught the tail end of Rosemary II asking Andy when we'd hit a deer.

"What?" I asked. "What are you talking about?"

"Your insurance adjuster was here yesterday. He wanted to see your car. He said you were the fourth deer strike he was called out on this week. When did you hit a deer?"

"Never," Andy said. She looked at me. "Did you?"

"Not me. Must be some mistake."

"Is there any damage on the car?" Andy asked, a little less pale, a little more focused.

"None that I saw."

"Maybe we should check it over anyway," Andy suggested. I caught a hint of tension in her voice.

The notion that O'Bannon had been here crossed my mind.

"When was the guy here?" I asked Rosemary II.

She cast her eyes up at an imaginary clock and said, "Morning. First thing after I opened. Bob Thanning was here putting out driveway markers and the two of them were standing out in the parking lot, carrying on about the big storm coming." Rosemary II made it sound like they knew each other.

Morning. Yesterday morning, O'Bannon was in Chicago. I tried to shake off the idea of a connection but worried that O'Bannon had not yet run out of associates.

Ten minutes later, Tom Ceeves pulled into the parking lot. Andy and I said our goodnights to the Essex County Air Service office crew. Rosemary II traded hugs with Andy and announced that she was shutting down. All the birds were in the nest. Pidge popped out of the pilot's office long enough to say goodnight to Andy and throw me a wink, which I ignored.

Outside, we threw our bags in Andy's car, then walked around it. Fat snowflakes, thrown by a ragged wind, slapped against our coats.

"I don't see anything," I said. She agreed. I waved her off. "Go! See you at home!"

Andy trotted to Tom's SUV. She climbed into the right front seat. Greg LeMore waved at me from the back seat, apparently along for the ride to the Lewis home. I waved back, thinking it was nice that he got to take a victory lap with Andy. Nice that he had a chance to meet Sarah. There were many ways this could have turned out differently without him. I like the guy.

"Just don't bring him home for dinner," I said to Andy through my teeth as they pulled away.

Tom rolled out of the parking lot and headed west, disappearing quickly in the blowing snow. I brushed accumulated snow from Andy's car, then hopped in. The heater had done its job. Lights and wipers on, I backed out of the parking space.

The car didn't explode.

62

The taillights skewed all wrong.

With each slap of the wiper blades, the scene became clearer as I rolled through unplowed snow toward our driveway.

Taillights, glowing red through the dark-gray twilight, sat oddly spaced where the end of the driveway joined the road. From my perspective, they should have been close together, then separating as I approached. These were the full width of a vehicle and remained so.

Not until I closed the distance to less than one hundred feet did the scene clarify.

The car wasn't on our driveway. It sat on our lawn, straddling the ditch and culvert at the end of the driveway. Our mailbox had disappeared. Probably under the car.

I eased Andy's car to a near stop, then turned in the open driveway. I pulled ahead a bit and stopped.

The driver had missed the turn. It was understandable. Near whiteout conditions and the fact that neither the road nor driveway had been plowed reduced the chances of getting it right, especially if you weren't familiar with the layout.

This driver wasn't. She had only been there once before.

Pregnant Not-Andy opened the door to her Mercedes and stepped out in the deepening snow.

"How many points do I get for a mailbox?" Lydia asked.

"Ten, but only if you stay on the road and keep going. Doesn't count if you wind up in the ditch."

I hurried to where she was struggling up the small slope where the culvert ran under the end of the driveway. I took her hand and helped her to level ground.

"The bad news is, I think it's a federal crime."

"I'm so sorry," she said waving at the scene. "I don't know the first thing about installing mailboxes, but I think my credit card knows how to buy a new one."

"Have you been here long? You must be freezing." I hooked her arm in mine and began guiding her toward the house.

"Not long. Not freezing. Heated seats," she said. She patted her belly. "Heated baby, remember? I take it Ka—Andy—isn't with you. I called the airport. The lady, Rosemary, said you were on your way here. I was passing by and…"

Rosemary II must not have heard Andy tell me about her side trip with Tom.

"Police business," I said. "She might be a while."

"I guess I'm oh for two on the ambush," Lydia sighed. "This might not have been my brightest idea."

"Let's get inside. There could be hot cocoa."

"Yes, but do you have marshmallows?"

THE HOUSE WAS COLD. Andy rules the thermostat and can control it from her phone. She must have lowered the temperature when we were on the road. That's my girl, taking care of the family budget while she chases bad guys.

I ran the risk of my wife's ire and poked at the digital thermostat until the display read seventy-five. In the basement, the furnace woke up.

Lydia remained inside her coat but removed a pair of elegant leather gloves and began fumbling in her purse.

"How soon do you think we can get a tow out here?" She pulled out her phone.

"In this weather, my guess would be tomorrow—if you're lucky." I wasn't joking. Chances were excellent that AAA would answer its phone with a recording telling you to go someplace warm and have a drink. Maybe not the drink part.

"Oh, no," Lydia stopped in mid-cell-phone dial. "That's not good. Do you think we can get the car out? You and me?"

I laughed. "Me, maybe. You, no."

I was struck once again by the strange experience of looking at Andy who wasn't Andy, of seeing the subtle differences in the sisters.

"Well, this is not good," she said. I looked for the lower lip, but Lydia doesn't have her sister's underbite. She heaved a frustrated sigh.

"Trouble?"

"I suppose I should bring you up to speed, Will." Now she slipped off her coat. I wasn't ready to shed mine yet. The kitchen remained cold. I put a kettle on the stove and turned on the burner.

She slid onto one of the counter-height chairs at the kitchen table.

"I rented a house on Leander Lake. On the east side of the lake, which isn't that far from here. I told you—I wanted to be close to Andy. We drove in yesterday, me and the kids. The ones I didn't kill on the road trip, anyway."

"That's…um…wonderful? Is it wonderful?"

"It's scaring the shit out of me, but yes, it's wonderful. Mom and Dad are freaking out, but in that very superior way, you know? Where they might call me once every hour, but when they do it's to ask me things like 'Did you have someone check the furnace? Does the house have an alarm system?' Like they know I'm blowing up my life, but they still have this little checklist for me."

"Wait. You said, 'the kids.' Where are the kids? Are your parents up here?"

"God, no! Andy would be investigating a murder-suicide if they came up here. The house is furnished. I have groceries—well, they're in the car —but I want to vibrate to a halt before I leap off another cliff and let Mom and Dad come here."

"So where are the kids?" I felt heat blowing from the register under the kitchen sink. I slipped off my coat.

"They're with the nanny," Lydia said with the innocence a five-year-old with chocolate on her face might deploy to deny breaking into the candy box.

"The nanny? *The* nanny?"

Lydia shrugged.

"What could I do? She's all alone in this country. She wants the child born here. She has no health insurance. Her parents don't have money. She loves the kids, and they love her. Hell, I love her, maybe even more after my asshole husband screwed her. What the hell! We can be birthing buddies!" She forced a laugh.

"Wow," I said. "My hat's off to you."

"Oh, don't let me overplay the I'm-so-benevolent card, Will. I need her. Someday I want to be that super single mom who can do it all and build rockets on the side, but I have a long way to go. Plus, I plan to drink heavily once this one is out of the oven. Somebody needs to be sober to put the kids to bed. And speaking of which, I won't win Mom of The Year for leaving my kids alone with their pregnant teenaged nanny in a strange house in a snowstorm. This was supposed to be a grocery run with a quick stop here. Can we see about getting my car out? I'm so sorry about all this! Jesus, I sound like a broken record around you!"

"I'm not so sure I can get your car out. I think it's hung up on the culvert, and I might do some damage if I try. Better to have a tow truck do it right. Why don't I drive you home? The roads are terrible."

"The roads I can handle. My father is a lifetime member of the Audi club. I can't tell you how many times I took the Ice Driving Course."

"Uh-huh…"

"What? I'm a great winter driver! I just didn't know where your driveway was. Now I know."

The kettle started to boil, so I pulled it off and looked for hot cocoa mix in the cupboard. Naturally, we had none. But to be fair, we had no marshmallows either.

"Seriously," she said, rising and putting on her coat, "I should go. But I will not let you go to all that trouble. Let me take Andy's car. I know how this looks, but I'm a much better driver than...well, than this!" She waved at the front of the house and the car in the ditch in our yard. "I'm the one who taught Andy how to drive!"

"Andy has a lead foot."

"Who do you think taught her that?" Lydia smiled triumphantly. "Besides, if we can get Andy to focus on me committing grand theft auto, maybe she'll overlook the fact that I pissed all over being a decent sister."

My silence derailed her. She cast her eyes at my feet.

"Sorry. I meant that to be funny. It's not so much. So, if we're going to be serious, then seriously, I will not allow you to drive me. Keys, sir." She held out her hand.

I can't win with these Taylor women. We traded key fobs.

I shrugged into my jacket. "Let me at least get our bags out of the car and your groceries out of your car."

"Thank you."

"Andy will obviously know you were here. Since you're stealing her car. Plus, I told her about your plans."

"Sorry for throwing you under the bus again. Tomorrow, after the storm is over, bring her to the house for dinner. That's what I had in mind coming here. I didn't want to invite you over the phone. You know. Because..."

"Yeah."

She pulled on her gloves and a knit hat and followed me back out into the storm. As we approached Andy's car, a set of headlights broke through the stunted visibility. The lights rode high, mounted above a snowplow on the front of a pickup truck.

"Great timing," I said to Lydia over the wind. I held her arm as we trudged toward Andy's car. "That's the guy that plows for us. Although I don't know why he'd bother this early in the storm."

"Where was he half an hour ago?" she laughed. "I might have found your driveway."

I helped her into the car. She started it while I pulled our overnight bags from the back seat. Instead of hustling them into the house, I put them on the side of the driveway in the snow, feeling an urgency to get Andy's car out of the driveway so that Bob could plow. I wondered why he planned to do it now. He would sure as hell have to come back in the morning. Seemed a bit of a waste to me.

When I turned back to jog down to Lydia's Mercedes and retrieve her groceries, I noticed that Bob had continued down the road. His taillights brightened and became brake lights, but he didn't stop before the falling snow swallowed him up.

"Okay," I muttered to myself, "maybe not."

Using Lydia's key fob, I popped the Mercedes' trunk to retrieve her groceries.

"Just like her sister," I observed. The trunk was filled to excess with paper grocery bags. Andy likes to keep the cupboards stocked. Except for hot cocoa, I guess. Then again, Lydia had a small army to feed.

Lydia deftly backed Andy's car out of the driveway onto the road and maneuvered the rear end close to me. I think she tried to show me she could handle a car in the snow. She released the trunk from inside.

Squinting against pelting snowflakes, I transferred the bags. Then I hurried around to her door. She rolled down the window and held up her phone. "Tell me your number. I'll text you the address."

"Don't. I lost my phone. Just tell me."

She did, and I spent a moment repeating it, first aloud, then in my head.

"Got it. Drive safely!"

"No worries. I've had my motor vehicle screw-up for this month. Tell Andy...well, you know…"

"It's gonna work out," I found myself saying, again realizing that I was pulling for Lydia.

She gave me an appreciative look.

She raised the window and pulled away into the blinding snow. Her taillights slowly vanished as I walked the driveway back toward the house.

A moment later I heard Bob coming back. I hurried to grab the overnight bags and get into the house before he started ramming snow up and down the driveway. But before I reached the house, he rolled past and disappeared in the direction Lydia had gone.

"Jesus, Bob, make up your mind."

63

I let the snow on the suitcases melt in the mudroom while I slipped off my coat and wiped the moisture off my boots with paper towels. An unfamiliar rattling and chirping caught my ear. I looked around the house for the offending device, then realized it came from my hip pocket. I pulled out the burner phone. Up until now I had only taken calls through the earpiece. I wasn't sure I knew how to answer the thing.

I stroked a finger across the green button on the screen and hoped for the best.

"Hello?"

"Hey," Andy said. Something sounded off. "I won't be home for a while."

"Everything okay?" A black thought crossed my mind. "How's Sarah?"

In the time it took Andy to answer, my mind conjured images of Sarah Lewis holding the big revolver in her hand.

"Sarah's fine." I blew out a breath in relief. "No, it's something else."

"What's going on?"

I heard a sudden noise in the background. It sounded like someone wailing. Andy must have cupped her hand over the phone, or turned away, because the sound became more distant and Andy's voice became stronger, yet quieter.

"Linda Thanning found Bob dead. In his garage."

I jumped to the immediate conclusion for a man forty pounds overweight.

"Heart atta—?" I stopped myself. "Wait! Bob? Bob Thanning?"

"It wasn't a heart attack. A bad accident. I have to—"

"Andy!"

"What?"

"Bob Thanning! He was just here! He just drove past!"

"Will, I saw him. He's dead."

"How?"

"He must've been fiddling with that monster snowblower of his. It looks like he got caught in it. It's bad."

"Andy, no! He was just here. His truck just went by. Twice! He—"

I stopped cold. I felt like someone who just grabbed an electric power line and couldn't move as the shock solidified muscle.

"His truck isn't here," Andy said. "Will, what are you—?"

"No no no no no no!" I heard myself saying over and over.

"Will, talk to me!"

"Andy, Bob's truck just drove by here. Twice. Oh, Christ! I think he's following your car!"

"My car?"

"Lydia was here. She got stuck in the driveway, so I gave her your car. I'll explain later. She's taking your car back to the house she rented."

"What house?"

I gave her the address I memorized. "Andy, I don't think Bob had an accident. I think someone took his truck. I think whoever took his truck is following Lydia because he thinks it's you! It's got to be O'Bannon! Or somebody that works for him! You've got to go!"

"Where?!"

"Lydia! Get to Lydia!"

There was no click and no dial tone to tell me the call had ended. I blinked at the stupid phone for a moment, then jammed it in my pocket. I grabbed the keys to my car and started to reach for my coat.

No. Not fast enough.

My car sat in the yard, cold and buried under a layer of snow. I would lose too much time clearing it. Too much time getting on the road. Too much time holding to a speed that would keep me on pavement.

I hurried to the mudroom and pulled open my overnight bag. Tossing aside loose clothing, I found the last unused propulsion unit.

No coat, no gloves, no hat. I grabbed the ski goggles and pulled them on.

The storm door slammed behind me. Cold bit through my shirt and snow slapped at my face. I planted my feet on the back steps, nearly slipped, then leaped into the air.

FWOOOMP! I pushed hard. The cool sensation snapped in place while I still had an upward trajectory. In a split second, weightless, I began to soar over the snow-covered driveway. The wind jerked me away from the house. My thumb slid the power control to the full forward stop. The unit screamed its angry wasp song and pulled me into the darkening sky. Night fell fast and early under the dense blanket of cloud and heavy snow.

I aimed for the tops of the trees lining the edge of the property. The power unit pulled me across the yard.

Clearing the treetops, I barely made out the road. Tire tracks that should have been fresh were already fading away under fast-falling snow. I stayed as high as possible without losing sight of the ground, knowing that power lines would become a factor at the next junction.

For an instant, I thought about cutting the corner. I knew the route Lydia intended to follow to Leander Lake. The address she gave wasn't all that far away. Twenty-five, maybe twenty minutes from our house. Ten if I cut across fields and over wooded land. But what if he caught up to her on the road? I had no choice. I had to follow her route as he had.

Snow pelted me. I gained speed. Vision would have been impossible if not for the eye protection.

Forty. Fifty knots. The fastest I've gone yet, faster than the concrete-slab-bombing run in Chicago. Almost too fast. In the low visibility, I nearly missed the stop sign at the end of the road, where Lydia turned right.

Two sets of tracks made the right turn.

I threw my hand to the right. The power unit pulled me into a tight turn.

The road ran north, straight and true, for a country mile. The snow allowed me to see only a fraction of that distance. Another stop sign appeared, and the tracks made another right. Still two sets.

The tracks took the county road east. A mile later, they turned left, onto Sunset Circle Road, a two-lane blacktop that swept north through marsh and wooded countryside for ten miles before swinging around Leander Lake.

Once again, I wished for a way to cut the corners. The road carved a scenic path through the landscape, sometimes snaking back and forth almost senselessly. In the fall, streams of Harley riders choose this route for the view and the thrill of the curves. I wanted to cut across the curves to save time but could not go high enough to keep the road in sight. Each time I angled higher the world below faded and disappeared. Instrument flying is only possible with instruments. I had none.

Back and forth, I raced above the curves. Somewhere ahead, the trees thickened where the Lakes Region of Essex County beckoned to the wealthy. In summer, the homes ringing Leander Lake would be filled. Most of the structures sit unoccupied in winter.

I had no sense of time. Weaving up the road seemed to take forever. I tried to plot out what the driver of the truck was thinking. Would he follow her to the lake house? Would he follow her inside? Would he figure out, once he saw her, that it wasn't Andy? Then what?

Headlights jerked me out of my panicked war-gaming. High-mounted above a snowplow, the headlights of a pickup truck appeared below me, moving southbound out of the snow-shroud. I shot over the twin beams in a flash. In the cab, I spotted a driver, but no passenger.

I couldn't see his face, but there was no mistaking Bob Thanning's truck.

I started to flick my hand around for a tight circle to go after him, but immediately cancelled the idea.

Lydia!

What if he caught up to her? What if—?

I let the truck disappear into the snow and night behind me.

The pavement cut through the band of woods that surrounds the lake, taking the road to the shoreline before curving sharply to the right to begin its circle around Leander Lake.

The address Lydia gave wasn't far now. The home she rented, she said, was on the east side of the lake. Just a few more seconds and the lake would come into view. A few more seconds and I would cut to the right and follow the road to a driveway, and in that driveway find Lydia struggling with groceries, and then everything would be fine.

Nothing was fine.

The curve in the road appeared ahead and below. The lake appeared, white and frozen over with an early layer of thin, snow-covered ice.

Tire tracks told me the worst.

They left the road and became mixed and muddy on a path to the shoreline. Broken brush littered the path. Sharp brown grooves stood out against the snow where wheels cut into the soil and scribed dark lines toward the lake.

Beyond the shoreline, a black hole littered with jagged pieces of bobbing broken ice extended outward from the tracks.

Below the ragged edges of the ice, in the black water, red taillights glowed briefly, then winked out as if the Devil closed his eyes.

He pushed her in!

I shot over the curve and out over the lake, frantically reversing the power unit. When I finally stopped, I backed myself over the gaping hole in the ice.

No choice. From thirty feet up—

Fwooomp!

Gravity took me at once. I dropped and hit the water hard. Chunks of ice clawed at my legs as I sliced through the surface.

Cold like no cold I've ever felt stunned my nervous system, sending signals of agony to my brain. I lost orientation at once in the black. My downward drop continued, but I couldn't be sure how deep. Pressure in my ears added to the pain attacking me from all sides.

I'm a good swimmer and I can do the length of a standard-sized pool entirely under water after a series of strong cleansing breaths. Not only did I forget to suck in air on the way down, the jolt of cold seemed to punch what little air I had from my lungs.

I had no air. I had no time.

I stopped descending. I swept my arms and pulled myself toward what I thought was down. My left hand slammed into something hard.

If not for the pain already enveloping me, I would have known that half the fingernail in my center finger had been torn away.

I groped. Hard. Smooth. Vertical. It had to be the side of the car. Better yet, the driver's side!

I slapped at it. I felt a smooth surface. I felt a line, a molding. I reached up, trying to find the seam between the windows and the door but it didn't make sense. When my hands reached the upper edge of the smooth surface, it abruptly ended.

The top of the car was gone.

My chest screamed for air.

I groped into the empty space where the window should have been. How could this have happened? Where was the window? The roof?

Upside down, dummy! The car is upside down!

I frantically pushed down and felt for the bottom of the door. There, I found the seam, then the window. Pounding at the metal with my palm, I found the door handle.

Please, God, let it not be locked!

Andy's car locks the doors when it hits nine miles per hour in Drive. Lydia would not have been familiar with the car, and chances were good she wouldn't have had the presence of mind to unlock the car doors as she plunged into the lake.

My lungs raged at me to abandon her.

I jerked at the door handle.

Locked.

I resolved to try and kick in the window and reached for purchase against the metal when my hand hit the wheel well. The rear wheel well.

This is the back door!

I pushed away from the wheel well, past the rear door, and rammed my head into the edge of the driver's door, which hung open. The jolt sent flickers of light into the darkness enveloping my vision.

She got the door open!

Too late. I couldn't do it.

I kicked hard for the surface, clawing at the water until I broke through floating chunks of ice.

I heaved air into my lungs, tasting gasoline. The cold seared my throat. My muscles wanted to surrender to the thousands of pins stabbing into my skin.

I heaved the air out. Then in. Then out. Then in again.

Down.

I flipped myself and arm-stroked downward, praying I had kept my position and my orientation.

Once again, my left hand hit first, striking something hard and sharp. I didn't feel the gash that cut through the fleshy side of my palm.

I groped at the object, found the bottom of the car, traced a line to the edge, then worked my way forward, and found the bottom of the open driver's door.

So close! Yet the effort sapped my air. I wanted to kick for the surface again, but I knew that this was my last trip.

I used the door scuff panels to pull myself down and groped at the seat, then lower, and found soft flesh. Lydia!

Upside-down. Leg. Abdomen. The mound of baby.

I pawed until I found the strap for the seatbelt, still angled across her body. She didn't respond to my touch. I frantically followed the strap up to the latch, I jabbed my fingers into the latch, thinking I was screwed and Lydia was dead if this didn't release.

It snapped open easily. I jerked it clear and she floated free of the seat, motionless, inverted. I grabbed anything. Coat. Arm. I pulled, and she bumped toward me, then stopped. I had no idea if her legs were now entangled with the steering column, or her coat was caught or if she had one arm snagged in the shoulder strap.

I wiggled and shoved, moved her back and forth, and twisted her toward the open door. Something gave, and she came toward me in the darkness. I kicked away from the car and pulled. More of her came free. I worked to rotate her body, then slipped my hands under her arms and wrapped them around her chest above the baby bump. I pulled.

We both floated backward into a void.

Out of air. Again, my lungs screamed at me. White sparks ignited at the edges of my vision.

I had no idea which way was up. If there was a bottom, I couldn't feel it.

Buoyancy. Lane Franklin's matter-of-fact voice spoke calmly in my head. *Buoyancy, Will. It won't matter which way you swim; a bubble will only go up.*

The notion, like a wave of warm calm, spread across me—and with it, a tide of overwhelming peace. *What a smart girl,* I thought, deeply appreciating Lane.

I felt all urgency slipping away.

Buoyancy, Will! Lane screamed at me. *OMG! What are you waiting for!*

I had let go. Of panic. Of effort. Of Lydia. Her body floated at my fingertips. I threw my arms and legs around her again—

FWOOOMP! The sound roared at me in the deep silence of the water.

Something rushed around me. Water stroked every part of my body. Ice hit the top of my skull and jarred me, and I heard cracking. Rigid edges scraped my face and tore at my arms.

We broke through the thin ice like some awkward sea beast breaching. We shot up, ejected from the water, scattering shards of ice, rising fast.

Air. I spit and took it in, sucking in water drops that made me cough and nearly cost me my grip on Lydia. She had vanished with me, but I felt her in my arms, weightless and motionless. I held her with her back to me. I adjusted my grip and pressed my hand to her chest to see if she also drew air.

I felt nothing.

Frantic, I pushed my hand inside her coat, over a wet sweater, to where I prayed her heart would be pounding.

Nothing.

NOTHING!

I screamed out profanity. We rose into the blowing snow and began drifting in the wind, away from the shore, farther over the ice. Snow falling heavily around us muted the sound of my curses.

Except for my grip on Lydia, my hands were empty. The propulsion unit lay somewhere in the lake below. The ski goggles were gone, too; torn off when I hit the water.

Up. We continued, soon to be enveloped in night, the earth beneath us obscured by snow. She lifeless, me helpless.

I considered dropping again. We would break through the ice below and from there I might pull her to safety. But carried on the wind, we had drifted farther over the lake, over the ice that would bar us from ever reaching the shore.

Even if I reached land, then what? I didn't know CPR. I had no idea how to revive her. She needed much more than I had to offer. How long had she been without air now? What was happening to her? To the baby?

What good am I!?

Utter desperation became black rage.

STOP!

Not a thought. Rage sculpted into reaction.

We stopped.

Now what?

We were too high to drop safely into the ice again. We were too far from shore in any event. I couldn't take the time to play with folded currency to get us down.

Do something!

Lydia would die without medical attention that was, at best, half an hour away on roads barely passable. I couldn't call for help. My phone was a saturated piece of useless plastic in my pocket.

DO SOMETHING!

Rage again—shaped into motion.

GO!

Something firm at my center took us. The ice below moved rapidly. An acceleration unlike anything I felt with the propulsion units swept us toward the south end of the lake.

First the shoreline, then trees appeared below me in the snow. The road. We moved. Fast. A solid pressure tugged at the center of my body. Like a muscle I didn't know I had. It flexed and sent us hurtling above the trees, into a maelstrom of relative wind that burned my eyes. I caught a glimpse of the curving Sunset Circle Road below.

We flew arrow straight.

DOWN!

We dipped. The landscape blurred beneath us. Snowflakes pricked my face and body as they collided with us.

LEVEL!

Pivoting on the firmness in my center, we resumed a level course. I guessed our speed at close to sixty knots. Wind tore at our clothing. My eyes streamed tears, squinting to see.

UP!

Power lines and transmission towers flew toward us. I felt my course alter, shifting directly toward the nearest tower, and up and over it in a shaved second. It hadn't been a conscious effort. It happened because— that's what you do.

You always fly over the towers.

We dropped again to just above treetop height.

Please please please please please, I prayed. I fixed my mind on the one destination that might save her. In my head, I saw the structure, drab and rectangular. I saw the helipad extending from one wing of the building. I saw the entrance where I had been carried just six months ago, injured and unaware.

Essex County Memorial.

In the restricted visibility, with eyes all but shut, I lost all sense of where we were. Landmarks I should have known went by so fast I couldn't make them out. The wind tore at my face.

Helpless to do anything for her, I rotated Lydia's limp body until she faced me. I pulled her into an embrace to shield the child between us. Her head fell against my shoulder. Her wet hair streamed after us like a transparent banner.

Light broke through the dark veil of snow. Streetlights formed lines in geometric patterns ahead, looking like runway lights, starkly contrasting the darkness, making the sky black. I saw a gas station I knew. It passed below at remarkable speed.

Not much farther.

A neighborhood swept by below. Cars followed headlight cones filled with sparkling snow. For a split second I smelled diesel exhaust as we shot over a semi, rolling slowly on an unplowed street.

The hospital came up fast, materializing out of the snow like a special effect. For a terrifying moment I realized I had no idea how to stop or get down safely, but it wasn't up to me. The image had formed and whatever drove us flew to that image as if it had been programmed into a navigation system.

We dropped from the sky toward the Emergency Entrance at Essex County Memorial. Despite a dramatic drop in speed, the landing was terrible.

Fwooomp! Gravity took us.

My feet hit the pavement and failed me. I stumbled forward and for a horrifying moment thought I would crash down on Lydia and the baby. I twisted hard to put the pavement at my back and brought her down on me. Her limp body blew the air from my lungs.

We skidded through the snow until my shoulder slammed into the glass automatic doors with a loud thud. Activated, the door scraped past me.

I gasped. Lydia sprawled on top of me.

Footsteps rattled the snow-catcher flooring of the entrance.

Someone dropped into my vision, but with eyes full of tears I saw only a shape. I felt a hand on my shoulder.

"*Help her!*" I tried to say, but it came out hoarse and thin. I sucked in a load of air and tried again. "Drowned! Not breathing!"

More hands. More shapes. Someone lifted Lydia off me.

"Drowned! Not breathing!" I rasped. "Pregnant!"

"Get her inside!" someone shouted. Lydia rose in urgent arms and floated out of my blurred field of vision. More footsteps. Someone new dropped beside me.

"Where are you hurt?" A woman's voice. Hands probed my body.

"Okay—I'm okay—help her!"

"We are. We're helping her. Just lay still." The hands worked their way down my arms. Across my torso. Down my legs. "Are you hurt?"

"No." I tried to rise, but a firm hand pressed me down.

"We're going to get a board."

I coughed. Something wet tickled my esophagus. I coughed again and couldn't stop. The hand wanted to hold me down, but I pushed it aside and got up on one elbow. I used my free hand to wipe the blur from my eyes. I coughed and spit.

"Phone! I need a phone."

"Let us get you—"

"NOW!" I closed a grip on the helping hand. I squinted to see. A nurse. A young woman. "Please! *Call the police!*"

64

Andy found me in one of the ER cubicles. They had me on a bed, soaking through the sheets. She pushed past a nurse working to fit a blood pressure cuff on my arm. She pulled me into a tight embrace.

"I'm okay," I said into her hair.

She popped back up and looked at me with furious intensity. The look was all Andy, all worry.

"Lydia," I said. I didn't know where to begin and a hard knot formed in my throat. I couldn't speak. On top of that, the room started to blur again. "Shit!" I managed to say.

"They're working on her," Andy said urgently, touching my face. "She's breathing. She's alive, Will." Her eyes clouded up. Which in turn messed up my vision even more. Neither of us could speak. We pulled each other close. My eyes burned.

"Shit! I'm getting you all wet."

I felt her let loose a laugh, an explosive burst powered by tension and fear. She pulled away from me and sniffled loudly.

"What happened?!"

I threw a quick glance at the nurse, who seemed bent on getting my blood pressure.

Andy turned and held up her badge. "Would you give us a minute?"

The nurse didn't appreciate being asked to interrupt her duties but eased out of the room after registering a complaint with rolled eyes.

Andy closed the sliding glass door.

I swallowed a few times to get control over my throat.

"O'Bannon. Somehow, he had Bob's truck. Came to the house. When he saw your car pull out, he followed it." I told her the rest. The part about getting to the hospital was hard. I didn't know how to describe it.

"Up," she said.

"What?"

"*Up.* Like the motel room in Sioux Valley. You did that thing. You did it again in Chicago. When we—when we were falling. That time it was *Stop.* I heard it. In my head. Like you were *inside* my head."

"Yeah, like that. Only lots more of it. This time—I don't know—it was—like an autopilot. Like navigation. Like it knew where to take us. I didn't *command* any of it, Dee. I just—*it* just went!"

She dropped onto a stool by the bed and put her hands over mine.

Damned lump jammed up my throat again because now I had to tell her the worst of it.

"I'm so sorry! It's my fault. The money. I fucked with him and took his money, and now he's coming after us. After you. Pidge. Lydia. God, he thought she was you! The baby! I'm—so—" I couldn't finish. I closed my eyes, unable to look at Andy.

She touched my cheek. I looked up. Her head moved slowly from side to side.

"Will, they arrested O'Bannon two hours ago in St. Louis. Chief Schulz called. Chicago Chief Schultz."

I swallowed hard, fighting the raging knot in my throat, fighting the sour blockage that dammed up my words.

"They got him!" she said emphatically.

"How?"

"He tried to get through security on a passport under another identity. Facial recognition tagged him. They got him."

Her words didn't make sense. She read the complete lack of comprehension in my face. She leaned into me and said it again.

"It wasn't O'Bannon!"

65

"You need to stop visiting us." Sam Morrissey looked at me with naked disgust. "And we need to get you out of those wet clothes."

I wasn't the least bit interested in what the young doctor had to say about me.

"How is she?" Andy and I asked in unison.

Morrissey looked pointedly at Andy. "Your sister is fine. The baby is fine."

Andy made a sound; I'm not sure if it was a cry of relief or her idea of cursing, or laughter. It simply escaped from her. She squeezed my right hand to the point of inflicting pain. My left had been wrapped up because of a gash in the flesh on the outside of the palm.

Morrissey turned around and slid the door closed behind him.

"We need to talk." He fixed an appraising eye on me, a mildly accusatory eye. "You seem to associate yourself with miracles, Will." Sam Morrissey had been the ER doctor who attended to me when I arrived at this same ER after my plane crash six months ago. "How's the pelvis?"

"Hurts when I fall down on concrete."

"About that…"

I didn't like where this was going, or the lies I would need to tell when it got there.

"Staff tells me you said she had drowned."

He let it hang. I didn't fall for it. After a moment, Morrissey gave up. He said, "She did. She drowned. We found fluid in her lungs. Her heart was beating, but she wasn't breathing. Do you mind telling me where and how this happened?"

I glanced at Andy for help.

"Doctor, that might be a problem," she said.

"You may be right. Because unless it happened at the water fountain down the hall, it is a problem. Your sister has all the symptoms of someone pulled out of a lake. Except we don't have a lake around here. We all assumed you had to transport her here, but nobody can tell me how that happened." Morrissey let the statement hang as a fill-in-the-blank. Again, neither of us fell for it. "Regardless," he went on, "transport of any kind would have taken time. Time without oxygen reaching your sister's brain. Did you administer CPR, Will?"

"Sorry. I don't know how."

"Did you administer oxygen?"

"Didn't have any with me."

Morrissey nodded and ran his fingers through his sandy brown hair.

"Well, somehow your sister arrived here with blood oxygen levels *above* normal. Better than we could ever hope for, even if a team of EMTs immediately administered pure oxygen and performed CPR."

"What does that mean?" Andy asked.

"It means she's okay. Better than okay," he said. "It means she drowned—and it had very little effect on her. So how is it that she fell in a lake and drowned, and then fell out of the lake onto our sidewalk with oxygen-rich blood?"

Again, he let the question hang.

"You're not going to tell me, are you?"

I shook my head slowly. I felt bad about it. I like Sam Morrissey.

He held a long pause, then retreated to doctor-mode.

"She runs a slight risk of pneumonia, but we're treating her for that. And we're giving her antibiotics. She might have inhaled impurities with the water that got in her lungs. There was a hint of gasoline."

He stopped and stared.

"You're really not going to tell me, are you?"

I shook my head again.

"I suppose there's not much point in reporting this to the police," he said to Andy.

"Consider it done," she said. "Can I see her? Is she awake?"

"Sedatives are contraindicated for someone in her condition, so she is, in fact, awake and I see no reason why you cannot see her."

I started to swing my legs off the bed.

"Oh, no! You stay here. We're going to stitch up that hand and give you some antibiotics. You smell like gasoline, too."

Andy kissed me quickly and hurried out of the room.

Damn.

I missed the reunion.

66

They tried to keep me. I refused. My clothes were soaked and began to chafe. They wanted to get them off me. I refused. They gave me towels and I dried myself as much as I could. Morrissey stitched up my hand. It hurt like hell. I think he enjoyed that.

I couldn't get my boots back on, so I carried them and walked in spongy socks covered by pale blue booties. They let me look in on Lydia for a moment. I poked my head in just long enough to see two sisters holding on to each other as if letting go meant letting go of life. Neither spoke. I didn't intrude.

My damned eyes started to sting again. Must have been the gasoline.

I slipped out and ran into Mike Mackiejewski. Mike had been at the Thanning house with Andy. They had been more than halfway to Leander Lake when the call from the hospital caught up with her.

I told Mike she would be a while. He seemed a little shaken by what he'd seen at the Thanning house. I asked him to give me a ride home. It gave him something to focus on. After telling the nurse to tell Andy I'd be back for her, I left.

On the way home, I used Mike's phone and called Sandy Stone. I asked her to drive down to Lydia's lake house, introduce herself and stay there with the nanny and Lydia's kids. Sandy didn't question.

In dry clothes and my own car, I returned to the hospital almost two hours later. The roads, which were bad when Lydia had been pushed into the lake, were a nightmare by the time I got back to the hospital. The wind peaked and drove the snow sideways. Visibility shrank to zero at times.

It took some effort to find Andy. Lydia had been moved to a room and I had no phone. The hospital system hadn't quite caught up with events, and the front desk could not find her name or room number. Only after tracking down Sam Morrissey in the ER was I able to get directions.

"You're really not going to tell me," he said again after giving me Lydia's room number.

"Nope."

Andy saw me when I arrived at the room. She gestured for me to be quiet. Lydia slept. Andy gently kissed her sister on the head and slipped out. I put my arm around Andy's shoulder. She slipped her arm around my waist.

"I don't want to go, but they won't let me stay," she said.

We said little as we walked out to my car. The wind would have blown the words away. Snow fell heavily around us.

"I want to be here first thing in the morning," Andy said in the compressed silence of the car.

"We will."

I reached behind the seat and handed Andy her laptop.

"What's this doing here?"

"We have a stop to make," I said.

I explained.

ROSEMARY II ANSWERED the door and hurried us into her home. Andy had called from the car as we drove to the small house Lane shared with her mother. Rosemary II seemed to think nothing of a late-night request to visit in the middle of a snowstorm. She assumed we were on a mission to see her daughter.

"Please, come in! Let me get Lane!"

"No, wait," Andy said. "We're here for you. I want to show you something."

Standing in Rosemary II's tiny living room, Andy slipped off her gloves and opened her laptop. She brushed a strand of hair from her eyes, but it dropped back in place with determination. Andy touched the screen several times to bring up an image. She turned the laptop toward Rosemary II.

"Is this him? The insurance adjuster who wanted to see my car?"

Rosemary II didn't hesitate.

"That's him." She put on a look of concern because the image was a prison mug shot. A band below the photo read Evergreen Reform. The man in the photo aimed cold, dead eyes at the prison photographer. "Who is he?"

Andy and I traded looks. I had expected Rosemary II's affirmation. Getting it still packed a punch.

Andy closed the laptop.

"A ghost."

DIVISIBLE MAN—THE SECOND GHOST
December 3, 2017 to February 11, 2018

The following short story
comes from the manifests
of Essex County Air Services.

"Angel Flight" forms the bridge
to the next DIVISIBLE MAN novel.

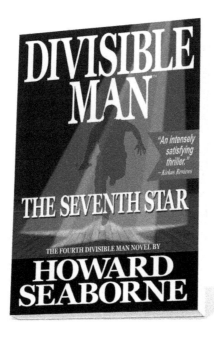

ANGEL FLIGHT

ANGEL FLIGHT

"Mistletoe?"

Andy looked up at me. I watched her sleepy eyes squeeze, attempting to focus on the sprig of leaf and berry I had taped to my forehead.

Her hair spread on the pillow, framing her face in sweet symmetry.

"Damn, how did that get there?" I asked.

She let a pair of dimples peek from the corners of her mouth.

"Bring it in, Pilot," she said, almost purring. "But we're going to have to be quick. I'm taking a patrol shift today."

"I don't think I can do quick." I lifted the covers and slid into the warm bed beside her.

"Right. You just keep on believing that."

Challenge accepted.

I made a point of not being quick. She did not protest.

* * * * *

Andy did that thing she does, the one where she rushes around the house performing half a dozen tasks simultaneously. She worked her hair into a bun, put on her belt, poured coffee into a thermos, holstered her weapon, and located her patrol uniform hat after asking me where she put it. I sat in the kitchen at the counter-height table and sipped my own coffee, feeling a certain pride in the fact she was running late.

"Are you going to the airport?" she asked on the move from somewhere in the living room.

"Thought I'd play Santa," I called back. "Although I don't know if anyone will be there in this weather. If they shut everything down, I may have to deliver house to house. Santa old school."

I glanced out the kitchen window. Still couldn't see the barn. People who don't fly often ask me what it's like being in a cloud. Stand outside on a foggy day. That's what it's like.

"Don't take Lane's gift, okay?" Andy blew into the kitchen in full uniform. Despite her promotion to detective, the scheduling needs of the department still required her to take an occasional shift as patrol sergeant. Especially around the Christmas holiday. "And don't take Rosemary II's. I want to drop them off on the way to Lydia's tonight."

"That's the opposite direction," I pointed out. "Maybe we should just go hang out with Lane and Rosemary II tonight instead."

The idea got no traction.

I didn't hide my trepidation about Christmas Eve at Lydia's. Had it been simply Andy and Lydia and I, sipping wine (in Lydia's pregnant case, grape juice) and watching Lydia's little girls jumping out of their skin in anticipation of Santa's visit—that I would have loved.

Such was not the plan.

Lydia, flush with the success of reuniting with her sister Andy, had plunged ahead on the path of restoring peace in the family. She invited her parents and her brother and his wife for a family Christmas. Holidays bear a stress load all their own without attempting to implement an armistice in a six-year war—The Shitstorm, as Andy and I called it. Six years of Andy rejecting her father's wishes, and he in turn rejecting her.

Lydia decided the time had come to end it.

I did not foresee this going well.

"We have to give this a chance," Andy said, slipping into her Essex PD jacket. "We'll have Lane and her mom over for dinner this week. But tonight—tonight will be tonight."

Well, that makes it all better.

I'd been pulling for Lydia. But my opinion, which is as weightless as I am when I vanish, was that Lydia had campaigned a bridge too far. I was surprised by Andy's willingness to participate in Lydia's peacemaking. I thought she might want to firm up her new alliance with her older sister before taking on their father. I chalked it up to holiday spirit. And maybe Lydia's recent near-death experience.

Andy scooped up her keys and pulled me into a kiss.

"Thanks for the mistletoe," she hummed in my ear.

"There's more on the vine."

"Good."

I followed her to the door.

"Be safe out there. It's zero-zero."

"Roger that."

* * * * *

After Andy left, I finished the last-minute Christmas wrapping I traditionally save for Christmas Eve (and sometimes Christmas morning). In other words, Andy's gift.

This year, Andy's gift was easy. She strongly hinted for a rail-mounted laser sight compatible with her Beretta Model 92A—as in she e-mailed me a link to the item on the manufacturer's website. The compact box proved easy to wrap, but before I did so, I removed the laser sight and replaced it with a small, velvet-lined box containing a thin chain and a single tiny diamond framed in a stylized heart. I caught Andy admiring the necklace at Shinamon's Jewelers the night of the Essex Winter Festival. We had been walking from shop to shop under city-hung Christmas lights when Andy stopped at the window. I asked if she wanted to try it on, but she declined. Not in the family budget, she claimed. I protested that you only adhere to a budget if you have actual money. She claimed that I just proved her point. Of course, she didn't know I'd been salting away a few dollars here and there all year for precisely this sort of emergency. Now I looked forward to scoring extra points not only for the gift, but for the frugal foresight and the whole noticing-that-she-liked-it thing.

I planned to give her the gift tonight before we set off for Lydia's. I wasn't about to jeopardize my shot at Hero Husband status by waiting until the holiday lay in ruins.

Andy managed the rest of the gift wrapping, which I deemed only fair since she's the one who did all the shopping. There were gifts for Lydia and her two little girls. Gifts for Pidge and Dave Peterson, fellow pilots at Essex County Air Services. Something for Andy's boss, Tom Ceeves. Andy found something for Rosemary II—I'll be honest, I didn't pay attention when Andy described it to me. We purchased a Bluetooth speaker for Lane. Andy bought something for our friend, Sandy Stone—and again, I have no clue what. (It's a condition I call Girl Gift Blindness, and I insist it's a real thing.)

My second-favorite gift was a framed photo of Earl Jackson standing in front of his newly acquired King Air 90. Andy snapped the picture surreptitiously, catching my boss in a rare moment of introspection in the shadow of a beautiful airplane. Honestly, the intimacy of the photo stuns me. Earl is a human built on a gargoyle mold, with a head as bald as a boulder and a perpetual scowl on his face. The intimidating exterior makes perfect camouflage for a heart so big it requires a solid fireplug body to contain it. Yet the photo reveals a man connected to a machine and the sky beyond it in ways that perhaps only a pilot would understand.

I argued that Andy should be the one to give him the photo. I reasoned there would be less chance Earl would throw it back at her. Earl doesn't like gifts, but he has a giant soft spot for my wife.

I slipped into the afternoon by spending time reloading and fine-tuning the latest version of my flashlight-battery-powered propulsion units. The newest editions had detachable propellers, making them easier to carry in my flight jacket. The propellers simply snapped on and locked in place. I've learned to keep at least one of the compact power units at my fingertips at all times.

"Ladies and gentlemen, I give you the FLOP!" I announced to a capacity crowd cheering in my head. "Flight Launching Operational Propulsion!" I couldn't wait to tell Andy the new name. Maybe when I give her the diamond.

A little after two p.m. I loaded the Christmas packages in my car and edged my way into the fog.

Early December brought several icy Alberta Clippers through Wisconsin—fast-moving low-pressure systems followed by giant masses of frigid Canadian air. Starting the first weekend of the month, we had snowfall after snowfall, almost guaranteeing a white Christmas. Two days before the holiday, a warm air mass crept into the state, drawn by a broad low-pressure system that trudged east in no particular hurry. Temperatures rose above freezing. Snow melted by day, then refroze in the night as sheets of ice. Warm air flowed across a snow-covered landscape, which caused moisture in the air to condense as fog. Dense fog stretched from central Illinois all the way to the Canadian border. Holiday travelers at every major airport in the Midwest found themselves stranded as the airlines cancelled flights in record numbers.

Exiting our driveway, I glanced back. I couldn't see the house. There was no question in my mind. Nobody but Santa Claus would be flying today. I felt sure I'd find the offices at Essex County Air Service empty.

Wrong.

* * * * *

"What's the Mojave doing on the ramp?" I asked Rosemary II the moment I cleared the tinted glass doors.

She held up her just-a-minute hand and then touched the earpiece on her headset to send me her on-the-phone gesture.

She wore a grim expression.

I deposited the cardboard box containing Christmas gifts on the floor under the artificial tree in the corner. Colored tree lights along with the scent of fresh coffee warmed the flying service office. Rosemary II makes superb coffee. I helped myself to a cup while she carried on her largely silent side of what seemed to be a troubling conversation.

I finished a third of the heavenly brew before Rosemary II ended the call.

"Oh, dear," she said. She's not much older than me but she projects a potent mothering influence on everyone at Essex Air. We love her for it.

"What's going on?"

"That was Earl. He's been trying to work out an Angel Flight all morning, and it's going badly."

Earl Jackson donates his airplanes and pilots to Angel Flight, an organization that provides private aircraft transportation to families needing to travel long distances for medical treatment. I've flown a few Angel Flights for him. The missions are both fulfilling and heartbreaking, especially when transporting children.

"Jesus, nothing's flying in this," I said, but I had a bad feeling, noting again that the Piper Mojave had been pulled out of the hangar. Even from the office, just a few hundred feet away, fog softened the outline of the airplane.

"That's the problem," Rosemary II said. She suddenly remembered something and hurried through the inner office and out the door which put her on my side of the front counter. Almost spilling my coffee, she threw a big hug around me.

"Merry Christmas, Will," she whispered in my ear. "And thank you."

She squeezed me in a deep and appreciative embrace, then backed away, leaving the scent of her perfume between us.

"Merry Christmas to you, too," I fumbled, feeling awkward.

She gave me a long look with dark brown eyes, then nodded and went back the way she came.

Six months ago, I had a hand in saving her daughter's life. One Thank-You would have long-since covered it, but I guess the holiday spirit reignites memories of the episode for Rosemary II.

"You were saying?" I sought a quick change of subject.

Rosemary II returned to her station behind the counter.

"Earl had an Angel Flight scheduled for this morning. Pick up at Milwaukee Mitchell, then up to Marshfield." Angel Flights to Marshfield and its world-famous research clinic were not uncommon.

"Well, that's not happening," I said, feeling grateful that someone employed sound decision-making.

Rosemary II drew a long breath and tipped her head from side to side.

"Tell me that's not happening."

"Oh, it's fucking happening!" Pidge marched out of the pilot briefing office with her flight bag in one hand and an iPad in the other. She wore her work uniform, which made her look like a teenaged girl dressed up as a pilot. At twenty-three she holds every rating including Airline Transport Pilot, and she flies everything Earl owns. She and Earl get along like fire and gasoline vapor, but the one thing they can both agree on is that she's the best pilot either of them knows.

"You can't be serious," I said. "Marshfield is as low as we are."

"Two hundred and a quarter, last hour," Pidge informed me. "Icing in the clouds."

"So, this is not happening," I said again, making it sound more like a command. I had been Earl's chief pilot before the FAA suspended my license. I still carried some authority.

Rosemary II issued one of her motherly sighs.

"There's a little girl," she said. And like the cold, heartless sonofabitch I can be, I thought *of course, it had to be a little girl*. "She has a blood disease. She was supposed to be treated two days ago, but she couldn't travel. She's taken a turn. Now it's a matter of life—"

"Don't say life or death," I warned Rosemary II. "Not when pilots have to make a go or no-go decision."

"Oh, that decision's already been made," Pidge said.

"What do you mean?"

Both women looked at me, leaving the question hanging. Rosemary II finally answered.

"Earl set up the flight for this morning, but the fog cancelled it. They decided to transport her by ambulance."

"Sounds like the right idea to me," I said.

"Twenty minutes ago, they called Earl, and Earl called Andy, and now they're coming here," Rosemary II said.

"Wait. What?"

"They called Earl because they got as far as Essex County, but there's a huge pile-up and the highway is closed. They thought maybe a helicopter could meet them on the highway and make the rest of the trip. But of course, that's impossible. So, Earl called Andy and got her to go out to the highway and find them and bring them here."

"Why here?" I didn't like where this was going.

"Because Earl told them I'd fucking fly them to Marshfield," Pidge said. Pidge drops F-bombs on everything, but even so, I knew from her tone she didn't like the idea. Not one bit.

"You can't. This is very bad shit."

"I can," she said, matter-of-factly. "I agree with you. It's very bad shit. But I can. And you know I can."

"Where's Earl?" If he was orchestrating all this, I wanted to speak to him.

"Once it looked like the flight wouldn't go, he hopped in his car and drove to Milwaukee. I think he planned on driving the family to Marshfield himself, but the girl is so bad off they need an ambulance and an attending nurse."

"Jesus," I said. "Does he know this family?"

Rosemary II gave me a look meant to shame me. "It's Christmas, Will. Everybody knows everybody."

"What about a detour? Can't they get around the pile-up?"

"It's Christmas, Will," Pidge said, piling on. "Granny and all the fucking uncles are taking the detour. It's a knot. That's why Earl called Andy for a police escort."

I turned to Pidge.

"You know the rules, Pidge. Angel Flight or not, the pilot cannot allow the need to infect his judgment."

"*Her* judgment, dumbass," she punched at my shoulder. "Yeah, I know the fucking rules."

But you're doing this anyway, I thought. *This is not good.*

Pidge busied herself with her flight kit, but it was a ploy. The way she had everything organized told me she had already filed a flight plan and finished the preflight.

"How much gas are you taking?" I asked.

"All of it," she said.

"Well," I said grimly. "You will need it. Because when you can't get into Marshfield, you may have to fly to Nebraska to find a place to land."

* * * * *

I didn't want anything to do with this.

My holiday delivery had been made. My work here was done. I didn't want to be around to see this emergency unfold. A big part of me feared Pidge was about to do something monumentally stupid.

I decided to finish my coffee and get out of the way.

Just as soon as I helped Pidge load her things in the plane.

"What are you doing?" she asked when I joined her on the ramp.

"Helping you load up."

"Then why am I fucking carrying all this shit?"

"Because you're pilot-in-command of this dumbass idea."

We walked to the airplane without continuing the conversation. Shining and damp, the Mojave sat on the ramp looking the way all airplanes look to me—like a glorious creature restrained. Like its landing gear and wheels represented chains locking her sleek body to the earth.

Pidge pulled down the door which served as a stair and climbed in. I waited on the ramp. While she thumped through the cabin toward the cockpit, I pressed my hand against the aluminum skin of the airplane. I closed my eyes and tried to feel something meaningful while my hand traded heat for cold with the airplane. I tried to feel the future—as if a touch could join me to this flying machine and tell me everything would be okay. Or tell me it would not.

I strained to hear machine whispers. I searched the insides of my eyelids for a vision of wheels touching down on damp pavement after a challenging but safe flight. The airplane protected its mysteries and revealed no prescient secrets to me. I broke the bonding touch, leaving the question unanswered.

I was about to take up the weather argument with Pidge when the distant sound of sirens cut through the fog. I recognized the warble of an Essex PD cruiser, but it harmonized with off-key notes from a second unit. Both grew louder, and the fog on the other side of the hangar soon throbbed with flashing heartbeats of blue and red.

The sirens abruptly stopped, and the lights grew brighter, eventually rounding the buildings. Andy nosed her cruiser up against the hangar. A large, square rescue squad ambulance pulled up behind the airplane.

An EMT hopped out and hurried to the back of the unit. The driver, another EMT, rounded the front fender and walked toward me. Andy came up close behind him.

"Are you the pilot?" the driver asked.

I thumbed toward the cabin and said, "She is. In the cockpit."

The driver glanced back at his unit, at the drama unfolding behind the rear doors. Then he leaned toward the aircraft door to look for Pidge.

"She's not really going to do this, is she?"

"She won't do anything unsafe, if that's your question," I answered a bit defensively. Andy correctly read my tone as unhappy and bounced a worried look in my direction.

The first EMT hustled up with a heavy case in hand. "This goes in the cabin with the kid."

"How much does it weigh?" I asked.

"About seventy pounds," he said. He strained against the weight. I leaned into it and grabbed one side of the case. Together we heaved it up into the cabin.

"I got it," I said, and I pushed it behind the last seat. I automatically estimated its effect on the aircraft weight and balance, considering that Pidge had loaded full fuel. The calculation grew more critical when the co-driver produced two more heavy, hardshell cases. I helped load them. I leaned in the cabin and called up to Pidge to give her the numbers for a revised weight-and-balance estimate.

By the time I stepped back onto the ramp, both EMTs had gone to the rear of the ambulance. I watched them help a nurse pull a gurney from the back of the unit. An IV bag hung above the figure on the gurney.

So small.

The child had been wrapped in blankets for protection against the cold. She lay almost entirely hidden. Even with the blanket bulk, she looked tiny. A lock of brown hair peeked from her wrap. Someone, a civilian, a woman with worry etched deep in her skin, hurried to tuck the blankets around the child and over her face as the gurney rolled.

Andy looked at me with pain shading her green eyes.

"Oh, this is not good," I muttered to the only person listening. Me.

The cluster of attendants rolled the gurney up to the Mojave.

"That won't fit," I said of the stretcher on wheels. People think all airplanes have the interior dimensions of an airliner. "She'll have to be carried up and she'll have to be in a seat. We can recline it, but she'll have to be strapped in."

After a split second of hesitation, they set about untangling the child. The nurse detached the IV bag and readied herself to carry it alongside the girl. The EMTs rearranged the blankets, then slid their hands under the girl and effortlessly lifted her. One tucked the girl's head against the other's shoulder to ensure she would not be bumped against the door frame.

"Take the back seat on the left," I instructed them. I hurried up into the cabin ahead of them and positioned myself in the seat across the aisle.

The EMT carried the child up the steps embedded in the door. Hunched over, he squeezed into the cabin and swung her into the seat. I leaned over and grabbed the seatback mechanism, reclining it two notches. Any farther and it would interfere with the door.

The nurse entered the cabin with the IV bag. She looked around for somewhere to hang it. The smooth moldings in the cabin roof offered no anchor points.

"Andy!" I called out. "Go get a wire coat hanger from Rosemary II!"

A minute later Andy handed a coat hanger through the cabin door. The nurse passed it to me. I did a little bending, then jammed it into the plastic molding above the seat. The nurse fixed the IV bag in place, then set about unpacking portable monitors from the hardshell cases. She meticulously unwound leads and made connections. After several minutes, two of the complex devices beeped and filled their screens with data.

After ensuring that the IV tubes were not pinched or obstructed, the nurse backed out of the cabin to let the co-driver and me out. The mother barely allowed us to clear before she hurried up into the cabin to be with her daughter.

I touched the nurse on the sleeve and beckoned her toward the tail of the airplane.

"This looks bad," I said in the lowest possible voice. It was a question. The expression on the nurse's face telegraphed her answer.

"She should have been at the clinic three days ago," she said. "Her condition has become...aggressive. We agreed to drive her but to be honest, especially in this fog..." she shook her head. "Can the pilot really get us there?"

I looked at the mist floating all around us. "If it's like this in Marshfield, no. And she can't bring you back here. She's going to have to fly on to find someplace above minimums to land. This is a very bad idea."

"This is the only idea," the nurse said. "I hate to put it that way. I know how these things work. If I were you, I wouldn't make the flight."

"And what's her outcome if we call it off?"

"I refuse to answer that."

"Okay."

I gave her a pat on the shoulder, and she hurried back to the stairs to take her place in the cabin. I backed away with Andy.

Pidge appeared in the cabin doorway. She reached down for the straps on the door.

"Wait!" I called out. I turned to Andy.

Her eyes told me she saw this coming.

"I guess this proves I'll do anything to avoid the big dinner tonight," I said.

She put her hands on either side of my face and planted a kiss.

"I know."

I broke away from wanting another kiss and hurried to the cabin door.

"You're going to need a hand," I told Pidge. I expected a smart-ass reply, but she simply nodded, then worked her way up to the pilot's seat.

I hunched my way into the cabin and took a knee beside the mother, who sat directly across the aisle from the child. The nurse had taken the seat behind the pilot's seat, facing aft toward her patient.

I put a hand on the mother's arm.

"Ma'am," I said. "You need her to arrive in Marshfield quickly and safely."

She nodded at me. Her eyes were wet.

"That pilot up front may not look like it, but she's the best there is. But this flight is going to be tough, and as good as she is, she's going to need help. We also need all the fuel we can carry. We're loaded up and we're going to pick up ice. You have a tough choice. You can go along, which means I have to get off. Or I can take the co-pilot's seat and increase the chances of getting her there. But if I do that, it has to be without you. Because we can't both go. We'll be overloaded."

It was a flat-out lie.

The woman's face quivered and wrinkled. Tears spilled. "But—but she's my—*she's my baby!*"

I took her hand. She had more to say but couldn't get the words out. She knew the potential dark side of this decision, of leaving her child. I knew it, too. I knew I might be stealing a mother from her child's final moments. But I also knew there was little chance we were going to land this flight in Marshfield.

"Let us do this for her. Like she was our own," I said.

* * * * *

Pidge ignited the right engine while I secured the door. On the way back up the aisle I gave the nurse a reassuring nod, entirely false. By the time I strapped in the co-pilot's seat, Pidge had the left engine running. She let the Mojave roll at once. We wheeled around on the ramp and rolled for a departure on Runway 13. As we taxied, I saw Andy standing beside her cruiser, holding the mother by the shoulder as the woman shook, sobbing.

I gave Andy an apologetic thumbs-up while working the radios to copy our IFR clearance. ATC cleared us direct and added the latest weather from Marshfield, as if to make a point. I read back their instructions and received an immediate release, with a request to report airborne on Center frequency.

You can know an airport intimately, but when low visibility steals your orientation, even the most familiar taxiways and runways become alien environments. Pidge and I strained to see the yellow taxi line that took us toward the runway. At the Hold Short line, I worked through the pre-takeoff checklist while Pidge performed each check. During the run-up, she took an extra minute to listen to the engines with her eyes closed.

"Zero-zero takeoff," I said through the intercom. We'd been through this before, recently, in a snowstorm, but this time our roles were reversed. This time Pidge sat in the command seat. She would fix her attention on the instruments while I maintained a visual orientation to the runway, holding us on the centerline with the rudder pedals until I called for her to rotate.

We finished the pre-takeoff checklist. Pidge back-taxied into position on the runway. I made the departure announcement over the silent radio frequency for Essex County. Pidge lined us up and slowly worked the throttles forward while holding the brakes. The engines sang. The airframe shuddered. When the manifold pressure reached twenty inches, she let the brakes go and pushed the throttles to the stops. The Mojave surged forward.

We both held the control yoke. I firmly worked the pedals, guiding the nosewheel down the runway centerline.

"Power check," Pidge called out.

"Suction," Pidge called out.

I fixed my eyes on the runway ahead. I barely saw the white lines below the nose as we raced forward into the blinding mist.

"Airspeed's alive," Pidge called out.

The runway lights ticked past us, ever faster. I watched the needle swing on the airspeed indicator.

"Rotate!" I called, giving us an extra five knots for comfort.

Pidge pulled the yoke and the Mojave leaped free of the runway. My world, the world over the nose, went white. Pidge glued her eyes to the instruments.

"Blue line. Gear up," she said. I pulled the handle and monitored until the light said all three wheels were tucked in.

"Positive rate," I reported.

I switched to the air traffic control frequency. "Chicago Center, Angel Flight One One Kilo with you, climbing to six thousand."

* * * * *

The cruise portion of the flight unfolded uneventfully. It may have been the Angel Flight call sign, or it may have been the utter absence of other aircraft on the frequency, but we seemed to get priority treatment from air traffic control. Direct routing put us close to Marshfield in less than an hour, far faster than an ambulance.

Not fast enough.

Just as we began our descent, the nurse touched my shoulder. I turned around and she met my eyes with a dark expression.

"She's not doing well. Not at all. How much longer?"

Pidge had accepted vectors for an instrument approach into Marshfield. We chose runway 16, which is fifteen hundred feet longer than the only other option. The best instrument approach into Marshfield could only lower us to within 400 feet of the ground. I didn't think the visibility in any direction was much more than 400 feet. On top of everything, we were accumulating ice. The surface temperature at Marshfield hovered above freezing, putting the freezing level just above the ground. If we were lucky, we might shed ice once we reached minimum descent altitude, but we'd be collecting it throughout the approach.

I looked back at the nurse. She didn't have headphones on, so I pulled mine off to avoid shouting over the intercom into Pidge's ears.

"Close. Another ten minutes," I said. She shook her head as if that might not do. I found myself trying hard not to look at the bundle wrapped up in the rear seat. As the nurse drew a deep breath and started to turn away, I caught her arm. "That's if we break out. It doesn't look good."

"Then what?"

"We try again," I said. "But it means picking up a lot of ice. We can't keep trying indefinitely."

She let it sink in.

"It might not matter," she said. She delivered a pointed look, then turned back to her charge.

352

I put the headphones back on.

"What's the story?" Pidge asked.

"Not your concern," I said.

"Fuck that," Pidge answered. "I'm taking us down to two hundred. Fourteen forty MSL."

Instrument pilots flying a blind approach follow strict procedures. The ironclad rule is to descend to the prescribed altitude. If you do not see the runway environment or find yourself in a position from which you can land safely, you execute the missed approach procedure. You don't descend one inch below the prescribed Minimums. Period. No other option exists.

Except the very dangerous practice of busting Minimums. Pidge just announced her intention to do exactly that, cutting our safety margin in half.

"I'll put us there. Needles crossed. You find our way out of this fucking muck," Pidge added.

"Affirmative."

* * * * *

We tracked inbound on the approach course. The one blessing hidden in this mass of stagnant, cold, wet air was an absence of turbulence. Except for the steady song of the engines, we might have been sitting in someone's living room. The Mojave rode through the air like a skater on glass.

I called out the final approach fix and dropped the landing gear. Pidge configured for the descent, adjusting speed, trim and attitude. The moving map display showed us dead center on course. The crossed needles on the navigation instruments told us we were aligned precisely on the glide path. Shades of darkness in the fog indicated the day had grown old.

"Five hundred above Minimums," I called out to Pidge.

Her hands moved the controls microscopically.

"Four hundred above Minimums."

Nothing but white in every direction.

"Three hundred."

Airspeed nailed.

"Two hundred. Final gear check. Three green."

"One hundred."

Steady. On course. Needles perfectly crossed.

"Minimums."

My eyes darted between the windshield and the altimeter.

"Minus one hundred."

Nothing. Nothing but white. Not even the hint of a light.

"Minus two hundred!"

"Anything?" Pidge demanded. I felt her flinch on the yoke to arrest the descent.

"Nothing! Missed approach!"

She powered up slightly but held the altitude for a second. Any other time, I would have criticized her. Instead, I grabbed the extra second and frantically searched ahead and directly below. For an instant, I thought I saw a runway light. Then another. But it did us no good.

Pidge went to full throttle for the Missed Approach climb. I retracted the gear and called out the speed. I contacted Minneapolis Center and reported the bad news. They asked our intentions. I said we would try again.

"She's starting to handle like a pig," Pidge said. I glanced at the ice building on our windshield frame and on the wings. Pidge hit the deicing boots. Pieces flew into the slipstream, but not all of them.

"One more and we're done," I said. "We stay down here too long, and we won't be able to climb out of it." I double-checked to ensure that the prop and windshield de-icing systems remained on.

I glanced back at the cabin. The nurse had unstrapped and now knelt in the aisle beside the child. She had the seat fully reclined and leaned over her patient, working frantically with what I took for a syringe. She must have felt my gaze, because she turned to me and shook her head sharply.

Center called. "One One Kilo, we have a request from Marshfield for you to contact them on CTAF. Frequency change approved. Report back on."

I acknowledged and switched over to the Marshfield frequency.

"Marshfield Unicom, Mojave One One Kilo."

"One One Kilo, this is Marshfield. We heard you go over. You need to know, we're down to zero-zero. Repeat. Down to zero-zero."

My heart sank.

"Roger, Marshfield. Thanks."

"Will," Pidge spoke in my head, the way headphones do.

I turned in my seat and looked at Pidge. She looked at me.

"We're not going to get this thing down," she said.

I said nothing.

"I'm willing to try," Pidge said. "But I know how it's going to go."

"Affirmative."

I fought the urge to look at the bundle in the back.

I didn't know this child. I didn't know her story, her illness, her family. I didn't know what she wanted for Christmas except maybe just to wake up on Christmas morning. What I really needed to know, however, was if that was *just too God damned much to ask*? Just to wake up one more day? Just to wake up on Christmas morning?

I surrendered to the urge and looked back, but I couldn't see the girl. The nurse had flipped up the seat armrest and worked herself into a position in the aisle, so she could hold the child in her arms. She had nothing else to give her but the touch of another human.

It's Christmas, Will. Everybody knows everybody.

"Pidge, level off. Right here. Hold eighteen hundred!" I commanded.

Pidge didn't question. She had configured for a climb back to three thousand, but she cut the power and leveled the aircraft at one-thousand-eight-hundred feet.

I grabbed the iPad from the flight bag.

"Where's the Marshfield clinic? The pediatric hospital?"

"The fuck should I know!"

I worked the iPad, stabbed at the screen, did a quick search on the non-aviation map page and found the prestigious and utterly useless—to us at this moment—clinic. I memorized the location and switched over to the ForeFlight navigation application. In a moment, switching to aerial view, I located and marked the building. Then I backed out to see where we were in relation to the clinic.

On the screen, the small airplane icon tracked northwest. Pidge had reversed our course for another attempt at the approach. The clinic, located near the center of town, lay ahead and to our left beneath the blanket of fog, almost directly under the approach course for runway 23.

"Pidge line up for the RNAV Two Three. Stay at this altitude. We've got towers all over hell here, but the highest is seventeen-oh-nine. Don't go below eighteen hundred."

I unstrapped.

"Sure. Ninety feet. No problem. What the fuck are you doing?"

I paused. She looked sharply at me.

"I'm going to take the kid and bail out."

Pidge gave me as much blank stare as she could afford while throwing her attention between me and the instrument panel.

"Oh," she said. "I was afraid you were going to do something fucking stupid."

I levered my way out of the cockpit, taking my headphones and the iPad with me. To get around the nurse, still occupying the thin aisle, I had to climb over the seat opposite the girl. I positioned myself at the rear of the cabin and hooked up the intercom again.

"Pidge hold the reciprocal course for the RNAV Two Three Approach. I'll call out when you should turn inbound."

"Got it."

I pulled off the headset and laid it aside. By now the nurse was looking at me, so I gestured for her to come close.

"How is she?" I asked, speaking up over the engines.

She shook her head. "She doesn't have long. Can we get down?"

Now I shook my head. She clutched her lips together, fighting tears. I waved them away.

"Listen to me," I said, taking her shoulders in my hands. "Do you believe in Christmas miracles?"

Her eyes grew wetter. She gave a helpless shrug.

"I'm going to do something you will find impossible to believe. I don't have time to explain it, but it may help her make it. I may be able to get her down there. Are you willing?"

She nodded emphatically.

"What's your name?" I asked.

"Christie," she said.

"Christie, I'm Will. There's only one catch to this. But it's a deal-breaker. You can't tell anyone what happens here tonight. No matter who it is, no matter how they ask. You can't tell anyone what you're about to see. Ever. Can you do that?"

I think she thought we were about to do something as prosaic as breaking a regulation because she nodded quickly.

"No, I'm serious. This is going to shake you up. You have to promise me, swear to me, on the life of this child!"

"I swear!" she said quickly. "Anything we can do to get her there, please."

"Okay. I'm going to show you something now. You won't believe it."

I made sure I had her eyes locked on me.

Fwooomp! I vanished.

It gave her a jolt, a small one. She blinked.

"You can't see me," I told her. "But I'm still here."

Fwooomp! Reappearing startled her, and now it sank in. Her eyes went wide.

"Listen to me!" I took her shoulders again before she became absorbed in a tangle of impossible thoughts. "I can do that. And I can also fly. Like freakin' Tinkerbell. Don't ask how. I can fly, and I want to take that girl with me and jump out of this perfectly good airplane right over the clinic and deliver her. It's the only way we can get her down. There's no way to land the plane."

Her mouth worked open and closed. Nothing came out.

"You have to swear to me, you will never tell anyone what happens here. Swear to me!" I gently shook her shoulders. "On the life of this child!"

"Uh! I swear! How—?"

"Secret government experiment gone bad," I said quickly. "This is going to work. Get her ready! Go!" I shook her shoulders again and she snapped out of her gawking. She turned quickly and busied herself with the patient.

I put on the headset.

"Pidge!"

"Right here."

"Turn us inbound. Line up on the Two Three approach course."

"Roger that. Are you seriously fucking doing this?"

"Slow us down, as slow as you can. And if you can throttle back the left engine, that will help. I'm going to open the door and that's going to create some serious yaw. Be ready. When I say so, I want you to cut the left engine for a count of five. Don't try to hold altitude. After I go out, power up and take it up a few thousand and put it on autopilot—slow but not too slow. You'll have to come back here and close the door. Get the nurse to sit up front for balance or you'll be way out of C.G."

"Fuck!"

I pulled up the iPad and checked the track. Pidge had gone about ten miles northeast of Marshfield. The tiny airplane icon turned to intercept the inbound course for the RNAV 23 approach. I wondered what in the world ATC was thinking of all this. Probably getting ready to call us a crash. I had no doubt they were already pitching altitude warnings at Pidge.

Christie gestured at me to indicate that the safety belts around the girl had been released. She removed the IV connection and disconnected the myriad electronic leads, setting off monitor warnings. She moved out of the aisle. I took her place.

I collected my first close look at our passenger.

"Jesus Christ," I said aloud.

The girl seemed impossibly small. I couldn't guess her age. She seemed smaller than Lydia's five-year-old. But this girl had older-girl features. Her face wore thin, almost translucent skin. Her closed eyes lay slightly sunken, and her forehead ran high. She seemed to glow in serene defiance of whatever ruthless killer she carried in her body. I felt a stab in the heart, seeing this beautiful child in such a state. I couldn't tell whether she slept peacefully or had simply begun to let go of life.

I tore my gaze away and checked the map. Pidge had aligned us with the RNAV 23 inbound approach course. We were just five miles from the center of town where my waypoint marked the clinic.

"Slow us down, Pidge. I'm opening the door."

I felt the change in pitch. The engine song changed. A vibration shuddered through the airframe as Pidge lowered the flaps. I felt the asymmetrical thrust and Pidge's counter pressure on the rudder as she reduced power on the left engine. The unsynchronized props sent a throbbing vibration through the airframe.

I scrambled back to the door and released the interior latch.

A door opening in flight is an emergency, but not a fatal emergency. Pilots tend to make door-release incidents fatal by failing to fly the airplane first and dealing with the door second. I knew of doors for this type of aircraft that had come open, and in one case of a small boy who had nearly fallen out. The airplane would continue to fly—at low speed, with skewed thrust, and burdened by ice on the wings—as long as Pidge maintained her deft touch.

Any pilot other than Pidge and I would have had doubts.

I threw the latch. The door blew open. It nearly pulled me out. I grabbed the door frame. The wind roared in the cabin, blinding and cold.

Christie's expression turned to horror. She had to be rethinking this. Someone was about to jump out of the airplane with her little patient and this mad act did not hold up to scrutiny in her logical mind.

I scrambled back up the aisle and looked directly at her.

"I can do this!" I shouted at her. I forgot about the intercom.

"Jesus, Will! Not in my ears!" Pidge scolded me. "Holding Vmc plus five. If you're going to do it, fucking do it!"

Christie nodded at me, clutching the seat's armrests.

I glanced at the iPad. Three miles.

I knelt beside the girl and slid my arms under her body. When I lifted, I nearly threw her. She had no body weight. I folded the blanket around her and felt extra hands helping. Christie leaned forward and tucked the blanket tightly in place as I positioned the child against my shoulder.

I gave her an appreciative nod. She sat back in her seat, put her hand across her mouth and began to cry.

Not much I could do about that.

The iPad indicated less than two miles to go.

"Five degrees left, Pidge."

Pidge didn't answer over the intercom, but I felt the airplane yaw.

I edged my way back to where the door hung open. The white fog had gone dark. Night seeped into the endless mist. Wind screamed past the cabin door at over a hundred miles per hour.

I held the girl tightly against my shoulder with my left arm. I took one last look at the iPad, at the aerial imagery showing the location of the pediatric hospital. I noted the large space identified as a cemetery across the street from my destination. That space would be an unlighted void among the city lights. It was the best available beacon, since I couldn't take the iPad with me. If I made the tablet vanish with me, I couldn't see it. If I made it reappear, it would have weight, and that weight would take us down at terminal velocity. Either way, it was useless to me.

I set the device on the rear right-side seat.

A low glow seeped into the cabin from below. The city lights of Marshfield radiated up through the fog.

"In ten seconds cut the left engine, Pidge! Then I'm out. Good luck!"

"Merry fucking Christmas!"

I threw off the headset, turned and dropped on my butt. I scooted toward the door with my legs out. The instant I extended my feet out the door the hundred-mile-per-hour wind pressure tried to tear them away.

My plan had been to vanish and fly out the door, but I couldn't hold the child and pull myself with my hands. In any case, the moment I vanished, wind blowing into the cabin would have pushed me against the opposite side of the airframe. Weightless, I'd never get out the door.

I would have to jump first, then vanish.

I suddenly realized I needed one more thing and almost blew the whole operation by nearly forgetting it.

I fixed a right-handed grip on the girl. Her legs dangled on either side of my thighs. With my left, I groped in my jacket for a FLOP unit. One-handed, I struggled to fix the propeller in place. In the gale-force wind I nearly fumbled the whole works out the door. This was not a well-thought-out plan.

Snap! The prop seated itself. I tested the power. It worked.

I glanced back at the iPad on the seat cushion.

Over the target. Pidge cut the left engine. The slipstream weakened.

Shit!

I heaved myself out the door, clutching the tiny child against my chest as the force of the wind tore us away from the airplane.

FWOOOMP! I put all I had into snapping *the other thing* around us.

Things happened fast.

The initial blast of wind roared like an angry sky creature and ripped us away from the door. Almost instantly, the gale died to nearly nothing, as if the beast lost its breath.

The Mojave engines thundered as Pidge restored the power to climb away.

We fell into a featureless gray void. I slid the FLOP power control to full forward thrust and held it opposite the wind generated by our fall. The FLOP sang its angry wasp song and arrested our descent. When the relative wind dropped to nothing, I eased the power to neutral. We floated in silence, wrapped in the cool sensation that comes with disappearing. Mist encircled us, but I had no problem with orientation. The Marshfield city lights radiated up from below. Dark night sky hung above us.

I angled my wrist and gently powered up the FLOP. A breeze stroked us as we descended into the glowing mist.

Streetlights emerged from the fog below like luminous bugs floating to the top of a creamy liquid. Bright Christmas lights added color to the fog, like sprinkles melted into white pastry frosting. Icicle lights traced the outlines of houses. Holiday lights turned trees into beacons.

Ahead and to my right, a dark patch nestled in the surrounding light. I aimed the power unit toward that darkness, the cemetery across from the clinic. Shapes and structures took form through the fog. Residential homes gave way to a campus of large buildings. I'd never seen the Pediatric Hospital wing of the expansive Marshfield clinic but felt reasonably certain I was on target.

We crossed a parking lot. Evenly spaced lamps all around us cast down cones of lighted mist, creating a magical misty forest of transparent Christmas trees. I felt the girl move. Her small arms around my neck applied a weak but steady embrace. Her head rose from my shoulder. She looked around. I wondered if somehow her vanished and weightless state gave her strength.

I aimed for what looked like an emergency entrance.

I eased us onto the concrete outside broad glass doors. A final pulse of the FLOP stabilized and stopped us. In the distance, I heard the airplane high above the fog. Engine song faded into the silent night.

Fwooomp! Gravity reacquired us. I settled onto my feet.

I looked down at the bundle in my arms. Wide, bright eyes stared up at me from an expression so serene, so at peace, it took my breath away.

"Are you an angel?" she asked.

"No, honey." I smiled down at her. "That's all you."

ANGEL FLIGHT
February 23, 2018

ABOUT THE AUTHOR

HOWARD SEABORNE is the author of the DIVISIBLE MAN series of novels and a collection of short stories featuring the same cast of characters. He began writing novels in spiral notebooks at age ten. He began flying airplanes at age sixteen. He is a former flight instructor and commercial charter pilot licensed in single- and twin-engine airplanes as well as helicopters. Today he flies a Beechcraft Bonanza, Beechcraft Baron and a Rotorway A-600 Talon experimental helicopter he built from a kit in his garage. He lives with his wife and writes and flies during all four seasons in Wisconsin, never far from Essex County Airport.

Visit www.HowardSeaborne.com to join the Email List and get a FREE DOWNLOAD.

ALSO BY HOWARD SEABORNE

DIVISIBLE MAN

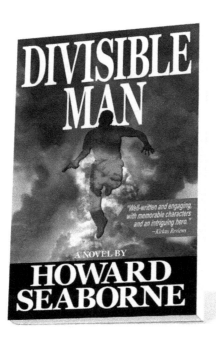

The media calls it a "miracle" when air charter pilot Will Stewart survives an aircraft in-flight breakup, but Will's miracle pales beside the stunning after-effect of the crash. Barely on his feet again, Will and his police sergeant wife Andy race to rescue an innocent child from a heinous abduction—*if Will's new ability doesn't kill him first.*

Available in print, digital and audio.

Learn more at **HowardSeaborne.com**

ALSO BY HOWARD SEABORNE

DIVISIBLE MAN: THE SIXTH PAWN

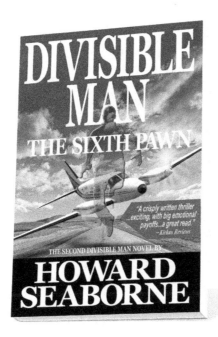

When the Essex County "Wedding of the Century" erupts in gunfire, Will and Andy Stewart confront a criminal element no one could have foreseen. Will tests the extraordinary after-effect of surviving a devastating airplane crash while Andy works a case obstructed by powerful people wielding the sinister influence of unlimited money in politics.

Available in print, digital and audio.

Learn more at **HowardSeaborne.com**

ALSO BY HOWARD SEABORNE

DIVISIBLE MAN: THE SECOND GHOST

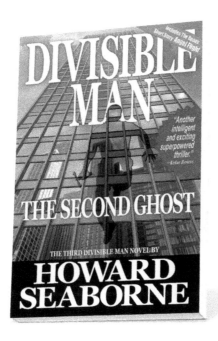

Tormented by a cyber stalker, Lane Franklin's best friend turns to suicide. Lane's frantic call to Will and Andy Stewart launches them on a desperate rescue. When it all goes bad, Will must adapt his extraordinary ability to survive the dangerous high steel and glass of Chicago as Andy and Pidge encounter the edge of disaster. **Includes the short story, "Angel Flight," a bridge to the fourth DIVISIBLE MAN novel that follows.**

Available in print, digital and audio.

Learn more at **HowardSeaborne.com**

ALSO BY HOWARD SEABORNE

DIVISIBLE MAN: THE SEVENTH STAR

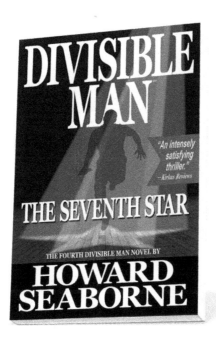

A horrifying message turns a holiday gathering tragic. An unsolved murder hangs a death threat over Detective Andy Stewart's head. And internet-fueled hatred targets Will and Andy's friend Lane. Will and Andy struggle to keep the ones they love safe, while hunting a dead murderer before he can kill again. As the tension tightens, Will confronts a troubling revelation about the extraordinary after-effect of his midair collision.

Available in print, digital and audio.

Learn more at **HowardSeaborne.com**

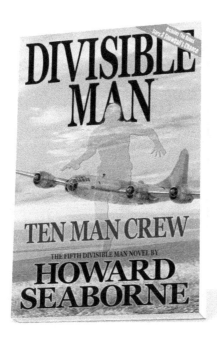

ALSO BY HOWARD SEABORNE

DIVISIBLE MAN: THE THIRD LIE

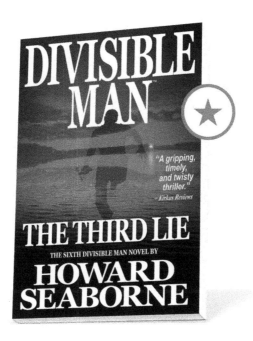

Caught up in a series of hideous crimes that generate national headlines, Will faces the critical question of whether to reveal himself or allow innocent lives to be lost. The stakes go higher than ever when Andy uncovers the real reason behind a celebrity athlete's assault on an underaged girl. And Will discovers that the limits of his ability can lead to disaster.

A Kirkus Starred Review.

A Kirkus Star is awarded to "books of exceptional merit."

Available in print, digital and audio.

Learn more at **HowardSeaborne.com**

ALSO BY HOWARD SEABORNE

DIVISIBLE MAN: THREE NINES FINE

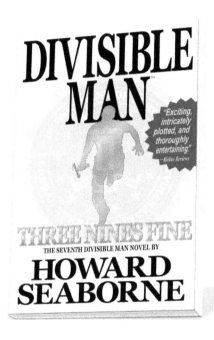

A mysterious mission request from Earl Jackson sends Will into the sphere of a troubled celebrity. A meeting with the Deputy Director of the FBI that goes terribly wrong. Will and Andy find themselves on the run from Federal authorities, infiltrating a notorious cartel, and racing to prevent what might prove to be the crime of the century.

Available in print, digital and audio.

Learn more at **HowardSeaborne.com**

ALSO BY HOWARD SEABORNE

DIVISIBLE MAN: EIGHT BALL

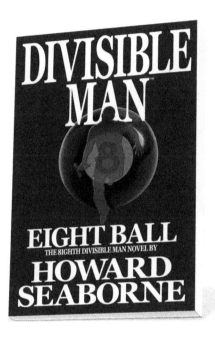

Will's encounter with a deadly sniper on a serial killing rampage sends him deeper into the FBI's hands with costly consequences for Andy. And when billionaire Spiro Lewko returns to the picture, Will and Andy's future takes a dark turn. The stakes could not be higher when the sniper's true target is revealed.

Available in print, digital and audio.

Learn more at **HowardSeaborne.com**

ALSO BY HOWARD SEABORNE

DIVISIBLE MAN:

ENGINE OUT AND OTHER SHORT FLIGHTS

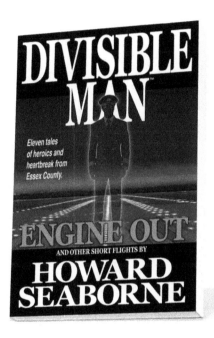

AVAILABLE: JUNE 2022

Things just have a way of happening around Will and Andy Stewart. In this collection of eleven tales from Essex County, boy meets girl, a mercy flight goes badly wrong, and Will crashes and burns when he tries dating again. Engines fail. Shots are fired. A rash of the unexpected breaks loose—from bank jobs to zombies.

Available in print, digital and audio.

Learn more at **HowardSeaborne.com**

ALSO BY HOWARD SEABORNE

DIVISIBLE MAN: NINE LIVES LOST

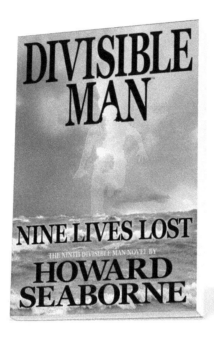

AVAILABLE: JUNE 2022

A simple request from Earl Jackson sends Will on a desperate cross-country chase ultimately looking for answers to a mystery that literally landed at Will and Andy's mailbox. At the same time, a threat to Andy's career takes a deadly turn. Before it all ends, Will confronts answers in a deep, dark place he never imagined.

Available in print, digital and audio.

Learn more at **HowardSeaborne.com**

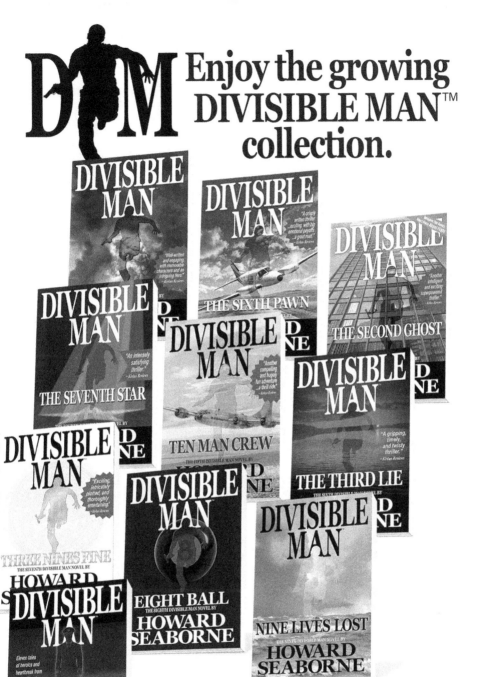

CPSIA information can be obtained
at www.ICGtesting.com
Printed in the USA
LVHW081235180922
728646LV00025B/1009/J

9 781958 005361